"Go!" Kith-Kanan cried, his heart pounding in his throat. The single syllable reverberated in the air.

Hiddukel backed away a pace and spun on one toe. His cape swirled around like a flame. Faster and faster the god whirled, until his elven form vanished, replaced by a whirling column of red smoke and fire. Kith-Kanan threw up an arm to shield his face from the virulent display. The voice of Hiddukel boomed in his head.

"The time of wonders is at hand, foolish king! Forces older than the gods surround you! Only the power of the Queen of Darkness can withstand them! Beware!"

# THE DRAGONLANCE® SAGA

Elven Nations Trilogy
Volume Three

DragonLance® SAGA

# The
# Qualinesti

Paul B. Thompson
& Tonya R. Carter

TSR Inc.

# DRAGONLANCE® Saga
## *Elven Nations*

### Volume Three

## The Qualinesti

Copyright ©1991 TSR, Inc.
All Rights Reserved.

First Printing: November 1991
Printed in the United States of America
Library of Congress Catalog Card Number: 90-71493

9 8 7 6 5 4 3 2 1

ISBN: 1-56076-114-8

TSR, Inc.
P.O. Box 756
Lake Geneva, WI
53147 U.S.A.

TSR Ltd.
120 Church End, Cherry Hinton
Cambridge CB1 3LB
United Kingdom

For Mickey

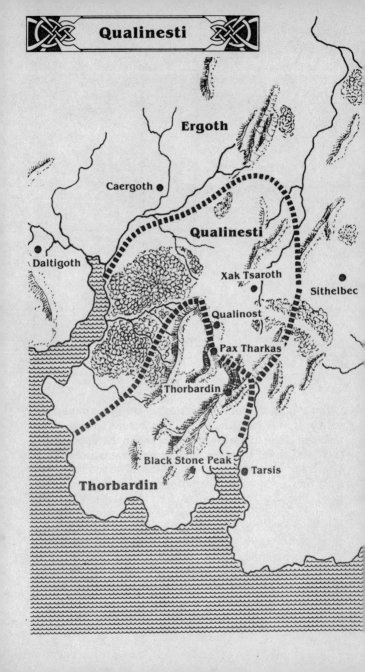

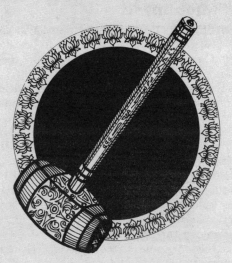

# ✒ Prologue ✒

## The Cornerstone

---

*Ten thousand footsteps rattled in the quiet mountain* valley. It was early morning, just before sunrise, and mist still clung to the low places between the slopes. Five thousand elves, dwarves, and humans were assembling in this remote mountain pass. Many were warriors, resplendent in burnished armor and flowing capes, who had battled in the long years of the Kinslayer Wars, elf against man, man against dwarf, and elf against elf. So protracted had been the time of bloodshed that sons and daughters of warriors had grown up to bear arms alongside their parents.

This was an army of peace, gathered in the Kharolis Mountains. They had come from the kingdom of Thorbardin and the realm of Qualinesti to seal a bargain and to erect a fortress. Pax Tharkas, it was to be called; the name had already been agreed upon. In the elven tongue, it meant "Citadel of Peace."

From the southern end of the pass came the delegation of dwarves, led by their new king, Glenforth Sparkstriker. It was he who had led the doughty dwarven armies against the humans of Ergoth, checking their advance in the high mountain passes around Thorbardin. The Battle of Raven's Hook had cost Prince Glenforth an eye, but it had also put an end to the Emperor of Ergoth's plan to subjugate the dwarves. Now, with his eye patch of beaten gold and his magnificent coal-black beard rippling across his mailed chest, King Glenforth led his people in an even greater endeavor.

Behind the king came the most powerful thanes, those of Glenforth's own Clan Hylar. Richly dressed in crimson velvet and glittering with all the jewels they could possibly wear, the Hylar each bore a ceremonial hammer on his shoulder. Close behind the Hylar came the Daewar, for this great occasion wearing midnight blue tunics, yellow sashes, and great wide-brimmed hats of brown leather. The Daewar carried gilded rock chisels, as long as each dwarf was tall.

The thanes of the other clans, the Klar and the Neidar, less richly dressed but still proud, followed in the wake of their more powerful cousins. The Klar carried ceremonial trowels, and the Neidar picks.

Where the valley floor began to slope upward, King Glenforth raised a hand. The councillors and thanes halted and waited in respectful silence.

The delegation from Qualinesti approached the dwarves from the north end of the valley. Most of the delegation were formerly of Silvanesti, and had the chiseled features and light coloring of that ancient elven race. But sharp eyes could see the mingled characteristics of the Kagonesti, the elves of the forest, and even the broad features of humans. The new elven kingdom of

Qualinesti had existed for just eighty years, and so far had proven the truth of its founder's dream: that elves and men and dwarves could live together in harmony, peace, and justice.

The founder himself led his nobles and notables to meet the Thorbardin thanes. In middle age now, as elves reckon time, the Speaker of the Sun was by far the most commanding figure in the valley. Age and toil had sent a few streaks of silver through his white-blond hair, but the clear, noble features of the House of Silvanos were unaltered by all the years of strife.

Kith-Kanan, the Speaker of the Sun, the founder of the nation of Qualinesti, stopped his entourage twenty paces or so from the dwarves. Alone, he went forward to meet King Glenforth of Thorbardin.

The elf met the dwarf near a large boulder that rose up in the center of the path. Glenforth extended his thick, powerful arms.

"Royal brother!" he said heartily. "I rejoice to see you!"

"And I you, Thane of Thanes."

Tall elf and squat dwarf clasped hands about each other's forearms. "This is a great day for our nations," Kith-Kanan said, stepping back. "For all of Krynn."

"There were many times I didn't think I would live to see this day," Glenforth said frankly.

"I, too, have wondered if this new kingdom of ours could have been born without the blood and suffering of the war. My late wife used to say that all things are born that way—with blood and pain." Kith-Kanan nodded slowly, thinking of days gone by. "But we're here now, that's the important thing," he added, smiling.

"Praise the gods!" said the dwarf sincerely.

Kith-Kanan turned back the folds of his emerald green cape to free his left hand. Looking to his waiting entourage, he smiled and lifted his arm, gesturing two figures forward. Glenforth squinted his good eye and saw that the two were children, a golden-haired boy and a brown-haired girl.

"King Glenforth, may I present my son, Prince Ulvian, and my daughter, Princess Verhanna," Kith-Kanan said, pushing the children forward. Ulvian dragged his feet and hung back from the unfamiliar dwarf. Verhanna, however, approached the king and bowed deeply to him.

"You do me honor," Glenforth said, a smile flashing amidst his black beard.

"No, sire. I am the honored one," Verhanna replied, her high voice ringing clear in the mountain air. Her large, dark brown eyes appraised the dwarf frankly, with no sign of fear. "I've heard the bards sing of your greatness in battle. Now that I've met you, I see the truth of their songs."

"Memories of battle are a poor comfort when one grows old and tired. I would trade all of mine for a child like you," he said gallantly. Verhanna flushed at this praise, stammered a thank-you, and withdrew to her father's side.

"Go on," Kith-Kanan said to his son. "Make your greetings to King Glenforth."

Prince Ulvian took a small step forward and bowed with a quick, bobbing motion. "Greetings, Great King," he said, running his words together in his haste to get them out. "I'm honored to meet you."

His duty done, Ulvian stepped back and hovered just behind his father.

With a fond pat on Verhanna's cheek, Kith-Kanan sent his children back to the ranks of nobles. Turning once more to the dwarf, he said softly, "Excuse my son. He hasn't been the same since his mother died. My daughter never really knew her mother; it's been easier for her."

Glenforth nodded politely. Practically everyone from Hylo to Silvanost knew the tale of Kith-Kanan and his human wife, Suzine. She had died many years before, in one of the last battles of the Kinslayer War. Her children matured at a much slower rate than human children, but not as slowly as full-blooded elven offspring. In human terms, both were still quite young.

The two monarchs exchanged more polite trivialities before returning to the reason for their meeting this morning. At a sign from Glenforth, an elderly dwarf came forward carrying an object covered by a red velvet cloth. It was obviously very heavy, and he held it firmly in both hands. Glenforth took the parcel, holding it easily. The elderly dwarf bowed to his king and was introduced as Chancellor Gendrin Dunbarth, senior thane of the Hylar clan.

"My lord," Kith-Kanan said, scrutinizing the chancellor, "I once knew a wise dwarf called Dunbarth of Dunbarth. Are you by chance related to him?"

Gendrin mopped his brow with a coarse-looking handkerchief. "Yes, Highness. Dunbarth of Dunbarth, ambassador to the court of Silvanesti, was my father," replied the dwarf, puffing from exertion.

Kith-Kanan smiled. "I met him in Silvanost many years ago and remember him with esteem. He was an honorable fellow."

Glenforth cleared his throat. Kith-Kanan returned his attention to the king. In loud, ringing tones, audible to the assembled thanes and Qualinesti, the dwarf king declared, "Great Speaker, on behalf of all the dwarves of Thorbardin, I present you with this special tool. I know you will wield it justly, for the benefit of your people and mine."

He passed the velvet-wrapped burden to Kith-Kanan. The Speaker of the Sun whisked the cover away, revealing a large iron hammer, wrought in traditional dwarven style but made larger to fit the hands of an elf. The octagonal iron handle was banded with silver, and the sides of the massive flat hammerhead were gilded.

"It is called Sunderer," Glenforth explained. "Our priests of Reorx forged it in a slow fire, and quenched it in dragon's blood to give it a worthy temper."

"It is magnificent!" Kith-Kanan said in awed tones. He

turned the great hammer in his hands. "This is the tool of a demigod, not a mortal such as I!"

"Well, as long as it's good enough," the dwarf king said with a wry smile. He waved a beringed hand, and another Hylar thane came to him. This dwarf bore one of the long iron chisels banded with silver. He gave it to his king, then he and Gendrin Dunbarth withdrew.

Kith-Kanan and Glenforth walked in matched step to the boulder that lay in the center of the pass. As they proceeded with appropriate dignity, Kith-Kanan said softly, "Will you make the announcement, or shall I?"

"This was your idea," Glenforth replied in a low voice. "You do it."

"It's a joint project, Your Highness."

"Yes, but I'm no speechifier," said the dwarf. They stood by the boulder. "Besides, everyone knows elves are better talkers than dwarves."

"First I've heard of it," Kith-Kanan muttered.

The Speaker of the Sun turned to face the delegations. King Glenforth stood resolutely beside him, his hands resting on the long chisel as a warrior rests on his sword pommel.

Kith-Kanan listened for a moment to the stillness of the valley. The mist was vanishing, burned off by the rising sun. A flock of swifts darted and wheeled overhead. Somewhere in the distance, a dove made its mournful call.

"We have come here today," he began, "to erect a fortress. Not a stronghold for war, for we have too long followed that path. This fortress, which we of Qualinesti and our friends of Thorbardin shall build and occupy together, shall be a place of peace, a place where people of all races can seek haven and find protection and rest."

The Speaker paused as the first direct rays of the sun lanced over the mountain peaks into the valley. He was facing east, and the sunbeams warmed his face. A surge of resolution, of the rightness of what they were beginning here today, passed through Kith-Kanan.

"This boulder will be the cornerstone of Pax Tharkas, the Citadel of Peace. King Glenforth and I will carve it out ourselves, as a symbol of the cooperation and friendship between our countries."

He turned to the rock and set the great hammer Sunderer on his shoulder. Glenforth butted the chisel against the rock and steadied it with both of his thick, powerful hands.

"Swing true, Speaker," he said, half-jesting.

Kith-Kanan raised the hammer. Ulvian and Verhanna, standing with the Qualinesti nobles, stepped forward to get a better view of their father's work.

Sunderer came down on the chisel. A torrent of sparks fell across the boulder, spraying the dwarf king with fire. Glenforth laughed and urged Kith-Kanan to strike again. The third blow Kith-Kanan delivered was a mighty stroke indeed. It echoed through the valley like a roll of thunder and was quickly followed by the dry crack of cleaving rock. An entire side of the boulder fell away, leaving the rock with a face clean and straight. Cheers erupted from the onlookers.

Sweating in the cool mountain air, Kith-Kanan said to Glenforth, "Your hammer strikes nothing but true blows, Thane of Thanes."

"*Your* hammer, Great Speaker, like all tools, strikes only as its wielder aims," replied the dwarf thoughtfully. He blew on his hands and rubbed them together.

"What do you think of that, Ullie?" Kith-Kanan called, looking to his son. The boy had his head down, a hand pressed to his right cheek. The Speaker frowned. "What's wrong, son?"

Ulvian looked up slowly to meet his father's eyes. The boy's face showed pain. When he took his hands away, a small cut could be seen on his cheek. Gazing at the blood staining his fingers, Ulvian said softly, "I bleed!"

"A rock chip hit you," Verhanna said matter-of-factly. "Some landed on me, too." She shook the folds of her boyish clothes and bits of stone and grit fell out.

Prince Ulvian's face twisted in anger. "I bleed!" he cried. He backed away from his father and bumped into a wall of courtiers and nobles. They parted for him, and the panicked prince fled into the crowd.

"Ulvian, come back!" Kith-Kanan shouted. The boy did not heed him.

"Want me to catch him?" Verhanna offered, sure in the knowledge that she was swifter than her brother.

"No, child. Stay here."

Kith-Kanan summoned his castellan, the elf in charge of his household, Tamanier Ambrodel. The elderly, gray-haired elf, dressed in a gray doublet and mauve cape, stepped out of the crowd.

"Find my son, Tam, and take him to a healer if he needs one," said the Speaker.

Tamanier bowed. "Yes, Highness."

Kith-Kanan watched his castellan disappear into the crowd. Hefting the great hammer, he said, "Ullie will be all right." Glenforth cleared his throat and pretended to be studying the boulder before him.

Verhanna and the rest of the crowd stood back as the Speaker of the Sun and the King of Thorbardin resumed their places at the stone. The valley rang with the sound of iron on rock.

In short order, the stone became a cube, square on four sides and rough on top. King Glenforth wasn't tall enough to bring the chisel to bear on the top of the boulder, so his thanes formed themselves into a living stair, that he might climb onto the rock. It was quite a sight, all the richly bedecked dwarves of Clans Hylar and Daewar, their thick arms locked together, bent over and braced against the cornerstone. Glenforth set aside the chisel and climbed up their backs. Once he was atop the stone, the thanes passed the chisel to him.

"Well, Great Speaker," said the dwarf from his lofty perch, "now I am higher than you! Will your councillors elevate you as mine did me?"

Kith-Kanan tossed the hammer to the top of the boulder, then faced his people. "You heard the Thane of Thanes! Will the nobles of Qualinesti stoop so that their Speaker can rise to the occasion?"

Half a hundred elves and men surged to the rock, ready to aid Kith-Kanan. Laughing, the Speaker ordered them back, then chose three elves and three humans. They looped their arms around each others' waists and bent to the rock. As the others cheered, Kith-Kanan climbed nimbly atop the boulder. He and Glenforth stood side by side, and the cheering continued. Finally Kith-Kanan raised his hands and waved for silence.

"My good and loyal friends!" he cried. "Many times in the recent past I have wondered if our coming to this new land was wise. Many times I have asked myself, should I have stayed in Silvanost? Should I have fought to establish in our old homeland the ideals we now share?"

There were shouts of "No! No!" from the crowd.

"And now—" Kith-Kanan again waved for quiet. "And now, I see us here today—men, elves, and dwarves—working together where once we fought, and I know I could have done nothing less than lead you to this new land, to make this new nation. You have all suffered and struggled and bled for Qualinesti. So have I. We did not fight to make a country like my father's, where tradition and age count for more than truth and justice. I do not want to rule for centuries and see all my ideals grow hoary with time. Therefore, on this rock, with this great hammer, Sunderer, in my hand, I will make you this pledge: The day this fortress is finished, I shall abdicate in favor of my successor."

A loud murmur of surprise spread through the assembly. The dwarves stroked their beards and looked concerned. Some of the Qualinesti elves cried out that Kith-Kanan should rule for life.

"No! Listen to me!" Kith-Kanan shouted. "This is what we fought for! The ruler and the ruled must be bound by a solemn pact that neither shall suffer the other unwanted. Once this fortress of peace is complete, let a younger, fresher mind lead Qualinesti forward to greater happiness and glory."

He nodded to King Glenforth. The dwarf placed the chisel against the surface of the rock. The gilded head of Sunderer flashed in the sun. Sparks flew as it smote Glenforth's chisel, and the blow Kith-Kanan struck reverberated down through the boulder into the stony ground of Krynn. Every elf, every dwarf, every human present felt the mighty stroke.

# ❧ 1 ❧

## Shadow Talk

When kith-kanan led his followers west to found a new elven nation in the ancient woodland known first as Mithranhana, he had no goal, no plan in mind except that the mistakes of Silvanesti would not be repeated. By this he meant not only the autocratic, inflexible government of the first elven nation, but also the baroque, ornamental layout of the city of Silvanost itself.

The site of the first city in the new nation was chosen not by conscious thought, but by a lost deer. Kith-Kanan and his closest lieutenants were riding ahead of their column of settlers one afternoon when they spied a magnificent hart with ice-blue antlers and gray hide. Thinking the beast would make a fine trophy, as well as

provide much needed meat, Kith-Kanan and his lieutenants gave chase. The hart bounded away with great
leaps, and the elves on horseback were hard pressed to
keep up. The deer led them farther and farther from their
line of march, down a steep ravine. An arrow nocked,
Kith-Kanan was about to try a desperate on-the-fly shot
when the ravine ended at the precipitous edge of a river
gorge. Kith-Kanan pulled his horse up sharply and gave
a yell of surprise. The deer leapt straight off the cliff!

Astonished, the elves dismounted, hurried to the rim
of the gorge, and looked down. There was no sign of the
hart; no carcass lay smashed on the riverbank below.
Kith-Kanan then knew the animal had been a magical
one, but why had it deliberately crossed their path? Why
had it brought them here?

The answer soon became obvious as the elves surveyed
their surroundings. Across the wide gorge was a beautiful
plateau, lightly wooded with hardwoods and conifers.
After only a moment's reflection, Kith-Kanan knew this
was to be the site of their new city, the capital of their new
nation.

The plateau was bounded on the north, east, and west
by two rivers, which converged at the north end of the
plateau and became a tributary of the White Rage River.
These two streams ran through deep, wide gorges. The
south side of the roughly triangular escarpment was a
labyrinth of steep, rocky ravines, and the land rose
eventually to form the mountains of Thorbardin. From a
natural point of view, the place was ideal, offering beauty and natural defenses. And as for the gray hart—well,
the Bard King, Astarin, the god most revered by elves, is
sometimes known as the Wandering Hart.

So the city of Qualinost was born. For a time, there
was much sentiment to name the town after Kith-Kanan,
as Silvanost had been named after the great Silvanos,
august founder of the first elven nation. The Speaker of
the Sun would not hear of it.

"This city is not to be a monument to me," he told his

well-intentioned followers, "but a place for all people of good heart."

In the end, it was Kith-Kanan's friend and war companion, Anakardain, who named the city. That middle-aged warrior, who had fought beside Kith at the Battle of Sithelbec, remarked one night over dinner that the noblest person he'd ever heard of was Quinara, wife of Silvanos. The palace in Silvanost was called the Quinari, after her.

"You're right!" Kith-Kanan declared. Though Quinara had died before he was born, Kith-Kanan knew well the stories of his grandmother's virtuous life. Thereafter, the budding city in the trees was known as Qualinost, which in Old Elven means "In Memory of Quinara."

The ranks of the immigrants were swelled daily by arrivals from Silvanesti. A vast camp grew up along the bank of the east river as more permanent dwellings sprouted among the evergreens on the plateau. The buildings of Qualinost, formed from the rose quartz that occurred naturally there, were domelike or conical in shape, reaching like leafless trees to the heavens.

Greatest effort was reserved for the Tower of the Sun, a tremendous golden spire that was to be the seat of the Speaker of the Sun's reign. In general design, it resembled Silvanost's Tower of the Stars, but in place of cold, white marble, this tower was covered with burnished gold. The metal reflected the warm, bright rays of the sun. The shape of the Tower of the Sun was the only likeness Qualinost bore to the old elven capital; when it was done, and Kith-Kanan had been formally installed as Speaker of the Sun, then the break between East and West was complete.

\* \* \* \* \*

One spring morning in the two hundred and thirtieth year of the reign of Kith-Kanan, the calm of Qualinost was shattered by the tramping of massed hobnailed boots. City folk gathered outside their rose-hued homes, in the shade of the wide, spreading trees, and watched as nearly the entire Guard of the Sun, the army of Qualinesti, marched across the high-arched bridges that spanned the four corners of the city. Unlike human fortified towns, Qualinost had no walls; instead, four freestanding spans of wrought iron and bronze arched from tower keep to tower keep, enclosing the city in walls of air. The bridges were designed to aid in the protection of the city, yet not interfere with the free passage of traders and townsfolk. Not unimportantly, they were breathtakingly beautiful, as delicate as cobwebs but obviously strong enough to hold the troops that even now marched across them. The bronze of the cantilevered spans flashed fire in the sunlight, and at night, the black iron was silvered by the white moon, Solinari. The four keeps had been named by Kith-Kanan as Arcuballis, Sithel, Mackeli, and Suzine Towers.

That morning, the people stood with their faces turned upward as the companies of guards left the tower keeps and converged on Suzine Tower, at the southeast corner of the city. The elves had been at peace for over two centuries, and no such concentration of troops had been observed in all that time. Once the two thousand soldiers of the guard had gathered at the keep, quiet returned once more to the city. Though the curious Qualinesti watched for long minutes, nothing else seemed to be happening. The arched bridges were again empty. The people, their faith in their leaders and their troops strong, shrugged their shoulders and went back to their daily routines.

There were too many warriors to fit inside Suzine Tower, so many stood on the lower intersecting ends of the bridges. Rumors circulated through the ranks. What was happening? Why had they been summoned? The old enemy, Ergoth, had been quiet a long time. Tension existed with Silvanesti, and the frightening idea formed that the Speaker's twin brother, Sithas, Speaker of the

Stars, was attacking from the east. This grim story gained momentum as it spread.

In ignorance, the troops waited as the sun passed its zenith and began its descent. When at last the shadow of the Tower of the Sun reached out and touched the eastern bridge, the keep's doors opened and Kith-Kanan emerged, along with a sizable contingent from the Thalas-Enthia, the Qualinesti senate.

The warriors clasped their hands to their armored chests and cried, "Hail, Great Speaker! Hail, Speaker of the Sun!" Kith-Kanan acknowledged their salutes, and the soldiers fell silent. The Speaker of the Sun looked tired and troubled. His mane of blond hair, heavily shot through with silver, was pulled back in a crude queue, and his sky-blue robes were wrinkled and dusty.

"Guards of the Sun," he said in a low, controlled voice, "I have summoned you here today with a heavy heart. A problem that has plagued our country for some years has grown so much worse that I am forced to use you, my brave warriors, to suppress it. I have consulted with the senators of the Thalas-Enthia and the priests of our gods, and they have agreed with my chosen course."

Kith-Kanan paused, closing his eyes and sighing. The day was beginning to cool slightly, and a breeze wafted over the tired leader's face. "I am sending you out to destroy the slave traders who infest the confluence of the rivers that guard our city," he finished, his voice rising.

The guards broke out in subdued murmurs of surprise. Every resident of Qualinost knew that the Speaker had been trying to suppress slavery in his domain. The long Kinslayer War had, as one of its saddest consequences, created a large population of refugees, vagabonds, and lawless rovers. These were preyed upon by slavers, who sold them into bondage in Ergoth and Silvanesti. Since Qualinesti was a largely unsettled area between these two slave-holding countries, it was inevitable that the slavers would operate in Kith-Kanan's land. Slavers who drove their human and elven "goods" to market through Qualinesti territory frequently captured Qualinesti citizens as they went. Slavery was one of the principal evils Kith-Kanan and his followers had wanted to leave behind in Silvanesti, but the pernicious practice had insinuated itself into the new country. It was time for the Speaker of the Sun to put an end to it.

"Lord Anakardain will lead a column of a thousand guards up the eastern river to the confluence. Lord Ambrodel will command a second column of seven hundred and fifty mounted warriors, who will sweep the western branch and drive the slavers into Lord Anakardain's hands. As much as possible, I want these people taken alive for public trial. I doubt many of them will have the stomach to fight anyway, but I don't want them dealt with summarily. Is that clear?"

Most of the guards were former Wildrunners who had fought with Kith-Kanan against the Ergothians; they were the sons and daughters of Kagonesti elves who had been held in slavery in Silvanost for centuries. Slavers could expect little kindness from them.

Kith-Kanan stood back as Lord Anakardain began dividing the troops into the two forces, with the remaining two hundred fifty warriors to remain behind in the city. General Lord Kemian Ambrodel, son of Kith-Kanan's castellan, stood beside his sovereign.

"If you wish, sire, I can have Lady Verhanna assigned to the city guard," he said confidentially.

"No, no. She is a warrior the same as any other," Kith-Kanan said. "She would never want to be shown favoritism simply because she is my daughter."

Even in the crowd of two thousand troops, he could easily pick out Verhanna. Taller by almost a head than most of the Qualinesti warriors, her silver helm bore the red plume of an officer. A thick braid of light brown hair hung down her back to her waist. She was quite mature for a half-human. Never married, Verhanna was dedicated to her father and to the guards. Kith-Kanan was proud of his daughter's warrior skills, but some small fatherly portion of him wished to see her wedded and a mother before he died.

"I would prefer, however, that she go with you rather than Anakardain. I think she will be safer with the mounted troops," Kith-Kanan told Lord Ambrodel.

The handsome, fair-haired Silvanesti elf nodded gravely. "As you command, sire."

Lord Anakardain called his young subordinate to his side. Kith-Kanan watched Lord Ambrodel hurry away, and he was once more struck by the strong resemblance the young general bore to his elderly father.

As the guards broke up into their two units, the Speaker reentered Suzine Tower, trailed by several members of the Thalas-Enthia. With a notable lack of protocol, Kith-Kanan went to a table set beside the curved wall and poured himself a large cup of potent nectar.

The senators ringed round him. Clovanos, who was of an old, noble Silvanesti clan, said, "Great One, this act will cause great dismay to the Speaker of the Stars."

Kith-Kanan set down his cup. "My brother must deal with his own conscience," he said flatly. "I will not tolerate slavery in my realm."

Senator Clovanos waved a dismissive hand. "It is a minor problem, Great Speaker," he said.

"Minor? The buying and selling of people as if they were chickens or glass beads? Do you honestly consider that a minor problem, my lord?"

Senator Xixis, who was half Kagonesti, put in, "We only fear retribution by the Speaker of the Stars or the Emperor of Ergoth if we mistreat those slavers who happen to be their subjects. Our country is still very new, Highness. If we were attacked by one or both of those countries, Qualinesti would not survive."

"I think you gravely underestimate our strength," said a human senator, Malvic Pathfinder, "and overestimate the concern of two monarchs for some of the worst scum to walk this world!"

"There are deeper roots to this business than you

know," Clovanos said darkly. "Even within Qualinost, there are those who profit by this trade in flesh."

Kith-Kanan snapped around, his robes swirling about his feet. "Who would dare," he demanded, "in defiance of my edicts?"

Clovanos paled before the Speaker's sudden wrath. He backed up a step and stammered, "G-Great Majesty, one hears things in taverns, in temples. Shadow talk. Dark things without substance."

Xixis and Irthenie, a Kagonesti senator who still proudly wore the face paint popular with her wilder cousins, stepped between Kith-Kanan and the chastened Clovanos. Irthenie, whose intelligence and strong anti-slavery stance made her a confidant of the Speaker, declared, "Clovanos speaks the truth, Majesty. There are places in the city where money changes hands for influence and for slaves sold in other lands."

Kith-Kanan released the gold clasp from his long hair and combed through the pale strands with his fingers. "It never ends, does it?" he said tiredly. "I try to give the people a new life, and all the old vices come back to haunt us."

His gloomy observation hung in the air like dark smoke. Embarrassed, Clovanos and Xixis were the first to leave. Malvic followed, after offering words of support for the Speaker's stand. The half-human Senator Harplen, who seldom spoke, left with Malvic. Only Irthenie remained.

With much tramping and shouting, the two units of the Guards of the Sun dispersed. Kith-Kanan watched from the window as his warriors streamed over the bridges to the tower keeps and down into the city. He looked for, but didn't see, Verhanna.

"My daughter is going out with the guard," he said, his back to the Kagonesti woman. "This will be her first taste of conflict."

"I doubt that," said Irthenie flatly. "No one close to you can be unfamiliar with conflict, Kith. What I don't understand is why you don't send your son along, too. He could use some hard lessons, that boy."

Kith-Kanan rolled the brass cup back and forth in his hands, warming the nectar within. "Ulvian has gone off with his friends again. I don't know where. Probably drinking himself sick, or gambling his shirt on a roll of the bones." The Speaker's tone was bitter. A frown pulled at the corners of Kith-Kanan's mouth. He set his cup aside. "Ullie has never been the same since Suzine died. He was very close to his mother."

"Give him to me for six months and I'll straighten him out!"

Kith-Kanan had to smile at her declaration. Irthenie had four sons, all of whom were vigorous, opinionated, and successful. If Ulvian were younger, he might take Irthenie up on her offer. "My good friend," he said instead, taking her dark, age-worn hands in his, "of all the problems that face me today, Ulvian is not the worst."

She looked up at him, studying him closely. "You're wrong, Speaker," she said. "The fortress of Pax Tharkas is nearing completion, and the time is fast approaching when you vowed to abdicate. Can you in good conscience appoint a good-for-nothing idler like Ulvian the next Speaker of the Sun? I think not."

He dropped her hands and turned away, his face shadowed by concern. "I can't go back on my word. I swore I would abdicate once Pax Tharkas was finished." He sighed heavily. "I wish to pass on the mantle of leadership. After the war, and after building a new nation, I am tired."

"Then I tell you this, Kith-Kanan: Take your rest and give over the title to another, as long as it is anyone but your son," Irthenie said firmly.

The Speaker did not reply. Irthenie waited for several minutes, then bowed and left the tower.

Kith-Kanan sat down on a hard barrack chair and let the sunshine wash over his face. Closing his eyes, he gave himself over to deep and difficult thoughts.

\* \* \* \* \*

"Ho there, trooper! Close up your ranks!"

Sullenly the guards reined their horses about. They weren't usually so glum, but they happened to have been assigned to the strictest, most particular captain in the Guards of the Sun. Verhanna Kanan did not spare herself, nor anyone in her command.

Verhanna's troop was moving northward, patrolling the western slopes of the Magnet Mountains, a small but steep range of peaks west of Qualinost. The stream that flowed past the western side of the city originated in these mountains. The land was sparsely wooded this close to the range of hills. Lord Ambrodel had given Verhanna's troop the task of searching closest to the foot of the peaks, where the guards were vulnerable to ambush from above.

The captain kept her warriors close together. She didn't want any stragglers getting picked off. Her eyes never left the hillside. The red rock and brown soil were streaked with veins of black. These were deposits of lodestone, the natural magnets that gave the mountains their name. Kender shamans came from all across Ansalon to dig up the lodestone for protective amulets. So far on this sortie, the only living things Verhanna had seen were a few of the small kender race, working at the outcroppings of lodestone with deer antler picks.

Her second-in-command, a former Silvanesti named Merithynos, Merith for short, kept by her side as their horses picked their way slowly over the stony ground. The slopes were in shadow all morning.

"A futile task," Merith said, sighing loudly. "What are we doing here?"

"Carrying out the Speaker's command," Verhanna replied firmly. Her gaze rested on a dark figure nestled in a fold in the ground. She stared hard at it but soon realized it was only a holly bush.

Merith yawned, one hand pressed against his mouth. "But it's such a bore!"

"Yes, I know. You'd rather be in Qualinost, strutting down the street, impressing the maids with your sword and armor," Verhanna said dryly. "At least out here you're earning your pay."

"Captain! You wound me!" Merith clutched his chest and swayed as if shot by an arrow.

She scowled at him, a mock frown on her face. "Fool! How did a dandy like you ever get in the guards?" she asked.

"Actually, it was my father's idea. Priesthood or war-riorhood, that's what he told me. 'There's no room in Clan Silver Moon for wastrels,' he said—"

Verhanna stiffened and reined her horse up short. "Quiet!" she hissed. "I saw something."

With hand signals, the captain divided her troop of twenty in half, with ten warriors, including herself, dismounting. Sword and buckler at the ready, she led the guards up the gravelly slope. Their booted feet slid in the loose dirt. The climb was a slow one.

Suddenly a shape rose up in front of Verhanna and scampered away, like a partridge flushed by a spaniel.

"Get him!" the captain shouted. The small creature, which seemed to be wrapped in a white cloth, darted away but lost its footing and rolled downhill. It came to rest with a bump against Merith's booted feet.

He put the tip of his slender elven blade against the sheeted mound, pricking the creature until it lay still. "Captain," Merith called coolly, "I have him."

The guards closed around the captive. Verhanna took one edge of the white sheet and pulled hard, spinning the occupant around. Out popped a small, sinewy figure with flaming red hair and a face to match.

"Stinkin', poxy, rancid, dirty, lice-ridden—" he sputtered, rubbing his backside. "Who poked me?"

"I did," Merith said. "And I'll do it again if you don't hold your tongue, kender."

"That's enough, Lieutenant," Verhanna said sharply. Merith shrugged and gave the outraged fellow an insolent smile. The captain turned to her captive and demanded, "Who are you? Why did you run from us?"

"Wrinklecap is who I am, and you'd run, too, if you woke from a nap to see a dozen swords over you!" The kender stopped rubbing his backside and twisted around to look at it. An almost comical expression of outrage widened his pale blue eyes. "You made a hole in my trousers!" he said, glaring at them. "Someone's gonna pay for this!"

"Be still," Verhanna said. She shook out the sheet Wrinklecap had been sleeping in. A double handful of black pebbles fell from its folds. "A lodestone gatherer," she said. The disappointment in her voice was obvious.

"*The* lodestone gatherer," intoned the tiny fellow, tapping his chest with one finger. "Rufus Wrinklecap of Balifor, that's me."

The guards who were waiting below on horseback called out to their captain. Verhanna shouted back that all was well. Sheathing her sword, she said to the kender, "You'd better come along with us."

"Why?" piped Rufus.

Verhanna was tired of bandying words with the noisy kender, so she pushed him ahead. Rufus snatched his sheet from the elven captain and rolled it up as he walked.

"Not fair—big bunch of bullies—creepin', pointy-headed *elves*—" He grumbled all the way down the slope.

Verhanna halted and ordered her troopers to remount. She sat down on a handy boulder and waved the kender over. "How long have you been in these parts?" she asked him.

After a few seconds of hesitation, the kender took a deep breath and said, "Well, after Uncle Trapspringer escaped from the walrus men and was eaten by the great ice bear—"

The captain quickly clamped a hand over the kender's open mouth. "No," she said firmly. "I do not want your entire life history. Simply answer my questions, or I'll let Lieutenant Merith poke you again."

His long red topknot bobbled as Rufus swallowed hard. Verhanna was easily twice his size. Merith, from his mounted position next to them, was tapping the pommel of his sword meaningfully. The kender nodded. Verhanna released her hold on him.

"I've been here going on two months," Rufus said sulkily.

Verhanna remembered the loose stones he'd had. "You don't have much to show for two month's work," she commented.

Rufus puffed out his thin chest. "I only take the best stones," he said proudly. "I don't fill my pockets with trash like all them others do."

Ignoring for the moment the little fellow's last remark, Verhanna asked, "How do you live? I don't see any camp gear, cooking pot, or waterskin."

The kender turned innocent azure eyes on her and said, "I find what I need."

Merith snorted loudly. A smile touched Verhanna's lips. "Find, eh? Kender are good at that. Who have you 'found' things from?" she asked.

"Different people."

Verhanna drew a long, double-edged dagger from her belt and began to strop it slowly against her boot. "We're looking for some different people," she said carefully, making sure the kender followed every stroke of the bright blade. "Humans. Maybe some elves." The dagger paused. "Slavers."

Rufus let out his breath with a whoosh. "Oh!" he exclaimed, his high-pitched voice descending the scale. "Is *that* who you're after? Well, why didn't you say so?"

The kender launched into a typically random account of his activities of the past few days—caves he'd explored, wonders he'd beheld, and a secret camp he'd found over the mountains. In this camp, he claimed there were humans and elves holding other humans and elves in chains. Rufus had seen the camp just two days before.

"On the other side of the mountains?" Verhanna said sharply. "The eastern slope?"

"Yup. Right by the river. Are you going to attack them?" The kender's eagerness was unmistakable. His darting gaze took in their armor and weapons, and he added, "Well, of course you are. Want me to show you where I saw them?"

Verhanna did indeed. She ordered food and water for Rufus while she conferred with Merith about this new intelligence.

The kender wolfed down chunks of *quith-pa*, a rich elven bread, and bites of a winesap apple. "This little fellow may be a great help to us," she said confidentially to Merith. "Send a message to Lord Ambrodel informing him of what we've learned."

Merith saluted. "Yes, Captain." His expression turned grim as he added, "You realize what this means, don't you? If the slavers are on the other side of the mountain, then they are operating within sight of the city."

He turned on one heel and strode away to send the dispatch to Lord Ambrodel. Verhanna watched him for a moment, then pulled on her gauntlets and said to Rufus, "Can you ride pillion?"

The kender hastily lowered a water bottle from his lips, dribbling sweet spring water down his sunbrowned cheeks. "Ride a what?" he asked suspiciously.

Not pausing to explain, Verhanna swung onto her black horse and grabbed the kender by the hood attached to the back of his deerhide tunic. Yelping, Rufus felt himself lifted into the air and settled on the short leather tail of her saddle.

"That's a pillion," she said. "Now hold on!"

# ❧ 2 ❧

## The Raid

The kender led Verhanna's troop across the mountains to a bluff overlooking the River of Hope, which formed Qualinost's western boundary. The towers and bridges of the city rose up to the northeast not three miles away. The sun was setting behind the mountains at the warriors' backs. Its light washed the capital, and the arched bridges glowed like golden tiaras. Nestled in the light green of spring leaves, thousands of windows reflected the crimson sun. Brightest of all, the Tower of the Sun mirrored the fiery glow with a vigor that nearly burned Verhanna's eyes.

Verhanna gazed over the city her father had founded, and a deep sense of peace filled her. Her home was beautiful; the thought that dealers in elven and human misery operated within sight of Qualinost's beauty sent a wave of resolute anger washing over her.

Rufus broke her reverie. "Captain," he whispered, "I smell smoke!"

Verhanna strained until she caught a faint tang of wood smoke on the gentle breeze. It was coming from below, from the base of the bluff. "Is there a way down there?" she queried.

"Not on horseback. The path's too narrow," Rufus replied.

Quietly Verhanna ordered her troops to dismount. The horses were tethered among the rocks, and a group of five warriors was set to watch them. The remaining fifteen followed Verhanna to the path. She, in turn, followed Rufus Wrinklecap.

It was obvious that others had been using this path. Sand from the riverbank had been spread over the rocky ground, no doubt to soften footfalls. Now the sand served the guards as they crept down the path two abreast. They were careful to keep their shields from banging against anything. The smell of wood smoke grew stronger.

The base of the bluff was some thirty yards from the river's edge. Scrub pines dotted the landscape, and halfway out from the cliff, there was nothing but sand deposited by the river during spring floods. Verhanna caught Rufus by the shoulder and stopped him. The warriors crouched silently behind their captain, shielded from the camp by the small trees.

Voices drifted to them. Voices and sounds of movement.

"Can't see how many there are," Verhanna said in a tense whisper.

"I can find out," Rufus said confidently, and before she could stop him, he had eased out from under her hand and started forward.

"No! Come back!" the captain hissed.

It was too late. With the fearlessness, some might say foolishness, of his race, the kender scrambled forward a few paces, stood, and dusted the sand from his knees. Then, whistling a cheery air, he marched into the unseen slavers' camp.

Merith crawled to his captain. "The little thief will give us away," he murmured.

"I don't think so," she replied. "By the gods, he's a brave little mite!"

Moments later, rough laughter filled the air. Rufus's treble voice, saying something unintelligible, followed, then more laughter. To Verhanna's surprise, the kender came rolling through the scrub pines, knees tucked under his chin. He made a graceful flip onto his feet and flung out his arms. There was more laughter, and a spattering of applause. Verhanna understood; the kender was playing the fool, doing acrobatic tricks to amuse the slavers.

Rufus scuffed his feet on the sand and dove headfirst into a somersault. From her hiding place, Verhanna could just make out what he'd marked in the dirt. A one and a zero. There were ten slavers in the camp.

"Good fellow!" she whispered fiercely. "We'll rush them. Spread out along the riverbank. I don't want any of them jumping in the water and swimming away." Burdened by armor, her guards wouldn't be able to pursue the slavers in the river.

Swords whisked out of scabbards. Verhanna stood, silently thrusting her blade in the air. The last rays of daylight fell across her face, highlighting its mix of human and elven features. Almond-shaped elven eyes, rather broad human cheeks, and a sharp Silvanesti chin proclaimed the captain's ancestry. Her braid of light brown hair hung forward across her chest, and she flicked it behind her. She nodded curtly to her warriors. The guards swept forward.

As Verhanna hurried through the screen of scrawny trees, she took in the slavers' camp in a quick glance. At the foot of the cliff stood several huts made of beach stone chinked with moss. They blended in so well with their surroundings that from a distance no one would have recognized them as dwellings. Two small campfires burned on the open ground in front of the huts. The slavers stood in a ragged group between the fires. Rufus, his red topknot dripping perspiration and his blizzard of freckles lost on his flushed face, was standing on his hands before them.

The astonished slavers shouted when they saw the guards crashing toward them. A few reached for weapons, but most elected to flee. Verhanna pounded across the sand, straight at the nearest armed slaver. He appeared to be a Kagonesti, with dark braided hair and red triangles painted on his cheeks. In his hands he held a short spear with a wicked barbed head. Verhanna fended off the spear point with her shield and hacked at the shaft with her sword, lopping off the spearhead. The Kagonesti cursed, flung the wooden shaft at her, and turned to run. She was on him in a heartbeat, her long legs far swifter than his. The captain lowered her sword and slashed the fleeing slaver on the back of his leg. He fell, clutching his wounded limb. Verhanna hopped over him and kept going.

The slavers fell back, driven in toward the cliff base by the swords of the guards. Some chose to fight the Qualinesti, and these died in a brief, bloody skirmish. The ragged band was poorly armed and outnumbered, and soon they were on their knees, crying out for quarter.

"Down on your bellies!" Verhanna shouted. "Put your hands out flat on the ground."

She heard a warning shout from her left and turned in time to see one of the slavers sprinting for the river. He had too much of a head start for any of the guards to catch him, but he hadn't reckoned on Rufus Wrinklecap. The kender whipped out a sling and quickly loosed a pellet. With a *thunk*, the stone hit the back of the slaver's head, and the escaping human fell and lay still. Rufus trotted over to him, and his hands began moving through the fellow's clothing.

The fight was over. The slavers were searched and bound hand and foot. Of the ten in the camp, four were human men, four were Kagonesti, and two were half-humans. Merith remarked on the fact that the three who died fighting were all Kagonesti.

"They're not inclined to submit," Verhanna replied grudgingly. "Have those huts searched, Merith."

Rufus came sauntering up, swinging his sling jauntily. "Pretty good fight, eh, Captain?" he said cheerfully.

"More a pigeon shoot than a fight, thanks to you."

The kender beamed. Verhanna dug into her belt pouch and found a gold piece. Her father's graven image stared up from the coin. She tossed it to Rufus.

"That's for your help, kender," she said.

He caressed the heavy gold piece. "Thank you, my captain!"

Just then Merith shouted, "Captain! Over here!" He stood by one of the huts.

"What is it?" she asked sharply when she reached him. "What's wrong?"

Ashen-faced, he nodded toward the hut. "You—you'd best go inside and see."

Verhanna frowned and pushed by him. The door of the crude stone house was nothing but a flap of leather. She thrust a hand through and stepped inside. A candle burned on the small table in the center of the one-room dwelling. Someone was seated at the table. His face was in shadow, but Verhanna saw numerous rings on the hand that rested on the table, including a familiar silver signet ring. A ring that belonged to—

"Really, Sister, you have the most appalling timing in the world," said the seated figure. He leaned forward into the candlelight, and the hazel eyes of the line of Silvanos sparkled.

"Ulvian! What are you doing here?" Verhanna asked,

shock reducing her voice to a whisper.

Kith-Kanan's son pushed the candle aside and clasped his hands lightly on the tabletop. "Conducting some very profitable business, till you so rudely disrupted it."

"Business?" For a long moment, his sister couldn't take it in. The crude plates and utensils, the worn wooden table, the rough pallet of blankets in one corner, even the sputtering candle—all claimed her roving gaze before her eyes once more rested on the person before her. Then, with the force of a summer storm, she exploded, "Business! Slavery!"

Ulvian's handsome face, so like his mother Suzine's, twitched slightly. Full-blooded elven males couldn't grow beards or mustaches, but Ulvian kept a modest stubble as a sign of his half-human heritage. With a quick, distracted motion, he stroked the fine golden hair.

"What I do is none of your affair," he said, annoyed. "Nor anyone else's, for that matter."

Her own brother a trafficker in slaves! Eldest son of the House of Silvanos and the supposed heir to the throne of Qualinesti. Verhanna's face flamed with her disgrace and the knowledge of the shame and pain this would cause their father. How could Ulvian do such a thing? Then her mortification was replaced by anger. Cold rage filled the Speaker's daughter. Grabbing Ulvian by the front of his crimson silk doublet, Verhanna dragged him from behind the table and out of the hut. Merith was still waiting outside.

"Where are the slaves?" she rasped. Mutely Merith pointed to the larger of the two remaining huts.

"Come on, Brother!" growled Verhanna, shoving Ulvian ahead of her. Other guards saw the Speaker's son and gaped. Merith stormed at them.

"What are you gawking at? Mind those prisoners!" he ordered.

Verhanna propelled Ulvian into the slave hut. Within, a guard was removing a young, emaciated female elf's chains with a hammer and chisel. Other slaves slumped against the walls of the hut. Even with their deliverance at hand, they were broken in spirit, listless and passive. There were some half-human males, and to Verhanna's horror, two dark-haired human children who couldn't have been more than nine or ten years old. All the captives were caked with filth. The hut reeked of stale sweat, urine, and despair.

The guard hacked the elf woman's chain in two and helped her stand. Her thin, frail legs wouldn't support her. With only the faintest of sighs, she crumpled. The guard lifted her starved body in his arms and carried her out.

Verhanna knew she must get control of her emotions. Closing her eyes, she willed herself to be calm, willed her heart to slow its frenzied beating. Opening her eyes once more, she said with certainty, "Ulvian, Father will have your head for this. If he favors me, I'll gladly swing the axe."

One pale hand adjusting the lace at his throat, Ulvian smiled. "I don't think so, sweet Sister. After all, it wouldn't look good for the Speaker's heir to go around without a head, now would it?"

The captain slapped her brother. Ulvian's head snapped back. Slowly he turned to face his sister. She was four inches taller than he, and the prince tilted his head back slightly to stare directly into her eyes. The smirk was gone from his lips, replaced by cold-blooded fury.

"You will never be Speaker if I have anything to say about it," Verhanna swore. "You are unfit to utter our father's name, let alone inherit his title."

A single bead of blood hung from the corner of Prince Ulvian's mouth. He dabbed at it and said softly, "You always were Father's lapdog."

Sweeping the door flap aside, Verhanna called, "Lieutenant Merith! Come here!" The elegant elf hustled in, scabbard jangling against his armored thigh.

"Put Prince Ulvian in chains," she ordered. "And if he utters one word of protest, gag him as well."

Merith stared. "Captain, are you sure? Chain the prince?"

"Yes!" she thundered.

Merith searched among the heaps of chain in the slave hut and found a set of manacles to fit Prince Ulvian. Abashed, he stood before Kith-Kanan's son and held open the cold iron bonds.

"Highness," Merith said tightly. "Your hands, please."

Ulvian did not resist. He presented his slim arms, and Merith snapped the bands around his wrists. A hole in the latch would take a soft iron rivet.

"You will regret this, Hanna," the prince said in a barely audible voice as he stared at his manacled wrists.

\* \* \* \* \*

By the time Verhanna's warriors had the slavers' camp sorted out, Lord Ambrodel and his personal escort of thirty riders had come thundering up the riverbank, summoned by fast dispatch. The elves set up a double row of torches in the sand to light the riders' way. By the same light, they had sorted the wretched captives by race and gender. The slavers were chained together in one large band, and a guard of bow-armed warriors set to watch them.

Lord Ambrodel rode up, sand flying beneath his horse's hooves. He called out loudly for Verhanna. The Speaker's daughter came forward and saluted the younger Ambrodel.

"Give me your report," he ordered before dismounting.

Verhanna handed him a tally showing eight slaves found and freed, and seven slavers captured. "Three chose to fight and were killed," she added. Lord Ambrodel slipped the parchment under his breastplate.

"How were they moving the slaves?" he asked, surveying the cunningly concealed camp.

"By river, sir."

Lord Ambrodel glanced back at the moonlit water.
"My lord," Verhanna continued, "we found signs that
more slaves were sent on from this camp. The ones we
found here were too sick to travel. I'd like to take my
troop on and try to intercept the rest before they reach
the Ergoth border."

"You're far too late for that, I'm sure," Lord Ambrodel
replied. "I want to question the leader of the slavers. Did
you take him alive?" Verhanna nodded curtly. The warrior lord tugged off his leather gauntlets and slapped the
sand from his mailed thighs. "Well, Captain, show him
to me," he said impatiently.

Without a word, Verhanna turned on one heel and led
her commander toward the huts. The slavers lay on the
ground, their heads buried in their arms in despair or
else staring with hatred at their captors. Verhanna
yanked a torch from the sand and held it high. She held
the door flap open for Lord Ambrodel and thrust the
torch inside. The face of the figure seated before them
leapt into clarity.

Lord Ambrodel recoiled sharply. "It cannot be!" he
gasped. "Prince Ulvian!"

"Kemian, my friend," the prince said to the general,
"you'd best have these fetters removed. I am not a common criminal, though my hysterical sister insists on
treating me like one."

"Release him," said Lord Ambrodel. His face was
white.

"My lord, Prince Ulvian was caught engaging in the
forbidden commerce of slavery," Verhanna put in quickly. "Both my father's edicts and the laws of the Thalas-
Enthia demand—"

"Don't quote the law to me!" Lord Ambrodel
snapped. "I shall bring this matter to the attention of the
Speaker at once, but I will not drag a member of the royal family through the streets of Qualinost in chains! I

cannot disgrace the Speaker so!"

Before she could order it, Merith was at Verhanna's side, chisel in hand. She shoved her lieutenant's hands aside and grasped the cold iron clamps in her own bare hands. With the strength bestowed upon her by her elven heritage, Verhanna pried the manacles apart just enough so that Ulvian could slip his arms out. Impudently he handed the empty chains to his sister.

"Captain!" Lord Ambrodel said. "Return to your troop. Muster them for marching."

"My lord! To what destination?" she answered tersely.

"Southeast—to the forest. I want you to search for other slaver camps there. Lieutenant Merithynos will remain to report on the finding of the slavers."

Verhanna's gaze flickered to her brother, to Merith, and back to Lord Ambrodel. She was too disciplined in the ways of the warrior to disobey her commander, but she knew Lord Ambrodel was sending her away so he could handle the delicate business of Ulvian's crime and punishment. Kemian would not let the prince escape; he was too honest for that. But he would grant her brother every privilege, up to the moment he turned Ulvian over to Kith-Kanan himself.

"Very good, sir," Verhanna finally responded. With a curt nod, she departed, spurs ringing as her heels struck the packed sand.

Ulvian rubbed his wrists and smiled. "Thank you, my lord," he said. "I shall remember this."

"Save your gratitude, my prince. I meant what I said; you will be given over to your father's judgment."

Ulvian maintained his smile. The ruddy light of the torch made his blond beard and hair look like copper. "I'm not afraid," he said lightly. Indeed he wasn't. His father had never punished Ulvian for his errant ways in the past.

As Verhanna gathered her warriors together with hoarsely shouted commands, the kender reappeared. His pockets were bulging with plunder from the slavers' camp: knives, string, flints, clay pipes, brass-studded wristbands.

"Hail, Captain," Rufus called. "Where to now?"

Verhanna looped her reins around her left hand. "So you came back? I thought I'd seen the last of you."

"You paid me. I'm your scout now," Rufus announced. "I can lead you anywhere. From which horizon will we next see the sun?"

Verhanna swung into the saddle. Her eyes rested on the hut where her brother and Lord Ambrodel still tarried. Her brother, the slaver.

"South," she said, biting off the word as it left her tightly drawn lips.

\* \* \* \* \*

The Speaker's house was quite large, though far less grand than the Quinari Palace in Silvanost where Kith-Kanan had grown up. Built entirely of wood, it had a warmth and naturalness he felt was missing from the great crystal residence of his brother, the Speaker of the Stars. The house was more or less rectangular in shape, with two small wings radiating to the west. The main entrance was on the east side, facing the courtyard of the Tower of the Sun.

Lord Ambrodel, Lieutenant Merith, and Prince Ulvian stood in the lamplit antechamber where Kith-Kanan usually greeted his guests. As it was well past midnight, the bright moons of Krynn had already set.

Despite the late hour, the Speaker looked alert and carefully groomed as he and Tamanier Ambrodel descended the polished cherrywood staircase to the antechamber. His fur-trimmed robe swept the floor. The toes of his yellow felt slippers protruded from under the green velvet hem.

"What has happened?" he asked gently.

As senior officer present, it fell to Kemian Ambrodel to explain. When he reached the point in his story where

Verhanna had discovered Prince Ulvian in the slavers' camp, Kemian's father Tamanier gasped in astonishment. Kith-Kanan's gaze shifted to Ulvian, who pursed his lips and rocked on his heels in an obvious display of arrogance.

"Were the slaves you found badly treated?" asked the Speaker in clipped tones.

"They were sick, filthy, and ill-fed, Majesty. From what they told us, they were held back from a larger group of slaves sent on by river to Ergoth because they were deemed too feeble for hard work." Kemian fought down his disgust. "A few had been whipped, Speaker."

"I see. Thank you, my lord."

Kith-Kanan clasped his hands behind his back and studied the floor. The maple had a beautiful grain pattern that resembled the dancing flames of a fire. Suddenly, he lifted his head and said, "I want you all to swear to keep what happens here tonight strictly secret. No one is to know of it—not even your families. Is that clear?" The assembled elves nodded solemnly, except Ulvian. "This is a delicate matter. There are those in Qualinost who would try to profit from my son's—actions. For the safety of the nation, this must remain a secret."

Stepping down from the last stair, the Speaker stood nose-to-nose with his son. "Ullie," he said quietly, "why did you do it?"

The prince quivered with suppressed anger, tinged with fear. "Do you really want to know?" he burst out. "Because you preach about justice and mercy instead of strength and greatness! Because you waste money on beggars and useless temples instead of a proper palace! Because you were the most famous warrior of the age, and you've thrown all your glory away to idle in gardens instead of fighting your way to the gates of Silvanost, our rightful home!" His voice choked off.

Kith-Kanan looked his son up and down. The grief on his face was visible to all. The Speaker's great dignity asserted itself, however, and he said, "The war and the great march west left Silvanesti with an acute shortage of farmers, crafters, and laborers. To appease the nobles and clerics, my brother, the Speaker of the Stars, has sanctioned slavery throughout his realm. A similar condition exists in Ergoth, with similar results. But no amount of inconvenience justifies the bondage of living, thinking beings by others. I have made it my life's goal to stamp out the evil traffic in servitude in Qualinesti, and yet my own son—" Kith-Kanan folded his arms, gripping his biceps hard through the plush velvet of his robe. "Ulvian, you will be held under close confinement in Arcuballis Tower until—until I can think of a proper punishment for you," he declared.

"You don't dare." The prince sneered. "I am your son, your only legitimate heir! Where will your precious dynasty be without me? I know you, Father. You'll forgive me anything to keep from being the first and last Speaker of the Sun from the House of Silvanos!"

The aged Tamanier Ambrodel could contain himself no longer. He had been friend to Kith-Kanan ever since the Speaker was a young prince in Silvanost. To listen to this spoiled pup jeering at his father was more than mortal flesh could bear. The gray-haired castellan stepped forward and struck Ulvian with his open hand. The prince rounded on him, but Kith-Kanan moved swiftly, placing himself between his son and castellan.

"No, Tam. Stop," he said, his voice shaking. "Don't justify his hatred." To Ulvian, he added, "Fifty years ago you might have earned a beating for your insolence, but now I will not ease your conscience so readily."

Tamanier stepped back. Kith-Kanan beckoned to Merith, standing quietly behind Kemian Ambrodel.

"I have a charge for you, Lieutenant," Kith-Kanan said gravely. The Speaker's gaze unnerved the anxious young elf. "You will be my son's keeper. Take him to Arcuballis. Stay with him. He must see and speak to no one—no one at all. Do you understand?"

"Yes, Great Speaker." Merith saluted stiffly.

"Go now, while it is still dark."

Merith drew his sword and stood beside Ulvian. The prince glared sullenly at the naked blade. Speaker, castellan, and general watched the two leave for the tower keep that guarded the city's northeastern corner. When the great doors of the house closed behind them, Kith-Kanan asked Kemian where Verhanna was. Lord Ambrodel explained how he'd thought it best to separate brother and sister at such a crisis.

"A wise decision," Kith-Kanan said ruefully. "Hanna would wring Ullie's neck."

The Speaker bade Kemian return to the field and continue the hunt for slavers. The general bowed low, first to his sovereign and then to his father, and swept out of the hall. Once he was gone, Kith-Kanan sank shakily to the steps. Tamanier swiftly knelt beside him.

"Majesty! Are you ill?"

Tears glistened in Kith-Kanan's brown eyes. "I am all right," he murmured. "Leave me, Tam."

"May I escort Your Majesty to his room?"

"No, I want to sit awhile. On your way now, old friend."

Tamanier rose and bowed. The scuff of his sandals faded in the dimly lit corridor. Kith-Kanan was alone.

He realized his hands were clenched into fists, and he relaxed them. Five hundred years was not a long time to live, by elven standards, yet at that moment, Kith-Kanan felt very aged indeed. What was he to do with Ulvian? The boy's motives were a mystery to him. Did he need money so badly? Was it the thrill of doing something forbidden? No reason could excuse his conduct this time.

Once, after Ulvian had returned home half-naked and filthy after literally losing his shirt gambling, Verhanna had cornered her father. "He's no good," she had said.

"Isn't he? Who made him so?" Kith-Kanan had wondered aloud. "Can I blame anyone but myself? I hardly ever saw him till he was twelve. The war was going badly, and I was needed in the field."

"Mother spoiled him. She filled his head with a lot of nonsense," Verhanna said bitterly. "I can't count the times he's told me you were responsible for her death."

Kith-Kanan drew a hand across his brow. He couldn't count the times he'd told Ulvian the truth about Suzine, that she had sacrificed her life for her husband and his cause, but Ulvian never believed it.

What could he do? Ulvian was right; Kith-Kanan couldn't have his own son executed or banished. He was the Speaker's heir. After working so hard, sacrificing so much, to build this great nation, Kith-Kanan wondered, was it all to be lost?

A bell tolled somewhere far off. The priests of Mantis, called Matheri in old Silvanost, were ringing the great bronze temple bell, signaling the imminent dawn. Kith-Kanan raised his weary head from his hands. The sound of the bell was like a voice, calling to him. *Come, come,* it said.

Yes, he thought. I will meditate and ask the gods. They will help me.

# ❧ 3 ❧

## The Balance of Justice

_____

*The domed ceiling of the Tower of the Sun was deco*-
rated with an elaborate mosaic symbolizing the passage
of time and the forces of good and evil. One half of the
dome was blue sky, made up of thousands of chips of
turquoise, and a brilliant sun made from gold and diamonds. The opposite half was tiled with the blackest
onyx and sprinkled with diamond stars. The three
moons of Krynn were represented by discs of ruby for
Lunitari, silver for Solinari, and oxblood garnet for
Nuitari. Dividing these hemispheres was a rainbow
band set with crimsonite, topazes, peridots, sapphires,
and amethysts. The rainbow was a barrier and bridge
between the worlds of night and day, a symbol of the

intervention of the gods in mortal affairs.

Kith-Kanan meditated on the symbolism of the dome as he lay on his back on the rostrum in the center of the tower floor. Unlike its counterpart in Silvanost, this tower was not used as the throne room. The Tower of the Sun was mainly used when Kith-Kanan wanted to, as Verhanna put it, "impress the boots off a visitor."

Kith-Kanan pillowed his head on one hand. His silver-blond hair was loose and spread out around his head like a halo. Fixing his gaze on the ceiling of the tower, he opened his mind. The peace and balanced beauty of the Tower of the Sun calmed him, allowing him to consider difficult matters.

Rows of windows and mirrors spiraled up the height of the tower, letting in the sun and reflecting it in endless cascades. No matter where the sun was in the sky, the Tower of the Sun would always be brightly lit. The Speaker draped his free arm over his face. A cool breeze played over his arms as it whistled through the tower windows. Even that was soothing. On this day, the Speaker of the Sun needed every bit of peace he could find as he wrestled with the problem of succession.

Qualinesti must have an heir. Kith-Kanan had sworn, before the gods and the assembly at Pax Tharkas, that he would step aside when the fortress was complete. Weekly dispatches from the chief architect and master builder, the dwarf Feldrin Feldspar, kept him informed of the progress there. Pax Tharkas was ninety percent done; with good weather and no delays, the citadel would be finished in another two or three years. Kith-Kanan must name his successor soon.

For too long, the Speaker had consoled himself with the thought that his only son was merely wayward. But now there was no denying that the problems ran much deeper. His own son involved in the slave trade. . . .

With Ulvian obviously unworthy for the position of Speaker of the Sun, Kith-Kanan pondered other candidates. Verhanna? Not a good choice. She was brave, intelligent, and as honorable as any highborn Silvanesti, but also temperamental and sometimes prone to harshness. In spite of Kith-Kanan's dreams of equality in his kingdom, the fact that Verhanna was half-human would also weigh against her in the minds of some of his full-blooded elven subjects. These prejudices were kept carefully tucked away, out of plain sight, but the Speaker knew they existed still. Coupled with the fact that Verhanna was female, that bias would be too much to overcome.

"You could marry again," said a quiet voice.

Kith-Kanan descended the rostrum and looked around. The tower was pitch-dark, though he knew it wasn't yet midday. Standing to his left, between two of the pillars that ringed the chamber, was a strange elf, wreathed in yellow light.

"Who are you?" demanded Kith-Kanan.

The halo of light followed the stranger as he approached the rostrum, though the elf carried no lamp or candle. He was clad entirely in a suit of close-fitting red leather. A scarlet cape hung from one shoulder and brushed the floor. The stranger's ears were unusually tall and pointed, even for an elf, and his long hair was a vivid ruby red.

"I am one who can help you," the intruder said. He spoke with an air of supreme self-assurance. Now that he was closer, Kith-Kanan saw that his eyes were black and glittering, set in a face as dead white as dry bones. No lines at all touched the face; it might have been carved from purest alabaster.

"Begone from here," Kith-Kanan said sharply. "You intrude on my privacy!" He faced the stranger, his muscles tensed for fight or flight.

"Come, come! You're in a quandary about your son, aren't you? I can help. I have considerable power."

Kith-Kanan knew this elf must be, at the very least, a powerful sorcerer. The tower was wrapped in protective spells, and for any malign being to enter would require great mastery of magic. "What is your name?"

The red elf shrugged, and his cape rippled like waves in a scarlet sea. "I have many names. You may call me Dru if you like." With one hand at his slim waist and the other held out before him, Dru made a graceful, mocking bow. "You came here seeking help from higher powers, Great Speaker, so I have answered your call."

Kith-Kanan's brows arched. "Are you mortal?"

"Does it matter? I can help you. Your son has offended you, and you want to know what to do about it . . . yes? You are Speaker of the Sun. Condemn him," Dru said smoothly.

"He is my only son!"

"And yet you might have another, if you marry again. For a slight fee, I can procure for you the mate of your heart's desire." He smiled, revealing teeth as red as his hair. Kith-Kanan recoiled and moved quickly back to the rostrum, where the potent magic symbols set in the floor mosaic would protect him from evil spells.

"I will not bargain with an evil spirit!" he exclaimed. "Begone! Trouble me no more!"

The red elf laughed, the loud peals echoing weirdly in the black, empty tower. "Our bargain has already commenced, Great Speaker!"

Kith-Kanan was confused. Already commenced? Had he somehow summoned this odd being from the netherworld?

"Of course you did," Dru said, reading his thoughts. "I'm a busy fellow. I don't waste my valuable time appearing to just anyone. Here, son of Sithel. Let me demonstrate what I can do."

Dru brought his white hands together with a loud clap. Kith-Kanan felt a breeze rush by him, as if all the air in the tower gusted toward the strange elf. With a crackling hiss, a ball of fire appeared suddenly between Dru's palms, and he flung it to the floor, where it burst. The loud crack and blinding flash caused Kith-Kanan to stagger back. When his vision had cleared, he beheld a transformed scene.

Kith-Kanan no longer stood in the Tower of the Sun, though its rostrum was still solid beneath his feet. His surroundings were those of a smaller tower. By the stonework and the shape of the windows, he knew that it was in Silvanost. Tapestries in shades of pale green and blue hung on the walls, depicting woodland scenes and elegantly clad ladies. Sunlight filled the room.

A sigh caught his ears. He turned and saw a large, heavy wooden chair, its back to him, facing an open window. Someone was sitting in the chair. Kith-Kanan couldn't see who.

Suddenly the someone stood. Kith-Kanan glimpsed her beautiful red hair and his breath caught.

"Hermathya," he whispered.

"She cannot see or hear us," Dru informed him. "You see how she languishes in Silvanost, unloved and unloving. I can have her at your side in the blink of any eye."

Hermathya . . . the love of his youth. For many years the wife of his twin brother, Sithas. She stared straight through the spot where Kith-Kanan stood, piercing him unknowingly with her deep blue eyes. Her red-gold hair was piled up on her head in elaborate braids, showing the elegant shape of her upswept ears, and she wore a gown of the finest spider's-web gold, thin and clinging. Once he had proposed marriage to her, but his father, not knowing of their love, had betrothed her to Kith-Kanan's twin, Sithas. So much time had passed since that distant day. Now Sithas was leader of the Silvanesti elves, as Kith-Kanan ruled the Qualinesti.

Lonely and a bit self-pitying, Kith-Kanan felt himself sorely tempted. Always Hermathya's great beauty had been able to arouse him. An elf would have to be made of stone not to feel something in her presence.

Just as he was about to ask Dru his terms, Hermathya turned away. She lunged at the open window before her chair. Kith-Kanan cried out and reached for her.

Before she could hurtle through the high window,

Hermathya was brought up short. The harsh clank of metal shocked Kith-Kanan. Beneath the hem of her golden gown, he spied an iron fetter, locked about her right ankle and attached by a chain to the heavy chair. The chair was fastened to the floor. Though the fetter was lined with padded cloth, it gripped Hermathya's slender ankle tightly.

"What does this mean?" demanded Kith-Kanan.

Dru seemed vexed. "A minor problem, Great Speaker. The lady Hermathya suffers from despondency over the crippling of her son during the war and, I might add, over the loss of your love. The Speaker of the Stars has ordered her chained so that she won't harm herself."

Hermathya had been staring with palpable longing at the open window. Her face was as exquisitely lovely as Kith-Kanan remembered it. The high cheekbones, the delicately slender nose, and skin as smooth as the finest silk. Time hadn't marked her at all. Once more her faint sigh came to him, a sound full of sorrow and yearning. Kith-Kanan squeezed his eyes shut. "Take me away," he hissed. "I cannot bear to see this!"

"As you wish."

The dark embrace of the Tower of the Sun in Qualinost returned.

Kith-Kanan shuddered. Hermathya had been out of his thoughts, and out of his heart, for centuries. The break between him and his twin brother had been widened by the passion Kith-Kanan had felt for Hermathya. Time and other loves had practically extinguished the old fire. Why did he feel such longing for her now?

"Old wounds are the deepest and the hardest to heal," said Dru, once more answering Kith's thoughts.

"I don't believe any of this," the Speaker snapped. "You created that scene with your magic to deceive me!"

Dru sighed loudly and circled the rostrum, his yellow aura moving with him. "Ah, such lack of faith!" Dru said sardonically. "All I offered was true. The lady can be yours again if you meet my terms."

Kith-Kanan folded his arms. "Which are what?"

The red elf pressed his hands together prayerfully, but the expression on his face was anything but pious. "Permit the passage of slave caravans from Ergoth and Silvanesti through your realm," he said quickly.

"Never!" Kith-Kanan strode toward Dru, who did not retreat. The strange elf's yellow aura stopped the Speaker's advance. When he reached out to touch the golden shell, he snatched his fingers back as if they'd been burned. But the glow was bizarrely, intensely cold.

"You are brave," Dru mused, "but do not try to lay hands on me again."

At that moment, Kith-Kanan realized who Dru really was, and for one of the few times in his life, he was truly frightened.

"I know you," he said in a voice that wavered, though he fought to keep it steady. "You are the one who corrupts those beset by adversity." Almost too softly to be heard, he added, "Hiddukel."

The God of Evil Bargains, whose sacred color was red, bowed. "You are tiresome in your virtues," he remarked. "Is there nothing you want? I can fill this tower twenty times with gold or silver or jewels. What do you say to that?" His red eyebrows rose questioningly.

"Treasure will not solve my problems."

"Think of the *good* you could do with it all." Hiddukel's voice dripped with malicious sarcasm. "You could buy all the slaves in the world and set them free!"

Kith-Kanan backed away toward the rostrum. It was his safe haven, where not even the evil god's magic could reach him. "Why do you concern yourself with the slave trade, Lord of the Broken Scales?" he asked.

The god's elven form shrugged. "I concern myself with all such commerce. I am the patron deity of slavers."

The stone of the rostrum bumped against Kith-Kanan's heels. Confidently he climbed backward onto it. "I refuse all your offers, Hiddukel," he declared. "Go away, and trouble me no further!"

The look of malign enjoyment left the red-garbed elf's face. Addressed by his true name, he had no choice but to depart. His pointed features twisted into a hateful grimace.

"Your troubles will increase, Speaker of the Sun," the God of Demons spat. "That which you have created will come forth to strike you down. The hammer shall break the anvil. Lightning shall cleave the rock!"

"Go!" Kith-Kanan cried, his heart pounding in his throat. The single syllable reverberated in the air.

Hiddukel backed away a pace and spun on one toe. His cape swirled around like a flame. Faster and faster the god whirled, until his elven form vanished, replaced by a whirling column of red smoke and fire. Kith-Kanan threw up an arm to shield his face from the virulent display. The voice of Hiddukel boomed in his head.

"The time of wonders is at hand, foolish king! Forces older than the gods surround you! Only the power of the Queen of Darkness can withstand them! Beware!"

The fiery specter of Hiddukel flew apart, and in two heartbeats, the Tower of the Sun was quiet once more. The deep darkness that filled it remained, however. Sweating and shaking from his near escape from the Collector of Souls, Kith-Kanan sank to the floor. His body was wracked with spasms he could not control. A jumble of thoughts and images warred inside his brain— Ulvian, Hermathya, Suzine, Verhanna, his brother Sithas—all surmounted by the leering visage of Hiddukel. He felt as if his soul was the object of a deadly tug-of-war.

Kith-Kanan's entire body ached. He was limp, worn out, exhausted. Rest was what he craved. He must rest. His eyelids fluttered closed.

\* \* \* \* \*

"Sire? Speaker?" called a faint voice.

Kith-Kanan pushed himself up on his hands. "Who is

it?" he replied hoarsely, brushing hair from his eyes.

A glow appeared from the entry hall. This time it was the mundane light of a lamp in the hands of his castellan.

"I'm here, Tam."

"Great Speaker, are you well? We could not reach you, and—and the whole city has been plunged into darkness! The people are terrified!"

Concentrating his strength, Kith-Kanan struggled to his feet. Behind the agitated Tamanier were several silent Guards of the Sun. Their usual jaunty posture was gone, replaced by an attitude of tense fear.

"What do you mean?" the Speaker demanded shakily. "How long have I been in here? Is it night?"

Tamanier came closer. His face was white and drawn. "Sire, it is barely noon! Not long after you entered the tower to meditate, a curtain of blackness descended on the city. I came at once to inform you, but the tower doors were barred by invisible forces! We were frantic. Suddenly, only a few moments ago, they swung wide."

Kith-Kanan adjusted his rumpled clothing and combed his hair back with his fingers. His mind was racing. The tower seemed normal, except for the darkness cloaking it. There was no trace of Hiddukel. He took a deep, restoring breath and said, "Come. We will see what the situation is and then calm the people."

They went to the entrance, Kith-Kanan striding as purposefully as his nerves and throbbing muscles would allow. Tamanier hurried along with the lamp. The guards at the door presented arms and waited dutifully for the Speaker to pass. The great doors stood open.

Kith-Kanan paused, his feet on the broad granite sill. The gloom beyond was intense, far denser than ordinary night. In spite of the torches carried by Tamanier Ambrodel and several warriors, Kith-Kanan could barely see to the bottom of the tower steps. The torchlight seemed muffled by the jet-black fog. There were no lights to be seen in the gloom, though from this high vantage point, all of Qualinost should be spread out before him. Overhead, no stars or moons were visible.

"You say this happened just after I entered the tower?" he asked tensely.

"Yes, sire," replied the castellan.

Kith-Kanan nodded. Was this some spell of Hiddukel's, to coerce him into accepting the god's vile bargain? No, not likely. The Lord of the Broken Scales was a deceiver, not an extorter. Hiddukel's victims damned themselves. Their torment was thus sweeter to the wicked god. . . .

"It's very strange," Kith-Kanan said in his best royal manner. "Still, it doesn't seem dangerous, merely frightening. Is the prisoner still in Arcuballis Tower?" No need to bandy the prince's name about.

One of the guards stepped forward. "I can answer that, sire. I was at the tower myself when the blackness fell. Lieutenant Merithynos thought it might be part of a plot to free his prisoner. No such attempt was made, however, Highness."

"This is no mortal's spell," remarked Kith-Kanan. He swept a hand through the murk, half expecting it to stain his skin. It didn't. The gloom that looked so solid felt completely insubstantial, not even damp like a normal fog.

"Tell Merithynos to bring his prisoner to my house," Kith-Kanan ordered briskly. "Keep him sequestered there until I return."

"Where are you going, sire?" asked Tamanier, confused and unsure.

"Among my people, to reassure them."

With no escort and bearing his own torch, Kith-Kanan left the Tower of the Sun. For the next several hours, he walked the streets of his capital, meeting common folk and nobles alike. Fear had thickened the air as surely as the weird gloom. When word spread that Kith-Kanan was in the streets, the people came out of the towers and temples to see him and to hear his calming words.

"Oh, Great Speaker!" lamented a young elf woman. "The blackness smothers me. I cannot breathe!"

He put a hand on her shoulder. "It's good air," he assured her. "Can't you smell the flowers in the gardens of Mantis?" His temple was close by. The aroma of the hundreds of blooming roses that surrounded it scented the still air.

The elf woman inhaled with effort, but her face cleared somewhat as she did. "Yes, sire," she said more calmly. "Yes . . . I can smell them."

"Mantis would not waste his perfume in suffocating air," said the Speaker kindly. "It's fear that chokes you. Stay here by the gardens until you feel better."

He left her and moved on, trailed by a large crowd of worried citizens. Their pale faces moved in and out of the gloom, barely lit by the scores of blazing brands that had sprouted from every window and in every hand. Where the avenue from the Tower of the Sun joined the street that curved northwest to the tower keep called Sithel, Kith-Kanan found a band of crafters and temple acolytes debating in loud, angry voices. He stepped between the factions and asked them why they were arguing.

"It's the end of the world!" declared a human man, a coppersmith by the look of the snips and pliers dangling from his oily leather vest. "The gods have abandoned us!"

"Nonsense!" spat an acolyte of Astra, the patron god of the elves. "This is merely some strange quirk of the weather. It will pass."

"Weather? Black as pitch at noon?" exclaimed the coppersmith. His companions—a mix of elves and humans, all metal crafters—loudly supported him.

"You should heed the learned priest," Kith-Kanan said firmly. "He is versed in these matters. If the gods wanted to destroy the world, they wouldn't wrap us in a blanket of night. They'd use fire and flood and shake the ground. Don't you agree?"

The smith hardly wanted to contradict his sovereign, but he said sullenly, "Then why don't they do something about it?" He gestured to the half-dozen young clerics facing him.

"Have you tried?" Kith-Kanan asked the acolyte of Astra.

The cleric frowned. "None of our banishing spells worked, Highness. The darkness is not caused by mortal or divine magic," he said. The other clerics behind him murmured their agreement.

"How long do you think it will last?"

The young elf could only shrug helplessly.

The coppersmith snorted, and Kith-Kanan turned to him. "You ought to be grateful, my friend, for this darkness."

That caught the fellow off guard. "Grateful, Majesty?"

"It's pitch-black on a working day. I'd say you have a holiday." The crafters laughed nervously. "If I were you, I'd hie on over to the nearest tavern and celebrate your good fortune!" A broad grin brightened the coppersmith's face, and the disputants began to disperse.

Kith-Kanan continued on his way. Passing a side street on his right, he halted when he heard weeping coming from the dim alley.

The Speaker turned into the side street, following the sound of sobbing. Suddenly a hand reached out of the dark and pressed against his chest, stopping him.

"Who are you?" he said sharply, thrusting the torch toward the one who'd halted him.

"I live here. Gusar is my name."

The weak torchlight showed Kith-Kanan an old human, bald and white-browed. Gusar's eyes were white, too. Cataracts had taken his sight.

"Someone is in trouble down there," said the Speaker, relieved. An old blind man was hardly a threat.

"I know. I was going to help when you blundered up behind me."

Kith-Kanan bristled at the man's bluntness. "Get that brand out of my face, and I'll be on my way," the blind man continued.

The monarch of Qualinesti drew his torch back. Gusar moved off with the easy confidence of one used to darkness. Kith-Kanan trailed silently behind the blind man. In short order, they came upon a trio of elf children huddled by the closed door of a tower home.

"Hello," Gusar said cheerfully. "Is someone crying?"

"We can't find our house!" wailed an elf girl. "We looked and looked, but we couldn't see the daisies that grow by our door!"

"Daisies, eh? I know that house. It's only a few steps more. I'll take you there." Gusar extended a gnarled hand. The elf children regarded him with misgiving.

"Are you a troll?" asked the smallest boy, his blue eyes huge in his tiny face.

Gusar cackled. "No. I'm just an old blind man." He pointed a thumb over his shoulder. "My friend has a torch to help light your way."

Kith-Kanan was surprised. He hadn't realized the old man knew he was still there.

The girl who'd spoken got up first and took the human's hand. The two boys followed their sister, and together the children and the old human wandered down the lane. Kith-Kanan followed at a distance, until the little girl turned and announced, "We don't need you, sir. The old one can see us home."

"Fare you well, then," Kith-Kanan called. The bowed back of the aged human and the flaxen hair of the elf children quickly vanished in the inky air.

For the first time in days, the Speaker smiled. His dream of a nation where all races could live in peace was truly taking hold when three children of pure Silvanesti blood could fearlessly take the hand of a gnarled old human and let him lead them home.

## 🍃 4 🍃

# the lightning and the Rock

On the morning of what would have been the fourth day of darkness, a ball of red fire appeared in the eastern sky. The people of Qualinost swarmed into the streets, fearfully pointing at the dangerous-looking orb. Within minutes, dread turned to relief when they realized that what they were seeing was the sun, burning through the gloom. The darkness lifted steadily, and the day dawned bright and cloudless.

Kith-Kanan looked out over his city from the window of his private rooms. The rose-quartz towers sparkled cleanly in the newborn sunlight, and the trees seemed to bask in the warmth. All over Qualinost, in every window and every gracefully curving street, faces were upturned to the luxurious heat and light. As the Speaker looked south across his city, the songs and laughter of spontaneous revelry reached his ears.

The return of light was a great relief to Kith-Kanan. For the past three days, he had done nothing but try to hold his people together, reassuring them that the end of the world was not nigh. After two days of darkness, emissaries had arrived in Qualinost from Ergoth and Thorbardin, seeking answers from the Speaker of the Sun as to the cause of the fearful gloom. Kith-Kanan had his own ideas, but didn't share them with the emissaries. Some new power was rising from a long sleep. Hiddukel had said it was a power older even than the gods. The Speaker did not yet know what its purpose was, and he didn't want to spread alarums through the world based on his own flimsy theories.

From all over his realm, people poured into Qualinost, clogging the bridges and straining the resources of the city. Everyone was afraid of the unknown darkness. Fear made allies of the oldest enemies, too. From outside Kith-Kanan's enlightened kingdom came humans and elves who had fought each other in the Kinslayer Wars. During the darkness, they had huddled together around bonfires, praying for deliverance.

From his window overlooking the sunlit city, Kith-Kanan mused, Perhaps that was the reason for it—to bring us all together.

There was a soft, firm knock at the door. Kith-Kanan turned his back on the city and called, "Enter." Tamanier Ambrodel appeared in the doorway and bowed.

"The emissaries of Ergoth and Thorbardin have departed," the castellan reported, hands folded in front of him. "In better spirits than when they arrived, I might add, sire."

"Good. Now perhaps I can deal with other weighty matters. Send Prince Ulvian and the warrior Merithynos to me at once."

"At once, Majesty" was Tamanier's quiet reply.

As soon as the castellan had departed, Kith-Kanan moved to his writing table and sat down. He took out a fresh sheet of foolscap. Dipping the end of a fine stylus into a jar of ink, he began to write. He was still writing when Ulvian and Merith presented themselves.

"Well, Father, I hope this ridiculous business is over," Ulvian said with affected injury. He was still clad in the crimson doublet and silver-gray trousers he'd been captured in. "I've been bored silly, with no one to talk to but this tiresome warrior of yours."

Merith's hand tightened on the pommel of his sword. His cobalt-blue eyes stared daggers at the prince. Kith-Kanan forestalled the lieutenant's offended retort.

"That's enough," the Speaker said firmly. He finished writing, melted a bit of sealing wax on the bottom of the sheet, and pressed his signet ring into the soft blue substance. When the seal was cool, he rolled the foolscap into a scroll and tied it with a thin blue ribbon. This he likewise sealed with wax.

"Lieutenant Merithynos, you will convey this message to Feldrin Feldspar, the master builder who directs the work at Pax Tharkas," said the Speaker, rising and holding out the scroll. Merith accepted it, though he looked perplexed.

"Am I to give up guarding the prince, Majesty?" he asked.

"Not at all. The prince is to accompany you to Pax Tharkas."

Kith-Kanan's eyes met his son's. Ulvian frowned.

"What's in Pax Tharkas for me?" he asked suspiciously.

"I am sending you to school," his father replied. "Master Feldrin is to be your schoolmaster."

Ulvian laughed. "You mean to make an architect out of me?"

"I am putting you in Feldrin's hands as a common laborer—a slave, in fact. You will work every day for no wage and receive only the meanest provender. At night, you will be locked in your hut and guarded by Lieutenant Merithynos."

Ulvian's confident smirk vanished. Hazel eyes wide, he backed away a few steps, falling to one of the Speaker's couches. His face was pale with shock.

"You can't mean it," he whispered. More loudly, he added, "You can't do this!"

"I am the Speaker of the Sun," Kith-Kanan said. Though his heart was breaking with the punishment he was visiting on his only son, the Speaker's demeanor was firm and unyielding.

The prince's head shook back and forth, as if denying what he was hearing. "You can't make me a slave!" He leapt to his feet and his voice became a shout. "I am your son! I am Prince of Qualinesti!"

"Yes, you are, and you have broken my law. I'm not doing this on a whim, Ullie. I hope it will teach you the true meaning of slavery—the cruelty, the degradation, the pain and suffering. Maybe then you will understand the horror of what you've done. Maybe then you'll know why I hate it, and why you should hate it too."

Ulvian's outrage wilted. "How—how long will I be there?" he asked haltingly.

"As long as necessary. I'll visit you, and if I'm convinced you've learned your lesson, I'll release you. What's more, I will forgive you and publicly declare you my successor."

That seemed to restore the prince somewhat. His gaze flickered toward Merith, who was standing at rigid attention, though his expression reflected frank astonishment. Ulvian said, "What if I run away?"

"Then you will lose everything and be declared outlaw in your own country," Kith-Kanan said evenly.

Ulvian advanced on his father. There was betrayal and disbelief in his eyes, and rage as well. Merith tensed and prepared to subdue the prince if he attacked the Speaker, but Ulvian stopped a pace short of his father.

"When do I go?" he asked through clenched teeth.

"Now."

A roll of thunder punctuated Kith-Kanan's pronouncement. Merith stepped forward and took hold of the prince's arm, but Ulvian twisted out of his grasp.

"I'll come back, Father. I will be the Speaker of the Sun!" the prince vowed in ringing tones.

"I hope you will, Son. I hope you will."

A second crash of thunder finished the confrontation. Merith led the prince reluctantly away.

Hands clasped tightly behind his back, Kith-Kanan returned to his window. Melancholy washed over him in slow, steady waves as he gazed up at the cloudless sky. Then, even as his mind was far away, from the corner of one eye, he spied a bolt of lightning. It flashed out of the blue vault and dove at the ground, striking somewhere in the southwestern district of Qualinost. A deep boom reverberated over the city, rattling the shutters on the Speaker's house.

Thunder and lightning from a clear sky? Kith-Kanan's inner torment was pushed aside for a moment as he digested this remarkable occurrence.

The time of wonders was indeed at hand.

\* \* \* \* \*

Twenty riders followed the dusty trail through the sparse forest of maple saplings, most no taller than the horses. Twenty elven warriors, under Verhanna's command and guided by their new kender scout, Rufus Wrinklecap, rode slowly in single file. No one spoke. The muggy morning air oppressed them—that, and the cold trail they were trying to follow. Four days out of Qualinost, and this was the only sign of slavers they'd found. It hadn't helped that they'd had to flounder on in three days of total darkness. Rufus warned the captain that the tracks they were tracing were many weeks old and might lead to nothing.

"Never mind," she grumbled. "Keep at it. Lord Ambrodel sent us here for a reason."

"Yes, my captain."

The kender eased his big horse a little farther away from the ill-tempered Verhanna. Rufus was a comic sight on horseback; with his shocking red topknot and less than four feet of height, he hardly looked like a valiant elven warrior. Perched on a chestnut charger that was bigger than any other animal in the troop, he resembled a small child astride a bullock.

During their brief stopover in Qualinost, while the troops were reprovisioned and a horse was secured for him, the kender had bought himself some fancy clothes. His blue velvet breeches, vest, and white silk shirt beneath a vivid red cape made quite a contrast to the armor-clad elves. Atop his head perched an enormous broad-brimmed blue hat, complete with a white plume and a hole in the crown to allow his long topknot to trail behind.

They had passed through the easternmost fringe of the Kharolis Mountains onto the great central plain, the scene of so many battles during the Kinslayer War. Now and then the troop saw silent reminders of that awful conflict: a burned village, abandoned to weeds and carrion birds; a cairn of stones, under which were buried the bodies of fallen soldiers of Ergoth in a mass grave. Occasionally their horses' hooves turned up battered, rusting helmets lodged in the soil. The skulls of horses and the bones of elves shone in the tall grass like ivory talismans, warning of the folly of kings.

Once every hour Verhanna halted her warriors and ordered Rufus to check the trail. The nimble kender leaped from his horse's back or slid off its wide rump and scrambled through the grass and saplings, sniffing and peering for telltale signs.

During the third such halt of the morning, Verhanna guided her mount to where Rufus squatted, busily rubbing blades of grass between his fingers.

"Well, Wart, what do you find? Have the slavers come

this way?" she asked, leaning over her animal's glossy neck.

"Difficult to say, Captain. Very difficult. Other tall folk have passed this way since the slavers. The trails are muddled," muttered Rufus. He put a green stem in his mouth and nibbled it. "The grass is still sweet," he observed. "Others came from the east and passed through during the days of darkness."

"What others?" she said, frowning.

The kender hopped up, dropping the grass and dusting off his fancy blue pants. "Travelers. Going that way," he said, pointing to the direction they'd come from Qualinost. "They were in deeply laden, two-wheeled carts."

Verhanna regarded her scout sourly. "We didn't pass anyone."

"In that darkness, who knows what we passed? The Dragonqueen herself could've ridden by clad in cloth o' gold and we wouldn't have seen her."

She straightened in the saddle and replied, "What about our quarry?"

Rufus rubbed his flat, sunburned nose. "They split up."

"What?" Verhanna's shout brought the other troopers to attention. Her second-in-command, a Kagonesti named Tremellan, hurried to her side. She waved him off and dismounted, slashing through the tall grass to Rufus. Planting her mailed hands on her hips, the captain demanded, "Where did they split up?"

Rufus took two steps forward and one sideways. "Here," he said, pointing at the trodden turf. "Six riders, the same ones we've been chasing all along. Two went east. They were elder folk, like the Speaker." By this, the kender meant the two were Silvanesti. "Two others went north. They smelled of fur and had thick shoes. Humans, I'd say. The last two continued south, and they're tricky. Barefoot, they are, and they smell just like the wind. Dark elders, and wise in the ways of the chase."

"What does he mean?" Verhanna muttered to Tremellan.

"Dark elders are my people," offered the Kagonesti officer. "They probably work as scouts for the other four. They find travelers, or a lonely farm, and lead the slavers there."

Verhanna slapped her palms together with a metallic clink. "All right! Gather the troop around! I want to speak to them."

The elven warriors made a circle around their captain and the kender scout. Verhanna grinned at them, arms folded across her chest.

"The enemy has made a mistake," she declared, rocking on her heels. "They've split themselves into three groups. The humans and Silvanesti are headed for their homelands, probably carrying the gold they made selling slaves. Without their Kagonesti scouts, they don't stand a chance against us. Sergeant Tremellan, I want you to take a contingent of ten and ride after the Silvanesti. Take them alive if you can. Corporal Zilaris, you take five troopers and follow the humans. They shouldn't give you much trouble. Four warriors will come with me to find the Kagonesti."

"Excuse me, Captain, but I don't think that's wise," Tremellan said. "I don't need ten warriors to catch the Silvanesti slavers. You should take more with you. The dark elders will be the hardest to catch."

"He's right," chimed in Rufus. His topknot bobbed as he nodded vigorously.

"Who's captain here?" Verhanna demanded. "Don't question my orders, Sergeant. You don't imagine I need numbers to track the woods-wise Kagonesti, do you? No, of course not! Stealth is what's needed, Sergeant. My orders stand."

A rumble of thunder rolled across the plain and was ignored. Without further discussion, Tremellan collected half the warriors and redistributed food and water among them. He formed his group around him while

Verhanna gave him final orders.

"Pursue them hard, Sergeant," she urged. Her blood was up, and her brown eyes were brilliant. "They've a week's head start, but they might not yet know anyone is after them, so they won't be moving fast."

"And the border, Captain?" asked Tremellan.

"Don't talk to me about borders," snapped the captain. "Get those damned slavers! This is no time for faint hearts or half measures!"

Tremellan suppressed his irritation, saluted, and spurred his horse. The troop rode off through the maple saplings as thunder boomed at their backs.

Verhanna felt a tug on her haqueton. She turned and looked down, seeing Rufus standing close beside her. "What is it?"

"Look up. There are no clouds," he said, turning his small face heavenward. "Thunder, but no clouds."

"So the storm is over the horizon," Verhanna replied briskly. She left the kender still staring at the clear blue sky. Corporal Zilaris took his detachment and headed north after the human slavers. Verhanna was watching them recede in the distance when suddenly a bolt of lightning lanced down a scant mile away. Dirt flew up in the air, and the crack of thunder was like a blow from a mace.

"By Astra!" she exclaimed. "That was close!"

The next one was closer still. With no warning, a column of blue-white fire slammed into the ground less than fifty paces from Verhanna, Rufus, and the remaining warriors. The horses screamed and reared, some falling back on their startled riders. Verhanna, still on the ground, kept a tight hand on her straining mount's bridle. Rufus had just remounted, and when his horse began to snort and dance, the kender climbed onto its neck to get a better hold. His cape flopped over the horse's eyes, a fortuitous accident, and the beast calmed.

The shock of the lightning strike passed, and the elves slowly recovered. One warrior lay moaning on the ground, his leg broken when his horse fell on him. Verhanna and the others set to binding his shattered limb. Rufus, not being needed, wandered over to the crater gouged by the lightning.

The hole was twenty feet across and nearly as deep. The sides of the pit were black and steaming. Tiny flames licked the dry prairie grass around the rim of the hole. Rufus stamped on the fires he saw and gazed with awe at the gaping pit. A shadow fell over him. He turned to see that Verhanna had joined him.

"Someone's hurling thunderbolts at us, my captain," he said seriously.

"Rot," was her reply, though her tone was uncertain. "It was just an act of nature." The next flash of lightning came in an instant. Verhanna uttered a brief warning cry and threw herself down. The bolt struck some distance away, and she sheepishly raised her head. Rufus was shading his eyes, staring at the southern horizon.

"It's moving that way," he announced.

Verhanna stood up and brushed dirt and grass from her haqueton. Her cheeks were stained crimson with embarrassment, and she was grateful that the kender ignored her nervous dive for cover. "What's moving away?" she asked quickly.

"The lightning," he replied. "Three strikes we've seen, each one farther south than the last."

"That's crazy," said Verhanna dismissively. "Lightning is random."

"Ain't no ordinary lightning," the kender insisted.

The warriors made their injured comrade comfortable, and when Verhanna and Rufus rejoined them, she ordered one of the warriors to remain with the injured elf to help him back to Qualinost.

"Now we are four," she remarked as they formed up to resume their hunt. A glance at Rufus caused her to amend her statement. "Four and a half, I mean."

"Not good odds, captain," one of the warriors said.

"Even if I were alone, I'd go on," stated Verhanna firmly. "These criminals must be caught, and they will be."

To the south, where the plain seemed to stretch on endlessly, the flash and crack of lightning continued. It was in that direction the little band rode.

\* \* \* \* \*

The audience hall of the Speaker's house was crammed with Qualinesti, all talking at once. The breeze stirred up by the roiling crowd had set the banners hanging from the high ceiling to waving gently. The scarlet flags were embroidered in gold, hand-worked by hundreds of elven and human girls. The crest of Kith-Kanan's family—the royal family of Qualinesti, not the old line in Silvanost—was a composite of the sun and the Tree of Life.

In the midst of this maelstrom, the Speaker of the Sun sat calmly on his throne while his aides tried to sort out the confusion. However, his inner conflict showed in the small circular movements of his thumbs on the creamy wooden arm of his throne. The wood was rare, a gift from an Ergothian trader who called it vallenwood and said it came from trees that grew to enormous size. Once polished, the vallenwood seemed to glow with an inner light. Kith-Kanan thought it the most beautiful wood in the world. It felt smooth and comforting under his nervously moving fingers.

Tamanier Ambrodel was arguing heatedly with Senators Clovanos and Xixis. "Four towers have been toppled by lightning strikes!" Clovanos said, his voice becoming shrill. "A dozen of my tenants were hurt. I want to know what's being done to stop all this!"

"The Speaker is attending to the problem," Tamanier said, exasperated. His white hair stood out from his head as he ran his hand through it in distraction. "Go home! You are only adding to the problem by being hysterical."

"We are senators of the Thalas-Enthia!" Xixis

snapped. "We have a right to be heard!"

All through this mayhem, thunder boomed outside and flashes of lightning, mixed with the bright morning sun, gave the hall eerie illumination. Kith-Kanan glanced out a nearby window. Three columns of smoke were visible, rising from spots where trees had been set afire by lightning. After two days of lightning, the damage was mounting.

Kith-Kanan slowly rose to his feet. The crowd quickly fell silent and ceased their nervous shuffling.

"Good people," began the Speaker, "I understand your fear. First the darkness came, weakening the crops and frightening the children. Yet the darkness left after causing no real harm, as I promised it would. Today begins our third day of lightning—"

"Cannot the priests deflect this plague of fire?" shouted a voice from the crowd. Others took up the cry. "Is there no magic to defend us?"

Kith-Kanan held up his hands. "There is no need to panic," he said loudly. "And the answer is no. None of the clerics of the great temples has been able to dispel or deflect any of the lightning."

A low murmur of worry went through the assembly. "But there is no threat to the city, I assure you!"

"What about the towers that were knocked down?" demanded Clovanos. His graying blond hair was coming loose from its confining ribbon, and small tendrils curled around his angry face.

From the rear of the hall, someone called out, "Those calamities are your fault, Senator!"

The mass of elves and humans parted to let Senator Irthenie approach the throne. Dressed, as was her custom, in dyed leather and Kagonesti face paint, Irthenie cut an arresting figure among the more conservatively attired senators and townsfolk.

"I visited one of the fallen towers, Great Speaker. The lightning struck the open ground nearby. The shock caused the tower to fall," announced Irthenie.

"Mind your business, Kagonesti!" Clovanos growled.

"She is minding her business as a senator," Kith-Kanan cut in sharply. "I know very well you expect compensation for your lost property, Master Clovanos. But let Irthenie finish what she has to say first."

A flash of lightning highlighted the Speaker's face for a second, then passed away. Chill winds blew through the audience hall. The banners suspended above the assemblage flapped and rippled.

More calmly, Irthenie said, "The soil near Mackeli Tower is very sandy, Your Majesty. I recall when Feldrin Feldspar erected that great tower keep. He had to sink a foundation many, many feet in the ground until he struck bedrock."

She turned to the fuming Senator Clovanos, eyeing him with disdain. "The good senator's towers are in the southwestern district, next to Mackeli, and they had no such deep foundations. It's a wonder they've stood this long."

"Are you an architect?" Clovanos spat back. "What do you know of building?"

"Is Senator Irthenie correct?" asked Kith-Kanan angrily. Before the fire in his monarch's eyes and the dawning disgust evident in the faces around him, Clovanos reluctantly admitted the accuracy of Irthenie's words. "I see," the Speaker concluded. "In that case, the unhappy folk who lived in those unsafe towers shall receive compensation from the royal treasury. You, Clovanos, shall get none. And be thankful I don't charge you with endangering the lives of your tenants!"

With Clovanos thus humbled, the other complainants fell back, unwilling to risk the Speaker's wrath. Sensing their honest fear, Kith-Kanan tried to raise their spirits.

"Some of you may have heard of my contact with the gods just before the darkness set in. I was told that there would appear wonders in the world, portents of some great event to come. What the great event will be, I do not know, but I can assure you that these wonders, while frightening, are not dangerous themselves. The darkness came and went, and so shall the lightning. Our greatest enemy is fear, which drives many to hasty, ill-conceived acts.

"So I urge you again: Be of stout heart! We have all faced terror and death during the great Kinslayer War. Can't we bear a little gloom and lightning? We are not children, to cower before every crack of thunder. I will use all the wisdom and power at my command to protect you, but if you all go home and reflect a bit, you'll soon realize there is no real danger."

"Unless you have Clovanos for a landlord," muttered Irthenie.

Laughter rippled in the ranks around her. The Kagonesti woman's soft words were repeated through the ranks until everyone in the hall was chortling in appreciation. Clovanos's face turned beet red, and he stalked angrily out, with Xixis on his heels. Once the two senators were gone, the laughter increased, and Kith-Kanan could afford to join in. Much of the tension and anxiety of the past few days slipped away.

Kith-Kanan sat back down on his throne. "Now," he said, stilling the mirth swelling across the hall, "if you are here to petition for help due to damage caused by the darkness or the lightning, please go to the antechamber, where my castellan and scribes will take down your names and claims. Good day and good morrow, my people."

The Qualinesti filed out of the hall. The last ones out were the royal guards, whom Kith-Kanan dismissed. Irthenie remained behind. The aged elf woman walked with quick strides to the window. Kith-Kanan joined her.

"The merchants in the city squares say the lightning isn't in every country as the darkness was," Irthenie informed him. "To the north, they haven't had any at all. To the south, it's worse than here. I've heard tales of ships being blasted and sunk, and fires in the southern forests all the way to Silvanesti."

"We seem to be spared the worst," Kith-Kanan mused. He clasped his hands behind his back.

"Do you know what it all means?" the senator asked. "Old forest elves are incurably curious. We want to know everything."

He smiled. "You know as much as I do, old fox."

"I may know a deal more, Kith. There's talk in the city about Ulvian. He's missed, you know. His wastrel friends are asking for him, and rumors are rampant."

The Speaker's good humor vanished. "What's being said?"

"Almost the truth—that the prince committed some crime and you have exiled him for a time," Irthenie replied. A sizzling lightning bolt hit the peak of the Tower of the Sun, just across the square from the Speaker's house. Since the strange weather had begun, the tower had been struck numerous times without effect. "His exact crime and place of exile remain a secret," she added.

Kith-Kanan nodded a slow affirmation. Irthenie pursed her thin lips. The yellow and red lines on her face stood out starkly with the next lightning blast.

"Why do you keep Ulvian's fate a secret?" she inquired. "His example would be a good lesson to many other young scoundrels in Qualinost."

"No. I will not humiliate him in public."

Kith-Kanan turned his back to the display of heavenly fire and looked directly into Irthenie's hazel eyes. "If Ulvian is to be Speaker after me, I wouldn't want his youthful transgressions to hamper him for the rest of his life."

The senator shrugged. "I understand, though it isn't how I would handle him. Perhaps that's why you are the Speaker of the Sun and I am a harmless old widow you keep around for gossip and advice."

He chuckled in spite of himself. "You are many things, old friend, but a harmless old widow is not one of them. That's like saying my grandfather Silvanos was a pretty good warrior."

The Speaker yawned and stretched his arms. Irthenie noticed the dark smudges under his eyes and asked, "Are you sleeping well?" He admitted he was not.

"Too many burdens and too many anxious dreams," Kith-Kanan said. "I wish I could get away from the city for a while."

"There is your grove."

Kith-Kanan clapped his hands together softly. "You're right! You see? Your wits are more than a little sharp. My mind is so muddled that I never even thought of that. I'll leave word with Tam that I'm spending the day there. Perhaps the gods will favor me again, and I'll discover the reason behind all these marvels."

Kith-Kanan hurried to his private exit behind the Qualinesti throne. Irthenie went to the main doors of the audience hall. She paused and looked back as Kith-Kanan disappeared through the dark doorway. Thunder vibrated through the polished wooden floor. Irthenie opened the doors and plunged into the crowd still milling in the Speaker's antechamber.

*   *   *   *   *

There were no straight streets in Qualinost. The boundary of the city, laid out by Kith-Kanan himself, was shaped like the keystone of an arch. The narrow north end of the city faced the confluence of the two rivers that protected it. The Tower of the Sun and the Speaker's house were at that end. The wide portion of the city, the southern end, faced the high ground that eventually swelled into the Thorbardin peaks. Most of the common folk lived there.

In the very heart of Qualinost was the city's tallest hill. It boasted two important features. First, the top of the hill was a huge flat plaza known as the Hall of the Sky, a unique "building" without walls or roof. Here sacred ceremonies honoring the gods were held. Convocations of the great and notable Qualinesti met, and festivals of the seasons were celebrated. The huge open square was paved with a mosaic of thousands of hand-set stones. The mosaic formed a map of Qualinesti.

The second feature of this tall hill, lying on its north slope, was the last bit of natural forest remaining within Qualinost. Kith-Kanan had taken great care to preserve this grove of aspens when the rest of the plateau was shaped by elven spades and magic. More than a park, the aspen grove had become the Speaker's retreat, his haven from the pressures of ruling. He treasured the grove above all features in his capital because the densely wooded enclave reminded him of days long past, of the time when he had dwelt in the primeval forest of Silvanesti with his first wife, the Kagonesti woman Anaya, and her brother Mackeli.

His time with Anaya had been long ago . . . four hundred years and more. Since then he had struggled and loved, fought, killed, ruled. The people of Qualinost were afraid of the darkness and lightning that had fallen upon them. Kith-Kanan, however, was troubled by the impending crisis of his succession. The future of the nation of Qualinesti depended on whom he chose to rule after him. He had to keep his word and step aside. More than that, he really wished to step aside, to pass the burden of command on to younger shoulders. But to whom? And when? When would Pax Tharkas be officially completed?

The grove had no formal entrance, no marked path or gate. Kith-Kanan slowed his pace. The sight of the closely growing trees already calmed him. No lightning at all had touched the grove. The aspen trees stood bright white in the morning sun, their triangular leaves shivering in the breeze and displaying their silvery backs.

The Speaker slipped the hood back from his head. Carefully he lifted the gold circlet from his brow. This simple ring of metal was all the crown Qualinesti had, but for his time in the grove, Kith-Kanan did not want even its small burden.

He dropped the crown into one of the voluminous pockets on the front of his monkish robe. As he passed between the tree trunks, the sounds of the city faded behind him. The deeper he went into the trees, the less the outside world could intrude. Here and there among the aspens were apple, peach, and pear trees. On this spring day, the fruit trees were riotous with blossoms. Overhead, in the breaks between the treetops, he saw fleecy clouds sailing the sky like argosies bound for some distant land.

Crossing the small brook that meandered through the grove, Kith-Kanan came at last to a boulder patched with green lichen. He himself had flattened the top of the rock with the great hammer Sunderer, given to him decades before by the dwarf king Glenforth. The Speaker climbed atop the boulder and sat, sighing, as he drank in the peace of the grove.

A few paces to his right, the brook chuckled and splashed over the rocks in its path. Kith-Kanan cleared his mind of everything but the sounds around him, the gently stirring air, the swaying trees, and the play of the water. It was a technique he'd learned from the priests of Astra, who often meditated in closed groves like this. During the hard years of the Kinslayer War, it had been moments like this that preserved Kith-Kanan's sanity and strengthened his will to persevere.

Peace. Calm. The Speaker of the Sun seemed to sleep, though he was sitting upright on the rock.

Rest. Tranquility. The best answers to hard questions came when the mind and the body were not fighting each other for control.

A streak of heat warmed his face. Dreamily he opened his eyes. The wind sighed, and white clouds obscured the sun. Yet the sensation of heat had been intense. He lifted his gaze to the sky. Above him, burning like a second sun, was an orb of blue-white light. It took him only half a heartbeat to realize he was staring at a lightning bolt *that was falling directly toward him.*

Shocked into motion, Kith-Kanan sprang from the boulder. His feet had hardly left its surface when the lightning bolt slammed into the rock. All was blinding flash and splintered stone. Kith-Kanan fell facedown by the brook, and broken rock pelted his back. The light and sound of the bolt passed away, but the Speaker of the Sun did not move.

* * * * *

It was after sunset before Kith-Kanan was missed. When the Speaker was late for dinner, Tamanier Ambrodel sent warriors to the grove to find him. Kemian Ambrodel and his four comrades searched through the dense forest of trees for quite a while before they found the Speaker lying unconscious near the brook.

With great care, Kemian turned Kith-Kanan over. To his shock and surprise, the Speaker's brown eyes were wide open, staring at nothing. For one dreadful instant, Lord Ambrodel thought the monarch of Qualinesti was dead.

"He breathes, my lord," said one of the warriors, vastly relieved.

Eyelids dipped closed, fluttered, then sprang open again. Kith-Kanan sighed.

"Great Speaker," said Kemian softly, "are you well?"

There was a pause while the Speaker's eyes darted around, taking in his surroundings. Finally he said hoarsely, "As well as any elf who was nearly struck by lightning."

Two warriors braced Kith-Kanan as he got to his feet. His gaze went to the blasted remains of the boulder. Almost as if he was talking to himself, the Speaker said softly, "Some ancient power is at work in the world, a power not connected with the gods we know. The priests and sorcerers can discern nothing, and yet. . . ."

Something fluttered overhead. The elves flinched, their nerves on edge. A bird's sharp cry cut through the quiet of the aspen grove, and Kith-Kanan laughed.

"A crow! What a stalwart band we are, frightened out of our skins by a black bird!" he said. His stomach rumbled loudly, and Kith-Kanan rubbed it. There were holes burned through his clothing by bits of burned rock. "Well, I'm famished. Let's go home!"

The Speaker of the Sun set off at a brisk pace. Lord Ambrodel and his warriors fell in behind him and trailed him back to the Speaker's house, where a warm hearth and a hearty supper awaited.

## ✦ 5 ✦

# the Citadel of Peace

*The blazing sun provided little heat in the thin air of* the Kharolis Mountains. Under that dazzling orb, twenty thousand workers labored, carving the citadel of Pax Tharkas out of the living rock. Dwarves, elves, and humans worked side by side on the great project. Most of them were free craftsmen—stonecutters, masons, and artisans. Out of the twenty thousand, only two thousand were prisoners. Those with useful skills worked alongside their free comrades, and they worked well. The Speaker of the Sun had made them this bargain: If the prisoners performed their duties and kept out of trouble, they would have their sentences reduced by half. Outdoor work at Pax Tharkas was far preferable to

73

languishing in a tower dungeon for years on end.

Not all the convicts were so fortunate. Some simply would not conform, so Feldrin Feldspar, the dwarf who was master builder in charge of creating the fortress, collected the idle, the arrogant, and the violent prisoners into a "grunt gang." Their only task was brute labor. Alone of all the workers at Pax Tharkas, the grunt gang was locked into its hut at night and closely watched by overseers during the day. It was to the grunt gang that Prince Ulvian was sent. He had no skill at stonecarving or bricklaying, and the Speaker had decreed that he should be treated as a slave. That meant he must take his place with the other surly prisoners in the grunt gang, pushing and dragging massive stone blocks from the quarry to the site of the citadel.

Ulvian's one meeting with Feldrin had not gone well. The chained prince, now dressed in the green and brown leathers of a forester, had been led by Merith to the canvas hut where the master builder lived. The dwarf came out to see them, setting aside an armful of scrolls covered with lines and numbers. These were the plans for the fortress.

"Remove his chains," Feldrin rumbled. Without a word, Merith took Ulvian's shackles off. Ulvian sniffed and thanked the dwarf casually.

"Save your thanks," replied Feldrin. His thick black beard was liberally sprinkled with white, and his long stay in the heights of the Kharolis had deeply tanned his face and arms. He planted brick-hard fists on his squat hips and skewered the prince with his blue eyes. "Chains are not needed here. We are miles from the nearest settlement, and the mountains are barren and dry. You will work hard. If you try to run away, you will perish from hunger and thirst," the dwarf said darkly. "That is, if my people don't hunt you down first. Is that clear?"

Ulvian rolled his eyes and didn't answer. Feldrin roared, "Is that clear?" The prince flinched and nodded quickly. "Good."

He assigned Ulvian to the grunt gang, and a burly, bearded human came to escort the prince to his new quarters.

When they were gone, Merith's shoulders sagged. "I must confess, Master Feldrin, I am exhausted!" he said, sighing. "For ten days, I have had the prince in my keeping, and I haven't had a moment's rest!"

"Why so, Lieutenant? He doesn't look so dangerous."

Feldrin stooped to retrieve his plans. Merith squatted to help.

"It wasn't fear that spoiled my sleep," the warrior confided, "but the prince's constant talk! By holy Mantis, that boy can talk, talk, talk. He tried to convert me, make me his friend, so that I wouldn't deliver him to you. He's engaging when he wants to be, and clever, too. You may have trouble with him."

Feldrin pushed back the front flap of his hut with one broad, blunt hand. "Oh, I doubt it, Master Merithynos. A few days dragging stone blocks will take the stiffness out of the prince's neck."

Merith ducked under the low doorframe and entered the hut. Though the walls and roof were canvas, like a tent, Feldrin's hut had a wooden frame and floor, sturdier than a tent. The mountains were sometimes wracked by fierce winds, blizzards, and landslides.

Feldrin clomped across the bare board floor and dropped his scrolls on a low trestle table in the center of the room. He turned up the wick on a brass oil lamp and settled himself on a thick-legged stool, then proceeded to rummage through the loose assortment of parchment until he found a scrap.

"I shall send a note back to the Speaker," he said, "so that he will know you and the prince arrived safely."

The lieutenant glanced back at the door flap hanging loosely in the still, cool air. "What shall I do, Master Feldrin? I'm supposed to guard the prince, but it seems you don't really need me."

"No, he won't be any trouble," muttered the dwarf,

finishing his brief missive with a flourish. He shook sand over the wet ink to dry it. "But I may have another use for you."

Merith drew himself up straight, expecting an official order. "Yes, master builder?"

Stroking his thick beard, Feldrin regarded the tall elf speculatively. "Do you play checkers?" he asked.

\* \* \* \* \*

Bells and gongs rang through the camp, and all over Pax Tharkas workers set down their tools. The sun had just begun to set behind Mount Thak, which meant only an hour of daylight remained. It was quitting time.

Ulvian dragged along at the rear of the ragged column of laborers known as the grunt gang. His arms and legs ached, his palms were blistered, and despite the cool temperature, the stronger sun at this high elevation had burned his face and arms cherry red. The overseers—the mute, bearded human Ulvian had met his first day in camp and an ill-tempered dwarf named Lugrim—stood on each side of the barracks door, urging the exhausted workers to hurry inside.

The long, ramshackle building was made from slabs of shale and mud, and the rear wall was sunk in the mountainside. There were two windows and only one door. The roof was made of green splits of wood and moss, and the whole barrack was drafty, dusty, and cold, despite the fires kept burning in baked-clay fireplaces at each end.

Inside the dim structure, the grunt gang members headed straight for their rude beds. Ulvian's was near the center of the single large room, as far from either fire as it could be. Still, he was so tired that he was about to fall on his bunk when he noticed the man who slept on his right was already in bed, where he had apparently lazed all day. Ulvian opened his mouth to protest.

The prince froze two paces from the bed. The human's

head and right leg were swathed in loose, bloodstained bandages. His hands hung limply over the sides of the narrow bunk.

"Poor wretch won't live the night," rasped a voice behind the prince. Ulvian whirled. A filthy, rag-clad elf stood close to him, staring at him with burning gray eyes. "He was taking a hod of bricks up the tower, and the scaffold broke. Broke his leg and cracked his skull."

"Aren't—aren't there healers to take care of him?" Ulvian exclaimed.

A dry rattle of laughter issued from the throat of the sun-baked elf. He was nearly as tall as Ulvian, and very thin. When he looked down at the human on the bed, dust fell from his blond eyebrows and matted hair. "Healers?" he chortled. "Healers are for the masters. We get a swig of wine, a damp cloth, and a lot of prayers!"

Ulvian recoiled from the loud elf. "Who are you?"

"Name's Drulethen," said the elf, "but everyone calls me Dru."

"That's a Silvanesti name," Ulvian said, surprised. "How did you come to be here?"

"I was once a wandering scholar who sought knowledge in the farthest corners of the world. Unfortunately when the war started, I was in Silvanesti, and the Speaker of the Stars needed ablebodied elves for his army. I didn't want to fight, but they forced me to take up arms. Once out in the wilderness, I ran away."

"So you're a deserter," said Ulvian, understanding dawning.

Dru shrugged. "That's not a crime in Qualinesti," he said idly and sat down on the nearest bed. "While I wandered the great plain, I found it was easier to take what I wanted than work for it, so I became a bandit. The Wildrunners caught up to me, and the Speaker of the Sun graciously allowed me to work here rather than rot in a Qualinost dungeon." He held out his slender hands palms up. "So it goes."

No one had spoken at such length to Ulvian since his

arrival at Pax Tharkas. Dru might be a coward and a thief, but it was obvious he had a certain amount of education, which was as rare as diamonds in the grunt gang. Sitting down on his own bed, the prince asked Dru a question that had been bothering him. "Why can't we get closer to the fires?" he said in a low voice. Dru laughed nastily.

"Only the strongest ones get a place by the chimneys," he said. "Weaklings and newcomers get stuck in the middle. Unless you want a beating, I suggest you don't dispute the order of things."

Before Ulvian could broach another question, Dru moved to his own bunk. Dropping down on the bed, he turned his back to the prince and in seconds began to snore lightly with each intake of breath. Ulvian threw himself across his own bed, which consisted of strips of cloth nailed to a rough wooden frame. It stank of sweat and dirt even more strongly than the barracks as a whole. The prince locked his hands together behind his head and stared at the crude ceiling overhead. The orange-tinged sunlight filtered in through the chinks in the roof slats. While he pondered his fate, he dozed fitfully.

Something thumped against the prince's feet, which hung over the end of his short bunk. Ulvian snapped to a sitting position. Dru had bumped him on his way to the injured human's bed, where he now stood. Skinning back the man's eyelid with his thumb, Dru shook his head and made clucking sounds in his throat.

"Frell's gone," he announced loudly.

An especially tall human came to the dead man's bed and hoisted the body easily over his shoulder. He strode across the room and kicked the front door open. The red wash of sunset flowed into the gloomy barracks. The tall human dumped the corpse unceremoniously on the ground outside. Before he could close the door again, a dozen gang members were already picking the dead man's bed clean. They took everything, from his scrap of blanket to the few personal items he'd stowed under the bunk. The press was so great that Ulvian was forced to move away. He spied Dru leaning against the wall near the water barrel. Slipping through the crowd, he finally faced the Silvanesti.

"Is that it?" he asked sharply. "A man dies and he gets dumped outside?"

"That's it. The dwarves will take the body away," Dru replied, unconcerned.

"What about his friends? His family?" insisted the prince.

Dru took a small stone from his pocket. It was a four-inch cylinder of onyx the thickness of his thumb. "Nobody has friends here," he said. "As to family. . . ." He shrugged and didn't finish. His fingers rubbed back and forth over the piece of black crystal.

Just as night was claiming the mountain pass, the sound of metal against metal sent the grunt gang storming toward the door. Outside was a huge iron cart wheeled by four dwarves. The cart bore a great kettle, and when one of the dwarves removed its lid, steam poured out. Ulvian let the rest of the gang press ahead of him, having no desire to be trampled for a dish of stew.

When he got outside, he shivered. A raw wind whistled down the pass, knifing through the clothing the prince wore. He watched the laborers, clay bowls in hand, mill around the food wagon while the dwarves served the steaming stew and doled out formidable loaves of bread to each worker. The aroma of roasted meat and savory spices drifted to Ulvian's nose. It drew him toward the wagon.

He was promptly shoved away by a Kagonesti with a shaved head and two scalp locks that hung down his back. Ulvian bristled and started to challenge the wild elf, but the hard muscles in the fellow's arms and the definite air of danger in his manner held the prince back. Ulvian slinked to the rear of the poorly formed line and waited his turn.

By the time he reached the wagon, the dwarves were scraping the bottom of the kettle. The ladle-bearing dwarf, warmly dressed in fur and leather, squinted down from the cart at Ulvian.

"Where's your bowl?" he growled.

"I don't know."

"Idiot!" He swung the ladle idly at the prince, who ducked. The copper dipper was as big as his hand and stoutly formed. The dwarf barked, "Get back inside and find yourself a bowl!"

Chastened, Ulvian did so. He searched the room until he saw Dru, who was leaning against the wall by the water barrel, eating his stew.

"Dru," he called, "I need a bowl. Where can I get one?"

The Silvanesti pointed to the fireplace at the south end of the room. Ulvian thanked him and wended his way through the crowd to the fireplace. Up close, he saw that the hearth was dominated by the same Kagonesti who had shoved him away from the food cart.

"What do you want, city boy?" he snarled.

"I need a bowl," replied Ulvian warily.

The Kagonesti, who was called Splint, set down his bowl. Glaring at the prince, he said, "I'm no charity, city boy. You want a bowl, you got to buy it."

The Speaker's son was perplexed. He had nothing to trade. All his valuables had been taken from him before he left Qualinost.

"I don't have any money," he said lamely.

Harsh laughter rang out around him. Ulvian flushed furiously. Splint wiped his mouth with the end of one of his long scalp locks.

"You got a good pair of boots, I see."

Ulvian looked at his feet. These were his oldest pair of boots, scuffed and dirty, but there were no holes in them and the soles were sound. They were also the only shoes he had.

"My boots are worth a lot more than a clay dish," Ulvian said stiffly.

Splint made no reply. Instead, he picked up his bowl and started eating again. He studiously ignored Ulvian, who stood directly in front of him.

The prince fumed. Who did this wild elf think he was? He was about to denounce him and tell everyone in earshot that he was the son of the Speaker of the Sun, but the words died in his throat. Who would believe him? They would only laugh at him. Hopelessness welled up inside him. No one cared what happened to him. No one would notice if he lived or died. For a horrible instant, he felt like crying.

Ulvian's stomach rumbled loudly. A few of the gang around him chuckled. He bit his lip and blurted out, "All right! The boots for a bowl!"

Languidly Splint stood up. He was the same height as Ulvian, but his powerful physique and menacing presence made him seem much larger. The prince shucked off his boots and was soon standing on the cold dirt floor in his stockings. The Kagonesti slipped his ragged sandals off and pulled on the boots. After much stamping of his feet to settle them into the unfamiliar footwear, he pronounced them a good fit.

"What about my bowl?" Ulvian reminded him angrily.

Splint reached under his bunk next to the fireplace and brought out a chipped ceramic bowl, enameled in blue. Ulvian snatched the dish and ran to the door, leaving gales of coarse guffaws in his wake. By the time he threw open the door and dashed out, the dwarves and the food wagon were gone.

The grunt gang was still laughing when he returned moments later. He stalked through them to the crackling fire, where Splint sat warming himself.

"You tricked me," Ulvian said in a scant whisper. He was afraid to raise his voice, afraid he would start shrieking. "I want my boots back."

"I'm not a merchant, city boy. I don't make any exchanges."

The barracks were quiet now. Confrontation was as

thick in the air as smoke.

"Give them back," demanded the prince, "or I'll take them back."

"You truly are an idiot, pest. Go to sleep, city boy, and thank the gods I don't beat you senseless," Splint said.

Ulvian's pent-up rage exploded, and he did a rash thing. He raised a hand high and smashed the empty bowl against the Kagonesti's head. A collective gasp went up from the workers. Splint rocked sideways with the blow, but in a flash, he had shaken it off and leapt to his feet.

"Now you got no boots and no bowl!" he spat. His fist caught Ulvian low in the chest. The prince groaned and fell against one of the spectators who had gathered, who promptly flung him back to Splint. The Kagonesti delivered a rolling punch to Ulvian's jaw, sending him spinning into the wall. Splint followed the reeling prince.

Ulvian's world swam in a sea of red fog. He felt strong hands grasp his shirt and drag him away from the support of the wall. More blows rained on his head and chest. Every time he was knocked down, someone picked him up and tossed him back to receive more abuse. Vainly he tried to grapple with Splint. The wild elf broke his feeble grip with little more than a shrug, kicking him in the stomach.

"He's had enough, Splint," Dru said, stepping between the prostrate Ulvian and the raging Kagonesti.

"I ought to kill him!" Splint retorted.

"He's new and stupid. Let him be," countered Dru.

"Bah!" Splint spat on Ulvian's back. He rubbed his throbbing knuckles and returned to his place by the fire.

Dru dragged the semiconscious prince to his bed and rolled him into it. Ulvian's face was bruised and battered. His left eye would soon be invisible behind a rapidly swelling lid. Eventually the pain of his injuries gave way to sleep. Hungry and beaten, Ulvian sank into forgiving darkness.

During the night, someone stole his stockings.

## ᛥ 6 ᛞ

## Bards and Liars

---

*The lightning lasted three days, then suddenly ceased.*
The next day, exactly one week after the darkness had
fallen across the world, the sky filled with clouds. No
one thought much of it, for they were ordinary-looking
gray rain clouds. They covered the sky from horizon to
horizon and lowered until it seemed they would touch
the lofty towers of Qualinost. And then it began to
rain—brilliant scarlet rain.

It filled the gutters and dripped off leaves, a torrent
that drove everyone indoors. Though the crimson rain
had no effect on anyone save to make him wet, the uni-
versal reaction to the downpour was to regard it as unnatural.

"At least I am spared the hordes of petitioners who sought an audience during the darkness and lightning," Kith-Kanan observed. He was standing on the covered verandah of the Speaker's house, looking south across the city. Tamanier Ambrodel was with him, as was Tamanier's son, Kemian. The younger Ambrodel was in his best warrior's garb—glittering breastplate and helm, white plume, pigskin boots, and a yellow cape so long it brushed the ground. He stood well back from the eaves so as not to get rain on his finery.

"You don't seem upset by this new marvel, sire," Tamanier said.

"It's just another phase we must pass through," Kith-Kanan replied stoically.

"Ugh," grunted Kemian. "How long do you think it will last, Great Speaker?" Scarlet rivulets were beginning to creep over the flagstone path. Lord Ambrodel shifted his boots back, avoiding the strange fluid.

"Unless I am mistaken, exactly three days," said the Speaker. "The darkness lasted three days, and so did the lightning. There's a message in this, if we are just wise enough to perceive it."

"The message is 'the world's gone mad,' " Kemian breathed. His father didn't share his concern. Tamanier had lived too long, had served Kith-Kanan for too many centuries, not to trust the Speaker's intuition. At first he'd been frightened, but as his sovereign seemed so unconcerned, the elderly elf quickly had mastered his own fear.

Restless, Kemian paced up and down, his slate-blue eyes stormy. "I wish whatever's going to happen would go ahead and happen!" he exclaimed, slamming his sword hilt against his scabbard. "This waiting will drive me mad!"

"Calm yourself, Kem. A good warrior should be cool in the face of trial, not coiled up like an irritated serpent," his father counseled.

"I need action," Kemian said, halting in midstride.

"Give me something to do, Your Majesty!"

Kith-Kanan thought for a moment. Then he said, "Go to Mackeli Tower and see if any foreigners have arrived since the rain started. I'd like to know if the rain is also falling outside my realm."

Grateful to have a task to perform, Kemian bowed, saying, "Yes, sire. I'll go at once."

He hurried away.

*     *     *     *     *

Red rain trickled down Verhanna's arms, dripping off her motionless fingertips. Beside her, Rufus Wrinklecap squirmed. She glared at him, a silent order to keep still.

Ahead, some thirty feet away, two dark figures huddled by a feeble, smoky campfire. Rufus had smelled the smoke from quite a distance off, so Verhanna and her two remaining warriors had dismounted and crept up to the camp on foot. Verhanna grabbed the kender by his collar and hissed, "Are these the Kagonesti slavers?"

"They are, my captain," he said solemnly.

"Then we'll take them."

Rufus shook his head, sending streams of red liquid flying. "Something's not right, my captain. These fellows wouldn't sit in the open by a campfire where anyone could find them. They're too smart for that."

The kender's voice was nearly inaudible.

"How do you know? They just don't realize we're on their trail," Verhanna said just as softly. She sent one of her warriors off to the left and the other to the right to surround the little clearing where the slavers had camped. Rufus fidgeted, his sodden, wilting plume bobbing in front of Verhanna's face.

"Be still!" she said fiercely. "They're almost in position." She caught a dull glint of armor as the two elf warriors worked their way into position. Carefully the captain drew her sword. Muttering unhappily, Rufus pulled out his shortsword.

"Hai! Qualinesti!" shouted Verhanna, and bolted into the clearing. Her two comrades charged also, swords high, shouting the battle cry. The slavers never stirred. Verhanna reached them first and swatted at the nearest one with the flat of her blade. To her dismay, her blow completely demolished the seated figure. It was nothing but a cloak propped up by tree limbs.

"What's this?" she cried. One of her warriors batted at the second figure. It, too, was a fake.

"A trick!" declared the warrior. "It's a trick!" A heartbeat later, an arrow sprouted from his throat. He gave a cry and fell onto his face.

"Run for it!" squealed Rufus.

Another missile whistled past Verhanna as she sprinted for the trees. Rufus hit the leaf-covered ground and rolled, bounced, and dodged his way to cover. The last warrior made the mistake of following his captain rather than making for the edge of the clearing nearest him. He ran a half-dozen steps before an arrow hit him in the thigh. He staggered and fell, calling out to Verhanna.

The captain crashed into the line of trees, blundering noisily through the undergrowth. When she reached her original hiding place, she stopped. The wounded elf warrior called to her again.

Breathing hard, Verhanna sheathed her sword and put her back against a tree. The red rain coursed down her cheeks as she gasped for breath.

"Psst."

She jumped at the sound and whirled. Rufus was on his hands and knees behind her.

"What are you doing?" she hissed.

"Trying to keep from getting an arrow in the head," said the kender. "They was waitin' for us."

"So they were!" Furious with herself for walking into the trap, she said, "I've got to go back for Rikkinian."

Rufus grabbed her ankle. "You can't!"

Verhanna kicked free of his grasp. "I won't abandon a comrade!" she said emphatically. Shrugging off her cloak, Verhanna soon stood in her bare armor. She drew a thick-bladed dagger from her belt and crouched down, almost on all fours.

"Wait, I'll come with you," said the kender in a loud whisper. He scampered through the brush behind her.

Verhanna reached the edge of the clearing. Rikkinian, the wounded elf, was now silent and unmoving, lying facedown in the mud. The other warrior sprawled near the phony slavers. Curiously, the stick figures and cloaks had been re-erected.

"Come here, Wart," the captain muttered. Rufus crawled to her. "What do you think?"

"They're both dead, my captain."

Verhanna's gaze rested on Rikkinian. Her brisk demeanor was gone; two warriors had paid for her mistake. Plaintively she asked, "Are you certain?"

"No one lies with his nose in the mud if he's still breathing," Rufus said gently. He squinted at the propped-up cloaks. "The archers are gone," he announced. Again Verhanna asked him if he was sure. He pointed. "There are two sets of footprints crossing the clearing over there. The dark elders have fled."

To demonstrate the truth of his words, Rufus stood up. He walked slowly past the fallen elves toward the smoldering fire. Verhanna went to Rikkinian and gently turned him over. The arrow wound in his leg hadn't killed him. Someone had dispatched him with a single thrust of a narrow-bladed knife through the heart. Burning with anger, she rose and headed for her other fallen comrade. Before she reached him, she was shocked to see Rufus raise his little sword and fall on the back of one of the propped-up cloaks. This time the cloak didn't collapse into a pile of tree limbs. Arms and legs appeared beneath it, and a figure leapt up.

"Captain!" Rufus shouted. "It's one of them!"

Verhanna fumbled for her sword as she ran toward the campfire. The kender stabbed over and over again at the cloaked figure's back. Though not muscular, Rufus possessed a wiry strength, but his attack appeared to have no effect. The cloaked one spun around, trying to throw the pesky kender off. When the front of the hood swung past Verhanna, she froze in her tracks and gasped.

"Rufus! *It has no face!*" she shouted.

With one last prodigious shake, the cloaked thing hurled Rufus to the ground. The kender's small sword flew into the woods as Rufus landed with a thud. He groaned and lay still, crimson rain beating down on his pallid face.

Verhanna gave a cry and slashed at the faceless figure, her slim elven blade slicing through the cloth with ease. She felt resistance as the blade passed through whatever lay beneath the cloak, but no blood flowed. Under the hood, where a face should have been, there was only a ball of grayish smoke, as if someone had stuffed the hood with dirty cotton.

Cutting and thrusting and hacking, Verhanna soon reduced the cloak to a tattered mass on the muddy ground. Shorn of its garment, the thing was revealed to be a vaguely elf-shaped column of dove-colored smoke. Two arms, two legs, a head, and torso were visible, but nothing else—only featureless vapor. Realizing she was exhausting herself to no avail, Verhanna stood back to catch her breath.

Rufus sat up slowly and clutched his head. He shook the pain aside and looked up at the smoky apparition standing between him and his captain. His hat had been trodden in the mud, and rain streamed from his long hair. Rufus glanced from the wispy figure to the dying campfire. Only a single coil of vapor, as thick as his wrist, snaked upward from the damp wood, and it twisted and writhed oddly in the still air.

Suddenly the kender had an inspiration. He dragged the other, unoccupied cloak to the fire and threw it over the smoldering wood. The sodden material soon extinguished the last of the sparks, and the fire died. As it did, the smoky figure thinned and finally vanished.

There was a long moment of silence, broken only by Rufus's and Verhanna's heavy breathing. At last Verhanna demanded, "What in Astra's name *was* that infernal thing?"

"Magic," Rufus replied simply. His attention was centered on retrieving his hat from the mud. Sorrowfully he tried to straighten the long, crimson-stained plume. It was hopeless; the feather was broken in two places and hung limply.

"I know it was magic," Verhanna said, annoyed. "But why? And whose?"

"I told you those elves were clever. One of them knows magic. He made the ghost as a diversion, I'll bet, to keep us busy while they escaped."

Verhanna slapped the flat of her blade against her mailed thigh. "E'li blast them! My two soldiers killed and we're diverted by magic smoke!" She stamped her foot, splashing blood-colored puddles over Rufus. "I'd give my right arm for another crack at those two! I never even *saw* them!"

"They're very dangerous," said Rufus sagely. "Maybe we should get more soldiers to hunt them down."

The Speaker's daughter was not about to admit defeat. She slammed her sword home in its scabbard. "No, by the gods! We'll take them ourselves!"

The kender jammed his soggy blue hat down on his head. His new clothes were ruined. "You don't pay me enough for this," he said under his breath.

\* \* \* \* \*

How empty the great house seemed with Verhanna gone. And Ulvian, sent off to toil in the quarries of Pax Tharkas. Lord Anakardain was away from the city, with the lion's share of the Guards of the Sun chasing down the last stubborn bands of slavers. Kemian Ambrodel was out questioning new arrivals in Qualinost about the red rain and other marvels of days past.

So many friends and familiar faces gone. Only he, Kith-Kanan, had remained behind. He had given up his freedom to roam when he accepted the throne of Qualinesti. After all these centuries, he finally understood how his father, Sithel, had felt before him. Bound up in chains like a prisoner. Only a Speaker's chains weren't made of iron, but of the coils of responsibility, duty, protocol.

It was hard, very hard, to remain inside the arched bridges of Qualinost, just as it was hard to keep inside the walls of the increasingly lonely Speaker's house. Sometimes his thoughts were with Ulvian. Had he done right by his son? The prince's crime was heinous, but did it justify Kith-Kanan's harsh sentence?

Then he thought of Verhanna, probing every glade and clearing from Thorbardin to the Thon-Thalas River, seeking those whose crimes were the same as her brother's. Loyal, brave, serious Hanna, who never swerved from following an order.

Kith-Kanan rose from his bed and threw back the curtains from his window. It was long after midnight, by the water clock on the mantle, and the world outside was as dark as pitch. He could hear the bloody rain still falling. It seeped under windowsills and doors.

A name, long buried in his thoughts, surfaced. It was a name not spoken aloud for hundreds of years: "Anaya."

Into the quiet darkness, he whispered the name of the Kagonesti woman who had been his first wife. It was as if she was in the room with him.

He knew she was not dead. No, Anaya lived on, might even manage to outlive Kith-Kanan. As her life's blood had flowed out of a terrible sword wound, Anaya's body had indeed died. But undergoing a mysterious, sublime transformation, Anaya the elf woman had become a fine young oak tree, rooted in the soil of the ancient Silvanesti forest she had lived in and guarded all her life. The forest was but a small manifestation of a larger, primeval force, the power of life itself.

The power—he could think of nothing else to call it—had come into existence out of the First Chaos. The sages of Silvanost, Thorbardin, and Daltigoth all agreed that the First Chaos, by its very randomness, accidentally gave birth to order, the Not-Chaos.

*Only order makes life possible.*

These things Kith-Kanan had learned through decades of studying side by side with the wisest thinkers of Krynn. Anaya had been a servant of the power, the only force older than the gods, protecting the last of the ancient forests remaining on the continent. When her time as guardian was ended, Anaya had become one with the forest. She had been carrying Kith-Kanan's child at the time.

Kith-Kanan's head hurt. He kneaded his temples with strong fingers, trying to dull the ache. His and Anaya's unborn son was a subject he could seldom bear to think about. Four hundred years had passed since last he'd heard Anaya's voice, and yet at times the pain of their parting was as fresh as it had been that golden spring day when he'd watched her warm skin roughen into bark, when he'd heard her speak for the final time.

The rain ended abruptly. Its cessation was so sudden and complete it jarred Kith-Kanan out of his deep thoughts. The last drop fell from the water clock. Three days of scarlet rain were over.

His sigh echoed in the bedchamber. What would be next? he wondered.

\* \* \* \* \*

"Thank Astra that foul mess has stopped!" exclaimed Rufus. "I feel like the floor of a slaughterhouse, soaked in blood!"

"Oh, shut up. It wasn't real blood, just colored water," Verhanna retorted. For two days, in constant rain, they had tracked the elusive Kagonesti slavers with little result. The Kagonesti's trail had led west for a time, but suddenly it seemed to vanish completely. The crimson rain had ceased overnight, and the new day was bright and sunny, but Kith-Kanan's daughter was weary and saddle sore. The last thing she wanted to listen to was the kender complaining about his soggy clothes.

Rufus prowled ahead on foot, leading his oversized horse by the reins. He peered at every clump of grass, every fallen twig. "Nothing," he fumed. "It's as if they sprouted wings and flew away."

The sun was setting almost directly ahead of them, and Verhanna suggested they stop for the night.

Rufus dropped his horse's reins. "I'm for that! What's for dinner?"

She poked a hand into the haversack hung from the pommel of her saddle. "Dried apples, *quith-pa*, and hard-boiled eggs," Verhanna recited without enthusiasm. She tossed a cold, hard-boiled egg to her scout. He caught it with one hand, though he grumbled and screwed his face into a mask of disgust. She heard him mutter something about "the same eats, three times a day, forever" as he tapped the eggshell against his knee to crack it—then suddenly let it fall to the ground.

"Hey!" called Verhanna. "If you don't want it, say so. Don't throw it in the mud!"

"I smell roast pig!" he exulted, eyes narrow with concentration. "Not far away, either!" He vaulted onto his horse and turned the animal.

Verhanna flopped back the wet hood of her woolen cape and called, "Wait, Rufus! Stop!"

The reckless, hungry kender was not to be denied, however. With thumps of his spurless heels, he urged his horse through a line of silver-green holly, ignoring the jabs and scratches of the barbed leaves. Disgusted, Verhanna rode down the row of bushes, trying to find an opening. When she couldn't, she pulled her horse around and also plunged through the holly. Sharp leaf edges raked her unprotected face and hands.

"Ow!" she cried. "Rufus, you worthless toad! Where are you?"

Ahead, beyond some wind-tossed dogwoods, she spied the flicker of a campfire. Cursing the kender soundly, Verhanna rode toward the fire. The foolish kender didn't even have his shortsword anymore. In the fight with the smoke creature, Rufus's blade had been broken.

Serve him right if it was a bandit camp, she thought angrily. Forty, no, fifty bloodthirsty villains, armed to the teeth, luring innocent victims in with their cooking smoke. Sixty bandits, yes, all of whom liked to eat stupid kender.

In spite of her ire, the captain kept her head and freed her sword from the leather loop that held it in its scabbard. No use barging in unprepared. Approaching the campfire obliquely, she saw shadowy figures moving around it. A horse whinnied. Clutching her reins tightly, Verhanna rode in, ready for a fight.

The first thing she saw was Rufus wolfing down chunks of steaming roast pork. Four elves dressed in rags and pieces of old blankets stood around the fire. By their light hair and chiseled features, she identified them as Silvanesti.

"Good morrow to you, warrior," said the male elf nearest Rufus. His accent and manner were refined, city-bred.

"May your way be green and golden," Verhanna replied. The travelers didn't appear to be armed, but she remained on her horse just in case. "If I may ask, who are you, good traveler?"

"Diviros Chanderell, bard, at your service, Captain." The elf bowed low, so low that his sand-colored hair brushed the ground. Sweeping an arm around the assembled group, he added, "And this is my family."

Verhanna nodded to each of the others. The older, brown-haired female was Diviros's sister, Deramani. Sitting by the fire was a younger woman, the bard's wife,

Selenara. Her thick hair, unbound, hung past her waist, and peeking shyly out from behind the honey-golden cascade was a fair-haired child. Diviros introduced him as Kivinellis, his son.

"We have come hither from Silvanost, city of a thousand white towers," said the bard with a flourish, "our fortunes to win in the new realm of the west."

"Well, you've a long way to go if Qualinost is your goal," Verhanna said.

"It is, noble warrior. Will you share meat with us? Your partner precedes you."

She dismounted, shaking her head at Rufus. He winked at her as Diviros's sister handed Verhanna a trencher of savory pork. The captain stabbed the cutlet with her knife and bit off a mouthful. It was good, sweet flesh, as only the Silvanesti could raise.

"What sets you wandering the lonely fields by night, Captain?" asked Diviros, once they were all comfortable around the campfire. He had a thin, expressive face and large amber eyes, which gave emphasis to his words.

"We're on an elf hunt," blurted Rufus between mouthfuls.

The bard's pale brows flew up. "Are you, indeed? Some dire brigand is haunting these environs?"

"Naw. They're a couple of woods elves wanted for slaving." Food had restored the kender's natural garrulousness. "They ambushed some of our warriors, then used magic to get away."

"Slavers? Magic? How strange!"

Rufus launched into an animated account of their adventures. Verhanna rolled her eyes, but only when he nearly revealed Verhanna as the daughter of the Speaker of the Sun did she object.

"Mind your tongue," she snapped. She didn't want her parentage widely known. After all, traveling across the wild country with only a chatty kender for company, the princess of Qualinesti would make an excellent hostage for any bandit.

Planting his hands on his knees and glancing at his family, Diviros told his story in turn. "We, too, have seen wondrous things since leaving our homeland."

Rufus burped loudly. "Good! Tell us a story!"

Diviros beamed. He was in his element. His family sat completely still as all eyes fastened on him. He began softly. "Strange has been the path we have followed, my friends, strange and wonderful. On the day we left the City of a Thousand White Towers, a pall of darkness fell over the land. My beautiful Selenara was sore afraid."

The bard's wife blushed crimson, and she looked down at the tortoiseshell comb in her hand.

Diviros went on. "But I reasoned that the gods had draped this cloak of night over us for a purpose. And lo, the purpose was soon apparent. Warriors of the Speaker of the Stars had been turning back those who wished to leave the country. His Majesty feared the nation was losing too many of her sons and daughters to the westward migration, and he—But I digress. In any event, the strange darkness allowed us to slip by the warriors unseen."

"That was lucky," Verhanna said matter-of-factly.

"Lucky, noble warrior? 'Twas the will of the gods!" Diviros said ringingly, lifting a hand to heaven. "That it was so was shown five days later as we traversed the great southern forest amid a tempest of thunderbolts, for there we beheld a sight so strange the gods must have preserved us that we might be witness to it!"

Verhanna was growing weary of the bard's elaborate storytelling and showed it by sighing loudly. Rufus, however, was in awe of so spellbinding a speaker. "Go on, please!" he urged, a forkful of pork halted midway to his mouth.

Diviros warmed under the kender's intense regard. "We had stopped by a large pool of water to refresh ourselves. Such a beautiful spot, my little friend! Crystalline water in a green bower, surrounded by a snowy riot of blooming buds. Well, as we were all partaking of the icy cold liquid, a monstrously large bolt of lightning struck not a score of paces from us! The flash was brighter than the sun, and we were all knocked completely senseless.

"It was Selenara who roused first. She knows well the sound of a child in distress, and it was just such a sound that brought her awake—a mewling noise, a crying. My good wife wandered up the wooded hillside into a large meadow, and lo! there a great oak tree had been hit by the lightning, blasted into more splinters than there are stars in the heavens! Where the broad trunk had split open, she found the one who cried so piteously."

Diviros paused dramatically, gazing directly into Verhanna's impatient eyes. "It was a fully grown male elf!"

Rufus and his captain exchanged a look. Verhanna set aside her empty trencher and asked, "Who was it—some traveler sleeping under the tree when it was hit?"

The bard shook his head solemnly, and once more his voice was low and serious as he replied, "No, good warrior. It was clear that the fellow had been *inside* the tree and that the lightning had released him."

"Bleedin' dragons!" sighed the kender.

"My good spouse ran back to the pool and raised us from our stupor. I hurried to the shattered tree and beheld the strange elf. He was slick with blood, yet as my wife and sister washed him, there was not a cut, not even a scratch, anywhere on him. Moreover, there was an oval hollow in the tree, just large enough for him to have fitted in with his legs drawn up."

Verhanna snorted and waved a hand dismissively. "Look here," she said kindly, "that's quite a tall tale you've spun, bard, but don't carry on so hard that you begin to believe it yourself! You are a tale-spinner, after all, and a very good one. You almost had yourself convinced."

Diviros's mobile face showed only the briefest flash of annoyance. "Forgive me. I did not intend to deceive, only to relate to you the marvel we encountered in this elf who seemed born from a tree. If I offended, I apologize."

He bowed again, but Kivinellis blurted, "Tell them about his hands!" Everyone stared at the child, and he retreated once more behind his mother's back. Rufus hopped up from the log he'd been sitting on.

"What about his hands?" asked the kender.

"They were discolored," Diviros said casually. "The elf's fingers, including his nails, were the color of summer grass." His tawny eyes darted to his son, and the quick look was not kind.

"What happened to the green-fingered elf?" Rufus wondered aloud.

"We cared for him a day or two, and then he wandered off on his own."

Verhanna detected a note of resistance in his voice. In spite of Rufus's obvious enjoyment of the story, the bard was suddenly reluctant to speak. The captain had never known a bard to be reticent before an attentive audience. She decided to press him. "Which way did this odd, green-fingered fellow go?"

There was a momentary hesitation, barely discernible, before Diviros answered, "South by west. We have not seen him since."

The Speaker's daughter stood. "Well, we thank you, good bard, for your tale. And for our dinner. We must be off now."

She tugged Rufus to his feet.

"But I haven't finished eating!" protested the kender.

"Yes, you have."

Verhanna hustled him to his horse and sprang to her own saddle. "Good luck to you!" she called to the family. "May your way be green and golden!"

In a moment, they'd left the group of elves staring in surprise after them.

Back on the trail, cloaked by the robe of night, Verhanna brought her horse to a stop. Rufus bounced up beside her. The kender was still babbling about their abrupt departure and the premature end of his meal.

"Forget your stomach," Verhanna ordered. "What did you make of that strange encounter?"

"They had good food," he said pointedly. When she raised a warning eyebrow, Rufus added hastily, "I thought the bard was all right, but the others were a little snooty. Of course, a lot of the elder folk are like that—your noble father excluded, my captain." He flashed an ingratiating smile.

"They were afraid of something," Verhanna said, lowering her voice and tapping her chin thoughtfully. "At first I thought it was us, but now I think they were afraid of Diviros."

The kender crinkled his nose. "Why would they be afraid of him?"

Verhanna wrapped her reins tightly around her fist. "I have an idea."

She turned her horse back toward the bard's campfire. "Get your knife out and follow me!" she ordered, putting her spurs to work.

Her ebony mount bolted through the underbrush, its heavy hooves thrashing loudly. Puzzled, Rufus turned his unwieldy animal after his captain, his heart pounding in excitement.

Verhanna burst into the little clearing in time to see Diviros shoving his small son into the back of one of their carts. The bard whirled, eyes wide in alarm. He reached under the cart and brought out a leaf-headed spear—hardly bardic equipment. Verhanna shifted her round buckler to catch the spear point and deflect it away. Diviros planted the heel of the spear shaft against his foot like an experienced soldier and stood while the mounted warrior charged toward him.

"Circle around them, Wart!" the captain cried before ducking her face behind the rim of her shield. Verhanna and Diviros were seconds from collision when the young elf boy stood up in the cart and hurled an earthenware pot at his father. The thick clay vessel thudded against Diviros's back. He dropped his spear and fell to his knees, gasping for air. Verhanna reined in her mount and presented the tip of her sword at his throat.

"Yield, in the name of the Speaker of the Sun!" she declared. Diviros's head dropped down in dejection, and he spread his hands wide on the ground.

Rufus clattered up to the cart. The boy scrambled over the baggage and bounced up and down in front of the kender.

"You've saved us!" he cried joyously.

"What's going on here?" Rufus asked, his confusion evident. He looked up at Verhanna. "Captain, what in darkness is going on?"

"Our friend Diviros is a slaver." Verhanna prodded Diviros with her sword tip. "Aren't you?" The elf didn't answer.

"Yes!" the boy said. "He was taking us all to Ergoth to be sold into slavery!"

The two elf women were released from their cart, where Diviros had bound and gagged them. Gradually the whole story came out.

The Guards of the Sun, under Kith-Kanan's orders, had so disrupted the traffic of slaves from Silvanesti to Ergoth that slave dealers in both lands were resorting to ruses like this one. Small groups of slaves, disguised as settlers and held by one or two experienced drivers, were being sent on many different routes.

Verhanna ordered Diviros bound. The elf women did her bidding eagerly. Once the erstwhile bard was secured, Rufus approached her and said, "What do we do now, Captain? We can't keep trailing the Kagonesti with a prisoner and three civilians in tow."

Disappointment was written on Verhanna's face. She knew the kender was right, yet she burned to bring the crafty Kagonesti slavers to justice.

"We can resume the hunt," she said firmly. "Their trail was leading west, and we'll continue in that direction."

"What's in the west?"

"Pax Tharkas. We can turn Diviros over to my father's

guards there. The captives will be taken care of, too."

She looked up into the starry sky. "I want those elves, Wart. They ambushed my soldiers and made a fool of me with their smoke phantom. I want them brought to justice!" She drove her mailed fist into her palm.

They bundled Diviros into one of the carts and set Deramani, the older elf woman, to watch him. The younger woman, Selenara, volunteered to drive their wagon. Rufus tied Diviros's horse to the other cart and climbed in beside Kivinellis. Once Verhanna was mounted, she led the caravan out of the clearing and headed west.

The elf boy told Rufus and Verhanna that he was actually an orphan from the streets of Silvanost. Then he proceeded to shower them with questions about Qualinesti, Qualinost, and the Speaker of the Sun. He'd heard tales of Kith-Kanan's exploits in the Kinslayer War, but since the schism between East and West, even the mention of Kith-Kanan's name was frowned upon in Silvanesti.

Verhanna told him all he wanted to know—except that she was the daughter of the famous Speaker.

Then Rufus posed a question to Kivinellis. "Hey, was that story about the elf coming out of the tree true?" he asked.

"Don't be ridiculous," put in Verhanna. "Diviros was lying, playing the part of a bard."

"Oh, no, no!" said the boy urgently. "It was true! The green-fingered elf appeared just as he said!"

"Well, what happened to him?" queried the kender.

"Diviros tried to feed him a potion in order to steal his will so he could sell him in Ergoth as a slave. But the potion had no effect on him! In the night, while we all slept, the green-fingered one vanished!"

Verhanna shrugged. "I don't believe it," she muttered.

The red moon, Lunitari, set at midnight. The freed slaves slept in the carts, but Verhanna and Rufus remained awake, and the caravan continued to move west through the night.

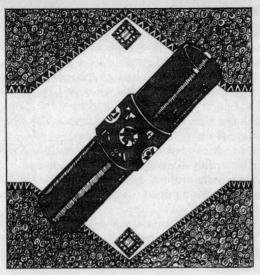

## 7

# The Black Amulet

"Clear away! Clear away there! Do ya want to be mashed to jelly? Get out!" The dwarf overseer, Lugrim, bellowed down at one of the workers pushing a granite block ten feet long, eight feet wide, and six feet high. It didn't help the grunt gang that the rotund dwarf stood on top of the block, adding his own weight to their overall burden. The block was sliding slowly down an earthen ramp. Other workers, human and half-human boys, skipped back and forth in front of the stone, sweeping the wave of displaced dirt out of the way with shovels and rakes. Theirs was a dangerous job; the block could not be stopped once in motion, and if the boys got caught or fell while sweeping, the stone would crush

them. Only the most nimble worked as sweepers. Ulvian was embedded in a mass of sweating, straining
bodies, his hands flat on the block and his bare toes dug
into the dirt. The red rain had stopped just two days before. Its remains were evident all over Pax Tharkas in
the form of crimson puddles, and now the damp soil
gripped like glue. Five days he had been at Pax Tharkas.
Five days of exhaustion, toil, and fear.

"Push, you laggards!" Lugrim exhorted. "My old
mother could push harder than you!"

"I knew your mother," Dru shot back quickly, face to
the ground as he strained. "Her breath could move solid
rock!"

The overseer turned and glared in the direction from
which the voice had come. A squat fellow, even by
dwarven standards, he could barely see over his thick,
fur-wrapped belly. "Who said that?" he demanded, his
eyes darting over the gang.

"All together, lads," grunted Splint. As one, the convicts gave a hard, sudden shove. The block slid forward,
skewing to the left. The dwarf atop the stone lost his
footing and toppled over the side. He let out a loud
"Oof!" and lay stunned. The block ground inexorably
onward.

Merith appeared, elegantly clad in burnished armor
and a fur mantle, his fair hair clean and neatly combed.
Helping the fallen dwarf to his feet, he asked, "Are you
all right?"

"Aye." Lugrim braced his arms against his back and
winced, then turned ponderously to face the grunt gang,
who were watching him. "You think you're clever, don't
you, scum?"

"Yes, Master Lugrim," they replied in unison, sing-
songing their words like naughty children.

Merith easily picked out Ulvian in the crowd of twenty convicts. The prince didn't meet his glance but kept
his legs driving forward in the blood-colored mud. In
spite of his growing blond beard, the marks of his beat-

ing by Splint still showed. Gossip had told Merith what happened, but the warrior refused to intervene. Kith-Kanan's son had hard lessons to learn if he was to survive.

Below the pinnacle where Merith stood, the two square tower keeps that were the innermost defense of the fortress rose to unequal heights. Construction on the west tower was farther along than on the east. Its parapets were already in place. From this distance, Merith could see tiny figures walking on them and on the great wall that connected the two towers.

The camp was situated in the valley behind the fortress. In front of the citadel, farther down the pass, two curtain walls had been erected as the first lines of defense against any attacker. Tall, single gates of hammered bronze were the only openings in the walls. They stood open now, propped apart by huge timber balks. Workers and artisans poured in and out like streams of ants around a bowl of fruit.

Looking down on all this, Merith could well believe the completion of Pax Tharkas was not far away. A year, perhaps less. Feldrin Feldspar had done a magnificent job, building the citadel not only quickly but also well.

The night before, the master builder had shown him detailed drawings of the underground galleries that were being hollowed out of the mountainside beneath each tower. Enough food and water to last for years could be stored there, making Pax Tharkas resistant to any siege. An elaborate throne room, suitable for either the King of Thorbardin or the Speaker of the Sun, was also being constructed. Details such as these might take a few more years to finish, but the basic fortress would be ready to occupy much sooner than that.

A shadow fell across Merith; a cloud had covered the sun. As he turned from his study of the fortress, tiny particles peppered his face, and he inhaled grit. Vibrations tingled the soles of his shoes. It was an odd, tickling sensation, and Merith shifted his weight, looking down at his boots. Then he became aware of a deep humming sound, like the bass drums the priests of E'li sometimes played during festivals. The dust cloud was thickening. Below, workers scrambled in confusion.

"Landslide!" someone shouted.

Merith whirled and saw behind and to his left what he had only felt before. Boulders and rain-soaked chunks of wet soil were rolling down the east face of the mountain. Paralyzed, the elf warrior could only stare in amazement as tons of rock and dirt hurtled toward the quarries in the high pass. The noise increased to a deafening roar, and the ground shook so that he lost his footing and fell.

Screams filled the air, piercing the thunder of the avalanche. Merith rolled about like a pea shaken in its pod. He clawed at the stony earth, trying to keep his balance.

The landslide hit the pass. Rock chips and boulders flew, crushing everything they hit. Merith watched helplessly as a huge stone bowled over half a dozen quarry workers. A pall of reddish dust descended over the scene. The roar faded. The sobbing of the terrified and injured was everywhere.

"Help!" A loud cry sliced through the moans of the injured and dying. "Help, somebody! Help me!"

Merith stumbled to his feet and ran down the earthen ramp. The overseer was lying on the path on this side of the block. The convicts had scattered, as had the sweeper boys. Merith knelt beside the dwarf. Lugrim had an ugly bleeding gash on his forehead. His heart beat strongly, however, so the elf warrior knew he was only knocked unconscious.

"Help, in the names of the gods! The stone is moving!" The shout came again, nearer this time. Merith looked up and caught his breath in a gasp. The severe vibrations from the landslide had twisted the path of the granite block. It was teetering on the edge of the ramp, and people lay prostrate in the very shadow of the rock.

Merith left the dwarf where he lay. A few paces closer,

he saw two gang members close to the block. One was a Silvanesti he didn't know; the other was Prince Ulvian. The prince's pant leg was caught under the block! The granite had run over his trailing hem and was dragging him along. Only one of his comrades remained behind to help him.

"Merithynos! Help me!" screamed Ulvian. He kicked vainly at the huge stone with his left leg. His other was hard against the rock. The block crept forward on its own, driven by the slope of the ramp and its skewed position. In another yard or two, it would be far enough off the ramp that it would topple over on its side. Anything or anyone in its way would be crushed.

Merith and the Silvanesti pulled on Ulvian's arms, trying to tear him free. The prince's forester clothing was made of deerhide and was very tough. The warrior drew his knife and sawed at the leather. Too slow, too slow!

"Do something!" Ulvian pleaded, tears streaking his face.

"I'm trying, Your Highness!" Merith replied. The other elf stiffened for a moment, staring at Merith.

The lieutenant sawed harder at the deerhide and finally succeeded in making a small slit.

The block ground a sweeper's broom into the stony ramp. The crushing sound of the wooden handle being pulverized sent fresh paroxysms of terror through the prince. "Please don't let me die!" he groaned piteously. "Save me, Merith, Dru!"

The enormous cube of granite wobbled on the edge of the ramp. Merith cursed and tore at the leather pants with his hands. Ulvian's lower body already hung over the rim of the ramp, while he was pinned on his back.

The Silvanesti, Dru, grabbed Merith by his cloak and dragged him away. "Go to the tent of Feldrin Feldspar," he shouted at the warrior's horrified face. "Get the onyx ring he keeps on a thong around his neck!" When Merith continued to regard him with utter incomprehension, Dru shook him and roared, "Go now, if you hope to save your royal charge!"

Merith scrambled up the ramp and sprinted toward the master builder's tent. Mobs of dazed workers clustered around it, seeking Feldrin's attention. Merith had to whip out his sword in order to convince them to part to let him through.

Feldrin stood at the door of his hut, a cold wet cloth pressed to his head. He took it away and dipped it in a bowl of fresh water. There was a goose-egg-size bruise over his left eye.

"Quick! Give me the ring!" Merith demanded.

"What?" rumbled Feldrin. Merith thrust a hand into the dwarf's collar and found the onyx ring on a thong, just as Dru had said. It was made of black crystal, slightly larger than a finger ring, square cut, with odd glyphs engraved around the edge. Just then a shriek pierced the air. Merith yanked the ring from Feldrin's neck and took off at a run. The master builder bellowed for him to stop.

If the prince dies, it will be my fault, Merith thought desperately. Not only Ulvian, but also perhaps the entire dynasty of the House of Silvanos might come to an end under that block of gray stone. Dru was a few feet from the block, kneeling, his eyes mere slits, his hands clasped around the four-inch-long cylinder of onyx he constantly carried with him. Ulvian was calling out to the gods, begging for a merciful, quick death. As Merith approached, he saw the near end of the stone begin to lift off the ramp, about to topple over.

"Here!" he cried, thrusting the black crystal ring into Dru's fingers. The elf's eyes snapped open. Not even the terror of the moment could overcome Merith's shock at seeing the Silvanesti's eyes. They were solid black, with no white at all.

Dru took the ring from the thong and fitted the cylinder of onyx into its center hole. The result was an object that looked very much like a child's top—indeed, Dru balanced the two onyx pieces on the tip of the cylinder and removed his hand. The piece didn't topple over, but instead began to spin. All by itself.

A roaring filled Merith's ears. The air above the spinning top coalesced into a tight vortex, like a miniature whirlwind. Dust whirled and spun, caught up by the racing air. Dru rose to his feet and walked straight into the vortex. Merith, trying vainly to shield his face from the flying grit, was pressed backward. Invisible hands shoved him to his knees and then onto his back. It was as if lumps of stone had been laid across his chest. He could barely move his head, and his breath came in ragged gasps.

Through a haze of flying dirt, Merith saw Dru step up to the granite block and, with his bare hands, turn it over! The black-eyed elf simply grasped the lower edge of the stone and lifted it, with no more strain than shifting an empty barrel. The block slammed down on the ramp. Ulvian was saved!

Dimly Merith saw figures move past him. Feldrin Feldspar, walking jerkily, slowly, went straight to where the onyx top still rotated. The dwarf pulled a sparkling silver cloth from a small leather pouch and dropped it on the top.

Instantly the tremendous magical force dissipated. Blessed air filled Merith's lungs with a rush. His straining muscles, freed from the terrible force, slackened, and he lay limply on the ground. Through a pounding headache, he discovered a dampness on his face that proved to be a nosebleed. Painfully he sat up.

Armed overseers seized Dru and shoved him to the ground. A large wooden fork was thrust around his neck, pinning him to the dirt. Ulvian dragged himself to the elf who had saved his life and demanded in a weak voice that Dru be released.

"That cannot be done," Feldrin said, grimly surveying the area. "He could slay us all."

Workers and artisans had gathered in a crowd around the scene. Feldrin bent down and scooped up the silver cloth and onyx top, being careful to keep the black crystals wrapped in the shiny covering. Merith hauled himself to his feet and stood swaying.

"Come with me," Feldrin told him. "The rest of you, return to your tents! The healers will come and tend to your injuries!"

Feeling quite battered, Merith sluggishly followed Feldrin back to his tent. The master builder put the onyx pieces and silver cloth in a small golden box and locked it. Then he poured the grateful lieutenant a mug of Qualinesti nectar. Merith gulped it down.

"That was a very dangerous thing you did," Feldrin said, crossing his powerful arms over his broad chest.

The room still seemed to Merith to be spinning like the magical onyx top, and he put a hand to his head. "I don't understand," he protested.

"That elf is Drulethen, the infamous sorcerer. For fifty years, he ruled a portion of the Kharolis Mountains from his hidden keep, and he used his terrible magic to kill and enslave anyone who passed by. Finally, the King of Thorbardin led an expedition of elves and dwarves against him. The clerics managed to defeat his spells only with great difficulty, but the warriors were finally able to storm the keep and take him prisoner."

Merith's mug was empty, and Feldrin refilled it. "It was discovered that his power was chiefly invested in a simple onyx amulet. When that was taken away, he was powerless. We didn't know about the other piece of onyx. Drulethen must've kept it hidden for just such an occasion."

The nectar was sweet and strong. It sent strength coursing through Merith's veins as his head cleared. "But—he saved the prince!"

Feldrin sighed gustily. "Yes, thank Reorx! I don't know why he did it, but I can't fault his deed."

"Why don't you destroy the amulet? Or send it to Thorbardin, or somewhere else where Dru can't possibly get at it?"

Feldrin smote the table top with his fist. "That's the trouble! We can't! My king originally took the ring to his palace in Thorbardin. While it was in his possession, he was so wracked by illness and his sleep so tormented by dreadful nightmares that in desperation he sent it back to me." The master builder lowered his voice, though they were alone in the tent. "You see, my friend, the amulet is *alive*. It sometimes talks to mortals, and indeed there are those who say it was fashioned by the Queen of Darkness herself. It cannot be destroyed. Only the silver cloth can confine it once its power has been unleashed."

Merith asked about the cloth. "One of the most sacred relics of my people," Feldrin informed him. "No less than a scrap of hide from the Silver Dragon, the same one who loved and fought with the great human warrior Huma Dragonsbane."

This revelation stunned the already woozy Merith. "By the gods," he breathed. "I had no idea who or what I was dealing with! My only thought was to save the prince!"

"No harm done, young warrior." Feldrin put a hand on Merith's shoulder. "The Speaker of the Sun and the King of Thòrbardin made a bargain to put the evil Drulethen to work. Personally, I would have struck his head off, but my royal master believes he can use the sorcerer's knowledge for his own benefit, and the great and wise Kith-Kanan thinks he can actually reform Drulethen!" Feldrin shook his head. "The Speaker is always trying to improve his enemies."

"Aye," Merith agreed. "Ofttimes I have heard him say, 'I used to kill my foes; now I make them my friends. A warrior needs as few enemies as possible, but a Speaker needs as many friends as he can make.' "

*   *   *   *   *

The barracks were quiet, save for the coughs of sleeping grunt gang members trying to expel the dust they'd breathed all day. Ulvian lay on his side, wide awake. Aside from some scrapes and an aching right leg, he was essentially unharmed by his brush with death, yet he could not sleep. Over and over he replayed the scene— the block teetering above him, Dru pushing it aside with his bare hands, the awesome presence of the power in the black crystal.

The prince sat up, wincing as his wrenched muscles protested. He padded on bare feet to Dru's bed. Peering through the darkness, the prince realized his savior was not lying down but sitting with his knees drawn up to his smooth chin.

"Dru?" he whispered. "I need to talk to you."

"If you answer one question for me. Are you in truth the son of Speaker Kith-Kanan?" Ulvian admitted he was. "I knew the Speaker had some half-human children," Dru said softly. A gruff voice nearby rumbled a demand for silence. The sorcerer rose and took Ulvian by the arm. He led the prince to the relatively open area by the water barrel, where they could talk more freely.

"I won't forget your deed," Ulvian began.

"I should hope not," Dru said dryly. He smiled, his teeth showing white in the darkness. "We are a natural pair of allies, are we not? A prince and a sorcerer, both sentenced to labor on this ridiculous mausoleum, both required to hide their true identities."

Dru lifted a dipperful of water to his lips. Once he'd taken a long drink, he asked, "What did you do to end up in such a place, Your Highness? Why did your infamously just father send you here to work like a dog?"

With some hemming and hawing, Ulvian explained his activities as a slave trader.

"It was a harmless diversion," he insisted. "A few wealthy traders approached me and asked for my patronage. I had influence and knew warriors who could be bribed to look the other way. It was a mere lark, an adventure to keep boredom at bay, but my enemies in Qualinost used my capture as an excuse to exile me!" His voice rose until Dru had to quiet him. "I will reclaim what is rightfully mine," the prince finished darkly. "I will fulfill my destiny!"

Dru squatted and began to idly trace elaborate designs in the dirt floor. Curving lines, loops, and squares took shape. "What enemies do you have, my prince? Who are they?"

Ulvian hunkered down across from his friend and said, "There is my sister, Verhanna, for one. The old castellan, Tamanier Ambrodel, thinks I'm immoral and wicked, and his son, General Lord Kemian Ambrodel, believes he is better suited to be Speaker than I. There is an old Kagonesti senator, Irthenie by name, who—"

"I see."

Dru brushed the designs away with his hand. "I think we should make common cause, Your Highness. Your father and the king of the dwarves put me here. I've had to keep my true identity hidden because some of the elves and dwarves we work alongside would kill me if they knew who I really was." The sorcerer thrust his face close to Ulvian's. "Together we can escape this place and regain the power and position we are destined to have."

"Escape?" Ulvian echoed weakly. "I—I can't. My father will declare me an outlaw if I flee the country."

"Who said anything about fleeing the country? You and I will go to Qualinost. There must be nobles, senators, and clerics who favor you, my prince. We'll rally them round you and demand a pardon. What do you say?"

Ulvian rubbed his palms together. Despite the cool mountain air, his hands were damp with sweat. "I—I don't know," he said faintly. Much as he loathed his current situation, the prince realized that such a plan was risky at best. "When would we leave?" Ulvian asked hesitantly.

"This very night," Dru said, and Ulvian actually started at the abrupt words. "Both parts of my amulet are in camp. We can break into Feldrin's tent and get them.

Then no power within a hundred miles can stop us!"

The prince sank back slowly on his haunches. Bracing himself with his hands, he said, "Feldrin won't just hand—"

"With your help, I'll kill the old stonebreaker," the sorcerer snapped.

"No." Ulvian stood up, looking around nervously. "I can't do that. I can't murder Feldrin. I plan to be vindicated and pardoned. I won't murder my way to freedom."

Dru stood and shrugged expressively. "As you wish, my prince. I've been here for many years, you only a short time. After you've broken your back working on this damn fortress for a while longer, perhaps you'll change your mind."

Ulvian was about to reply when Dru's head suddenly snapped around, as if he'd heard a strange noise. He held up one hand to forestall Ulvian's words. "Wait," he said. "Something's amiss."

Ulvian followed the sorcerer to one of the two windows in the barracks. It seemed brighter outside than it should be this late at night. As they watched, it grew brighter still. The outline of the camp became clearer. Silhouetted tents gained distinct features. To Ulvian's astonishment, the sun appeared in the sky directly overhead. At first, only a faint red glow was visible, but then it blazed more and more brilliantly until the mountain pass was bathed in the full light of noon.

"What—what's happening?" Ulvian cried, shading his squinting eyes from the sudden glare.

Dru stroked his dirty, pointed chin. "Someone is tampering with the balance of nature," he said coolly. "Someone—or something—very powerful."

Men and dwarves emerged from their huts to stare at the bright sky and scratch their heads in wonderment. By the water clocks, it was still two hours till sunrise, yet sunlight flooded the tents.

\*　　\*　　\*　　\*　　\*

Dust from the landslide tinted the sky over the Kharolis Mountains rusty red. The gritty fog hung in the still air, unmoving. The day after the avalanche, the sun burned like an orange ball through the haze. It hung fixed at the peak of the heavens. As measured by notched candles and water clocks, several hours had passed, yet the sun had never budged.

"Master Lugrim, what o'clock is it?" called Ulvian to the overseer, whose face was hidden by a dripping dipper of cool water.

Lugrim poured the last few drops on his brow, which was already wet with sweat. "Nigh time to work again," he growled. "Are you men or camels? How much do you plan to drink?"

"I'm no man," Splint said acidly, "and I'll drink how I please."

"'Tis fearful hot," added a human named Brunnar in a thick Ergothic accent.

Six hours had passed since the sun's abrupt appearance, and the temperature had been growing steadily warmer. The air was unusually dead; no breeze wafted through the pass, and no clouds shielded the workers from the sun. Only the ever-present dust diffused the sunlight, coating the workers' sweltering bodies.

At Feldrin Feldspar's hut, a crowd of overseers and guild masters had formed. There was much debate over the strange sunrise. Some in the group insisted that work be halted until the heat abated, while others argued that work should continue.

"Our covenant with the Speaker of the Sun calls for us to work till sunset," the chief mason complained. "We must honor our pledge."

"Our people can't work forever," objected the leader of the carpenters' guild.

"Quiet, you shortsighted fools!" rumbled Feldrin, waving his hands over his head. "The sun hasn't moved for hours. Merciful Reorx! A calamity is upon us, and you quibble about schedules and quotas!"

The overseers and masters lapsed into embarrassed silence. Merith appeared and stood on the fringe of the crowd. He'd shed his armor in the heat and wore a lightweight white tunic and baggy gray trousers.

"This must be yet another of the wonders," said the elf warrior. "Like the darkness, the lightning, and the scarlet rain."

That set off a fresh wave of contention in the group. Feldrin let them argue a while, then shouted for quiet again.

The chief mason wailed, "What are we to do?"

"Collect all the fresh water you can," ordered Feldrin. "Fill every pot and jar in Pax Tharkas. Tell the sewing women to make canopies—very large canopies. We will erect them over the quarry walls to shade the workers."

The master builder loosened his fur mantle and let it fall to the ground. "Let it be done. And tell everyone to get rid of his heavy garments!"

"Do we resume work?" asked Lugrim.

"In two hours, by the water clock."

Feldrin's assistants dispersed to carry out his bidding. The trumpets blew, signaling an end to work, and every worker in the pass hurried indoors, out of the broiling sun. Feldrin and Merith watched the teeming site become a ghost fortress in a matter of minutes. The last people in sight were the dwarves who had been working on the parapet of the west tower. They secured their hoist and winch, then ducked inside the massive stone structure. For some time after that, the hoist swung to and fro, the block and tackle creaking loudly.

The sight of the sun-baked, lifeless fortress bothered the master builder. It was unnerving. In a gloomy tone, he said as much to the lieutenant.

"Why so, my lord?" asked Merith, surprised.

"The other marvels were like conjurer's tricks—they seemed mysterious and impressive, but they were essentially harmless. This is different. A few days of unrelieved sun could be the end of us all."

Feldrin dabbed sweat from his brow with the sleeve of his yellow linen shirt. "I can't help but wonder who has the power to do this. Who can stop the course of the sun itself through the sky?"

"Drulethen?" the lieutenant suggested.

"Certainly not," Feldrin said firmly. "Even if he possessed both halves of his evil talisman, he could never do such a thing." The dwarf shook his head. "I wonder if even the gods themselves. . . ."

"Nothing is beyond the gods," Merith replied reverently.

"Perhaps. Perhaps."

The dwarf picked up his discarded cloak and draped it over one arm. Already his salt-and-pepper hair was clinging to his damp face. With a sigh, he said, "I shall retire indoors now. Can't have my brain getting scrambled in this blasted sun."

"A wise notion, master. I shall do likewise."

Elf and dwarf parted company. Merith crossed the winding road to the fortress site alone, the only living thing moving through the entire construction site. Overhead, the hoist continued to sway and creak. The lieutenant thought it a mournful, lonely sound.

## 8

# Greenhands

*Midnight in Qualinost was as bright as any noon.* There had been no night at all for two days, and the heat was appalling. Half the public fountains in the city had dried up during the first twenty-four-hour period of the strange daylight. The people of Qualinost filled the courtyards of the great temples, begging the priests and priestesses to intercede on their behalf with the gods. Incense burned and chants rose to the heavens, but the sun burned mercilessly on.

The water clock in the chamber of the Thalas-Enthia showed it was midnight, yet the senators of Qualinesti were all present. Seated in his place of honor on the north side of the circular room, Kith-Kanan listened to the representatives of the people debate the series of marvels they had experienced, including the current dangerous manifestation. Many of the senators bore the signs of lack of slumber; not only were their duties pressing in this time of crisis, but the lack of night made it difficult for many in Qualinost to sleep.

"Clearly we have offended the gods," Senator Xixis said, "though I have no knowledge of what the offense could have been. I propose that offerings be made at once, and that they be continued until these plagues cease."

"Hear! Hear!" murmured a group of senators sitting on the western side of the chamber. These were known as the Loyalists, because they were loyal to the old traditions of Silvanesti, especially in matters of religion and royalty. Most of the full-blooded elven senators were members of this extremely conservative faction.

Clovanos, senior senator of the Loyalists, descended from his seat to the floor. The Thalas-Enthia met in a squat, round tower, larger in diameter than even the Tower of the Sun, though far less tall. The floor of the meeting chamber was covered with a mosaic map of the country, exactly like the more famous and larger map in the Hall of the Sky. High on the wall, near the ceiling, more mosaics ringed the chamber. These were the crests of all the great clans of Qualinesti.

Clovanos held out his hand to his friend Xixis, and the latter handed him the speaking baton. A rod twenty inches long made of ivory and gold, the baton was passed to whomever was addressing the Thalas-Enthia.

Resting the baton in the crook of his left arm, a signal that he intended to speak at length, Senator Clovanos scanned the assembly. The so-called New Landers sat on the east side of the chamber. They were a loose association of humans, half-humans, Kagonesti, and dwarves who favored new traditions, ones that reflected their mixed society. On the south wall was the middle-of-the-road group that had come to be known as the Speaker's

Friends, people like Senator Irthenie, who preferred to follow the personal leadership of Kith-Kanan.

"My friends," Clovanos finally began, "I must agree with the learned Xixis. From the strange and terrifying wonders that have been visited upon our helpless world, it is quite obvious that a grave offense has been committed, an offense against the natural order of life, against the gods themselves. Now they seek to punish us. Our priests have divined and meditated; our people have prayed; we ourselves have debated continuously. All to no avail. No one can determine why this should be so. However, very recently I received some information—information that enabled me to ascertain what the dreadful sacrilege was."

A buzz of speculation swept the chamber in the wake of Clovanos's words. The senator allowed it to continue for a moment, then said, "The knowledge came to me from a strange place—a place close to the hearts of the Speaker's Friends."

"Speak up. I can't hear you," Irthenie droned mockingly. A scattering of laughter among the New Landers and Friends made Clovanos's heat-reddened face grow even more florid.

"My information came from Pax Tharkas," he said loudly, facing the calm Kagonesti woman, "that folly of a fortress the Speaker puts so much faith in."

"Get on with it! Tell us what you know!" chorused several impatient senators.

Clovanos brandished the baton. The cries declined. "I received a letter from a friend and fellow Loyalist," he said with heavy emphasis, "who happens to be at the site of the fortress. He wrote, 'Imagine my surprise when I saw the Speaker's son, Prince Ulvian, working as a common laborer in the crudest and most dangerous of jobs.'"

Having thus spoken, Clovanos turned quickly to face Kith-Kanan. The chamber erupted. New Landers and Loyalists stood and shouted at each other. Denunciations flew in the thick, hot air. Only the Speaker's

Friends sat quietly, waiting for Kith-Kanan to deny the report.

Slowly, with great deliberation, the Speaker rose and crossed the floor to where Clovanos had turned to hurl retorts at the ranks of New Landers seated above him. He tapped on the senator's shoulder and asked for the baton. Clovanos had no choice but to surrender the speaking symbol to Kith-Kanan. Stiffly, his face sheened with sweat, the Silvanesti senator climbed the marble steps to his place among the Loyalists.

Kith-Kanan held the baton over his head until the room grew still. Bare to the waist in the dreadful heat, his tanned chest bore pale scars from wounds he'd received in the great Kinslayer War. A simple white kilt, a wide golden belt, and leather sandals were all he wore, save for the circlet of Qualinost atop his head. Though past midlife, his face growing more lined, the white-blond of his hair now more than half silver, the Speaker of the Sun was still as vibrant and handsome as he had been centuries earlier when he led his people out of Silvanesti.

"My lords," Kith-Kanan said in a firm voice, "what Senator Clovanos tells you is true."

The chamber grews so quiet that a falling feather would have rung out like a gong. After Clovanos's long-winded oration, the Speaker's simple statement seemed blunt and harsh. "My son is indeed working as a slave at Pax Tharkas."

Xixis leapt to his feet. "Why?" he shouted.

Kith-Kanan turned slowly to face the senator. "Because he was taken during the campaign to stamp out slave-trading and found guilty of helping such traders cross Qualinesti territory."

Malvic Pathfinder, a human and a New Lander, called out, "I thought the penalty for slave-trading was death."

A dozen Loyalists booed him.

"No father wishes to sentence his own son to the block," Kith-Kanan replied frankly. "Ulvian's guilt was plain, but instead of a useless death, I decided to teach him a lesson in compassion. I believed, and still believe, that once he had experienced the wretched life of a slave, he would never again be able to look upon people as cattle that can be bought and sold."

Kith-Kanan's well-muscled frame might have been carved from wood or marble. His proud and noble countenance was so overpowering that no one spoke for some time.

Finally Irthenie broke the silence. "Great Speaker, how long will Prince Ulvian be held at Pax Tharkas?" she asked. Her words, spoken with quiet force, carried to every bench in the chamber.

"He remains at my discretion," Kith-Kanan replied, facing her.

"It is wrong!" Clovanos countered. "A prince of the blood should not be forced to work as a slave by his own father! *This* is the offense the gods are punishing us for!" The other Loyalists took up his refrain. The chamber echoed with their outraged cries.

"Your Majesty, will you recall the prince?" asked Xixis.

"I will not. He has been there only a few weeks," Kith-Kanan answered. "If I freed him now, the only lesson he would have learned is that influence is stronger than virtue."

"But he is your heir!" insisted Clovanos.

Kith-Kanan gripped the speaking baton tightly, his other hand clenched into a fist. "It is *my* decision!" he replied, his voice ringing through the chamber. "Not yours!"

All the arguments and accusations ceased abruptly. Kith-Kanan's blazing gaze was fastened on the unfortunate Clovanos. The senator, his body quivering with anger, stared balefully down at his sovereign. Breaking the tense silence, Xixis said unctuously, "We are naturally concerned for the safety and future of the royal house. Your Majesty has no other heir."

"Your time, my lords, would be better spent finding ways to soothe the troubles of the common folk, and not interfering with the manner in which I discipline my son!" Kith-Kanan turned on his heel, strode to the door, and departed.

Since the Speaker had taken the baton with him, that meant the Thalas-Enthia session was over. The senators filled the aisles, clustering in small groups to discuss Kith-Kanan's stand.

There was no debate between Clovanos and Xixis. The two elves were in complete agreement.

"The Speaker will ruin the country," breathed Xixis anxiously. "His stubbornness has already offended the gods. Does he think he can stand against their will? It will mean the end of us all!"

"He has already cost me plenty," Clovanos agreed. He couldn't forget the loss of his towers during the siege of lightning. "If only we could come up with some alternate plan."

The din in the chamber was considerable. Xixis leaned closer to his ally. "What do you mean?" he asked.

"I can't speak in certainties," Clovanos replied, his words barely audible, "but suppose the fortress is finished before the Speaker decides the prince has been rehabilitated? Kith-Kanan has sworn to retire once Pax Tharkas is done; if Prince Ulvian is still under a cloud, another candidate must be found."

Xixis's mouse-colored hair was limp with perspiration, and his flowing robe clung to his clammy skin. Blotting his face with one sleeve, his eyes darted around. No one was listening to them.

"Who, then?" he hissed. "Not that dragon of a daughter!"

Clovanos sneered. "Even the open-minded people of Qualinesti would balk at having a half-human female as Speaker of the Sun! No, listen. You are familiar with the name Lord Kemian Ambrodel?" Xixis nodded. Lord Ambrodel was a prominent figure. "He is pure Silvanesti in heritage and a notable warrior."

"But he is not of House Silvanos!" Xixis cried, and Clovanos shushed him.

"That's the beauty of my plan, my friend. If we begin a campaign to have Lord Ambrodel named as the Speaker's heir, then His Majesty will feel compelled to recall Prince Ulvian from Pax Tharkas."

Xixis regarded his companion blankly.

"Don't you see?" Clovanos went on. "Publicly the Speaker may denounce his son as a failure, a weak and cruel rogue who deals in slaves. However, Kith-Kanan won't deny his own family. He cannot, any more than he could have had Ulvian executed. No, the Speaker, for all his harsh words, wants only his own son, the direct descendant of the great Silvanos to ascend the throne of Qualinesti. If we agitate for another heir, it will force the Speaker's hand. He *must* recall the prince!"

Xixis didn't seem convinced. "I have known the Speaker for two hundred years," he said. "I fought with him in the great war. Kith-Kanan will do what he thinks is right, not what's best for his family."

Clovanos rose to go, smoothing his pale hair back from his face. Xixis stood also. Linking his arm in the arm of Xixis, Clovanos murmured sagely, "We'll see, my friend. We'll see."

\* \* \* \* \*

"This air is like dragon's breath!" complained Rufus, sagging on the seat of the cart. Beside him rode Verhanna on her coal-black horse, and behind the kender creaked the other cart containing the freed slaves. Two days had passed, and the sun had burned continuously for a day and a half now.

"Have some water," Verhanna suggested, licking her dry lips. She passed her waterskin to the kender. He put the spout to his lips and drank deeply. "How far do you think we've ridden?" she asked. Without the moons or

stars to go by, or even the passage of the sun across the
sky, they'd lost track of what hour or day it was.

Rufus pondered her question. His scouting skills had
grown fuzzy in the constant daylight and mounting
heat. "A horse can walk forty miles a day," he said slowly. His freckled face screwed itself into a fearsome
frown. "But how long is a day when the sun doesn't shift
and the stars don't shine?" He shook his small head,
lashing his damp topknot from side to side. "I don't
know! Is there anything more to drink?" The waterskin
was drained.

Verhanna sighed and admitted there was no more water. She'd shed her armor and cloak and was down to
wearing a thin white shirt and divided kilt. Her elven
heritage was ever more apparent in her long limbs and
pale skin. The subtle influence of her human blood
showed in her figure, more muscular than any elven
woman.

"Any problems back there?" she called over her shoulder. The boy, Kivinellis, and the elf woman, Deramani,
sprawled atop a mound of loose baggage in the second
cart, waved listlessly from their perch. Selenara, driving
the cart, was too weary even to acknowledge Verhanna's
call. Diviros himself was propped up in the first cart,
driven by Rufus, and his hands and feet were still tied, a
gag in his mouth.

No trace of the Kagonesti slavers had turned up during their drive west. Verhanna had resigned herself to the
fact that they had lost the slavers. Nevertheless, she felt
a strong sense of responsibility for the former slaves in
her care. Rufus, however, insisted he might still recover
their trail. Ahead lay the Astradine River, and the Kagonesti would have to cross it. There was no bridge, the
kender recalled, just privately owned ferries. Someone
would have seen the Kagonesti. Someone would remember them.

They rode on, their heads nodding as they drifted in
and out of heat-fogged sleep. The forest around them

was unnaturally quiet. Even the birds and beasts were oppressed by the heat.

As he bobbed along, the kender dreamed he was back in the snow-capped peaks of the Magnet Mountains, where the captain had first found him. In his mind, he climbed the highest slopes and threw himself down into the drifted snow. How good it felt! How sweet the wind was, how fresh the clear, cold air! The gods themselves knew no kinder home than the peaks of the Magnets.

No one had any business screaming in such a peaceful place.

A drop of sweat slid down Rufus's nose. He batted it away. Ah, to shiver as the chill air brought gooseflesh to his bare arms! The brilliance of the valley below . . . Screaming?

He forced his eyes open as the sound came again. Verhanna was also drowsing, and it took several tugs on her arm before Rufus could get her to open her eyes.

"What—what is it?" she asked languidly.

"Trouble," was his matter-of-fact reply. As if on cue, the scream rang out a third time. Verhanna sat up and pulled in her reins.

"By Astra!" she exclaimed. "I thought I'd dreamed that!"

Kivinellis ran up beside Verhanna's horse. Damp with sweat, his blond hair gleamed in the brilliant sunlight. "It sounds like a lady in distress!" he announced.

"So it does. Can you tell which direction, Wart?" Verhanna nervously drew her sword.

Rufus stood on the cart seat and slowly craned his head in a circle, trying to catch the source of the sound. His pointed, elflike ears were infallible. "Ha!" he crowed at last and bounced on his toes.

Verhanna listened hard. Sure enough, she heard a faint crashing sound, the sort of noise a person might make if he were running pell-mell through the woods. She thrust her dagger and shield at Kivinellis.

"Defend the carts!" she cried. The shrill scream split

the air once more. "Grab your horse, Wart. We're off!"

Rufus was off the cart and on his chestnut mount before the words had scarcely left his captain's mouth. They turned their horses south, off the narrow track they'd been following, and plunged into the forest proper. Saplings and tree limbs raked at their faces. Verhanna had her sword, but the kender was poorly armed for a fight. Aside from a sheath knife, his only weapon was a kender sling. It was a light, handy missile thrower, which he'd used to good effect in the fight at the slavers' camp, but it would be hard to use in the close-growing trees.

Indistinct shouts came from ahead, off to their left. Verhanna halted her horse and waited. Someone was running.

A black-haired human woman, clutching a baby to her breast, came stumbling through the undergrowth. Tears streaked her face. Now and again, she looked back over her shoulder and screeched in terror. Verhanna dug in her spurs and rode hard toward her. The woman saw the warrior maid on horseback, sword drawn, and screamed again—this time for pure joy. She threw herself at the horse's feet.

"Noble lady, save us!" she whimpered. The baby in her arms was bawling loudly, nearly drowning out her words.

Rufus rode up beside his mistress. "Who's after you?" he asked the frightened woman.

"Terrible creatures—monsters. They want to eat my child!"

Hardly had she finished this declaration when a trio of hideous, gnarled creatures appeared in the undergrowth, obviously following the woman's trail. Verhanna's lip curled in disgust.

"Goblins," she said with distaste. "I'll settle with them!"

They were indeed goblins, but of the most backward and gruesome sort. All wore necklaces of human or elven teeth and bones, and one wore a sort of helmet made from a human skull. Their long fangs protruded over their bottom lips. Even from ten yards away, it was impossible not to smell their rank odor. The goblins were armed with crude maces made from lumps of rounded stone tied to thick ironwood handles. The sight of Verhanna, sword in hand, did not seem to upset the angry creatures. They must be desperately hungry, the captain decided, or driven mad by the suffocating heat.

Verhanna rode straight at them while the kender fitted a pellet into his sling. Clutching her baby tightly, the human woman crawled through the dead leaves until Rufus's broad horse was between her and the goblins.

Leaning forward, Verhanna smote the nearest creature with her keen Qualinesti blade. The goblin gave an inarticulate gurgle and dropped his club, his chest split open from shoulder to breastbone. The captain planted a foot on his chest and withdrew her blade. The goblin was dead before he hit the ground.

The other two monsters separated, one on each side of the warrior woman's horse. They swept their maces back and forth, warding off her sword. The goblin on Verhanna's left tried to get by to reach the woman cowering in the leaves. Before the captain could turn to cut him off, Rufus had put a pellet in the center of the goblin's forehead. Stunned, the cannibal creature fell facedown.

"Nice shot!" Verhanna cried.

"Look out!" yelled the kender at the same time.

His warning came too late. Verhanna had been distracted by the first goblin and had turned her back on the other. The second creature, who wore the human skull on its pointed head, dropped its mace in favor of using its teeth and claws. Grabbing her with its taloned hands, he yanked the captain off her horse.

Rufus drew his knife and half fell from his mount. The goblin sank its fangs into Verhanna's shoulder. She yelled loudly enough to rattle the leaves on the trees, and together she and the goblin toppled to the ground. The creature wrapped its arms and legs around her, entwining its rubbery black toes together. As Verhanna tried to pry it off, they rolled over and over in the leaves, locked in deadly embrace.

When the goblin presented its back to him, Rufus rammed his iron blade into its body—once, twice, thrice. The ferocious creature howled and let go of Verhanna. It turned on the little kender, murder in its bulging red eyes. Rufus held out his short blade and looked startled. How would it feel to be torn to bits by a filthy, heat-crazed goblin?

Wounded but not out of the fight, the captain flung herself at her sword where it lay in the dead leaves. As the wounded goblin gathered itself to leap on the kender, Verhanna beheaded it with one two-handed blow. Then the blade fell from her hands and she collapsed.

Just then the goblin that Rufus had knocked out with a pellet stirred noisily in the leaves. The kender quickly dispatched it by cutting its throat, then rushed to Verhanna.

"Captain, can you hear me?" he shouted.

"Of course I can hear you, Wart," she muttered. "I'm not deaf."

Indignation spread over the kender's mobile face. "I thought you were dead!"

"Not yet. Help me up."

Rufus pulled on her arm until Verhanna was able to sit up. Aside from the bite wound on her right shoulder and a few cuts and bruises, she didn't seem to be seriously injured.

"Where's the woman and her baby?" she asked, pushing her tumbled brown hair out of her eyes. Rufus looked toward his horse; there was no sign of the woman. In the confusion of battle, she must have fled. He didn't blame her. For a moment, it had looked like the goblins were going to get the best of them.

"She skedaddled," he reported, wiping the noxious

goblin blood from his knife blade. "No sign of her or the baby."

"That's gratitude for you," grumbled Verhanna, wobbling to her knees. "Ugh! These goblins are the filthiest creatures I know."

Studying her shoulder dispassionately, the kender said, "Your wounds should be washed, but we haven't any water."

"Never mind. We'll be at the Astradine soon."

The captain put a hand on her scout's shoulder and heaved herself to her feet. The two of them remounted their horses, and Verhanna took one last look at the bloody scene before they moved on. Her shoulder burned as if a glowing coal had been set under the skin. Verhanna held her reins limply in her left hand, favoring her injured side.

"Wait a minute," said Rufus. "This isn't the way we came in."

"Are you sure?"

He scratched his head and looked all around. There was nothing but trees and brush in all directions. "Blind me with beeswax! Which way do we go?" Shielding his eyes with his hands, the kender squinted into the hazy sky. The immobile sun gave no clue which direction they should take.

"Can't you find the trail?" Verhanna asked hoarsely. "That's what I pay you for, to be a scout."

Rufus leapt to the ground. He sniffed the dead leaves and dry moss. He turned his head, straining for any sound. Finally, in desperation, he shouted, "Ho, Kivinellis! Can you hear me? Where are you?" In spite of repeated calls, there was no answer. At last the kender turned to Verhanna and shrugged helplessly.

"Wart," she said weakly, "you're fired."

Verhanna's eyes rolled up until only the white showed. Without another sound, she toppled from her saddle and landed squarely on the kender.

Mashed flat on his back, with only his head showing

under the prostrate warrior maiden, Rufus groaned loudly. "Ow! Feels like a bear fell on me!"

There was no response from his captain. Finally he managed to haul himself out from under her and rolled her over. Verhanna still breathing, but her face was deathly pale and her skin blazed hotter than the calm, radiant air.

\* \* \* \* \*

Rufus set to work. He hadn't lived so long by his own wits without learning a thing or two about sickness. His captain had been poisoned by the filthy goblin's fangs, and unless he could cool her off, the raging fever would be the death of her.

Among their camp gear was a short-handled spade. The kender used it to rake away the layers of leaves that covered the forest floor. Within seconds, he was down to black soil. Below the dry top layer, he knew the earth would be moist and cool. Disregarding his parched throat and sweat-stung eyes, Rufus dug a shallow hole six feet long, two feet wide, and eight inches deep. It was hard going. The forest soil was a tangle of roots, rocks, and chunks of decayed wood. The captain was his friend though, and Rufus intended to do everything he could to save her. An hour after she'd fallen from her horse, the hole was ready for her.

Dropping his shovel, the kender dragged the much larger half-elf woman to the shallow pit and rolled her in so she lay on her back. Collapsing over her unmoving form, he panted and puffed with the exertion. This was hard work, especially since it was like toiling in a blast furnace. Not, of course, that Rufus had ever toiled in a blast furnace. . . .

After a bit, he set about heaping damp dirt around her and scattering leaves on top of her. Her face he left uncovered. Steam rose from the ground, drawn out either by the hot, dry air or Verhanna's fever. Finished at last,

Rufus sat down near his captain's head and waited.

He prayed to the Blue Lady to heal Verhanna; to be fair, he also addressed the goddess of healing by her Qualinesti name, Quen. Perhaps if he prayed to both her incarnations, she would be more likely to heal his captain.

Verhanna shifted restlessly under her covering of leaves and moist soil. The kender patted her forehead distractedly and pondered his situation. If Verhanna died, should he return to Qualinost with the news, or go on with the hunt for the Kagonesti slavers? And if she lived, how could they go on? How could anyone find his way cross-country without the sun or moons or stars to guide him?

The kender chewed his lip while his mind raced. Briefly he wished that he was back in the Magnet Mountains. At least there he knew his way around. Of course, life there hadn't been nearly so exciting. Since meeting his captain, he had fought slave-traders and goblins, met the Speaker of the Sun, and had a chance to investigate the city of Qualinost. Unbidden, his hands explored the multitudinous pockets of his tunic and vest for all the trinkets he'd collected. Instead of rings or beads or writing styluses, Rufus's nimble fingers brought out a walnut-sized piece of lodestone. Surprise lifted his eyebrows. He'd forgotten he had that.

Something about lodestones made his nose itch. Rufus scratched. No, that wasn't it. Something about lodestones made his brain itch. Yes, there was something important about the little rock. Lodestones, mountains, and mines. What about mines? He'd once sold some stones to a band of dwarf miners. In Thorbardin, the dwarves had mines that ran for miles under the ground, where the tunnels and shafts and galleries were quite confusing. How did they navigate? They never saw the sun or stars down there.

Now the kender's ear itched. He swiped at it with one hand; then both ears started itching. It grew unbearable.

Grabbing the wide brim of his blue hat, Rufus yanked it from his head. Two ravelings from the sewn headband were hanging down and tickling his ears. He started to break off the annoying threads.

Threads!

In an instant, he remembered what he'd been trying to remember about lodestones. A dwarf had told him once, "To find your direction underground, hang a sliver of lodestone from a thread. It will always point north and south." Rufus had scoffed at the dwarf's tale. After all, how could a dumb piece of rock know directions?

Verhanna moaned loudly, interrupting the kender's darting thoughts. Recalling again what he had finally remembered before about the lodestone, Rufus brought out his knife and whittled the small stone, trying to get it long and narrow, like a pointer should be. His blade grew dull and several fresh nicks appeared, but before long, he had the stone roughly spindle-shaped.

Carefully he pulled a long raveling from his hatband. The woolen strand was about six inches long. He tied it around the center of the stone and let the black rock dangle from his fingers. The whittled stone turned round and round, then gradually slowed and stopped.

The kender realized he didn't know which way was north and which was south. And he wasn't entirely certain he could trust such a silly trick.

"What choice have you got?" Rufus asked himself aloud. None, he answered himself silently.

He tied Verhanna's horse's reins to his saddle. Then he set about uncovering his captain. She was noticeably cooler, thanks to his treatment, but still gravely ill. He had a dragon's own time getting the unconscious woman out of the hole. Grunting with effort, he braced her up in a sitting position on the ground.

Verhanna's fever-fogged eyes opened. "Wart," she muttered. "I thought I fired you."

"You haven't paid me yet, my captain. I can't leave till I get my gold!"

With much wobbling, Verhanna rose to her feet. Rufus boosted her into her saddle, his head and both hands pushing on her backside. In another time and place, it might have been a comical scene, but now Verhanna's life was literally hanging by a thread—a woolen thread from a kender's hat.

The warrior maid drooped over her horse's neck. Leaving her mount tied to his saddle, Rufus took his horse's reins in hand and began to lead them out. The track they'd been on with the carts lay to the north, so he chose a direction and hoped it was right. His eyes were glued to the sliver of lodestone he held in his other hand. He walked and walked and walked. So intent was he on keeping to his course that it was some time before he noticed it was getting harder and harder to see.

"Just my luck!" the kender exclaimed. "I'm going blind!"

But Rufus was not going blind. The sun, so long fixed overhead, was finally moving. Already it was low in the sky off to his left, sinking through the trees and confirming his route as northerly. Never unhappy for very long, the kender found himself feeling rather satisfied. He had chosen the right path. His lodestone pointer worked.

A few minutes later, he came to the track through the forest they'd left earlier. Rufus danced with joy. He was the best scout in the whole world! He climbed onto his mount and thumped his heels cheerily against its sides, turning its face toward the setting sun. There was no sign of the two carts or the former slaves, but Rufus was immensely relieved to be on the path again.

Crickets and birds, silent during the three days of noon, sang again as shadows lengthened on the trail. Rufus stopped now and then to see how his captain was doing. Her breathing was shallow and quick, and her face was too warm again. That was bad. How he wished he was in Balifor, where he knew several healing shamans! There was one on Peacock Street who had—

Water. The kender's button nose twitched. He smelled

water. In a few seconds, the horses detected it, too. The tired, parched animals shambled faster, eager for a refreshing drink. Agreeing with them completely, Rufus let them have their heads.

The trees thinned and finally disappeared. In the last of the daylight, the kender saw that a wide bed of mud lay before him. The horses walked laboriously across the mud, pulling their hooves free with loud sucking noises. Evidently the river had shrunk during the long heat wave. Rufus wondered if there was any water left. If so, he couldn't see it. A thick scroll of fog shrouded the center of the river.

As they entered the fog, Rufus heard a splashing sound. He looked down. The horses had found the water. They waded in up to their bellies. Rufus leaned over and drank some of the sweet liquid from his cupped hand. Then he stood in his saddle and clambered over to Verhanna's mount.

Her hands and feet trailed in the cool stream. Standing with one foot in her stirrup, the kender scooped up a hatful of water and held it to her lips. Only partly conscious, she drank.

Sounds from the opposite shore caught Rufus's attention: voices, axles creaking, horses whinnying. Incapable of ignoring something that sounded so interesting, Rufus slipped into the water and swam quietly toward the noises.

As the kender rose out of the river, his soaked topknot fell across his face. He pushed it aside. Only his head showed above water, and the fog hung close around him. When he felt the oozy bottom under his toes, he walked slowly to shore.

The figures in the fog resolved themselves into tall people, elves or humans, who were trying to push a heavily loaded wagon out of the mud. They had foolishly steered the conveyance too close to the water's edge, and now it was held fast by the thick muck. As far as Rufus could see by the light of their torches, they were unarmed. Mostly they were muddy, and from the sounds they were making, disgusted with their plight. He decided they must be immigrants bound for Qualinesti. Perhaps there would be a healer among them. He'd have to go back and get his captain.

When he returned to his horses, he remounted and started for the far shore, toward the immigrants. The very center of the stream was too deep for the animals to walk, but the Thoradin-bred chargers swam the short distance easily. Kender, horses, and the unconscious warrior maiden splashed ashore.

"Hullo there! Rufus! Rufus Wrinklecap!" called a high voice. The startled kender saw a small fellow break away from the others.

"Kivinellis? Is that you?" The elf boy yelped with delight and waved Verhanna's dagger over his head. The other elves froze in their tracks.

Rufus clapped the boy on the back, saying, "Good to see you! My captain's wounded. We had a fight with some goblins, then got lost in the woods."

He peered over the boy's head at the people beside the wagon. None of them looked familiar.

"Where're Diviros and the women?" he asked quickly. "Who are these folk?" The Kagonesti at the wagon broke ranks and came toward him.

"Oh, these are my friends," said Kivinellis. "When you and the warrior lady rode off, Diviros got his legs untied and jumped down from the cart. I chased him, but he ran into the woods and I was afraid to follow. Me and the womenfolk came to the river 'cause you didn't come back."

The Kagonesti settlers were close now, so Rufus hailed them. "Hello! My captain is sick with a goblin's bite. Is there a healer among you?"

One Kagonesti male, his face painted with a host of black and white dots, turned away from the kender and called over his shoulder, "They have come, just as you said!"

Puzzled, Rufus said to Kivinellis, "Who's he talking to?" The fair-haired elf boy merely shrugged.

A soft yet penetrating voice pierced the night. "Bring the woman to me."

A male voice, Rufus decided. A little farther up the riverbank.

Two sinewy Kagonesti lifted Verhanna from her horse and carried her ashore. Rufus and Kivinellis followed, and the boy explained that his female companions had gone on to Qualinost with another group of wagons. He had decided to wait at the river ford for a while to see if Verhanna and the kender turned up.

"Where are they taking my captain?" asked Rufus, loud enough for the elves to hear.

His answer came striding out of the dark. A head taller than the Kagonesti, the newcomer was also an elf, though fairer in complexion. His face wasn't painted. Yellow hair hung loose around his wide shoulders. A rough horsehair blanket, with a hole cut in the center for his head, covered his chest and arms. His legs were sheathed in leather trews.

He stopped where the grassy shore met the mud flats. "I can help you," said the stranger. His words were softly spoken, yet carried easily to Rufus.

"Are you a healer?" asked Rufus.

"I can help you," he repeated.

The tall, yellow-haired elf went to the Kagonesti and took Verhanna from their arms. He carried the strapping warrior woman effortlessly, but with great gentleness. He turned and started away from the river.

"Where are you going?" called the kender. He pushed between the Kagonesti and splashed through the mud till he was dogging the tall elf's heels. Kivinellis remained with the Kagonesti, conversing with the wild elves. Where a line of locust trees bordered the grassy bank, the stranger lowered Verhanna to the ground.

"A goblin bit her," Rufus said, panting. "The wound's poisoned."

The stranger's long fingers probed Verhanna's shoulder. She gasped when he touched the wound itself. Sitting back on his haunches, the tall elf regarded her with rapt attention.

"What're you waiting for? Make a poultice. Work a spell!" The kender wondered if this fellow was really a healer.

The stranger held up a hand to quell the impatient Rufus. By the light of Krynn's stars and two bright moons, the kender could see that his fingers were dark, as if stained with dye. Rufus's penetrating vision could just make out that the stain was green.

Green. Green fingers. In a flash, Rufus remembered Diviros's queer tale of the lightning splitting the oak and a fully grown elf falling from the broken tree—a fully grown elf whose hands were green.

"It's you!" the kender exclaimed. "The one from the shattered tree! Greenhands!"

"I have been waiting for you," said Greenhands. "Through days of red rain and endless sun."

He bent down and slipped his arms around Verhanna. Taking her limp form into his embrace, Greenhands closed his right hand over the ugly, swollen wound on her shoulder. Rufus could see the muscles in the tall elf's neck tighten as he drew Verhanna closer to him, as if he were embracing a lover.

"What're you—?"

She groaned once, then cried out in torment as the stranger dug his odd, grass-colored fingers into her wound. Verhanna's eyes flew wide. She stared over the strange elf's shoulder at Rufus. What was in her eyes? Terror? Wonder? The kender couldn't tell. She uttered a long, tearing wail, and Greenhands suddenly joined his voice with hers. The combined scream hammered painfully at the listeners, wrenching their hearts as it agonized their ears.

Kith-Kanan's daughter closed her eyes with a slow flutter. Greenhands lowered her carefully to the ground, straightened up, and walked away. Rufus went to his captain.

Her breast rose and fell evenly. She was asleep. Beneath the filthy shreds of her linen shirt, Verhanna's right shoulder was as smooth and unscarred as a baby's cheek.

The kender yelped in astonishment. He jumped up and stared after Greenhands, who was still walking away. "Wait, you!" he yelled. Not ten paces from where Verhanna lay, Greenhands sank to the ground. The kender and elves ran to him.

"Are you all right?" Rufus asked as he reached the elf. Kivinellis already knelt by the stranger. It was he who noticed the change.

"Look at his hand!" the boy gasped.

The tall elf's right hand, the one he'd healed Verhanna's wound with, was split open. A long, deep gash, from which blood oozed, ran across his palm. Black blood caked his green fingers, and the smell of the suppurating goblin bite rose up like foul smoke.

"He is *thalmaat*," said one of the Kagonesti in deeply reverent tones.

"What's that?" asked Kivinellis, unfamiliar with the old dialect.

Rufus glanced from the bloody green hand of the tall stranger to his captain, now peacefully resting. "It means 'godsent,' " the kender said slowly. "One who is actually sent by the gods."

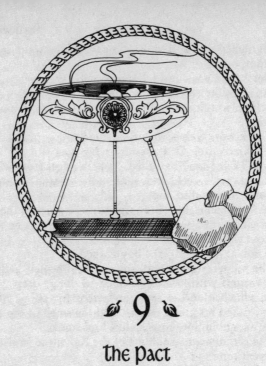

# 𝕖 9 𝕖

## the pact

Rain pattered on the dry streets of Qualinost. After three days of continuous sunshine, the rain was a blessing. The city dwellers, who had so fastidiously avoided the crimson downpour, stayed outside, luxuriating in the refreshing, clean liquid. The wide, curving streets were full of people.

Once the rain had abated to a soft shower and cool breezes flowed across his capital, Kith-Kanan rode with Senator Irthenie and Kemian Ambrodel through the busy streets. The Speaker of the Sun was surveying the city to see how much it had suffered in the three days of heat. Qualinost, he was relieved to see, didn't seem to have been much damaged by the burning sun.

His subjects noticed the Speaker riding among them. They tipped their hats or bowed as he passed. Here and there, Kith-Kanan came upon a gang of gardeners removing some tree or bush that had succumbed to the relentless heat. At the right hand of each of these groups waited a priest of Astra, ready to plant a new tree in place of the old. No, Qualinost had not suffered very much.

The market square was less cheerful. Kith-Kanan rode ahead of his two companions across the almost deserted plaza and saw all the empty stalls and ruined produce lying trodden on the cobblestones. One merchant, a burly human with a leather apron, was sweeping up some spoiled potatoes when Kith-Kanan reined in to speak with him.

"Hello there, my good fellow," called the Speaker. "How goes it with you?"

The man didn't look up from his work. "Rotten! All of it rotten! What's a man supposed to do with five bushels of dried-out, split-open, rotten vegetables?"

Irthenie and Kemian drew alongside Kith-Kanan. "So the sun ruined your crop?" asked the Speaker sympathetically.

"Aye, the sun or the darkness or the lightnin' or the flood of bloody rain. Makes no never-mind to me which it was. It happened." The man spat on the damp stones.

An elf woman with a basket of withered flowers under one arm heard their conversation. With a quick curtsy to her sovereign, she asked, "Why do the gods punish us so? What sin have we committed?"

"How do you know the gods are punishing anyone? These strange things might all be signs of some great wonder to come," Kith-Kanan suggested.

The human, squatting on the ground to gather his ruined potatoes into baskets, grumbled, "They say it's because Kith-Kanan has put his own son in chains to help build the fortress at Pax Tharkas." He still didn't realize to whom he was conversing. At his harsh words, the elf woman blushed, and Kemian Ambrodel cleared his throat loudly. The human lifted his head.

Even though the Speaker didn't wear the glitter and gold of state robes, the man recognized him. "Mercy," the man gasped. "Y-Your Worship, I'm sorry. I didn't know it was you!"

Grimly Kith-Kanan replied, "Have no fear. I would hear everything my people think of me."

"Is it true, Majesty?" asked the elf woman meekly. "Did you sell your own son into slavery just to finish that big castle?"

Kemian and Irthenie started to remonstrate with the woman for her blunt query. The Speaker held up his hands to silence them. Patiently he explained what Ulvian had done, and why he had sent him to Pax Tharkas. His earlier wish to keep Ulvian's crime from public gossip seemed hopeless. Now he felt it was more important for his people to know the truth and not entertain wild imaginings.

While he spoke, more people gathered—peddlers, tinkers, farmers, potters. All came to hear Kith-Kanan's story of the trouble he was having with his son. To his amazement, they all believed that Ulvian's exile and the twelve days of marvels were related.

"Where did you get these ideas?" Irthenie asked sharply.

The potato man shrugged. "Talk. Just talk . . . you know."

"Shadow talk," said Kith-Kanan, too faintly for most to hear. Kemian heard, and he glanced at the Speaker.

"Is Lord Kemian Ambrodel to be your son now?" shouted a voice from the crowd. The three mounted elves turned their heads to and fro, trying to spot the one who'd spoken.

"Will Lord Ambrodel be the next Speaker of the Sun?" the same voice demanded.

"Who said that?" muttered Irthenie. No one answered, but others in the crowd took up the cry. Keeping a steady hand on his fractious mount's reins, Kith-Kanan let the shouting grow a while. He wanted to measure the sentiment of his people.

Kemian, however, could not remain calm. "Silence!" the general roared. "Show respect for the Speaker!"

"Silvanesti!" someone shouted back at him, and it was like a curse. The young warrior, in an agony of embarrassment and anger, looked to his sovereign. Kith-Kanan seemed thoughtful.

"Sire," said Kemian desperately, "I think you'd best assure them I am not to be your successor." His voice was tight but earnest.

"Say something," Irthenie urged from the side of her mouth.

At last the Speaker held up a hand. "Good people," he said. The crowd instantly fell silent, awaiting his response. "I understand your concern for the throne. Lord Ambrodel is a faithful and valiant servant. He would make an excellent Speaker—"

"No! No!" the crowd erupted. "No Silvanesti! No Silvanesti!" they chanted. In his own shock at the Speaker's words, Kemian barely heard their insults.

"Have you forgotten that I am of the royal house of Silvanos?" Kith-Kanan said icily. "No one is more Silvanesti than I!"

"You are the Speaker of the Sun! The father of our country!" a male voice answered. "We don't want some Silvanesti courtier's boy to rule us. We want a ruler of your blood or none!"

"Your blood or none!" echoed a large segment of the crowd.

Kemian snatched at his reins, ready to charge into the mass of unarmed Qualinesti and put an end to these insults. Kith-Kanan leaned over and laid a hand on the warrior's arm. Eyes blazing, Kemian stared angrily at the Speaker, but he didn't try to evade his grasp. Reluctantly he relaxed, and Kith-Kanan let go of his mailed arm.

"Go back to the Speaker's house, General," Kith-Kanan said coolly. "I shall return shortly."

"Sire!" Kemian saluted and wheeled his prancing horse in a tight half-circle. The traders and farmers scattered from his path. The general let out a yell and spurred his mount. With a loud clatter of hooves, horse and rider tore across the market square and vanished down a curving street.

The people cheered his abrupt departure. Disgusted with them, Kith-Kanan was about to follow Kemian's exit when Irthenie abruptly got down off her horse.

"I'm too old to stay up that high for so long," she proclaimed loudly, rubbing her backside with exaggerated care. "For seven hundred and ninety-four years, I walked everywhere I needed to go. Now that I'm a senator, I'm not supposed to walk anywhere." Those nearest the Kagonesti woman chuckled. "One pays a price to sit in the Thalas-Enthia," she said gruffly. More people laughed.

Kith-Kanan slackened his reins and sat still, waiting to see what the foxy senator was up to. "You people," she said loud enough to carry to the fringes of the mob, "you stand here and say you don't want Kemian Ambrodel as the next Speaker of the Sun. I say, who told you he would be? It's the first I've heard of it." She stepped away from her dapple-gray horse, deeper into the crowd.

"He's a fine general, that elf, but you're right about one thing: We don't want a bunch of Silvanesti nobles ruling us, telling us we're not as good as they are. That's one reason we left the old country, to get away from so many lords and masters."

Irthenie's Kagonesti garb blended in well with the crowd, her leather and raw linen against their homespun wool and drab cotton. She literally rubbed shoulders with the people in the square. Irthenie was one of them.

"When I was younger and better-looking"—laughter rippled across the plaza—"I was taken from the forest by warriors. They were looking for wives, and their idea of catching one was to drag a net through the bushes and see what they flushed out." The senator stopped walking when she reached the center of the crowd. Every eye was on her. Kith-Kanan experienced a moment of nervousness at the sight of her small figure hemmed in on all sides by the mob. "I didn't much want to be a warrior's woman, so I ran away the first chance I got. They caught me, and this time, they broke my leg so I couldn't run again. Vernax Kollontine was hardly a loving husband. After he beat me for not washing his clothes often enough and not cooking his supper fast enough, I killed him with a bread knife."

There was a concerted gasp at this revelation. The Speaker of the Sun seemed just as surprised as his subjects, and he listened to the senator's tale just as intently. Irthenie held up a hand to calm the crowd, insisting, "No, no, it was a fair fight." Kith-Kanan smiled.

"The point of this long and boring story is that the Speaker of the Stars at that time, Sithel, ordered me sold into slavery as punishment for my crime. I lived as a slave for thirty-eight years. The great war freed me, and I was in the first band of settlers who came with Kith-Kanan to found Qualinost. This city, this country, is like no other in the world. Here every race can live and work, can worship, and can prosper or not as they please. That's freedom. That you and I enjoy it is mostly due to that fellow on horseback you see over there. It was his wisdom and judgment that got us here. If you're pleased with that, then you ought not doubt his wisdom regarding either his son or his successor."

The square remained quiet after she finished speaking. Only the soft patter of rain accompanied Irthenie's final words.

"Slavery is an evil, ugly thing," she concluded. "It degrades not only the slave, but the master as well. Like any good father, the Speaker is trying to save his son from a terrible mistake. You should pray for him as I often do."

Irthenie walked back through the calmed crowd to her horse. Kith-Kanan handed her the reins, and she climbed into the saddle with a grunt. "Damn leg," she muttered. "It always gets stiff when it rains."

The Speaker and the senator rode on across the square. The people parted, making way for them. Hats were doffed. Wool tams and felt hoods were removed in respect.

Kith-Kanan kept his gaze serenely ahead. What had been a potentially dangerous situation had been reversed by the words of his old friend.

The cool rain felt good on his face. The air smelled sweet. Though nothing had been decided or changed, Kith-Kanan felt a sudden rush of confidence. Whatever forces were at work, he felt sure they were in his favor. Hiddukel's dire prophecies in the Tower of the Sun seemed like remote threats now.

"A question," he said as they rode on. "Was that story you told the crowd true?"

Irthenie kicked her heels against her horse's sides. The gelding broke into a trot.

"Some of it was," she replied.

\* \* \* \* \*

Steam hung in the air where the cold rain hit the baked stones of Pax Tharkas. All outside work had ceased, as it was too dangerous to cut stone or move blocks when the ground was wet. The grunt gang was not allowed to lie idle, though. Feldrin Feldspar was anxious about his rate of progress, so he put the convicts to work enlarging the tunnels being sunk into the mountainside beneath the towering citadel.

Ulvian hobbled about on a makeshift crutch. His right leg, the one that had been caught by the runaway granite block, had stiffened to the point where he needed a crutch to get around. He wasn't excused from work, however, so he limped through the dim, limestone tunnels, carrying waterskins to the other grunt gang members.

Near the end of one long gallery, barely wider than his shoulders, he came upon Dru. Ulvian paused a few feet away from the laboring elf. A small lamp burned on the tunnel floor. In its brassy light, Dru's chalk-covered body appeared ghostly.

"Here, friend," said the prince. "Drink while the water's still cool."

Dru set aside his pick and took the skin. He pointed the spout at his lips and let a stream of cold water flow into his mouth.

"Don't take it all. There are others who will want a drink."

Dru let the prince take the nearly drained skin. "You puzzle me," the Silvanesti said, leaning against the wall. The lamp threw weird highlights from below, making the elf's lean, angular face look like a mask. "You are a prince, the son of a monarch, and yet you fetch and carry water like any base-born serf."

"Hold your tongue! You may have saved my life, but I don't have to endure a lecture from you!" snapped Ulvian, more like his arrogant, proud former self.

Dru smiled thinly. "That's better. That's what I want to hear." Clasping his pick, the sorcerer stepped over the lamp and stood nose to nose with the son of Kith-Kanan. "If you can behave like a prince and not a serf, we can be gone from this miserable prison. Are you with me?"

"In what?" was Ulvian's derisive reply. "Shall we run away to the mountains, just so Feldrin's watchdogs can hunt us down? I'm on my good behavior here. If I sacrifice that, I have no hope of gaining my father's throne."

"We have only to cause a little excitement. That will distract the camp long enough for us to get inside Feldrin's tent and get my amulet."

So they were back to that. Ulvian folded his arms, disgust evident on his face. "I won't murder Feldrin. He's a thickheaded old bore, but he's honest."

Dru's smile was nasty. He turned and went to the low niche he'd already hollowed out in the soft rock. He tossed his pick aside. It rang dully on the dusty floor. Slumping against the wall, Dru said, "When are you going to wake up, Highness?" His tone dripped irony. "I have waited a long time for someone with whom I could ally myself. No one else in the grunt gang has any wit or breeding. But you and I, my friend, can go far together. You spoke of enemies. I can help you defeat them. The throne of your father can be yours, not in ten years or a hundred, but in *two months.* Perhaps sooner. With your leadership and my magic, we can make Qualinesti the most powerful empire in the world!"

His words held the prince's attention. Without realizing it, Ulvian let the waterskin drop from his fingers. It sloshed to the ground.

"I've dreamed of the day I would see Verhanna and the Ambrodels groveling at my feet," Ulvian whispered. "And the Crown of the Sun on my head. . . ." The prince's eyes were distant, beholding future glory. Visions of the empire he would rule, of the grand and opulent palace he would build, filled Ulvian's mind. Power and glory, comfort and ease, riches beyond dreaming. His word would be law. The people would worship him as they now worshiped his father.

Cutting through Ulvian's golden dreams, a rough voice from farther back in the tunnel called faintly, "Waterboy! Where's that waterboy?"

Abruptly Ulvian focused once more on Dru. "If we can accomplish this without bloodshed, count me in," he said grimly.

Dru bowed his head. "As Your Highness wishes. I shall be very careful." Then he quickly gave Ulvian a precise list of the things he'd need. It was a short list, but a puzzling one.

"What on Krynn can you do with a pound of white clay, some chips of coal, a span of leather thong, and a copper brazier?" the prince asked, confused. "None of them is rare or guarded. Why don't you collect them yourself?"

The sorcerer's gray eyes glittered like diamonds in the half-light. "You may not realize it, my prince, but I am closely watched. No one dares kill me, but I dare not do anything to cause suspicion, or my limbs would be fettered and I would be consigned to a deep, dark hole." He gestured at the rough limestone walls. "Like this."

Ulvian left him there. As he wended his way to the main tunnel under the central citadel, he mulled over the possibilities. Dru was dangerous, but a potentially powerful ally. Ulvian smiled in the dark tunnel as he limped along. Let Dru believe he was a vainglorious fool. That was a useful illusion. The time might come when Ulvian would no longer require Dru's services. . . .

Rough hands seized his shirt front. "Here!" bellowed a harsh voice. "Here he is, lads!"

Ulvian was dragged into a side tunnel and flung to the floor. His bruised leg knifed with pain. Through the gloom, he saw three grunt gangers standing over him. Two he knew well—the Kagonesti Splint, and a human called Brunnar. The third was another Kagonesti he knew only as Thrit.

"We been waiting an awful long time for our water," snarled Splint. "The damn dust down here is thicker than soup." He planted a foot on Ulvian's back. "So where's the water?"

Painfully the prince dragged the waterskin from beneath him. It was snatched from his grasp by Thrit, who reported that it was empty.

"I think our little waterboy needs a lesson," Splint growled and kicked the prince in the ribs. The three tall figures closed in.

\* \* \* \* \*

Dru swung his pick energetically at the limestone around him. He had no interest in working hard for his captors; the physical activity was simply a reflection of the state of fevered excitement in his mind. His time in this unnatural prison could be measured in days, perhaps only hours! Soon he would be free! Surely his patron god had sent that fool of a prince to be the instrument of his deliverance.

A sound in the passage behind him made him pause. Pick in hand, Dru whirled. The feeble glow of the fat-burning lamp didn't penetrate beyond the bend in the tunnel some six feet away. He waited. The noise came again, a scraping, dragging sound. Carefully the sorcerer bent down to take up the lamp, his eyes never leaving the black passage.

A hand, pale and slim, came into view on the dusty floor. Dru crept forward until the lamplight fell across the form of Prince Ulvian, sprawled on the ground. Blood matted his unkempt beard, and one eye was swollen shut.

Dru knelt. "Your Highness! What happened?"

"Splint . . . Brunnar . . . Thrit . . . beat me. . . ." Ulvian's lips were swelling, making speech difficult.

Dru dragged the prince to the far end of the tunnel and propped him against the wall. After making certain no one was around, the sorcerer reached under the waist of his baggy trousers and brought out a small hide drawstring bag. He poured a little of its contents into his hand. A pungent, sweet smell filled the air.

"Take this," murmured Dru, putting his hand to Ulvian's purple lips. "It's an herbal mixture of my own. It will restore you."

The prince managed to swallow some of the ground herbs. In a few minutes, the swelling in his eye and lips began to subside. A modicum of strength flowed into his body. Though the pain of his injured leg eased, his ribs still ached from his beating.

Ulvian lifted clouded eyes to the sorcerer's face and struggled to his feet.

"Rest a bit longer, Highness."

"No." Ulvian struggled to his feet. The magic herbs hadn't healed all his pains, but he felt considerably better. "I want to proceed with our plans as quickly as possible," he informed Dru. "And I've added a condition of my own."

Dru tucked his herb bag away. "What's that?"

"Twice Splint has laid hands on me. I want revenge!"

"Easily done, Highness. Just get the items I need."

Ulvian pushed Dru aside and hobbled off down the tunnel. His voice echoed back to the pleased sorcerer. "I'll have it all for you tonight!" he declared grimly.

## ◈ 10 ◈

### the knowing child

Verhanna slept deeply for the rest of the night and
well into the next day. When at last she stirred and sat
up, she saw Rufus sitting on the ground beside her. A
cool compress of damp moss fell away from her forehead when she moved. "What—what is this? Where are
we?"

"The west bank of the Astradine River," said the kender.

Rufus gave her a strand of venison jerky he'd bought
from the Kagonesti settlers. Verhanna gnawed on the
tough meat in silence for a while, then finally said, "Now
I remember. The goblins! That rotten scab of a creature
bit me. The wound festered." Suddenly she twisted

around and lifted the horsehair poncho draped over her. "It's gone!" she shouted. Verhanna lowered the piece of blanket. "Who healed me? My muscles aren't even sore!"

The kender pointed away from their campsite. "Him," Rufus said simply.

Seated on a fallen log a dozen paces distant was Greenhands, bare-chested now since Verhanna was using his poncho. His hair, which had appeared yellow by torchlight, was revealed by the light of day to be of purest white. Kith-Kanan's daughter picked her way down the mossy riverbank toward him. The strange elf was gazing placidly across the sluggish stream, which was still depleted by the three-day onslaught of the sun.

Verhanna opened her mouth—to demand, question, challenge—but she closed it again without speaking. There was something unsettling about this elf, something compelling. He was not handsome by elven standards. His cheeks were broad, but not high; his chin and nose were not fashionably narrow; his lips were full, not thin; and his forehead was massive, almost human in proportion. However, he was unmistakably elven, with almond-shaped eyes, elegantly pointed ears, and exquisitely long, tapering fingers. The expression on his face was serene.

"Hello," the Qualinesti princess finally said. His green eyes left off their study of the river and found her. A chill passed through Verhanna. She'd never seen any elf with eyes that color, and his gaze was direct, unwavering and unnerving. "Can you speak?"

"I speak."

"Thank Astra." She paused, embarrassed at the debt she owed him and unsure what to say. After a long moment, during which the elf's eyes never left her, she added rather hastily, "Rufus tells me you healed me. I—I wanted to thank you."

"It needed to be done," replied Greenhands. The wild elves whose wagon had been stuck in the mud hailed them, and the elder Kagonesti male called for

Greenhands to join them.

"Come along," the Kagonesti said. "We're bound for Qualinost!"

The strange elf replied, "I cannot go." Still his eyes remained on Verhanna.

The Kagonesti father tied off his reins and jumped down from the wagon. "What's that? Is this warrior holding you back?" he asked, glaring at the warrior maiden.

"I am not," she replied tartly.

"I must go to the west," Greenhands said. He rose and faced in that direction. "To the High Place. They must come with me." He indicated Verhanna and Rufus, who had managed to join them quietly for a change. Kivinellis, riding in the wagon with the Kagonesti's family, jumped off and ran to Verhanna.

"I want to go, too!" he declared. The father protested strongly. A young boy couldn't wander around with a kender, a warrior, and a simpleminded elf.

Verhanna ignored the Kagonesti and turned to Greenhands. "Why do you have to go west with us?" she wanted to know.

His brow furrowed in thought. "I have to find my father," he said.

"Who is your father?"

"I do not know. I have never seen him."

In spite of these vague replies, Greenhands was obstinate. He must go west, and Verhanna and Rufus must go with him. Defeated, the Kagonesti returned to his wagon, propelling Kivinellis ahead of him. The elf boy complained all the way.

"Poor little fellow," said Rufus. "Couldn't we keep him, my captain?"

Verhanna's attention was all on Greenhands. "No, he's better off with a family," she said distantly. "Astra only knows where we're headed—" The creak of wheels interrupted her. The loaded wagon lurched onto level ground and pulled away. Kivinellis, his blond head shining among the dark elves, waved forlornly from the back of the wagon. He was securely held by the Kagonesti's wife. Verhanna returned the wave, then turned back to Greenhands.

"I need some answers," Verhanna declared. "Who are you?"

"I have no name" was the mild answer.

"Greenhands, that's your name," said the kender. He clasped the elf's grass-hued hand in both of his small ones. "Pleased to meetcha. I'm Rufus Wrinklecap, forester and scout. And that's my captain, Verhanna. Her father is Kith-Kanan, the Speaker of the Sun."

Greenhands seemed startled, even bewildered, by this flood of information.

"Never mind," said Verhanna, shaking her head. Awkwardly she put a hand on the elf's bare shoulder. His skin was warm and smooth. When she touched him, Verhanna felt a tingle shoot up her arm. She didn't know if it was due to some force passing between them or if it was simply her own nervousness. Greenhands didn't seem to notice anything odd.

Looking him directly in the eyes, Verhanna asked firmly, "Who are you? Really?"

He shrugged. "Greenhands."

A flush of irritation washed over the warrior maiden. She was intrigued by this odd fellow and deeply grateful that he'd saved her life, but his naive and evasive replies were getting under her skin.

"I guess you'd better come with us," she stated. "My father would want me to bring you to Qualinost."

"What about the slavers?" asked Rufus.

"This is more important."

Greenhands shook his head. "I cannot go with you. I must go to the High Place." He pointed west, toward the Kharolis Mountains. "There. To find my father."

Verhanna's eyes narrowed, and her jaw clenched. Rufus intervened quickly. "It's not so far off the track to Qualinost, my captain. We could swing by the mountains first. You know," he said, changing the subject completely, "my father was a famous pot thrower."

Suitably distracted, Verhanna hitched the horse blanket up on her shoulders and looked at her scout. "You mean he made pots—threw them—on a wheel?" she asked.

"No, he threw them at my Uncle Four-Thumbs. In the carnival."

Suddenly Verhanna realized Greenhands was no longer with them. He was twenty paces away, loping along with the morning sun at his back. She called out for him to stop.

"You must stay with us!" she shouted.

Wind stirred his long, loose hair. He stopped, eyes fixed on the western horizon, while Verhanna retired to a stand of trees to dress. Now that the perishing heat was over, she donned her breastplate, childrons, and greaves over a fresh haqueton. Rufus did one of his usual vaults to reach the broad back of his red-coated Thoradin mount, and together they rode to where Greenhands waited.

"Do you ride?" Verhanna asked, returning the poncho to Greenhands. "There's room behind Wart if you do."

"There's room for most of Balifor up here," opined Rufus.

Greenhands pulled the poncho on over his head. "I'll walk," he said.

"It's a long way to the mountains," she warned, leaning on the pommel of her saddle. "You'll never be able to keep pace with the horses."

"I'll walk," he repeated, with exactly the same intonation.

She shook her head. "Suit yourself."

They topped a low rise and were out of the shallow valley cut by the river and back on the grass-covered plain. To the south, the blue humps of the Kharolis foothills were plainly visible in the clear morning sky, but Greenhands went resolutely west.

So intent were Verhanna and Rufus on keeping their eyes on Greenhands that neither bothered to look back at the riverbank. What had been a mud flat the night before was now a blossoming meadow. Grass had sprung up knee high in a few short hours, and a thousand colors of wild flowers bloomed where once there had been nothing but mud and cattails. Moreover, this strange growth narrowed as it entered the upland. Eventually it thinned to a point—the exact trail where Greenhands trod.

\* \* \* \* \*

The day wore on, and Greenhands showed no signs of tiring.

Verhanna and Rufus ate in the saddle, passing a water bottle back and forth between them. Greenhands plucked a few stems of grass from the turf to nibble. He ate and drank nothing else.

By midafternoon the novelty of watching the strange elf had worn off. Rufus lay down on his horse's back, clasping his hands behind his head and shading his face with his travel-worn hat. He gave his reins to his captain, and soon high-pitched snores whistled from his lips. Verhanna nodded a bit, but she was too conscious of her duty to falter and fought the sleep that tried to claim her.

Fatigue and the lingering shock of her healed goblin bite proved too strong, though, and she, too, eventually nodded off. When her charger stumbled slightly over a gopher mound, Verhanna jolted awake. Greenhands was no longer forging ahead on foot. The warrior maiden reined in and looked back. In the high grass fifteen yards behind them, the tall elf was kneeling.

"Wake up, Wart," she called to the kender. Yawning, Rufus sat up and caught his reins as she tossed them.

"Hey," the kender said sleepily, "where'd all the flowers come from?"

Verhanna looked past Greenhands and saw the vast trail of blooms that widened as it stretched out behind him. Not only flowers, but the dry prairie grass in the area had grown a foot taller.

"Look you," she said, leaning down from the saddle. "What sort of magic is this?"

"Quiet," he murmured. "The children call me."

She bristled at his abrupt command. "I'll speak when I like!"

The strange elf's tense, prayerful posture suddenly relaxed. He inhaled deeply and said, "They come."

Verhanna was about to make a rejoinder when a faint rumbling sound reached her ears. Heavy vibrations in the ground caused her mount to shift his feet and stamp nervously. Rufus sat up and called, "Captain, look!"

To the south, a dark brown line appeared on the horizon. It bulked larger and higher, and the rumbling grew louder. Swiftly the brown mass resolved into elk— thousands of them. A gigantic herd, stretching far to the left and right, was coming straight toward them.

"By Astra, it's a stampede!" Verhanna cried. She twisted her horse around to ride hard in the same direction the elk were moving. Their only chance was to go with the flow and not fall under those churning hooves.

"Give me your hand!" she shouted to Greenhands. "We must flee!"

The elk were only a couple hundred paces off and gathering speed. Rufus turned his mount and urged it next to his captain's. Bouncing to his feet in the saddle, he crowed with delight, "What a sight! Have you ever seen so many deer? If only I had a bow, we'd have venison for dinner forever!"

"You idiot, we're going to be trampled!"

Then the elk herd was upon them like a living wall of hide, antlers, and sharp hooves. The musky smell of the animals mingled with the dry odor of trampled grass. Thinking first of her decision to bring Greenhands to Qualinost, Verhanna threw herself on top of the elf to shield him from harm. Only after an eternal, terrifying second did the realization sink in that the herd had split and was flowing around them. The patch of ground with Verhanna, Greenhands, Rufus, and the two horses had been spared.

Thousands of elk, with liquid brown eyes and gaping mouths, rushed past them, nose to flank, shoulder to hip. The noise of their passage was deafening. Verhanna raised her head just enough to see the kender, still standing on his quiescent horse, hands clamped over his ears. With great astonishment, the warrior maid discovered that the stupid fellow was *grinning*. His carroty topknot was whipped back by the wind of the herd's passage, and a huge smile lit his pale eyes.

It seemed hours before the herd thinned. Alone or in pairs, the last few animals bounded in wide zigzags. In minutes more, the receding herd was again a brown line on the horizon. Then there was nothing but flying dust and the fading rumble of ten thousand hooves.

"E'li be merciful!" Verhanna breathed. "We are truly blessed!"

"Move away," Greenhands grumbled from beneath her. "You smell terrible."

She rolled smartly aside, and he sat up. Verhanna slipped the mail mitten back from her hand and slapped the elf across the jaw. She was instantly sorry, because tears formed in his vivid green eyes and his lips quivered.

"It's the metal you wear," he sniffled. One tear traced a shining path down his cheek. "It smells—like death."

"Yippee!"

The two of them turned to look up at Rufus. The kender was capering atop his horse. "What a sight!" he caroled gleefully. "That must be the biggest herd of elk in the world! Did you feel the wind they kicked up? The ground shook like a jelly pudding! What do you suppose made them run like that?"

"Thirst," Greenhands said. He sniffed and touched a

hand to his wet cheek. The sight of his own tears seemed to confound him. "The heat of days past made them mad with thirst."

"How do you know?" Verhanna demanded.

"They called out to me. I told them how to get to the river."

"You *told* them? I suppose you told them not to trample us, too?"

"Yes. I told the horses to stand still, and the elk would go around us."

The tall elf rubbed his fingertips together till the tears were gone. Then he stood and walked slowly away, not west as they had been going, but veering south. Exasperated beyond words, Verhanna swung into her saddle and followed him. Rufus fell in beside her. He could hear her grumbling and grinding her teeth.

"Why so angry, my captain?" the kender asked, his eyes still bright at their encounter with the elk herd.

"We spend our time trailing after him like body servants!" She slapped her armored thigh. "And the lies he tells! He knows more than he's telling, mark my words!"

The kender turned down his hat brim to shade his eyes from the lowering sun. "I don't think he knows how to lie," he said quietly. "The elk herd might've split by coincidence, but my horse just stood like a statue. It wasn't even quivering. If you ask me my opinion, Greenhands did talk to the elk."

## 🌿 11 🌿

## Rising Son

*Kith-kanan watched the sun set from the hall of the* Sky. He'd been alone there for hours, thinking. Since the day Irthenie had calmed the crowd in the market square, there had been other demonstrations in the streets in favor of Ulvian. Kemian Ambrodel, who sought no higher office than the one he held, was berated everywhere he went. Once he was even pelted with overripe fruit. The Speaker had to order him to remain in the Speaker's house to protect the proud warrior from further humiliation or worse.

Clovanos and the Loyalists were discreet enough not to be seen leading the activities, but within the hall of the Thalas-Enthia, they trumpeted the popular sentiment and demanded the return of Prince Ulvian. Lengthy petitions, inscribed on parchment scrolls three feet long, arrived at the Speaker's house daily. The signatures on the petitions grew more numerous each time, with many of the New Landers joining the Loyalists in seeking Ulvian's confirmation as Kith-Kanan's heir. Disgusted with the senate's shortsightedness, Kith-Kanan repaired to the Hall of the Sky to ponder his choices. He half hoped that the gods would choose for him, that some meaningful sign would show him what to do. However, nothing so mystical happened. He remained in the great plaza, watching his city through the waving treetops, until at last Tamanier Ambrodel came from the Speaker's house.

The Speaker got up from his knees and crossed the vast mosaic map to greet his faithful castellan. In spite of the worries that clouded his mind, his step was springy; no one viewing the beauty of the sunset and the great elven city from this vantage point could fail to be moved, and some small measure of his strength had been renewed by his meditation.

"Good health to you, Majesty," Tamanier said, bowing and presenting Kith-Kanan with an embossed dispatch case.

By the seal pressed in the wax of the lid, Kith knew the dispatch case was from Feldrin Feldspar. He broke the seal with his knife tip, and while Tamanier held the box, the Speaker raised the lid and drew out the papers inside.

"Hmm . . . Master Feldrin's report on the progress at Pax Tharkas . . . the usual requests for food, clothing, and other supplies . . . and what's this?" From between the sheets of official correspondence, the Speaker pulled a small folded letter on fine vellum, sealed carefully with a ribbon and a drop of blue wax.

He returned the other documents to the box and opened the sealed letter. "It's from Merithynos," he said, surprised.

"Good news, sire?"

"I'm not sure." Frowning, Kith-Kanan read the brief

letter, then handed the vellum to his castellan. Tamanier read Merith's account of Ulvian's near death, his salvation at the hands of the sorcerer Drulethen, and the friendship that Merith had observed growing between the prince and Dru.

"Drulethen—isn't he the monster who ruled the high pass to Thorbardin during the Kinslayer War?" asked Tamanier.

"Your memory is still sharp. I'd forgotten the sorcerer was at Pax Tharkas. He shouldn't be allowed to cultivate my son's friendship; he's far too dangerous." The memory of another voice suddenly flashed into Kith-Kanan's mind. What was it the god Hiddukel had said when he'd manifested himself in the Tower of the Sun?

*You may call me Dru.* It couldn't be coincidence that the god had chosen the name of the evil sorcerer. Where the gods were concerned, little was left to chance.

Tamanier continued to stand holding the dispatch box. After a long moment of silence, Kith-Kanan's eyes focused once more on the old castellan. "Return to the house, Tam," he said briskly. "Prepare for a trip. Small entourage, with a light, mounted escort. I want to move quickly."

The castellan's brows lifted. "Where are you going, Great Speaker?"

"To Pax Tharkas, my friend. I'll leave as soon as Lord Anakardain can get back to Qualinost. I want him to keep order here while I'm gone."

Tamanier bowed and withdrew, head buzzing with the speed of events. Kith-Kanan remained in the Hall of the Sky awhile longer. Standing at the edge of the artificial plateau, he looked out over his city. One by one, lamps were being lit in towers and on street corners, until it seemed the star-salted sky was mirrored on the ground. As the Speaker watched, lights illuminated the sweeping arch of the northern bridge directly ahead of him, behind the Tower of the Sun. Kith-Kanan turned slowly to each point of the compass to see the other three bridges similarly lighted. They surrounded Qualinost in a sparkling embrace.

Despite this glorious vista, something gnawed at Kith-Kanan. The great forces he'd sensed behind the marvels of the past days now seemed overshadowed by evil. He'd believed the wonders to be portents of some great event; perhaps they were indeed portents, but of a darker nature.

\* \* \* \* \*

The bells clanged, signaling the end of another day of toil at Pax Tharkas. Ropes were tied off or dropped, tools piled on carts to be taken back to storage sheds, and cookfires blazed in the twilight. From the parapet of the west tower, Feldrin Feldspar surveyed the site as Merith stood close by.

"It will stand ten times a thousand years," declared the dwarf, clasping his stout arms behind his back. "An eternal bridge between Thorbardin and Qualinesti."

In the ruby glow of sunset, the stones of the citadel shone a soft pink. It was a magnificent yet lonely sight, the great gateway wedged between the slopes of the wide pass. Merith, who didn't care for heights, kept back from the unwalled edge of the tower top. Feldrin stood with his toes hanging over the edge, completely unconcerned about the long drop before him.

"How long until it's finished?" asked Merith.

"Barring strange quirks of weather and landslides, the east tower can be completed in six months. The fortress will be habitable then, though the inside details may take another year to dress out." Feldrin sighed, and it was like the grunt of an old bear.

He raised a hand to shade his eyes from the sun, setting behind the mountains to their left. Below, the pass was a narrow valley stretching away to the north. A small stream wended its way through the pass, shadowed now that the sun was nearly down. Staring up into the dark hollows of the high pass, the dwarf said, "Dust. Hmm . . . could be riders coming."

Merith moved as close as he dared to the edge of the parapet and looked up the valley. "From the north?" he queried. That meant Qualinost.

"Probably some dandified courtier or senator from the city who expects a guided tour of the fortress," growled Feldrin. "I guess this means I have to wash my hands and beard and put on a clean vest." He sniffed.

"It could be a courier from the Speaker," Merith suggested, "in which case you'll only have to wash your hands."

Feldrin caught the small smile on the fair-haired warrior's lips. "Very well! A compromise, lieutenant. I'll wash my hands and beard, but I won't change my vest!"

Chuckling, the two entered the stairwell sunk into the roof of the tower and descended the long set of steps. By the time they reached ground level and made their way outside, the rising plume of dust in the pass had been dispersed by the ever-present wind. There was no further sign of riders.

"Maybe they changed their minds and went home," joked Feldrin. He shrugged and added, "The dust must have come from a rockslide. All the better. Let's see what rubbish the cook has inflicted on us tonight."

In fact, Feldrin's cook was excellent. He did amazing things with the simple fare provided for the master builder's table. Dwarven food was usually too heavy for elves, but Feldrin's cook managed to prepare lighter dishes that Merith found quite delicious.

The lieutenant trailed after the fast-moving dwarf. Once more he looked up into the pass, where they had spotted the dust cloud.

"I wonder," he said softly. "Were they riders, or—?"

"Come, Merith! Why are you lagging?"

\*     \*     \*     \*     \*

There were no sentinels in Pax Tharkas. No night watch patrolled the sleeping complex of tent, huts, and sheds. None had ever been needed. Not even the grunt gang barracks were guarded once its single door was locked for the night. Thus it was that Ulvian slipped unseen out a window of the barracks and worked his way around the camp, collecting the items Dru had requested. From the plasterers' mixing shed, he got more than a pound of dry white clay, as fine and pure as cake flour. The prince dumped it in a wide-mouthed pottery jar and hurried on. He made for the long row of blacksmiths' sheds. Coal by the peck was available there, hard black coal from Thorbardin, which the dwarf smiths used to forge some of the hardest iron in the world. Ulvian crept up to the closest furnace. It still glowed dull orange from the day's fire. Squatting on the dirt floor, he picked through the rubbish that lay scattered around the hearth doors. He dropped several pieces of coal into the jar containing the clay.

The tanner's shed yielded a length of thong. Now . . . where to find a copper brazier? Dru had been quite specific; only copper would do. Hugging the pot of dry clay and coal to his chest, Ulvian ran across the open compound to the coppersmith's hut. Inside, he found an abundance of copper plates, nails, and ingots, but no brazier.

Outside once more, Ulvian huddled under the eaves of the hut for a moment, pondering where he might find what he needed. Only two kinds of people used copper fire pans: priests and cooks. There were no clerics at Pax Tharkas, but there were certainly cooks.

Half an hour later, Ulvian was back at the grunt gang barracks. He knelt by Dru's bed and reached a hand out to awaken the sorcerer.

Before Ulvian touched him, Dru said quietly, "Do you have it all?"

"Yes—and it wasn't easy."

"Good. Put it under my bed and go to sleep."

Ulvian was taken aback. "Aren't you going to do anything now?"

"At this hour? No indeed. Morning will be soon enough. Go to bed, my prince. Tomorrow will be a busy day, and you'll wish you had slept tonight." So saying, Dru rolled over and closed his eyes. Ulvian stared, mouth agape, at the sorcerer's back. With no other recourse, the prince shoved the pot, the cooking brazier, and the leather strap under Dru's bed and lay down on his own sagging, dirty cot. In spite of the excitement of the night's foray, he was asleep in a few minutes.

*     *     *     *     *

The soft sound of rattling chains caused Ulvian to open his eyes. A pair of scales was hanging in the air over his bed. The fulcrum of the scales was broken, and one of the golden pans was tilted, its chains sagging loosely. From the tilted pan, white powder fell, landing on Ulvian's chest. It looked like the clay powder he'd gotten for Dru.

"What's this?" he muttered, trying to sit up. Strangely he could not. A great weight seemed to settle on his chest, just where the powdered clay rested. But it was only a small heap of dust, his mind protested. It couldn't hold him pinioned in his bed.

The pressure grew and grew until the prince found it difficult to draw breath. He lifted a weak hand to deflect the stream of powder cascading down. When his fingers touched the golden scale pan, he snatched them back quickly. The pan was red hot!

"Help!" he gasped, continuing his efforts to rise. "I'm suffocating! Help!"

"Be still," said a soft, chiding voice. Ulvian opened his eyes and encountered blackness. He was lying facedown on his bunk, his nose and mouth buried in his dirty scrap of blanket. The prince bolted to his feet, flinging the blanket aside.

A wild glance around showed Dru sitting cross-legged on his own bed, mixing something in a wooden bowl. The grunt gang barracks were otherwise empty.

"What's the matter?" Dru asked, not looking up from his task.

"I—I had a bad dream," stammered the prince. "Where is everybody?"

"It's the half-day of rest," replied the sorcerer. "They're all at breakfast." He set aside his stirring stick and poured a bit more water into the bowl. The stick was thickly coated with gluey white clay.

Ulvian's breathing returned to normal, and he ran his fingers through his tousled hair. When he was calm, he went to see what Dru was doing. The sorcerer had made a ball of clay the size of two fists. He wet his hands and picked up the mass. The thong and copper brazier sat on the floor by his bed.

"One of the simplest kinds of spells is image magic," said Dru, sounding like some sort of schoolmaster. "The sorcerer makes an image and consecrates it as the double of a living person. Then whatever he does to the image happens to the living person." He rolled the clay into a long cylinder and tore off smaller bits, which he dropped into the bowl. "A more advanced spell creates an image that has no connection to the living. From that image, another double can be born."

Fascinated, Ulvian knelt on one knee. "Is that what you're doing?"

Dru nodded. "With this small figure, I will generate a much larger double that will do my bidding. Such clay creatures are called golems."

He had molded the rough form of a stocky body. To it, he attached clay arms and legs, and a round ball for a head. With chips of coal, Dru made eyes for the image. Laying the clay doll on the bed, he dipped the leather thong in the damp bowl.

The sorcerer tied the wet thong around the waist of the clay figure. Then he sent Ulvian to get some live coals and kindling from the fireplace. With a crackling fire laid in the brazier, Dru began dangling the clay figure over the flames.

"Rise up, O golem. Gather yourself from the dust and arise! I, Drulethen, command you! The fire is in you, the dust of the mountains! Gather yourself and do my will!" Unlike his usual soft tone, the sorcerer's voice was changing, deepening, strengthening.

Wind whistled through the chinks in the crude barracks walls. Outside, the grunt gang members lounging around the breakfast wagon grumbled loudly about the dust being whirled into their eyes. In the barracks, Dru twisted the thong in his fingers, making the clay doll spin, first left then right.

"Rise up, O golem! Your form is here! Take the fire I give you and arise!" Dru shouted. Ulvian felt his skin crawl as the sorcerer's voice boomed through the room. The rafters of the poorly built barracks rattled, and bits of dried moss fell through the cracks.

Steam began to rise from the white clay doll. The smell of burning hide filled the prince's nostrils, threatening to gag him. The air vibrated, sending a tingling all along the surface of Ulvian's skin. The walls of the building groaned, and suddenly the complaints of the workers outside ceased. In seconds, hoarse shouts replaced the muttered grumblings.

"What's happening?" whispered Ulvian.

Breathing heavily, Dru never ceased his turning of the clay figure in the flames. "Go and see, my prince!" he gasped.

Ulvian went to the door and threw it open. The astonished faces of the grunt gang were looking off to the left, toward the quarries and the tent city. When he turned his face in that direction, the prince saw that a whirlwind of white dust writhed heavenward near the open pits where the limestone was cut. Elves, men, and dwarves ran from the area, shouting things Ulvian couldn't understand.

As Dru's invocation continued, the whirlwind coalesced into a thick, white body, twice as tall as the tallest tents. The black eyes on the featureless face mimicked the coal chips on the sorcerer's doll.

"By the gods!" Ulvian exclaimed, turning to Dru. "You've done it! It's as big as a watchtower!"

The sorcerer's hand was nearly invisible, shrouded by the steam rising from the baking clay figure. "Go!" he hissed. "The confusion will cover you. Get my black amulet!" Dru clenched his eyes shut, and tears trickled down his cheeks. The steam was scalding his hand. "Go! Hurry!"

"I will, but remember our bargain. You know who I want punished!" As he left, Ulvian closed the barracks door behind him. The grunt gang were all gone, and the dwarves who managed the food wagon had taken refuge underneath it. The clay giant was moving, striding stiffly across the camp, smashing through tents and huts as it went. The ground shook each time it took a step. No one tried to stop it. The workers weren't soldiers, and what arms there were in camp were of little avail against a twenty-foot-tall golem.

Feldrin Feldspar was in the west tower when the giant appeared. He heard the commotion and came outside in time to see the monster plowing through his workers' homes.

"By Reorx!" he shouted. "What *is* that thing?" No one stopped to answer his question, though he bellowed at his scattering people to stand and fight. The dwarf stood at the base of the west tower, shouting, until Merith appeared, mounted and in full battle armor.

"What do you propose, warrior?" Feldrin said, yelling above the uproar.

"Repel the monster," Merith replied simply. He drew his long elven blade. His buckskin horse pranced nervously, upset by the tumult around them.

"That's no natural beast!" Feldrin cried. "You'd be better off to find Drulethen. He's got to be behind this!"

"You find him," replied Merith. His horse turned a full circle. Touching his spurs to his mount's side, Merith was off, moving against the flow of terrified workers. All the artisans and laborers streamed toward the finished section of the citadel, seeking shelter from the rampaging giant.

Once clear of the panicked workers, Merith reined in and studied the monster as it tramped on. As nearly as he could tell, it hadn't injured anyone yet, but it had smashed about half a dozen huts with its thick feet and legs. It zigzagged around the camp as if it were looking for something.

Merith urged his horse forward, but the animal wanted no part of the giant. It reared and danced, trying to unseat its rider. The elf warrior held on and drew a yellow silk handkerchief from beneath his breastplate. It was a gift from a female admirer in Qualinost, but it served to cover his horse's eyes and quieted the animal somewhat. Merith wrapped the reins around his mailed fist and spurred ahead.

The golem halted and bent stiffly at the waist. Bits of dried clay the size of an elf's palm flaked off the giant's joints and fell to the ground.

Merith watched, fascinated, as the monster's hand split apart into five thick fingers. It plunged the hand into the ruins of a row of huts, and when it stood erect again, there was someone struggling in its grasp. The giant had the fellow by the throat. Merith saw that he was a Kagonesti elf.

Snapping down the visor on his helm, he charged at the monster. It paid no attention to him at all, even when Merith struck it full force with his sword. A wedge of hard white clay flew from the wound, but the giant was uninjured. The impact of the blow stung the elf warrior's arm. Grimacing, he struck again. Another chip of clay flew, but to no avail; the poor wretch in the monster's hand ceased kicking. The giant's black eyes never blinked. Opening its fingers, it allowed the Kagonesti to drop to the ground close to Merith.

Crouched under the awning of a hut, Prince Ulvian took in the scene with satisfaction. The death of his tormentor, Splint, pleased him immensely. He also saw the warrior, Merithynos, trying to subdue the clay giant with his sword. The prince laughed out loud at the lieutenant's antics, chopping at the mass of hard clay with comic futility.

Ulvian dashed down the lane, behind the busy Merith, up the hill toward Feldrin's hut. The golem had stomped flat nearly every other structure around the master builder's home. Ulvian burst through the door flap.

The outer room was empty. He searched every box and chest, with no result. The structure was divided by a canvas wall, the other half being Feldrin's bedchamber. Ulvian bolted in and pulled up sharply. Feldrin himself stood guard over a small golden casket.

"So," said the dwarf coolly, "you have joined forces with Drulethen."

"Give me the amulet," Ulvian said in a commanding tone.

"Don't be a fool, boy! He's using you. Can't you see that? He'd promise anything to get his hands on that amulet again—and break every promise once he had it. He has no honor, Highness. He will destroy you if he has the chance."

"Save your entreaties for someone else!" Ulvian's voice was a harsh, angry rasp. "My father sent me here to suffer, and I've suffered enough. Drulethen has sworn to serve me, and serve me he will. You all think I'm a fool, but you'll find out differently." There was a loud crash nearby, and Ulvian added impatiently, "Now surrender the amulet, or the golem will crush you to jelly!"

Feldrin drew a jeweled shortsword from behind his back. "You will get it from me only after I'm dead," he said solemnly.

Ulvian was unarmed. Feldrin's keen sword and the steely look of determination in the dwarf's eyes discouraged any rash action.

"You'll regret this!" the prince declared, edging back toward the doorway in the canvas wall. "The golem won't stand and argue with you. Once he comes, you will die!"

"Then it is by Reorx's will."

Furious, Ulvian dashed out of the tent. He nearly bowled over Dru, who was coming in his direction. The sorcerer cradled his left hand to his chest, and his ragged robes were soaked with sweat.

"Did you get it?" he cried, desperation glazing his eyes.

"No, Feldrin is guarding it. Why aren't you with the brazier? Is the spell over?"

Dru mustered his strength; his spell had exhausted him. "I hung the doll over the brazier. The thong is almost burned in two. When it severs, the magic will end."

The giant figure of the golem came into view over Dru's shoulder. It had nearly reached the citadel. The parapets were lined with workers, many of whom were hurling stones at the unheeding monster.

"Can you control it?" asked Ulvian quickly. "If you can, then bring it here. It's the only way to scare Feldrin into giving up the amulet!"

Wordlessly the sorcerer slid to his knees. His eyelids fluttered closed. Ulvian thought he had fainted, but Dru's lips were moving slightly.

Abruptly the golem did a jerky about-face and came marching toward Feldrin's hut. Merith dogged its heels, no longer slashing with his sword, but keeping it in view. When the elf warrior spied Ulvian and Dru, he put his head down and rode hard toward them.

"Merith is coming!" shouted the prince.

Still the sorcerer chanted. The golem's wide, round head swiveled down to look at the mounted warrior. An arm the thickness of a mature oak limb swept down, knocking horse and rider to the ground. The horse let out a shriek and lay still. Merith struggled vainly but was pinned under his dead mount.

"That got him!" Ulvian cried, leaping into the air in his excitement.

"And I've got you," said Feldrin from the door of his hut. Startled, the prince stepped back.

The dwarf had been a fighter of some note in his youth, and he knew how to handle a sword. Raising the jeweled blade high, he advanced toward Dru. The sorcerer never flinched, so complete was his concentration. Ulvian flung himself at the dwarf and grappled with him. The golem was only a score of yards away, and its long stride ate up the distance rapidly.

"Let go!" roared Feldrin. "I've no wish to harm you, Prince Ulvian, but I must—"

His muscled arms pushed steadily against Ulvian's lighter strength. The prince's grip was slipping. Gleaming in the morning sun, Feldrin's sword was only inches from the sorcerer's skull.

A wall of white fell on the prince and the dwarf. Ulvian was knocked backward through the air, landing hard on a pile of torn canvas and broken tent stakes. The breath was driven from his body, and the world vanished in a red, roaring haze.

Hands propped the prince up. He gasped and fought for air, and at last breath whooshed into his lungs. His vision cleared, and he saw Dru kneeling beside him. Ulvian shook his head to clear it, for he saw a remarkable thing: The spell animating the golem had obviously ended and the giant had fallen on Feldrin's hut, breaking into several large clay pieces. From under a barrel-sized portion of the monster's torso, Feldrin's fur-wrapped legs protruded. His feet twitched slightly. A groan sounded from under the mass of clay.

Dru was shaking and drenched with sweat, but his voice was triumphant as he said, "Where's the amulet?" Ulvian stammered that Feldrin kept the onyx talisman in a golden box. The sorcerer dashed into the ruins of the master builder's hut.

A profound silence had fallen over the construction camp. Ulvian blinked and gazed across the wrecked site. The walls of the citadel were lined with workers, all staring at him. Already some were leaving the parapet, no doubt to hurry to Feldrin's rescue.

Dru was tearing through the broken bits of hut, muttering. Ulvian called out, "We must flee! The workers are coming!"

The sorcerer didn't even respond, but kept up his frantic digging. Feldrin groaned once more, louder. Ulvian picked his way through the chunks of lifeless golem. He pushed a heavy slab of clay off the dwarf and knelt beside him.

"I regret this, Master Feldrin," said the prince. "But injustice requires strong deeds."

The dwarf coughed, and blood appeared on his lips. "Don't go with Drulethen, my prince. With him lies only ruin and death. . . ."

"Aha!" shouted the sorcerer, falling to his knees. He flung aside a bit of canvas, revealing the gilded box. No sooner did Dru try to pick it up than he shrieked in pain and dropped it again.

"You filthy worm!" he howled at Feldrin. "You put my amulet in a charmed case!" But Feldrin had lost consciousness and was beyond Dru's maledictions.

"Come here!" the sorcerer barked peremptorily. "Pick up the box."

Ulvian glared at him. "I'm not your servant," he retorted.

The first band of workers from the citadel appeared at the end of the wrecked street. They were armed with hammers, staves, and mason's tools. Eight men went to lift the dead horse off the fallen Merith. The warrior got stiffly to his feet and pointed expressively toward Feldrin's tent.

"There's no time for false pride now!" Dru spat. "Do you think those fools are going to pat us on the back for what we've done? It's time to flee, and I can't touch that wretched box. Pick it up, I say!"

Reluctantly Ulvian did so. Then he and the shaken sorcerer ran for the corral near the foot of the eastern slope. The prince snared two horses, short-legged mountain ponies, and boosted the weakened Dru onto one of them. Bareback, the pair rode hell-for-leather out the gate, scattering the other animals as they went. By the time the outraged workers reached the corral, not a single horse remained, and the only sign of the fugitives was a rapidly rising cloud of dust.

\* \* \* \* \*

Merith stood by a crackling fire, which blazed in a wide stone urn outside Feldrin Feldspar's hut. In spite of his badly bruised left leg, he had insisted on standing guard personally outside the master builder's home. The entire camp was silent, and nothing stirred but the wavering flames before him. The lieutenant kept his cloak close around his throat to ward off a persistent chill.

The clip-clop of horse's hooves alerted him. Quickly he stepped back from the fire, back into the deep shadows cast by the hut's overhanging roof. Drawing his sword, he set his shield tightly on his forearm. The hoofbeats drew nearer.

A tall figure, mounted on a rather tired-looking sorrel, emerged from the night. The newcomer's face and figure were obscured by a long, monkish robe with a deep hood. The rider approached the fire and dismounted. He peeled off a pair of deerskin gloves and held his long, tapered fingers to the heat. Merith watched carefully. Short plumes of warm breath issued from the stranger's hood. Though he waited long minutes, the newcomer made no threatening moves. Warming his icy hands and body seemed to be his greatest concern. The lieutenant stepped out of the shadows and faced the robed figure.

"Who goes there?" he demanded.

"A weary traveler," answered the stranger. He spoke through the lower edge of the hood, and his words were muffled. "I saw your fire from a distance and stopped to warm myself."

"You are welcome, traveler," Merith said warily.

"A naked sword is a strange welcome. Are you troubled by bandits hereabouts?"

"Not bandits. A single elf did all this. A sorcerer."

The hooded one jerked his hands back from the fire. "A sorcerer! Why would a sorcerer trouble a lonely outpost such as this?"

"The evil one was a captive here, a prisoner of the King of Thorbardin and the Speaker of the Sun," Merith explained. "Through treachery, he regained his powers, wrecked the camp, and escaped."

The visitor passed a hand across his hidden brow. Merith caught the glint of metal at the fellow's throat. Armor? Or just a decorative torc?

The stranger asked how the sorcerer had escaped. The elf warrior told him briefly about the golem, though he didn't mention Ulvian's part in the affair. The visitor asked endless questions, and Merith found the late-night conversation tired him. His leg ached unmercifully, and his heart was heavy with the news he must send to his sovereign. The hooded stranger must be a cleric, he decided. Only they were so talky and inquisitive.

Weariness was banished instantly when Merith saw a pair of horses appear at the far end of the path. One of the riders was wearing armor. Merith lifted his sword and shield. The hooded stranger waved at him soothingly.

"Put down your weapons, noble warrior. These are friends of mine," he said. In a swirl of dark robes, the hooded one turned and hailed the two mounted fellows.

"Is something the matter, sire?" called the armored rider.

"Sire?" wondered Merith.

The stranger faced Merith and tossed back his hood.

Pale hair gleamed in the firelight. It was Kith-Kanan himself.

"Great Speaker!" Merith cried. "Forgive me! I had no idea—"

"Be at ease." Kith-Kanan waved, and Kemian Ambrodel and his father, Tamanier, rode up to the crackling fire.

"Are there just the three of you, Majesty?" asked Merith, scanning the path for more riders. "Where is your entourage?"

"I have a small party at the high end of the pass," Kith-Kanan explained. "I came down with the Ambrodels to find out what had happened. Even in the dark, the camp looks like a cyclone hit it."

Merith told the story of Drulethen, Ulvian, and the golem in detail, this time leaving out nothing. "I led a band of fifty trusted workers along the trail Prince Ulvian and Drulethen made," he finished, "but we couldn't hope to catch up on foot."

"Never mind, Lieutenant. Is Feldrin Feldspar well?" asked the Speaker.

"He has some broken ribs, but he will survive, sire." Merith managed a smile.

Kemian relieved the younger warrior and sent Merith to bed. Once the lieutenant was gone, Kith-Kanan shed his monkish habit, revealing full battle armor.

"I had a premonition something evil would happen," Kith-Kanan said grimly. "Now it is up to me to set things right. Tomorrow Lord Kemian and I will take the escort cavalry and go after Drulethen."

Tamanier said, "And Prince Ulvian?"

The silence in the camp was unbroken except by the soft snapping of the fire in the urn before them. The Speaker stared into the flames, the light giving his face and hair a ruddy glow. When the castellan was certain his sovereign wasn't going to answer, Kith-Kanan looked up and said evenly, "My son will face the consequences of his deeds."

# ☙ 12 ☙

## The Green and Golden Way

The high plains in summer were a harsh place. Dry and barren, they were frequently swept by grass fires that would burn right up to the stony bases of the Kharolis Mountains before dying out from lack of tinder. Yet as Verhanna, Rufus, and Greenhands ascended the sloping plain toward the distant blue peaks, the grassland was not only green, but also covered with flowers.

"Aashoo!" The kender sneezed loudly. "Where did all dese flowers come fum?" he muttered through a clogged nose. The air was thick with blowing pollen, released by the thousands of wild flowers. Verhanna wasn't much bothered by it, though she was startled by the vigor and variety of the flowers around them. The plain was an ocean of crimson, yellow, blue, and purple blossoms, all nodding gently in the breeze.

"You know, I've been this way before, on the way to Pax Tharkas," she said. "But I've never seen the grasslands bloom like this. And in the heat of midsummer!"

Ahead of them, his rough horsehair poncho coated with yellow dust, Greenhands walked steadily onward. His simple, sturdy features took on a special nobility in the warm light of day, and Verhanna found herself studying him more and more as they traveled.

"*Ushwah!*" barked Rufus. "Dis is tewwibuh! I cand bweathe!"

The warrior maiden dug deep into her saddlebag. In a moment, she brought out a thin red pod, shriveled into a curl. "Here," she said, tossing it to her scout. "Chew on that. It'll clear your head."

Rufus sniffed the tiny pod, but to no avail; nothing could penetrate his stuffy nose. "Whad is id?" he asked suspiciously.

"Give it back, then, if you don't want it," Verhanna said airily.

"Oh, all wide." The kender stuck the stem end of the seed pod in his mouth and chewed. In seconds, his look of curiosity was replaced by one of horror.

"*Ye-ow!*" Rufus's shriek rent the calm, flower-scented air. Greenhands halted and looked back, startled out of his unvarying gait. "Dat's hot!" protested the kender, his small face purpling in distress.

"It's a dragonseed pod," Verhanna replied. "Of course it's hot. But it will clear your head." Despite its fearsome name, dragonseed was a common spice plant grown in the river delta region of Silvanesti. It was used to make the famous *vantrea*, a hot, spicy dried fish that was beloved by southern elves.

Their horses overtook Greenhands. Verhanna reined in and said, "Don't worry. Wart was complaining about the pollen, so I did a little healing of my own."

Tears running down his cheeks, Rufus sluiced his tingling mouth out with water. Then he sniffed, and a pleased expression spread across his florid features. "What do you know! I can breathe!" he declared.

Greenhands had been standing between their two horses. Now he headed out once more, and they rode after him.

Verhanna urged her mount forward until she was alongside the silver-haired elf. The day was quite warm, and he had flipped back the front edges of his makeshift poncho, exposing his chest to the sun. In secret, sidelong glances, the warrior maiden admired his physique. With a little training, perhaps he could become a formidable warrior.

"Why do you stare at me?" asked Greenhands, intruding on the captain's thoughts.

"Tell me the truth, Greenhands," she said in a low voice. "How is it you're able to do the things you do? How did you heal my shoulder? How did you turn aside a herd of wild elk? Raise flowers out of dry soil?"

There was a long pause before he replied. Finally he said, "I've been thinking about those things. There seems to be something with me. Something I carry . . . like this garment." He passed a hand over the coarse fabric of the blanket he wore. "I feel it around me and inside me, but I can't set it aside. I can't separate myself from it."

Intrigued, Verhanna asked, "What does it feel like?"

Shutting his eyes, he lifted his face to the golden sunlight. "It's like the heat of the sun," he murmured. "I feel it, yet I can't touch it. I carry it with me, but I can't take it off." He opened his eyes and regarded her. "Am I mad, Captain?"

"No," she said, and her voice was soft. "You're not mad."

A piercing whistle cut her off. "Hey!" Rufus called from behind them. "Are you two going to walk right off the edge?"

Greenhands and Verhanna halted, taking in their surroundings. Not five paces in front of them was a deep ravine, cut through the grassy sod by some winter flood. They had been so absorbed in their conversation, neither had noticed the danger.

They turned and paralleled the rift for a dozen yards. Behind them, Rufus rode up to the lip of the ravine and gazed across. On the other side, the sere plain was covered with dry brown grass. At the kender's back, the landscape was carpeted with lush green grass and a riot of blooming flowers.

"*Wha-how!*" A neck-snapping sneeze wrenched the kender. His nose felt like it was filling even as he sat. Kicking his heels against his horse's red flanks, Rufus hastened after his captain. He hoped she could discover another dragonseed pod in her saddlebag.

\* \* \* \* \*

Late in the afternoon, the trio was well into the shadowed presence of the Kharolis Mountains. Peaks welled up on three sides, and the open ground was ever steeper in grade. Hereabouts there was only one path through the mountains wide enough for horses, and it funneled directly to Pax Tharkas.

Once the carpet of grass and flowers thinned, Rufus found his head much clearer. He occupied his time by tootling discordantly on a reed pipe he'd made back at the Astradine River. The shrill cacophony got on Verhanna's nerves, and finally she snatched the reed from the kender's lips.

"Are you trying to drive me mad?" she snapped.

He bristled. "That was a kender ballad, 'You Took My Heart While I Took Your Rings.'"

"Ha! Trust a wart like you to know a love song with theft in it." Verhanna tossed the reed flute away, but Greenhands detoured from his path to retrieve it. The warrior maiden sighed. "Don't you plague me with that thing either," she warned.

Unheeding, the elf put the flute to his mouth and blew a few experimental notes. His fingers ran up and down the scale, and the instrument trilled melodically. Rufus raised his head and peered down at Greenhands.

"How did you do that?" he asked. Greenhands shrugged, a gesture he'd only lately acquired from Verhanna. Rufus asked for his flute back. When he had it, he piped several notes. Verhanna grimaced; it still sounded like the death throes of a crow.

Before she could voice her protest again, Rufus thrust the reed flute back at Greenhands. "You keep it," he said generously. "It's not refined enough for kender music."

His captain snorted. The elf accepted the instrument gravely and walked along slowly, playing random notes. Without warning, a red-breasted songbird settled on his shoulder. The tiny bird regarded Greenhands curiously, its beady black eyes almost intelligent.

"Hello," Greenhands said calmly. Verhanna and Rufus stared. The strange elf put the flute to his lips and played a fluttering trill. Much to his companions' astonishment, his feathered friend imitated the sound perfectly.

"Very good. Now this." He sounded a slightly more complex series of notes. The redbreast repeated the notes exactly.

A second bird, slightly larger and duller in color, circled the elf's head and settled on the opposite shoulder. A funny sort of musical trio began, as Greenhands and the little songbird exchanged perfectly pitched notes, while the brown thrush added off-key harmonics.

"The big bird sounds like you," Verhanna commented to the kender. Rufus answered her with a rude noise.

The captain's mount danced in a circle. The green-fingered elf had attracted more and more birds; in seconds, he was wrapped in a cloud of wildly singing creatures. He seemed unworried by them, continuing to walk steadily forward as his flute trilled. However, the birds were unnerving the horses.

"Stop it!" Verhanna called to Greenhands. "Send them

away!" He couldn't hear her over the shrill sound of birdsongs. More and more birds appeared, zooming around the group, dipping, soaring, diving. Wing tips and tails grazed their faces. Their mounts bucked and danced.

"Yow!"

A sizable starling thudded into the kender's back. He yanked off his hat and began swinging it at the darting creatures without success. A careening purple martin flew too close to Verhanna and smacked solidly into her neck. She quickly pulled her visor down to protect her eyes. Though her hands were full trying to calm her frantic horse, she managed to draw her sword.

With a loud war cry, the captain drove her nervous mount hard at Greenhands. Birds thumped off her armored head and against her horse. Verhanna pushed through the swarm. Completely unaware of the havoc he was causing, the elf was walking along in the center of an avian maelstrom, playing Rufus's flute.

Verhanna struck the pipe from the elf's hands with the flat of her blade. The instant the notes ceased, the birds stopped their mad whirling and dispersed quickly in all directions.

Greenhands stared at the broken flute lying in the grass. He picked up the two halves and then turned accusing eyes upon Verhanna.

"Your playing drove those birds mad," she explained, panting. He clearly had no idea what she was talking about. "We could've been killed!"

Understanding dawned on his face, and he apologized. "I'm sorry. I didn't mean to make trouble."

Rufus rode up, brushing feathers from his topknot. "Blind me with beeswax! What was that all about?"

Verhanna pointed to the chastened Greenhands. "Our friend here doesn't understand the power he has."

Humbly he repeated, "I'm sorry."

They resumed their march, guided by Greenhands. Though he honestly disavowed any knowledge of the fortress, it was obviously their destination.

The flowering grassland gave way to piles of boulders spotted by patches of dark green lichen. Coolness crept into the warm air of daytime, promising a brisk night. The sun sank behind the mountain peaks, washing the sky in gold, crimson, and finally deepest burgundy. As the last of the light was dying from the day, Verhanna dismounted. They had come to a wide spot in the pass, only a few hundred paces from the entrance. "We can camp here for the night," she decided.

The kender and the elf were agreeable. They tethered their horses and built a campfire. Rufus did the cooking for the little band. Considering a kender's ideas about dinner, things weren't bad. He busied himself warming a soup of dried vegetables, bread crumbs, and water while his captain curried their animals.

Greenhands settled down by the fire, staring unblinking into the flames. The yellow light made his green eyes and fingers stand out against the dark background of his poncho. Verhanna found herself peering at him over the back of her horse. Her right hand, wielding the curry comb, slowed and stopped in its motion as her scrutiny of the elf intensified. The light tan of his skin was deepened by the golden glow of the firelight. Though at rest, his well-formed body showed a lithe grace and beauty she found arresting. His profile was somehow quite attractive. Strong brow, rather a long nose, firm lips, a good chin. . . .

She brought herself up short. What was she doing? So many unfamiliar thoughts tumbled in her head. But one, quite odd, idea took precedence.

Could Greenhands be the husband she never thought she'd find?

A smile tugged the corners of her mouth upward. Wouldn't her father be surprised? He'd wanted her to marry for a long time. Though he never pushed openly, the warrior maiden knew he longed for her to be wife and mother. As quickly as this thought occurred to her, a sharp chill set her to shuddering. The mountain air had cooled rapidly with the setting of the sun.

When she'd finished with the horses, Verhanna wrapped her bedroll around her shoulders and settled by the fire. The kender was just downing the last of his soup. He handed her a bowl and, while she ate, he skipped around the campsite, humming his tuneless kender songs.

"What are you so happy about?" Verhanna asked him with a smile.

"I like the mountains," he said. "When the air is thin and the nights are cold, then Rufus Wrinklecap is at home!"

Verhanna laughed, but Greenhands' eyes were closed, and gentle snores issued from his mouth. Though still sitting upright, the elf had fallen fast asleep.

The kender scaled a pile of boulders resting against the sheer wall of the mountain behind the warrior maiden. When she asked what he was doing, Rufus replied, "In these parts, it's not wise to lie on low ground."

Her brow wrinkled in thought. "Why not?"

"Falling rocks, sudden floods, prowling wolves, poisonous snakes. . . ." The kender spoke a cheerful litany of disaster. He stopped and added a blithe "Good night, my captain. Sleep well!"

How well could she sleep after his listing of all those dangers? Her brown eyes searched the darkness beyond their dying fire. Moonlight and starlight washed the mountain pass, and the air was filled with the faint but normal sounds of night. The warrior maiden set her empty soup bowl down and sidled around the fire until she was close to Greenhands. Laying her head down by his crossed legs, she reasoned that since he seemed so connected to the wild, then he was probably safe from any natural disasters or creatures of the night.

The strange elf still slept upright, his head drooping toward the embers. The white light of Solinari washed his hair in silver. The dying firelight tinged the silver with rose. A single coral-hued strand had fallen across his closed eyes. Verhanna put up a hand to brush it away, but as her finger drew near, she shivered violently. It wasn't the cold of the night, for under her bedroll, by the fire, she was quite warm.

It must be tiredness, she decided, and the lingering effects of the goblin bite. The Qualinesti princess withdrew her hand and put her head down to sleep.

Verhanna's rest was troubled. She wasn't usually prone to disturbing dreams, but on this occasion, visions appeared in her mind, images of magic and power in a dark forest peopled by her father, Ulvian, Greenhands, and some others she didn't recognize. One countenance appeared frequently—a Kagonesti woman unknown to her. The wild elf woman had eyes the same brilliant green as Greenhands, and her face was painted with yellow and red lines. Her expression was ineffably sad, but in spite of the barbaric face paint, it was also regal and proud.

A faint noise intruded on Verhanna's visions. The warrior maiden's trained senses brought her fully awake. Only her eyes shifted as she tried to discover what had disturbed her. The fire was out, though a thin ribbon of white smoke rose from the bed of cinders. Her half-human eyes weren't as sharp as those of her full-blooded elf kin, but they were better than any human's. The moons had set, but the light of the stars was enough for her to make out a dark shape hovering over their pile of baggage, only a few yards from where she lay.

Kender, if you're trying to scare me, I'll have your topknot for a feather duster! she vowed silently. The black shape rose from its crouch. It was far too tall to be Rufus Wrinklecap.

In a flash, Verhanna rolled to her feet and drew her sword. She'd been lying on it, just in case Rufus was right about wolves. The intruder flinched and backed away. She heard hooves striking the stony ground. Her opponent must be mounted.

"Who are you?" Verhanna demanded. A strong animal smell invaded her nostrils.

More hoofbeats thumped in the shadows beyond Verhanna's line of sight. She was getting worried; there was no telling how many foes she faced. Advancing to the firepit, she kicked some of the kindling Rufus had piled up onto the coals. The dry bark caught quickly and blazed up.

"*Kothlolo!*" With a loud bass cry, the thing near their baggage threw up an arm to shield its eyes. Verhanna gasped when she saw it clearly—it had the head, arms, and torso of a man, but four legs and a swishing horse's tail. A centaur!

"*Kothlolo!*" shouted the centaur again. The circle of firelight caught the movement of other centaurs a few paces away. Verhanna shouted to Rufus and Greenhands to wake up.

"Rufus! Rufus, you dung beetle! Where are you?" she called.

"Here, my captain." He was just behind her. She wrenched her gaze from the nearest centaur long enough to spy the kender sitting atop a large boulder. "Who are your new friends?" he asked innocently.

"Idiot! Centaurs murder travelers! Some of them are cannibals!"

"Ho," rumbled the nearest centaur. "Only eat ugly two-legs."

She almost dropped her sword in surprise. "You speak Elven?"

"Some." On Verhanna's left and right, half-man, half-horse creatures pressed in toward the fire. She counted seven of them, five brown and two black. They carried rusty iron swords and spears or crude clubs made from small tree trunks. The one who had spoken to Verhanna carried a bow and quiver of arrows slung across his body.

"You do not fight, we do not fight," he said, cocking his brown head at her. Verhanna put her back against the boulder and kept her sword ready. Above her, Rufus loaded his sling.

"What do you want?" asked the warrior maiden.

"I am Koth, leader of this band. We follow the *jerda*, we hunt them," said the centaur. He held up hairy brown fingers to his forehead to imitate horns. Understanding dawned on Verhanna. He meant the elk herd. "*Jerda* ran hard, and we lost them. *Kothlolo* are very hungry."

*Kothlolo* must be the centaur word for "centaur," Verhanna decided. "We haven't much food ourselves," she said. "We did see the elk herd. It was heading toward the Astradine River."

A black-coated centaur picked up her saddlebags and pawed through them. He found a lump of bacon and shoved it in his mouth. Immediately those nearest him swarmed over him, trying to snatch the smoked meat from his lips. The centaurs dissolved into a bucking, scrabbling fight, with only the bass-voiced Koth remaining aloof.

"They are pretty hungry," Rufus observed.

"And numerous," mumbled Verhanna. She couldn't very well start a fight with so many centaurs. She and Rufus might well end up as the main course at a losers' banquet.

"Where's Greenhands?" she said softly, looking around.

Through all the talking and squabbling over food, Greenhands had sat unmoving, lost in slumber. So complete was his sleep, Verhanna felt obliged to see if he was breathing. He was.

"By Astra, when he sleeps, he sleeps," she muttered.

A centaur found Rufus's store of walnuts in his ration bag. The others tore at his hand, scattering the nuts over the campsite. A few landed on Greenhands' head, and he finally stirred.

"You're alive," Verhanna said caustically. "I thought I was going to have to beat a gong."

The elf's face was blank. He licked his dry lips and

said, "I've been away. Far away. I saw my mother and spoke to her." Looking up at Verhanna, he added, "You were with me for a time. In the forest, with others I did not know."

Had they been sharing the same dream? At another time, Verhanna might have been curious, but just now she had other worries. "Never mind that now," she said to the elf. "We've got a camp full of wild, starving centaurs."

Greenhands started in surprise. He jumped to his feet and walked right up to the centaur leader.

"Greetings, uncle," he said. "How fare you?"

As Rufus and Verhanna exchanged looks of consternation, Koth bowed and replied, "I am a dried gourd, my cousin. And my cousins here are likewise empty."

"My friends have little to eat, uncle. May I show you to a stand of mountain apples? They are nearby and very sweet."

The centaur laughed, showing fearsome yellow teeth. "Ho, little cousin! I am not so young in the world that I think there are apples in early summer!"

Greenhands pressed a hand to his heart. "They are there, uncle. Will you come?"

The sincerity of his manner won over the centaur's natural skepticism. He snapped an order to his squabbling comrades, and the band of centaurs formed behind Greenhands. Then, without a brand to light the way, he stepped into the darkness, up the far slope. The centaurs followed, their small, worn hooves fitting deftly into the clefts in the rocks.

Rufus jumped off his boulder and started after them. "You, too?" snorted the warrior woman.

"My captain, I doubt nothing about that elf."

Sheathing her sword, Verhanna found herself alone by the campfire. With a long-suffering sigh, she reluctantly followed the troop. Rufus made his way easily up the slope; the going was less easy for her, being larger and burdened with armor. Soon Rufus pulled away from her, and the only sign she had of him was the steady trickle of pebbles he dislodged on his way up.

The slope ended suddenly. A ravine plunged down in front of Verhanna, and she almost fell facefirst into it. She flung her hands wide on the crumbling, gravelly soil and cursed herself for following Greenhands in the middle of the night. Once she'd gotten to her feet and dusted the dirt from her palms, Verhanna looked down into the shallow ravine. She was amazed by what she saw. There, nestled close to the sheer wall of the rising mountain, was a stand of apple trees, heavy with fruit. The Qualinesti princess moved down for a closer look.

The ground around the trees was littered with fallen apples, some rotten-soft, and the air was spiced by their fermented odor. The centaurs appeared to esteem these, for they galloped up and and down the ravine, filling their arms with the fallen fruit. Greenhands, Rufus, and Koth, the centaur leader, were standing together under the largest apple tree. The ancient tree was warped by wind and frost, yet its gnarled roots gripped the stony earth tenaciously.

"How did you know these were here?" Verhanna asked.

Greenhands looked at the laden branches close to his head. "I heard them. Old trees have loud voices," he said.

Verhanna was speechless. His words seemed completely ridiculous to her, yet she couldn't dispute the find.

Rufus went to the tree and climbed up to a triple fork of branches. He inched out on a branch until he could just reach a ripe fruit still hanging from the tree. Before his fingers could close on it, Greenhands was there, his moss-colored fingers wrapping tightly around the kender's wrist.

"No, little friend," he chided. "You mustn't take what the tree has not offered."

Koth popped a whole apple in his mouth and chewed

it up—stem, seeds, skin, and all. He grinned at Verhanna. "Your cousin with the green fingers is one of the old ones," he said.

"Old ones" was a common epithet given to members of the elven race. Verhanna, still ill-at-ease around the centaur band, said, "He's not my cousin."

"All peoples are cousins," answered Koth. Bits of over-ripe apple flew from his mouth. The other centaurs were racing around the ravine, yelling and dancing. Verhanna realized that the fermented fruit was making them tipsy. Soon the centaurs were singing, arms looped around their fellows' shoulders. Their bass and baritone voices sounded surprisingly harmonious.

Koth sang:

> "Child of oak, newly born,
> Walks among the mortals mild,
> By lightning from his mother torn.
> Who knows the father of this child?
> Who hears music in the flowers' sway
> And fears no creature in the wild
> Shall wear a crown made far away
> And dwell within a tower tiled."

"You made up a song about Greenhands," Rufus said admiringly. "That part about crowns, though—"

"It is a very sad song," Koth interrupted. "My grandfather's grandfather sang it, and 'twas ancient then."

Verhanna was growing tired of the drunken, bumptious centaurs. When one thumped into her for the second time, she announced she was going back to get some sleep. She strongly hinted that Rufus and Greenhands should do likewise.

"Cousin," said Koth to Greenhands, "you travel far?"

The centaurs quieted down and gathered around the green-fingered elf. "Yes, uncle. My father awaits me in a high place of stone," replied Greenhands.

"Then take this with you, gentle cousin." Koth took a

ram's horn that hung by a strap around his neck and gave it to the elf. "If ever you need the Sons of the Wind, blow hard on this horn and we shall come."

"Thank you, uncle, and all my cousins," Greenhands said, looping the strap around his neck.

He led the warrior maiden and the kender back to their camp. No one spoke. The shouts of the centaurs echoed once more through the peaks, slurred now as they continued to eat the fermented apples. Greenhands returned to the same boulder he'd sat by before, and he was asleep nearly as soon as he sat down. Rufus climbed back up to his safe perch, and Verhanna curled up by the dying fire. The smell of the centaurs lingered in her nostrils a long time. So did the words to Koth's ancient song.

## ✒ 13 ✒

## The Great Stone House

Dru and Ulvian rode all day without stopping. The rugged mountain ponies were hardy beasts, but even they rebelled at such treatment. By evening, they were panting and balking. In a fury, Dru lashed at his mount with a cut sapling switch. The pony responded by throwing the short-tempered sorcerer to the ground and galloping away.

Ulvian, sitting calmly on his own mount, watched Dru's fall and the flight of the abused pony. Dru scrambled to his feet and shouted, "After him! Worthless nag! I'll flay him if I ever get my hands on him!"

"Seems unlikely, from where I sit," remarked the prince. He slid off his horse, wincing. Riding bareback through the mountains for six hours had taken its toll on his aching backside.

Dru scowled and threw the hair back from his eyes. His manner had changed considerably since they left Pax Tharkas; his respectfulness, never sincere, had vanished completely. Sitting on a convenient boulder, he stared daggers in the direction of the fleeing pony.

All anger at the horse was forgotten, though, when Ulvian pulled the golden box out of his ragged cloak. The gilt flashed in the failing daylight. Dru licked his thin lips expectantly as Ulvian set the box on the ground between his feet. The prince produced the only tool he had, a mason's trowel he'd picked up near Feldrin's tent. He poked and scraped at the box. The gilt covering was supple, like leather, but the hard dwarven iron of the trowel didn't even scratch it. A charmed box indeed. Ulvian examined the hinges, the hasp in front, and the seal that held the box closed.

"Well?" Dru demanded peevishly. "What are you waiting for? Open it!"

"I shall. There's no sense blundering into it, though." The sorcerer slapped his thigh in frustration.

Ulvian lifted the seal on its silken string. He guessed that Feldrin wouldn't rely on a flimsy wax seal alone to protect the black amulet. Hooking the tip of the trowel inside the loop of silk, he broke the seal. Dru inhaled sharply.

"Now," he breathed. "Open it!"

The prince set the box down. The hasp was loose. Very gently he inserted the tip of the trowel under the lid and, with a sudden jerk, flipped the lid up. Something moved with blinding speed toward his hand. Ulvian recoiled and drove the trowel like a knife into the yellow-green thing that had leapt at him.

Dru peered over his shoulder. "What is it?"

Skewered neatly on the tool was a large spider, with a red rectangle on its belly.

"A headstone spider," Dru said. His tone was admiring. "One bite means certain death. Old Feldrin wasn't such a fool after all."

The prince flung the dead spider aside. Inside the box was a folded piece of silver cloth. Though there was little light remaining, the silver material threw off scintillas of light. When Ulvian touched it, its surface rippled with iridescent colors. The lumpy shape of the onyx amulet was obvious beneath the supple material. Without removing the cloth, he surreptitiously pushed the cylinder out of the ring, separating the halves of the magic talisman.

"Give it to me," Dru ordered imperiously. "Why are you so slow? Give me my amulet!"

Ulvian's hazel eyes glittered like cold metal as he looked at the sorcerer. "And if I don't? Will you flay me like the tired pony?"

The sorcerer balled his fists and nudged Ulvian sharply with his knee. "Don't be a fool!" he thundered. "The whole point of our escaping was to get my amulet back! It's of no use to you. Give it to me!"

Ulvian stood abruptly and presented the point of the trowel to Dru's throat. Reddish blood, the poisonous blood of the headstone spider, covered the tool's sharp tip. Dru blanched and turned his head away.

"You seem to forget that I am a prince," Ulvian snapped.

Dru swallowed hard and forced a smile. It was the ghastly expression of a grinning skull. "My friend," he said, striving for a soothing tone, "be at ease. I was—I am—very nervous about getting my property back. Did I not save you from the stone block? Didn't my golem avenge the insults inflicted on you by Splint? We are free now, my prince, but vulnerable. Only my magic can protect us from the wrath of your father and the dwarf king."

The trowel was lowered a few inches. "I am not afraid of my father. I have no intention of hiding from him," Ulvian said slowly. "My only thought in aiding you was to escape those thugs in Pax Tharkas who seemed bent on murdering me. Now that we are free, I intend to make my way back to Qualinost."

"But, Highness," Dru objected, "How do you know your father won't simply return you to Pax Tharkas? Your supposed crimes are now compounded by mayhem, murder, and escape. I would not trust the Speaker's mercy. Better to return with me at your side, my prince, fully armed with all my black arts and ready to defend you!"

Ulvian bent over and lifted the wrapped amulet. Dru's eyes bulged. Color flooded his face, and his breath hissed out. Ulvian shook the silver cloth, and a single piece of onyx—the ring—fell out into Dru's hands. He put the cloth back in the box and closed the lid.

"What's this?" Dru all but shrieked. "The other—"

"I don't trust you enough to give it all to you. If you behave and do as I tell you, then I'll give you the other half. Maybe."

A scream of outrage welled up in the sorcerer's throat, but it died before it could escape his lips. Instead, Dru closed his fingers around the black stone ring, and his tight lips pulled back in a smile. "As you wish, Highness. I, Drulethen, am your servant."

The sorcerer told Ulvian that the onyx ring solved his transportation problem; he no longer needed a pony. The ring allowed its possessor to shape-change. Before Ulvian's wide eyes, Drulethen the elven sorcerer expanded like a water-filled bladder. His skin split, and feathers sprouted. His fingers curved into talons as his arms were transformed into wings. A ripping scream issued from his swollen throat, and a hooked yellow beak burst through Dru's face. The sorcerer's eyes, as gray as storm clouds, were slowly suffused with a yellow tint. The transformation was too horrible to watch. When next Ulvian looked, a giant falcon stood before him, preening his shiny, golden-brown feathers.

So warlike was the expression in the great bird's eyes,

Ulvian fell back a pace. Uncertainly he asked, "Dru? Can you speak?"

"*Har!* Yes!"

Ulvian put the golden box under his cloak and walked to his pony, which was straining against its tied reins. The sight of the six-foot-tall hawk was unnerving it. As the prince mounted, he said, "Where shall we go?"

"*Har!* My home. Black Stone Peak. *Har!*"

So saying, the giant falcon spread its wings and lifted into the air. It was completely dark, but Dru's eyes glowed yellow, allowing Ulvian to mark his position. Calling out his harsh cries, the transformed sorcerer circled overhead, guiding Ulvian along the narrow path. A few hours ride, Dru promised, and they would reach his stronghold, the ancient pinnacle known as Black Stone Peak.

\* \* \* \* \*

Twenty elven warriors, armed with lance and shield, formed ranks in the pass above Pax Tharkas with Kemian Ambrodel and Kith-Kanan at their head. Each warrior carried three days' worth of water and dried food, a thin blanket roll, and a clay cup. Kith-Kanan told his soldiers that the eyrie occupied by Drulethen was at the very highest ridge of the Kharolis, up a steep trail. The warriors would need to travel fast and light.

The peak of his conical helmet flashed in the clean mountain sunlight. No ceremonial headpiece, Kith-Kanan's helmet had served him all through the Kinslayer War and bore its hammered-out dents and broken rivets with pride. Mounted on his snow-white charger, the Speaker looked back over his small band of fighters, none of whom had served with him against the armies of Ergoth. He marveled at their youthful seriousness. When the young blades of Silvanesti had first gone to war against the humans, they had done so with singing and shouting and tales of valor ringing in their ears.

Every one of them imagined himself a hero in the making. But these warriors with their solemn faces—where did these pensive young elves come from?

He raised his hand and ordered Kemian to lead the warriors forward. Tamanier called out, "When will you return, Great Speaker?"

"If you do not see my face five days hence, summon all the Wildrunners," Kith-Kanan replied. "And find Verhanna. She must know, too."

Touching his heels to his horse's snowy sides, Kith-Kanan cantered to the head of the double column. The old castellan watched the riders go. The constant breeze sweeping down the pass fluttered the small pennants on their lance tips. Tamanier was afraid, but he couldn't decide whom he feared most—his own son, Prince Ulvian, or Kith-Kanan.

Leaning heavily on his staff, the castellan walked back to the camp. It was alive with the sound of saws and hammers, as the damage wrought by the golem was being speedily repaired.

\* \* \* \* \*

The head of the pass gave onto three paths. One was the way down to Pax Tharkas; the one to Kith-Kanan's left, north, was the route to Qualinost; and trickling off to the Speaker's right, southward, was a narrow goat path that led to the higher reaches of the Kharolis Mountains. It was that way they must go.

"Single file. Tell the warriors," Kith-Kanan said in quiet, clipped tones. It was strange how easily the old ways of war and campaign came back, even after a long time.

"Who shall ride point?" asked Kemian.

"I will." The young general would have protested, but Kith-Kanan forestalled him by adding, "Drulethen and my son have had no time to set traps. Speed is the essential thing now. We must catch them before they reach the sorcerer's stronghold."

Kemian turned his horse around to spread the word to the others. He asked in parting, "Where is it this Drulethen is going? A castle?"

"Not exactly. It's called Black Stone Peak. The mountaintop was once a nest of dragons, who hollowed out the spire and made a warren of caves through it. Drulethen, with the help of his dark masters, took over the empty peak and made it his stronghold. You see, many years ago, during the great war, Drulethen extracted tribute from the dwarves as well as from any caravan crossing the mountains. He used to fly out on a tame wyvern and carry off captives to his high retreat. It took a concentrated assault by the dwarves and the griffon corps to overcome him."

"It must have been an amazing battle, sire. Why have I not heard of it? Why is it not sung?" he asked.

Unaccountably Kith-Kanan's eyes avoided his. "It was not a proud fight," he said, "nor an honorable one. I will say no more about it."

Kemian saluted and rode off to give the troopers their orders. The warriors strung out in a long, single-file line. The path was so narrow the riders' boots scraped rock on both sides as they negotiated the passage. Their lances proved troublesome in the close quarters as well. They were constantly banging against the overhanging wall of rock, making quite a clatter and bringing a barrage of pebbles down on the riders' heads. This narrow trail persisted for some hours, until Kith-Kanan emerged from it onto a small plateau. Once hemmed in by rock, the warriors were now exposed. The plateau was turtle-backed, paved with large stones worn smooth by centuries of wind and the runoff of melting ice. The heavy cavalry horses stumbled on the rocks. Dru's and Ulvian's ponies were far better suited to this terrain.

A cloud passed between the sun and the valley below. They were so high up, the cloud sailed along below them. The elves admired the view, and Kith-Kanan allowed them to rest for a few minutes while he scouted ahead. Kemian turned his horse to follow the Speaker.

"Any sign, Majesty?" he asked.

"Some." Kith-Kanan pointed to where moss had been scuffed off some stones by the hooves of ponies. "They are nearly a half day ahead of us," he reported grimly.

Water bottles were tucked away, and the ride resumed. They crossed the plateau to a steeply climbing trail. Kith-Kanan spotted a glint of metal on the ground. He raised his hand to halt the troopers and dismounted. With his dagger tip, he fished the object out from a cleft in the rocks. It was the broken lock from Feldrin's golden casket. A cold pressure constricted the Speaker's heart.

"They have opened the box," he said to Kemian. Standing, Kith-Kanan held the broken lock in his gauntleted palm and studied the surrounding slopes. "Yet there's no sign of any magic being unleashed. Perhaps Drulethen does not possess the amulet yet. . . ." Perhaps his son was smarter than he reckoned, Kith-Kanan silently added. The only hope Ulvian had for survival was to keep the talisman from the sorcerer's hands. The Speaker could only pray that his son realized that. Of course, Drulethen might be in such a hurry to reach his stronghold that he simply hadn't used the power he possessed.

The Speaker remounted and dropped the broken lock into his saddlebag. "Pass the word: Be as silent as possible. And quicken the pace."

Kemian nodded, his blood racing. This was far more challenging than rounding up bands of scruffy slavers. The chill air seemed charged with danger. The general rode down the line, conferring with the warriors in a hushed voice. The young fighters tugged at harness straps and armor fittings, tightening everything.

Kith-Kanan remained in the lead. He shifted his sword handle forward for easier drawing. Alone among all the rest, he was armed with sword and small buckler, instead of lance and full shield. His charger took the slope easily, its powerful legs propelling horse and rider up the hill. The warriors followed, but it was a slow process going up so steep a grade in single file. The column strung out until a half-mile separated Kith-Kanan and the last rider.

A covey of black birds started up in front of Kith-Kanan's horse. The animal snorted and tried to rear, but the Speaker's strong hands on his reins brought him down. With soothing pats and almost inaudible words, Kith-Kanan calmed his nervous mount. The black birds circled overhead, twittering. Staring up at the ebony whirlwind, Kith-Kanan experienced a sudden flash of memory, of a time long ago when crows had watched him as he struggled to find his way through a deep and mysterious forest. They had led him to the boy, Mackeli, who in turn had brought him to Anaya.

A shout from behind snapped Kith-Kanan's head around. One of the warriors had seen something. He twisted his horse around in time to see the elf lower his lance and charge into a small passage Kith-Kanan had passed a hundred paces back down the trail. There was a fearful scream. The nearest warriors crowded into the passage. Kith-Kanan rode hard down the slope, shouting at them to clear the way.

Just before he reached the mouth of the side ravine, the warriors sprang apart, some losing their lances in the process. A dark brown form hurtled by, veered between the tall chargers, and bolted down the trail. Seconds later, a sheepish-looking warrior appeared, unharmed, from the narrow passage.

"Your Majesty," said the elf, scarlet to his ear tips. "Forgive me. It was a stray pony."

The warriors, keyed up for a fight or to face some unknown horror, began to chuckle. The chuckles grew into guffaws.

"Brave fellow!" "How big was the pony's sword?" "Did he kick you with his little hooves?" they gibed. Kith-Kanan called them down, and they rapidly fell silent. The Speaker glared at them.

"This is not a pleasure ride!" he snapped. "You are in the field, and the enemy could be near! Deport yourselves like warriors!"

He ordered the soldier who'd charged the pony to report exactly what had happened.

"Sire, I saw something large and dark move. I called out, and it didn't answer. When I challenged it again, it looked like it was trying to avoid being seen. So I couched my lance and went after it."

"You did correctly," Kith-Kanan replied. "You say it was a pony?"

"Yes, sire. Its mane was clipped short, and there was a brand on its left flank—a hammer and square."

"The royal brand of Thorbardin," Kemian observed. "The pony came from Pax Tharkas."

Kith-Kanan agreed. "It must be one of the stolen ones. Why is it free, I wonder?" he mused. It didn't make sense for two escaping prisoners to abandon one of their mounts. The animal must have gotten away by accident.

"Luck is with us!" he announced. "Our quarry has lost half its mobility. If we ride without pause, we should overtake them!"

The elves hurried to their mounts. Kith-Kanan scanned the sky. The sun was subsiding in the west, throwing long shadows across the western peaks. They moved on, traveling into the setting sun, which made seeing distant objects difficult. However, the lost pony was a good omen. Drulethen could hardly be in full possession of his powers if he let a small horse get away.

A leaden sensation hit Kith-Kanan's stomach like a hammer blow and his hands clenched the reins. Suppose the pony hadn't bolted. Suppose Dru simply didn't need it anymore. Because Ulvian wasn't with him. Because Ulvian was already dead.

Kith-Kanan's heart argued against it. The sorcerer had no reason to dispense with the prince yet. They had found no body, no sign of struggle, along the trail. Ulvian *must* be alive.

"Sire?"

Kith-Kanan turned to Kemian Ambrodel. "Yes?"

"The peak, sire. It's in sight!"

Kith-Kanan looked up. Glowering down at them from its towering height, Black Stone Peak rose above the surrounding mountains. Clouds clung to its lower slopes, but the spire itself was washed by the orange sunset. No details were visible at this distance; the peak was at least twenty miles away.

"Keep the warriors moving," Kith-Kanan said. The sight of the black pinnacle steeled his courage. For all their differences, there was a bond of blood between the Speaker and his son. If Ulvian had come to harm, Kith-Kanan would have sensed it. His son must still be alive. While he lived, there was hope. Separating him from the clutches of the sorcerer Drulethen, however, promised to be a difficult and dangerous task.

## ᦿ 14 ᦿ

### the Clash of Stars

Verhanna, Rufus, and Greenhands broke camp in early morning while heavy fog in the higher parts of the Kharolis still clung to the trail. It hampered their progress greatly. Fearing unseen crevices and crumbling paths, the trio crept slowly ahead, keeping their backs to the slope of Mount Vikris, the second highest peak in the mountain range. As the day wore on, the fog worsened, until the warrior maiden finally called a halt sometime in midafternoon.

"We'll walk into a ravine if we continue," Verhanna said, vexed. "It's better to wait out the fog."

"We don't get stuff like this in the Magnet Mountains," Rufus observed. "No, sir, we never get fog like this."

"I wish we weren't getting it here," was her waspish reply.

Greenhands passed his fingers through the drifting mist, closing them quickly as if snatching something. Bringing his hands to his face, he opened his fingers and studied them closely.

"What're you doing?" Verhanna asked.

"I cannot feel this gray thing around us, yet it dampens my hand," he said, puzzled. "How is that?"

"How should I know?"

As he turned his serene gaze on her, perhaps to respond to her rhetorical question, Verhanna stepped away from the steep wall of the mountain and peered upward into the murk. "I wish there was some wood about! We could go on if we could make torches."

There was no wood, so there was nothing to do but wait out the confounding mist. Patience had never been one of Verhanna's virtues, and she chafed at the delay. Greenhands perched on the ground, his back propped against a square boulder. Rufus took a nap.

Eventually the sky darkened and the air cooled. The fog fell as a heavy dew, soaking the travelers, their horses, and all their baggage. Rufus's hat sagged around his ears. Verhanna wiped futilely at her armor, muttering dire predictions about rust. Only the green-fingered elf remained unconcerned. His long hair hung in thick, damp strands, and water dripped from the hem of his poncho.

"Let's move," Verhanna said at last. "As I figure it, we're only a couple hours' ride from Pax Tharkas."

Once more Greenhands took the lead. He seemed to know where he was going, though he'd never been this way before. Verhanna and Rufus let their mounts pick their way several paces behind him. The violet dusk quickly changed to purple twilight. Solinari, the silver moon, rose above the mountains. The top of the pass was in sight, no more than twoscore paces ahead.

The warrior maiden jiggled her reins, urging her horse

to a faster walk. Greenhands was nearly to the top of the pass. His right foot came down on the ridge of rock and dirt that marked the highest point in the pass, and he abruptly stopped. Verhanna pulled up beside him.

"What is it?" she asked.

"Wait," he replied. "It's coming."

"What now?"

She looked up and down the pass, alert for stampedes or rampaging goblins or anything.

Greenhands' placid expression had changed to one of great excitement. His eyes danced as he pointed upward and said, "Look!"

The starry vault of the sky was crisscrossed by brilliant streaks of light. Dazzling fireballs began at one horizon, streamed upward to the zenith of heaven, and vanished in explosions of color. From every corner, to every corner, the sky was gridded with fiery trails that left ghostly glowing imprints on the watchers' eyes.

Rufus halted on Greenhands' other side. "Shooting stars," he breathed, awestruck.

The celestial pyrotechnics raged on, utterly silent and blindingly brilliant. At times, two streaming fireballs would collide, making a doubly bright burst. Tiny streaks and broad, cometlike meteors were born, chased each other, and died in every color of the rainbow. Red fireballs left yellow trails. Blue-white comets fell toward the ground, only to burst soundlessly overhead.

"What does it mean?" Rufus wondered, rubbing his neck, stiff from staring up so long.

"Who says it means anything?" replied Verhanna.

"Perhaps it's an omen, or a warning from the gods, my captain."

Greenhands smiled. "Do not always look for the worst, little friend. Perhaps this is simply the gods making merry. Maybe the gods need amusement, too. This might be a celebration, not a dire warning of doom."

No one disputed his words, but Verhanna and Rufus shared a vague feeling of apprehension. This seemed but one more of the inexplicable, and therefore frightening, phenomena that had afflicted their world lately.

"Well, I can see the lamps of Pax Tharkas from here," said Verhanna, "We'll be there soon, and you can hunt for your poppa all over the camp."

Greenhands pointed away from the site of the fortress. "No, this way," he said and set off on the steep southern trail.

Verhanna maneuvered her horse in front of him. "Look here," she fumed, "we've followed you across nowhere long enough. There's nothing up this way. If your father is anywhere in these mountains, Pax Tharkas is the place to look. Besides, we're low on food and water."

"He is near," said the green-fingered elf. Greenhands moved to go around the horse. Verhanna let her mount drift forward, cutting him off again. Finally the strange elf put his arms under the black charger's belly.

"Hey!" Verhanna said sharply. "What're you—?"

Greenhands planted his feet and lifted. Horse and rider together came off the ground. The animal remained strangely calm, though its feet dangled in midair. Verhanna remained quiet as well; she was dumbstruck. With a few grunts and only the slightest evidence of strain, the green-fingered elf raised the enormous load off the rocky ground, turned a half-circle, and set it down on the trail behind him.

"Yow! Do that again!" cried the kender. Greenhands was already on his way, climbing the path.

Stunned, Verhanna called for him to stop. When he didn't, she said, rather illogically, "Stop him, Rufus! Don't let him go that way!"

The kender gave her look of supreme disgust. "How do you reckon I'll stop him, my captain? Shall I tell him a funny story?"

Verhanna spurred her horse after the rapidly disappearing elf. She rattled up the sloping path, and out came her longsword. She had no desire to hurt him, but his confounding actions and sudden display of strength had shamed her. Raising her weapon, the warrior maiden intended to use the flat of the blade to stun Greenhands.

When she was only yards from the elf, there was a sudden glare of blinding light. For an instant, the mountainside was as bright as noon. Rufus yelled shrilly, and Verhanna felt searing heat on her neck and upraised sword arm. A roar filled her ears, a sizzling sound hissed nearby, and all was white light and throbbing pain.

Eventually cool darkness returned, and Verhanna found herself looking up into the unhappy face of Greenhands.

"Are you all right, my captain?" he said worriedly.

"Y-Yes. Ow!"

Her sword arm burned and ached. "What hit me?"

"Nothing hit you," said Rufus, his head showing over the kneeling elf's shoulder. "One of those fireballs blasted into the mountain just above your head. The strike flung you off your horse and did this."

He tossed the stump of her sword down beside her. Verhanna numbly grasped the handle. It was still hot to the touch, and the blade had been melted off, leaving only a misshapen nub of iron above the crossguard.

"Where's my horse?" she asked groggily.

Rufus shook his head sadly and glanced over his shoulder toward the precipitous drop down the side of the mountain. He quickly said, "You can have mine, though. It's too big for me. I feel like a pea on a boar's back."

They hoisted the stiff Verhanna to her feet and showed her the furrow plowed over the slope by the fireball. The steaming slash was melted at the edges. It was a mere foot or so above where her head had been.

Verhanna peered down the steep slope where her mount had perished. Shaking her head, she whispered sadly, "Poor Sable. You were a brave warrior." Greenhands was supporting her trembling body. When she stumbled over a stone, he steadied her effortlessly.

With a healthy boost from Greenhands, Verhanna was soon mounted on Rufus's chestnut horse. Their mobility was severely reduced by the loss of an animal, but the kender wasn't heavy and his horse carried the two of them easily.

"Do you know this trail?" the warrior maiden asked Rufus as they rode away from Pax Tharkas.

"No, my captain, though it seems to lead higher into the mountains." The kender scrutinized the stars through a screen of speeding meteors and announced they were headed south.

"Into Thorbardin," Verhanna mused. She cradled her sword arm, still numb from the shock of the fireball's near miss. For Greenhands' benefit, she said loudly, "Your father wasn't a dwarf, was he?"

Before the elf could reply, Rufus piped up, "Oh, that's impossible, my captain. He's much too good-looking—"

Verhanna jabbed the kender in the stomach with her elbow—her sore elbow. Drawing in her breath sharply, she cursed and groaned, "Shut up, Wart."

\* \* \* \* \*

Like one of the famed towers of Silvanost, Black Stone Peak stood out against the starry sky, tall, cold, and imperious. The darker openings on its face were entrances to its web of caves, first carved out of the hard black rock by wild dragons some two thousand years earlier. Ulvian halted his pony and stared up at the forbidding peak.

Dru had once more regained his human form. Now he pushed past the Qualinesti prince, eager to be home again.

"You'll have to dismount," said the sorcerer, his voice drifting back on the night air. "There's no true path into the caves, only some hand-cut steps."

Ulvian swung down and led the pony by the reins. The night was fiercely cold, and his worn clothes provided little protection. There was no wind around Black Stone Peak, unlike every other mountaintop Ulvian had ever visited. Here the air was still and pregnant with menace.

The trail ended, and the two started up an uneven set of steps chiseled from the living rock. The pony went along reluctantly, tugging at its halter as the steps became steeper and narrower. Ulvian warred with the frightened animal until the pony finally snatched the reins from his hand. It clattered over the steps and quickly fled down the steep, winding trail.

"It's no matter, my prince," Dru said genially. "There's no place for the beast to go."

Ulvian turned to continue his climb. In the darkness, he took a wrong step and slid off the rock stairway. His sudden gasp and the sound of scattering pebbles echoed loudly.

"We'll break our necks trying to climb this in the dark!" Ulvian declared.

Dru held out his left hand. As the sorcerer muttered some words in an unknown tongue, Ulvian saw that the ring of black onyx lying in his palm had begun to glow faintly orange, then cherry red. In seconds, a crimson aura had enveloped the sorcerer. The prince, his cuts and bruises forgotten, shrank back as Dru turned toward him.

The sorcerer smiled. "Don't be afraid, Highness. You wished for light, and I have provided it," he said smoothly. He climbed higher, approaching the vertical side of the peak. In the glow of the amulet, an oval opening came into sight. Dru ducked into the low cave, and Ulvian, rather reluctantly, followed behind.

The cave smelled old and dry, with a faint background aroma of decay the prince couldn't identify. A dragon's den should smell fetid, he knew, but this one had been vacant for two millennia. The floor was remarkably smooth and doubly difficult to walk on since it sloped seamlessly up to join the walls and ceiling.

As they moved through the passage, the bloody glow surrounding Dru now and again illuminated some object on the tunnel floor: a dead, desiccated bird, a broken clay lamp, some tatters of cloth.

The two moved hunchbacked for some distance. Suddenly Ulvian saw Dru straighten. In a pace or two, the prince had emerged from the low tunnel into a vast cavern hollowed out of the very center of the stone spire. The sorcerer kicked among some debris near the wall and found a torch. He muttered a word of magic over it, and the ancient timber burst into flame. Dru circled the great chamber, lighting other torches still held in iron wall brackets decorated with metal spikes. The smell of burning tarry pine filled the cold air.

When at last all the torches were lit, Dru tossed his into a firepit in the center of the room. Some debris and wood there crackled into flame.

Lighted, the chamber was hardly less fearful than when dark. Most of the furnishings were wrecked, destroyed when the sorcerer's stronghold fell to the dwarves and elves. Glancing upward, Ulvian could see a few stars through the smoke hole fifty feet above him.

A more gruesome sight met his gaze when he looked down again. Resting in niches around the circular wall were hundreds and hundreds of skulls—white, empty, dry skulls. Some belonged to animals: mountain bears, elk, lions. Others were more disturbing. The light, airy craniums of elves nestled beside the thicker, smaller skulls of dwarves. In fewer numbers were human heads, recognizable by their wide jaws and small eye sockets.

"Lovely decor," the prince said, sarcasm masking his nervousness.

Dru had righted a broken chair that could nonetheless bear his weight. "Oh, these are not my doing," he said with mock humility. "The original owners of the peak collected these little mementos, and I didn't have the heart to throw them away when I took possession." A smile parted his thin lips. "Besides, I think they lend a certain air to my humble domicile."

Ulvian shrugged and kicked through the shattered remains of Dru's former life. He threw a leg over a stove-in
barrel and sat. "Well, we're here," he said. "Now what?"

"Now you must give me the other half of my amulet."

The small golden box was hard and heavy inside Ulvian's cloak. "No," the prince replied. "I have no illusions
about how long I'll live once I do that."

"But, Your Highness, Feldrin will certainly send someone after us, perhaps even royal warriors of Thorbardin
and Qualinesti! I cannot possibly defend us with only a
half measure of my powers."

Half a hundred skulls leered over Dru's shoulders.
Here on his own ground, the ragged prisoner of Pax
Tharkas seemed to acquire new strength, greater self-
possession. "I didn't come here to withstand a siege. I am
bound for Qualinost," Ulvian declared. "As far as I'm
concerned, you've gotten all the reward you earned—
escape from Pax Tharkas and half your amulet."

Dru folded his hands, twining his fingers together. "It's
a long way to Qualinost, my prince. You have neither
horse, nor pony, nor royal griffon to take you there."

From the corner of one eye, Ulvian saw the pommel of
a sword lying on the floor, buried by torn parchment
and broken pottery. "Am I your prisoner?" he asked
coolly.

"I thought we were partners."

"A prince of the blood and a base-born sorcerer, partners? I think not, Master Drulethen. On the other hand,
if you wish to become my servant. . . ." Ulvian rubbed
his beard thoughtfully. The sword hilt was just beyond
easy reach.

"I would serve you gladly! But without my entire amulet, I am a poor spell-caster and not half the sorcerer I
could be for you, Highness."

As Dru finished speaking, Ulvian hurled himself at the
half-buried sword hilt. He skidded in the debris, and his
fingers closed over the rough, wire-wrapped handle. By

the time he'd rolled clumsily to his feet, Dru was gone.
The broken chair was still there, but the sorcerer had
vanished.

The prince whirled, searching wildly. Drulethen was
nowhere to be seen. Then his voice boomed out, echoing
in the vast circular hall. "You stupid half-breed! Do you
think you can get the better of me so easily? How disappointed your father must be, to have such a worthless,
stupid son. Will he weep, I wonder, when he learns of
your death?"

"Come out and face me!" Ulvian cried, his eyes flying
to and fro over the grisly trophies lining the wall.

"We could have worked together, you know," Dru
went on. "With your name and my power, we could
have forged a mighty empire. No one could have
stopped us—not the dwarves, nor the Speaker of the
Stars in Silvanost. But you had to be foolishly greedy.
You thought you could command Drulethen of Black
Stone Peak."

Ulvian stood by the firepit, turning constantly, keeping the sword always ready. It was an ancient dwarven
blade, short and thick and rather rusty, but still lethal.
The sorcerer's voice bounced off the walls.

"I am no one's tool!" the prince shouted. "Even my father will give way to me in time!"

Ten tunnel mouths opened into the central chamber
at floor level, and Ulvian could see nearly a dozen more
higher up. The prince didn't recognize the one he'd
emerged from with Dru. Sweat formed on his brow.

"I have only to wait," the sorcerer said silkily. "When
you fall asleep, the amulet will be mine."

"Liar! You can't touch the charmed box!"

"True enough, but I will have it, and I'll be rid of you.
Good night, my prince. Sleep well. I'll be waiting."

Then there was silence, except for the soft crackling of
the fire.

"Dru!" called Ulvian. No answer. "Drulethen! If you
don't come out, I'll pitch the box into a gorge so deep

you'll never find it!"

Still there was no response.

Furious and terrified, Ulvian strode to the nearest tunnel opening. As he stepped inside it, a wall of wind gushed forth, flinging him back into the circular chamber. It was impossible to resist the wind, as the slick, curving tunnel floor offered no purchase for his feet. Trash covering the floor whirled around him, and soon Ulvian was back by the firepit. The wind ceased abruptly.

The same thing happened when he tried two other tunnels. Dru wasn't going to allow him to escape with the box. Very well, resolved the prince silently. If he had to, he would smash the onyx cylinder himself rather than allow the sorcerer to possess it. The pommel of the dwarven sword was hard brass; it would do nicely as a hammer.

The torches blazed brightly in their wall sconces. Ulvian sank down by the soot-stained rim of the firepit, the sword held firmly in one hand and the golden box in the other. The cold of the mountain penetrated to his very bones. He huddled by the small fire burning in the firepit and tried to ward off sleep.

\* \* \* \* \*

Twenty warriors and their leaders crouched in a cold defile, screened on three sides by slabs of upright stone. Some watched the wild aerial display, mesmerized by the dash and clash of shooting stars. Others gripped their lance shafts tightly, feeling the strain of impending combat like a hollow ache in the pit of their bellies.

"I don't like this—this marvel," Kemian whispered. "Do you think it's the sorcerer's doing, Majesty?"

Kith-Kanan looked up at the dance of comets and shook his head. "That is beyond the power of any mortal to orchestrate," he said. "More likely, it's part of the other wonders we've seen." For no reason he could name, the Speaker felt a surge of elation as he watched the stars racing and crashing over their heads. It seemed almost a celebration of sorts. He turned his attention back to the dark pinnacle just ahead. Dru and Ulvian must be inside by now. Still, they couldn't simply storm in. There was no telling what might lie waiting for them.

Though the Speaker hadn't been part of the attacking force that originally captured Drulethen, General Parnigar had. Parnigar had reported that Drulethen's wyvern had slaughtered many good warriors who tried to fight it in the tight confines of the tunnels. At last, Parnigar and the noted dwarf hammer-fighter Thulden Forkbeard had gotten behind the monster and cut its head off.

"Here's what we will do," the Speaker whispered. The young warriors forgot the shooting stars and listened intently. "You will separate into five groups of four, and each group will enter a separate tunnel. They supposedly all converge on the center hall, but be careful! Be as silent as you can, and if you find Prince Ulvian, subdue him and bring him out."

"What if we find the sorcerer?" asked one of the warriors.

"Take him alive if you can, but if he resists, slay him." Twenty heads nodded in unison.

"Sire," Kemian said, "what about you and me?"

"We shall go in the main entrance," Kith-Kanan announced.

The warriors left their lances with their tethered horses and formed into their assault groups, daggers drawn. Kith-Kanan raised his hand, and the ones destined for the farthest cave opening started up the trail. A moment later, the second group set out, and when they had reached the base of Black Stone Peak, the Speaker and General Ambrodel drew their swords and started forward.

In the cold, still air, every sound was as clear as crystal—the click of spurs on stone, the squeak of armor joints flexing, the rush of each elf's breath. The peak loomed over Kith-Kanan. Memories tumbled through his head, brief flashes of his past like the flare of the exploding meteors overhead. The scene he'd created by baring a weapon in the Tower of the Stars in Silvanost. Scaling the Quinari Palace the night he left on his resulting exile. Arcuballis, his noble griffon, companion during his sojourn in the wilds. Sithas, his twin, whom he hadn't seen since the division of the elven nation. Flame-haired Hermathya. The vestiges of old shame still burned when he remembered how much he'd been tempted by her beauty, even though she was wife to his brother. His own wife, Suzine, who had perished in the war. Mackeli, his brother, if not by blood then by heart and soul. And as the black shadow of the peak covered him completely, Kith-Kanan recalled the face of Anaya, his first wife and greatest love, the dark Kagonesti woman he'd lost so long ago in the wild forest of Silvanesti.

The cave mouth was low, and both elves had to duck to enter. Kemian tried to go in ahead of his monarch, but Kith-Kanan gestured him back.

Compared to the brightly flashing display outside, the tunnel was velvet blackness. Kith-Kanan eased his feet along, sword point leading, as his eyes adjusted to the dark. The curving floor was like glass, and his iron-shod feet slid all too easily. Kemian lost his balance and fell backward, landing with a loud clang. Shamefaced, he rolled to his hands and knees and hissed, "Forgive me, Majesty!"

Kith-Kanan waved away his apology and asked, "Can you stand?"

The young general rose slowly. "Come," whispered the Speaker.

A yellow glimmer appeared far ahead. Kith-Kanan's breath froze on the chin guard of his helmet. The feeble light grew and picked out a thin coating of frost on the tunnel walls. No wonder it was so hard to walk! Kith-Kanan put out a hand to halt Kemian. The warrior stopped.

Carefully the Speaker replaced his sword in its scabbard. Tied to the upper hanger ring of the scabbard was a small leather bag, closed with a drawstring. Kith-Kanan removed the bag from its ring. It held powdered resin, which sword-armed warriors used to coat the grips of their weapons. During battle, blood and sweat conspired to make sword grips treacherous, so a generous layer of pine resin made a warrior's hold more secure.

Kemian watched, fascinated, as Kith-Kanan sprinkled resin on the soles of his metal-clad boots. The white powder clung to everything it touched. Kith-Kanan indicated that Kemian should imitate his action. The younger elf did so.

It was fortunate they applied the gum to their feet, for only a short way ahead, the tunnel floor sloped downward at such an angle that walking without the resin would have been impossible. By now, both elves could smell torches burning—and something else. They heard a low drone, not of conversation, but of a male voice singing.

The Speaker stopped short. He squatted, using his sword for balance. Far out in the center of the great chamber ahead, a lone figure huddled under a ragged brown cloak, rocking back and forth, humming.

"It's the prince!" Kemian breathed.

There was no sign of Drulethen, which worried Kith-Kanan greatly, though he was relieved to see his son alive. "Stay hidden, General. I will approach my son."

"No, sire!" Kemian caught the Speaker's arm. "It could be a ruse to draw you out!"

"He is my son." The Speaker's brown eyes bored into Kemian's blue ones. The general dropped his gaze and his restraining grip.

"The other warriors should be in position by now," Kith-Kanan said encouragingly.

He stepped down the passage, his sword still sheathed. Kemian braced his hands against the walls and waited in an agony of suspense, fearing something would spring out and attack the Speaker.

Kith-Kanan emerged into the chamber. The array of skulls, the detritus of Drulethen's former furnishings failed to distract him. In a moderate tone, he called out, "Ulvian?"

The prince's sagging head jerked up, and he swiveled his neck to face his father. Cuts and bruises marred his bearded face. Ulvian's eyes narrowed. "Oh, that's clever," he said, his words slurred and rather high-pitched. "Assuming the shape of my father, eh? Well, it won't work!"

He slashed at the air with an antique shortsword.

Kith-Kanan glanced at the other tunnel mouths. The dark circles were all empty. He saw no sign of his other warriors.

"Son, it's truly me. Where is Drulethen?"

Ulvian staggered to his feet. He needed two hands to keep the sword pointed at his father. "I won't give you the amulet," he snarled. "I won't!"

Kith-Kanan walked slowly forward, hands wide and devoid of weapons. "Ullie, this is your father. I've come to save you. I've come to take you home." He spoke soothingly, and the prince listened, his head hanging like a ponderous weight on his shoulders. The Speaker came within an arm's length of his son.

"You're not my father," croaked the exhausted Ulvian. Awkwardly he thrust at Kith-Kanan. The Speaker easily sidestepped the blow and grappled with his bleary son. Kemian and all the other warriors, still hidden in the tunnels, burst from the openings, believing their Speaker was in danger. No sooner had they shown themselves than a blast of wind roared down from the ceiling, flattening the warriors and sweeping them head over heels back into the tunnels. Their cries echoed from far up the passages. The wind ceased blowing, and Kith-Kanan and Ulvian were alone in the chamber. Almost.

"Well, well," said the voice of Dru. "The sovereign of

Qualinesti has come to see me. I'm flattered. I knew there would be pursuit, but I hardly dared imagine the Speaker of the Sun himself would seek me out."

"Show yourself, Drulethen," Kith-Kanan commanded. "Or do you prefer to hide like some eavesdropping servant?"

"Here I am!"

Kith-Kanan whirled awkwardly, supporting Ulvian in his arms. The sorcerer had appeared behind them, on the opposite side of the firepit. Drulethen now wore a crimson robe. A band of shining black silk flowed across his chest and over his shoulder, trailing on the floor behind him. A ruby pin glittered in the silk on the sorcerer's left breast, and his blond hair was shiningly clean and combed back from his forehead. All trace of the slave of Pax Tharkas called Dru was gone. He was Drulethen of Black Stone Peak once more.

"By your command, Great Speaker," he said mockingly. He wore the onyx ring portion of the amulet around his neck on a strand of braided black silk. He bore no obvious weapons.

"You will surrender now to the authority of the Speaker of the Sun and the Thalas-Enthia of Qualinesti," Kith-Kanan said. "Surrender or face the consequences."

Dru chuckled. "Surrender? To one elf and one halfbreed? I think not. Your troops are scattered, Speaker, and cannot enter this place unless I wish it. And you cannot compel me to do anything."

Never taking his eyes from the sorcerer, Kith-Kanan lowered Ulvian to the floor. The prince was unconscious from sheer exhaustion. The Speaker drew his own formidable blade.

"Swords don't frighten me! I have only to wish it, and I'll go where you'll never see me or find me. That will leave you and your worthless son to fall asleep or starve. In either case, you will be at my mercy."

The Speaker stared hard at Drulethen's face. He knew from experience that magical disappearance was an illusion, a misdirection of the watcher's attention. The sorcerer wasn't going to fool him easily.

"So why don't you go?" asked Kith-Kanan.

Drulethen stepped down from the hearth and circled around, coming closer. His scarlet raiment rustled softly. Kith-Kanan kept himself between the sorcerer and Ulvian. "I merely hoped that you could be reasonable," purred the Silvanesti. "Perhaps we can come to a mutually beneficial agreement."

Stall. Think, thought Kith-Kanan. Give Kemian a chance to do something. "Such as what?" the Speaker said.

"Inside your son's shirt is a small golden box. It holds the other half of my amulet, and I cannot get it myself. If you give me the rest of my amulet, I will swear to serve you for, say, fifty years."

"Serve me how? I do not traffic in black magic."

Drulethen smiled pleasantly. He looked sleek and well groomed in his new attire, not at all like the wretched prisoner who had hauled stones from the Kharolis quarries. "If it's definitions that bother you, then I'll stipulate that I shall perform only the whitest of magic, exactly as Your Majesty orders. Isn't that fair?"

Torchlight flashed off the ruby pinned to the black silk on Drulethen's chest. Kith-Kanan's eyes flickered to it and back to the sorcerer's face. What had the magician just said? Ah, yes. He remembered now. "So for fifty years' service to me, you get a lifetime of power for yourself," he said. "Assuming you even honor your oath to me. I don't think the world would thank me, Drulethen."

The sorcerer's gray eyes were flinty. "Then your answer is no?"

"It is no."

The ruby flashed fire again. This time Kith-Kanan's attention strayed too long, and Drulethen suddenly wasn't there. The Speaker crouched, ready for an attack, then cut through the air with his sword. From above came thin, eerie laughter.

"Father and son are so alike!" chortled Drulethen. "I shall leave you to a common fate. Farewell, son of Sithel! I only wish my wyvern were here. He did so enjoy eating the flesh of highborn Silvanesti—" The laughter took a long time to fade away.

Kith-Kanan knelt and found the hard lump that was Feldrin's box inside Ulvian's clothing. The prince never stirred.

Circling the room, the Speaker searched for a way out. No wind rushed in at him unless he got within a pace of an opening. Lying just inside the tunnels were daggers and helmets dropped by his lancers.

An idea came to him. Cupping his hands to his mouth, Kith-Kanan shouted, "Hello! Kemian Ambrodel, can you hear me?"

Nothing. He moved to the next tunnel, always standing back to avoid triggering the magic wind. "Hello, this is the Speaker! Can you hear me?" he cried. After trying six holes, he finally received a reply.

"Yes, we hear you," came the faint answer. It was one of his warriors. Soon the Speaker heard Kemian's shout.

"Get all the rope you have," Kith-Kanan ordered. "Tie it together, then tie one end to a large rock. Roll it into the tunnel. It should follow the downslope to me, then I'll be able to use the rope to climb out against the wind!"

"Understood!"

"It won't work," said Dru's bland voice. "No rope in the world can withstand the Breath of Hiddukel."

Kith-Kanan planted his fists on his hips and said sarcastically, "You don't mind if we try, though, do you?"

He returned to his sleeping son and gathered him in his arms. He lay Ulvian's slack form near the entrance to the tunnel where he'd heard his warriors. As he did so, Kith-Kanan recalled Drulethen's reference to Hiddukel. That must be the evil sorcerer's patron deity. Weeks ago, when Hiddukel had appeared to him in the Tower of the Sun, he'd given his name as Dru. Had the god been hint-ing at the part his infamous disciple would play in the lives of the Qualinesti?

"There's no way out for you." Dru's voice was sharp. "Give me my amulet, and I'll spare your life."

"My life? A while ago you offered to be my slave for fifty years."

The sorcerer said no more. Kith-Kanan drew a tattered piece of tapestry over his son and sat down to wait. His nerves were singing with tension, but he knew that if the warriors took too long, fatigue would surely set in.

And nothing would stand between Drulethen and his black amulet.

# ✑ 15 ✑

## the fertile seed

"**ARE YOU SURE THIS IS THE WAY?**"

Rufus Wrinklecap's high voice split the cold night air. He, Verhanna, and Greenhands were following the steep, south-leading pathway up into the mountains. Verhanna had convinced Greenhands to let the kender take the lead to scout the narrow path for them. After some grumbling about having to walk instead of ride, Rufus complied. He quickly grew excited as he detected signs that others had passed along the trail very recently.

"Who were they?" asked Verhanna.

"Qualinesti, on shod horses," the kender replied. He sniffed the scant hoofprints, barely indented in the stony soil. "Warriors. At least twenty of them."

She scoffed, "How can you tell they were warriors?"

Rufus stuck his small nose in the air. "I can smell their iron, my captain."

Verhanna pondered the significance of the warriors' presence. They surely weren't hunting runaways from Pax Tharkas; Feldrin Feldspar had dwarven brigades to do such work. Intrigued, she moved on, following the kender.

Greenhands had barely spoken at all since they'd begun to climb. Not even the continued panorama of fiery comets overhead broke his profound silence.

At last they reached a small level patch on the upward slope, and Verhanna called a pause for rest.

Rufus dropped where he stood, worn out by his nose-to-the-ground scouting. Greenhands remained upright, his eyes fastened on the slope before them. Now he started off again. Verhanna, chewing on a piece of venison jerky, called him back.

"My father is near," he replied, glancing back at her. "I must go."

Wearily the warrior maiden dropped her half-eaten snack in her saddlebag. "Come on, Wart. His Majesty is going."

"What's the hurry?" complained the kender. Verhanna offered him a hand, and he swung onto the saddle pillion. "Where are we going? That's all I want to know—and what's the hurry?"

"Don't ask me," Verhanna said, clucking her tongue to urge the tired horse forward. "But I tell you this, Wart: If we don't find something significant by sunrise, I'm turning back, and to Darkness with Greenhands!"

The trail made several sharp turns and climbed at an even greater rate, so that they lost sight of Greenhands, who was keeping some paces ahead of them. Verhanna and Rufus passed a deeply shadowed defile on their left, and the horse halted on its own. It danced and snorted, tossing its head and refusing to go on, no matter how Verhanna coaxed or used her spurs.

The sky went dark.

The sudden cessation of the darting stars was startling and left the landscape much blacker than before. No moons shone; only the glimmer of starlight illuminated their way.

Rufus tugged at Verhanna's elbow. "The horse is calm now," he said. "Let's go."

"No, wait. Don't you feel it?"

Her voice was a whisper, and Verhanna sat stiff and still in the saddle.

"Feel what?" the kender asked impatiently.

"Like a storm is about to break. . . ."

Rufus replied tartly that he felt nothing, and Verhanna touched her heels to the horse's flanks. They went on. Around a turn, the sharp spire that was Black Stone Peak jutted into view, blotting out an area of stars.

"I feel cold," said Rufus, wiggling closer to Verhanna's back.

"I hear voices!" she hissed, and urged the horse to a brisker pace. Up the final stretch of trail, kender and warrior maiden rode hard. They burst onto a scene of frantic activity. A score of white faces turned to her, and she recognized them as fellow Guards of the Sun.

Kemian Ambrodel appeared out of the night. "Lady Verhanna!" he exclaimed. "This is amazing! How come you to be here?" He offered a gauntleted hand to her.

She shook his hand and said frankly, "My lord, I'm no less shocked to see you. My scout and I were led here by an extraordinary fellow, a tall, flaxen-haired elf we call Greenhands. He must've passed you only moments ago."

"He is here. I put him aside, as we are too busy to deal with newcomers at present." Kemian lifted his chin to indicate a boulder a few paces away. On it was seated the green-fingered elf. His attention was not directed at the warriors or Verhanna, but at Black Stone Peak.

Verhanna dismounted, and Rufus hopped to the ground behind her. "What's going on here?" piped the kender.

The warriors were tying hank after hank of rope together. Most of it was in short lengths, used to tether horses on a picket line at night.

"Your father is in there," Kemian said gravely, sweeping a hand toward the black spire of rock behind them. Quickly the young general sketched the situation.

"Will two extra pairs of hands help, my lord?" she asked.

Kemian grasped her shoulder. "More than help, lady."

Verhanna and Rufus began tying what line they had to the end of the warriors' supply. While thus engaged, they didn't notice Greenhands slide off the boulder and walk straight up the ramp toward the caves in the spire. Rufus glimpsed him and shouted, "Hey!"

"Stop!" Kemian commanded. Greenhands was almost at the mouth of one of the cave openings. At any second, the awful wind would rise and sweep him back. It might also scatter their hard-won loops of rope. "Stop at once, I say!" bellowed Lord Ambrodel.

Greenhands spared a brief look at the elves and kender, then stepped into the opening. Kemian Ambrodel clenched his jaw, his body tensing in anticipation.

No wind boiled forth. The night was quiet and cold, and not a breath of breeze stirred.

Kemian gaped. "Who is this elf? A sorcerer?"

"A very strange fellow," Rufus said. He struggled with the rope he was tying. It was thick and stiff. "He's got all kinds of power, but he never works a spell."

Lord Ambrodel looked to Verhanna. "Wart's right," she agreed. "If anybody can reach my father, this Greenhands can."

"We can't risk the Speaker's life on some vagabond's tricks. Get the rope ready!" barked Kemian.

The warriors gathered up the rope and hastened to the main tunnel mouth. Rufus had wrapped the tough rope around his small hands, the better to wrestle with a last knot, and he was dragged all the way to the base of the peak.

*  *  *  *  *

Kith-Kanan tapped the flat of his sword blade against the palm of his hand. Dru had made no sound or appearance in an hour or more, and the torches around the great circular room were burning out one by one. Half were gone when he heard the distant ring of shouting outside. He called up the tunnel in reply, but all was silence once more. The Speaker didn't want to make too much noise for fear of encouraging Dru to think he despaired of his situation.

Ulvian lay completely immobile at Kith-Kanan's feet. Father regarded son with mixed feelings. It was Ulvian's willfulness and pride that had brought them here. He had not only dealt in slaves, but also had fled the Speaker's justice and helped an evil sorcerer to escape. Yet Kith-Kanan's expression softened as he watched him sleep, curled up on the floor like a harmless child. This was his son, the baby boy he and Suzine had rejoiced in. He might be fully grown, but his heart was as a child's— a boy who adored his mother and seldom saw his father.

Tiredly Kith-Kanan rubbed his temples and tried not to dwell on what might have been.

"You are not alone."

Kith-Kanan whirled. A quarter of the way around the room, a solitary elf stood. It wasn't Dru. This elf was tall, fair-haired, young. He wore a rough horsehair poncho and leather trews. His gaze on Kith-Kanan was intense.

"Who are you?" demanded the Speaker, stepping over Ulvian. "Is this another of your guises, Drulethen?"

The stranger didn't respond. Instead, he continued to regard Kith-Kanan with an unsettling stare. His face bore such a look of rapt joy that the Speaker was momentarily distracted from his own worry. With a shake, as if coming to himself suddenly, Kith-Kanan lifted his sword point a bit higher and demanded, "Answer me!

Who are you?"

"I am Greenhands. At least, that's what my captain calls me."

"Green—" Kith-Kanan's eyes traveled downward, noticing the colored fingers for the first time. The room was growing dimmer as more of the torches flickered and died, but the grassy hue of the elf's hands was plainly visible.

"How did you get in here? Why didn't the wind blow you out?" asked the Speaker sharply.

"I simply walked in. I have been looking for you for a long time." The stranger moved a few paces closer, and a smile lightened his face. "You are my father."

Kith-Kanan was taken aback. His first reaction to this astonishing statement was puzzlement. If this was some trick of the sorcerer's, what was its purpose? Perhaps this elf was some feeble-minded innocent, a dupe of Drulethen's.

Again Greenhands moved nearer to the one for whom he had searched. Kith-Kanan's shifting thoughts were stilled as he looked into the strange elf's eyes. They were brilliantly, shiningly green, brighter than the clearest emeralds. His face seemed familiar somehow—the full-lipped mouth, the high forehead, the shape of his nose. It reminded the Speaker of— Kith Kanan rocked back on his heels, stunned by the thought that had exploded across his mind. Anaya! The tall elf reminded him of Anaya. The features, the eyes, were identical, even his green-tinged skin. Anaya's skin had changed just so when she had begun her transformation into a mighty oak. Lowering his sword, he moved forward to meet Greenhands halfway, near the now cold firepit. Their height was identical.

"Hello, Father," Greenhands said happily.

Kith-Kanan couldn't believe what he saw. It seemed impossible, yet he only had to look at this young elf to see his amazing resemblance to Anaya, to know that he spoke the truth. Somehow, by some miracle, his and

Anaya's son had come here, to Black Stone Peak.

The Speaker's voice was uncertain, so strong were the emotions that gripped him. "Your coming was foretold to me centuries ago," he whispered. "Only I did not understand then." He lifted a shaking hand to touch Greenhands' face. The elf smiled broadly, and Kith-Kanan enveloped him in a warm embrace. "My son!"

The happy moment was brief. Danger remained all around them. Kith-Kanan wiped away the tears that dampened his cheek and held Greenhands out at arm's length.

There was a rush of air overhead, a beating of unseen wings. Alarmed, Kith-Kanan stood back and raised his sword. Only a quarter of the torches in the room still burned, and in the half-light he saw a winged thing circle and dip in and out of the fitful light.

"Son, do you carry a weapon?" he asked, swiftly donning his helmet.

Greenhands held out empty arms. "No, Father."

The Speaker kicked among the debris on the floor. The winged creature swooped near him, and he slashed hard at it, missing. The beast soared away, and Kith-Kanan squatted long enough to pick up a stout piece of wood, a leg broken from a dining table.

"Take this," he said, tossing it to Greenhands. "If anything comes at you, hit it!"

An eerie laugh floated through the chamber. Kith-Kanan glanced at Ulvian. The prince was still unconscious. Overhead, the laugh sounded again.

"A fine weapon for a fine-looking warrior," said Drulethen. His voice caromed off the stone walls, making it difficult to determine where he was. "A worthy addition to the House of Silvanos!"

"Indeed he is," Kith-Kanan retorted. "He got in past your spells, didn't he?"

"How do you know I didn't let him in intentionally? I'm collecting royal Qualinesti!" he snarled nastily.

With hand gestures, Kith-Kanan indicated that

Greenhands should go around the other side of the chamber, away from him. The elf complied with commendable stealth. Kith-Kanan edged away from the unconscious Ulvian and talked to distract Drulethen.

"Well, great sorcerer, what do you intend to do with us?" he called out.

"My amulet. One of you is going to give me the other half of my amulet if I have to torture each of you in turn to convince you to do so." The sorcerer's voice had fixed in one place. Kith-Kanan peered at an upright, though broken, chair. A tall shadow had appeared there. He lowered his sword so the blade wouldn't gleam in the remaining torchlight.

"You cannot win, Drulethen. Ulvian might have helped you, but I will see to it you never have the amulet," he vowed. He stepped gingerly over some smashed crates, moving as silently as possible.

"Ulvian! That idle, untrustworthy wretch? He'll be the first to go, mark my words. I shall enjoy his torment."

Kith-Kanan's left shoulder bumped the wall. He was under one of the burned-out torches, and he slipped it from its bracket and sidled over to the next one, which still barely burned. He lit the stump and rushed toward the broken chair. As he did, the light from his brand fell upon Dru.

The Speaker froze in midstride, horrified. The thing perched on the chair was not an elf, nor was it a bird. It had golden-brown wings with red-tipped feathers, but instead of falcon's claws, two white elven hands gripped the back of the chair. Instead of a falcon's noble head, the thing was topped by a horrid mix, part elven, part bird. Dru's face and head bore feathers where hair had been. His eyes were large and black, like a falcon's, but set in elven eye sockets surmounted by feathery brows. Most hideous of all, instead of a nose, a large horny beak protruded from Dru's face.

"You see," hissed the sorcerer, "how much I need the rest of my amulet. The ring is the more powerful half, but it lacks refinement and control." He shuddered and hunched his head down between his shoulders. The awful face seemed to reflect a spasm of pain. "I find I can't control my transformations without the cylinder." The bizarre white fingers flexed over the broken chair's thick arm. "This is the last time I shall ask—give it to me!"

In reply, Kith-Kanan hurled the torch at the monster and lunged with his sword. Dru launched himself into the air, overturning the chair. He avoided Kith-Kanan's attack, but he didn't see Greenhands standing close by in the shadows, motionless. As he passed by, Greenhands swung his crude club. His strength was considerable, but his skill was not, and the blow was only a glancing one. Nevertheless, Dru was sent spinning, to land in a flurry of loose feathers on the other side of the chamber, near Ulvian. "Get him! Don't let him get up!" the Speaker cried.

He outran Greenhands to the fallen sorcerer, and he prodded the strange creature with his sword tip, ordering him to stand and surrender. The pile of feathers writhed and shifted, and a piercing shriek rose up from them. Greenhands arrived, and before their astonished eyes, the sorcerer changed shape once more.

The body of the bird lengthened, and the wings shriveled into feather-covered arms. Dru pushed himself onto his back and cried out again in agony. The beak on his white face and his black falcon's eyes remained the same. Feathers covered the rest of his body.

"Stand up!" Kith-Kanan ordered again.

"I—I cannot," the sorcerer wheezed. Sweat ran down his grotesque face in rivulets, and his body shook as if palsied. "I am—undone."

Just then Ulvian groaned and shifted on the stone floor. He moved to push himself up, inadvertently distracting Kith-Kanan. In a flash, the supposedly exhausted sorcerer had tripped Kith-Kanan. The Speaker went down hard. Before anyone could draw another breath, Drulethen's fingers locked around the Speaker's throat.

The sorcerer stood, dragging Kith-Kanan to his feet.

Blood roared in the Speaker's ears. The fantastic figure of the sorcerer was lost as Kith-Kanan's vision was suffused with a red haze. He tore at the hands that were throttling him, but Dru's grip was like iron.

"I know you have it!" he shrieked, shaking the Speaker violently. "Give me my amulet!"

Just as Kith-Kanan was losing consciousness, there was a crash and a scream. He felt himself falling, falling, until the hard floor met his back. He rolled aside, gasping, and let his vision clear. When he tried to grab for his sword, just out of easy reach, a wave of dizziness brought him down.

Greenhands was grappling with Dru. The sorcerer wasn't as strong as the Speaker's son, but he was infinitely more cunning. Twisting his body and breaking Greenhands' grip, Drulethen managed to wrest the table leg club from him. The thick pine flashed down and snapped across Greenhands' shoulders. He went reeling. Shouting with triumph, Dru picked up the Speaker's sword, put its tip to Kith-Kanan's throat, and felt in his clothing until he located the other half of the amulet. Kith-Kanan had secreted it beneath the breastplate of his armor.

"Ah!" Dru said, taking the black cylinder in his hand. "At last!"

"What's happening?" Ulvian asked, pulling himself up to a sitting position. His short sleep had left him confused.

Dru had moved away. Kith-Kanan crept on hands and knees to his son. "Drulethen," he managed to gasp.

"Father," said Greenhands, moving stiffly to join them, "the evil one is changing again."

Kith-Kanan staggered to his feet, retrieved his sword, and turned to face Drulethen. The sorcerer was across the room. He'd fitted the cylinder into the onyx ring he wore around his neck, and now the complete amulet dangled against his chest. His face was slowly swelling and turning purple; his feather-covered limbs were growing longer and more muscular. A slow laugh escaped his twisted lips.

"What a bargain," he rumbled from deep in his throat. "A thousand years of power for a thousand years of servitude. That's the deal I made with Hiddukel." A loud snapping and cracking sounded. Dru clapped his hands to his head and howled with pain. "Now that I have my amulet whole again, the world shall tremble at my name!"

Hard, pointed plates erupted through the skin of Dru's back. The feathers on his body dropped away as a thick tail, covered with scales, grew visibly before the elves' astonished eyes. The sorcerer's elven form grew and grew, hardening and thickening, until a winged, scaly monster filled the cavern deep inside Black Stone Peak.

Ulvian dragged himself close to his father. "By the gods," he gasped, "he's become a dragon!"

"No . . . a wyvern," Kith-Kanan said. "Just like the one he rode before, terrorizing the countryside."

The wyvern reared up twenty feet tall, green-black and glistening. Its catlike eyes were a poisonous yellow, and from its fanged jaws flicked a blood-red tongue. Horns sprouted from its head. For a moment, it looked wonderingly at its own ivory-clawed forepaws, then its wicked gaze returned to the three grouped beyond the center firepit.

"We must get out of here," Ulvian wheezed.

"If we can. The wind spell may not let us," answered his father. Kith-Kanan flexed both hands around the handle of his sword. He had little hope of getting close enough to kill the wyvern before it mauled him to death. He glanced at his newest son. "Greenhands can get out, though," he said.

Ulvian looked at the unknown, white-haired elf before him. There was no time for questions or answers, as the wyvern opened its hooked, leathery beak and hissed a challenge.

"Spread out and try the tunnels!" Kith-Kanan ordered.

The prince started for the nearest passage. His limbs felt strangely leaden. To his surprise, no blast of air came out of the passage to bar his way. He ducked his head and disappeared into the tunnel.

"Go!" Kith-Kanan urged Greenhands. "Save yourself!"

"I will stay and help you," he resolved. "I am strong."

The wyvern rushed the Speaker. Kith-Kanan backpedaled, slashing his sword back and forth to ward off the monster. From the side, Greenhands pried loose a paving stone in the floor and hurled it with all his might. The monster roared and hissed like a hundred boiling kettles as its left wing went limp. Its tail lashed out and swept Greenhands off his feet. The spearlike tail tip thrust at him, but the elf caught it in his hands and flung it back.

Kith-Kanan's sword scored a bloody line down the monster's torso. The wyvern returned its attention to the Speaker of the Sun. An iron-hard claw caught him in the chest, driving all the wind from him. Had he not been wearing armor, every bone in his chest would have been crushed. Kith-Kanan hurtled back. The wyvern's claw came down, but the Speaker drove his sword straight through the monster's paw, pushing and pushing until black blood flooded down the blade. The wyvern bellowed in pain and snatched its claw back, taking the Speaker's sword with it.

Kith-Kanan shouted at Greenhands that now was the time to flee. Then he himself backed into one of the tunnels. The monster was shaking its injured claw, finally dislodging the sword from it. As the Speaker disappeared into the tunnel, the wyvern snaked its neck down and thrust it into the opening. Kith-Kanan retreated out of reach.

The wyvern turned on Greenhands, the only remaining target. The green-fingered elf was markedly unafraid, and he dodged nimbly about the chamber, throwing enormous pieces of stone at the monster. From the tunnel, Kith-Kanan shouted over and over for him to abandon the room, to make his escape.

Greenhands fought on. The power that had made him and given him great strength had also bestowed upon him lightning-fast reflexes and an instinctive knowledge of how to hurt the beast. After one near miss by the wyvern's snapping beak, Greenhands found himself flat against the curving wall. A torch bracket was by his ear, and he reached up and snapped the black iron holder off the wall. The holder was ringed with iron spikes. With sufficient force, the points could pierce the wyvern's skull.

Kith-Kanan saw his newfound son leap at the monster. The wyvern's tail slashed around, destroying the last few burning torches in the room. Darkness seized the scene, though Kith-Kanan could still hear the sounds of the struggle. Now and then the iron bracket held by Greenhands would scrape on stone, and a fount of red sparks flared.

The wyvern howled—in pain or victory? Kith-Kanan couldn't tell. He had taken a step back toward the room when the smell and sound of the monster filled the end of the passage. It hissed at him and began to force its way in. Only its yellow eyes, each as big as the Speaker's head, shone in the darkness.

\* \* \* \* \*

"Try it again! Come on, put your backs into it!"

Verhanna, Rufus, and the warriors braced themselves against the back of a giant boulder, which they had managed to lever out of the mountainside. The scavenged rope was webbed about the rock, and now they were trying to roll it into the cave opening through which Kemian had heard the Speaker's voice. The boulder refused to budge more than an inch at a time.

"Weaklings!" Verhanna stormed, fear for her father manifesting itself in fury. And fear for Greenhands, to whom she owed her life. "You aren't true Guards of the Sun! The Speaker is in danger!"

Kemian snapped, "We know that! Do you think—?"

"Shh! Hear that?" Rufus said, interrupting Lord Ambrodel.

Strange sounds filtered out from the tunnel opening into the early morning air. They sounded like footsteps. Someone was coming out. The sun was a sliver on the eastern horizon, brightening the scene. Verhanna pushed forward to peer inside.

A slim figure staggered into view.

"Ulvian!" she exclaimed.

"Help!" he gasped. Two elves rushed forward to aid him. They supported him to the boulder and gently let him down. "Dru—he's become a wyvern! He's got both parts of the amulet!"

"Where's the Speaker?" demanded Kemian.

Ulvian closed his eyes and let his head sag against the rock. "Isn't he here?"

"No," Verhanna spat. "Neither is Greenhands!"

Kemian prodded the prince. "You left the Speaker to face a full-grown wyvern?"

"He told me to leave!"

The warriors and kender stared down at him. His face was still bruised from his beatings at the hands of the grunt gang, but his limbs were whole. Somewhere in the rear of the band, the word "coward" found voice.

Verhanna turned to Kemian. "The wind spell must be broken. We don't need the boulder and rope anymore. Let's go!"

"Wait. We can't just rush in. We must plan our attack!"

Kemian paused, then added more calmly, "Half will go in, the other half will stay and watch for the Speaker or Greenhands to emerge."

All except Ulvian volunteered to be in the contingent

that went inside. In the end, Kemian made the choices. The attacking party included himself and Verhanna, who made it plain she was going in whether or not he chose her. She ordered Rufus to remain outside.

"But why? I haven't ever seen a wyvern before," he complained.

"Because I said so, that's why. And I pay you." She glanced at Ulvian, who sat leaning against the boulder, eyes closed. "You can guard Prince Ulvian," she said contemptuously. "He's an escaped prisoner, after all."

Chagrined, the kender watched half the warriors file into the yawning cave. He shifted from one foot to the other, looking from the tunnel mouth to the remaining elves. They were as anxious as he to be part of the fight, but they stayed where they were, tense and expectant.

When the last elf entered the tunnel, Rufus could stand it no longer. He sprinted to an adjacent opening— and promptly collided with Kith-Kanan. "Your Mightiness!" burst out the kender. "We thought you were monster food!"

"Not yet, my friend. The beast is about twenty paces behind me."

"Yow!"

The kender darted around the Speaker to get a better look. The morning sun sent a roseate beam down the shaft, lighting the crawling monster's head and serpentine neck. Its mouth opened and a shrieking hiss reverberated down the passage.

"So that's a wyvern," Rufus said matter-of-factly.

"You'll get a much closer view if you don't get out of the way," Kith-Kanan stated. Kender and elf moved quickly away.

Kith-Kanan saw Ulvian scrambling to his feet by the rope-bound boulder. He also spied the unhappy warriors Kemian had left behind.

"Warriors! Get your weapons! The wyvern is coming!"

The ten elves ran to their horses and mounted, taking

their lances from the conical pile they'd been arranged in. The wyvern's head snaked out of the cavern opening. It saw Kith-Kanan and hissed in outrage.

"Go in and fetch Lord Ambrodel," Kith-Kanan ordered the kender. Rufus saluted and dashed inside a tunnel.

A warrior brought Kith-Kanan a horse and lance. The tired, battered Speaker climbed into the saddle and couched his lance. The monster's forelegs were free of the passage and it was wriggling the rest of its body out. The disk of the sun cleared the eastern mountains. The sky was bright blue.

The lancers charged the monster in ragged formation before it could get its wings, legs, and tail free. The first warriors scored hits on the wyvern's exposed chest, but it snapped its beak over their lance shafts and tossed the elves aside like dolls. One was thrown over the edge of the plateau, to vanish in the deep gorge below. A second was hurled against Black Stone Peak and slid to the ground dead, his neck broken.

"For Qualinesti!" Kith-Kanan shouted, charging forward.

Pushing with its powerful hind legs, the monster freed its wings. One of the leathery flying limbs hung limp, injured by Greenhands in the chamber; the other swept to and fro, upsetting horses and blinding riders. Kith-Kanan buried his lance in the wyvern's neck but was knocked from his horse. Two warriors shielded him from the enraged beast. The wyvern snatched the closest in both foreclaws and shook him as a terrier worries a rat, then hurled his lifeless body to the ground. The other warrior succeeded in driving his lance through the monster's uninjured wing. The elf let go of the weapon, turned his horse in a fast circle, and offered a hand to the fallen Speaker. Sore but spry, Kith-Kanan mounted behind the warrior.

The wyvern bled from half a dozen wounds and both its wings were damaged, but its strength hardly seemed diminished by the time it worked its legs free. The warriors drew off a short way on the lower plateau in order to form ranks and charge again. Kith-Kanan took the horse of a fallen fighter.

"Try to get behind it," he told the elves. "I'll try to distract it." The warriors settled into tight ranks. "Now!"

They galloped at the beast, then split into two columns and surrounded the wyvern. It lashed out from side to side with its barbed tail, slaying elf and horse alike. The great beast suffered more wounds, but no one came close to piercing its heart. Kith-Kanan dueled furiously with its beaked head, slashing with his sword at the ugly, snapping mouth. At one point, the wyvern caught the crest of his helmet. Kith-Kanan frantically tore at the strap buckle, releasing it before the wyvern could tear his head off.

"Fall back!" he shouted. "Fall back!"

Four warriors were able to comply. The other six were either dead or seriously wounded.

The monster let out a howl and stamped its feet. It flung the bodies of fallen warriors at Kith-Kanan and the survivors, a hideous gesture of contempt. Panting, sweating in the chill mountain air, the warriors clustered around their Speaker.

"We must kill it!" Kith-Kanan said grimly. "Otherwise its wings will heal, and it will be able to fly away."

A sharp whistle caught the Speaker's ear. He looked up at the peak, toward the source of the sound, and saw Rufus Wrinklecap, Verhanna, and some of the warriors who had entered the cave. They were standing in several higher tunnel mouths, forty feet above the Speaker.

Verhanna raised a hand, and the warriors in the caves began to shower the beast with stones and debris from inside the peak. The wyvern hissed loudly and leapt at them. Even with numerous lance wounds, it was able to jump three-quarters of the distance to the caves. On the third such leap, the monster dug its four clawed feet into the rocks and clung there. With its injured wings tightly furled against its body, the wyvern started to climb.

Kith-Kanan's heart leapt when he spied Greenhands at one of the cave openings. His son lived, praise the gods! In his hands, he held a loop of rope. All the others in the high caves had weapons of some kind, but not Greenhands. What was he up to?

The Speaker and the remaining elves on horseback sat ready, lances couched. Slowly the beast clawed its way up the peak, its talons leaving gray streaks on the black rock. Loose stones and pieces of Drulethen's furniture thudded off its head and body from above. Thick, horny eyelids blinked shut every time an object hurtled at the wyvern's eyes. Sword in hand, Kemian appeared in the tunnel mouth next to Greenhands.

"The monster will cut them to pieces in those tunnels," said one of the mounted warriors. "Shouldn't we go in and help them?"

"Stand your ground," Kith-Kanan said sternly. "Lord Ambrodel knows what he's doing." In fact, the Speaker was extremely worried, but he had to trust his general's judgment.

Greenhands leaned far out of the cave opening, the loop of rope in his hand. The wyvern was only a few feet below, its attention on those hurling debris at it. The others suddenly ceased their attacks and withdrew deeper into their caves. Hissing and howling, the wyvern raised its head to see what they were doing—and Greenhands dropped the loop of rope over its head, like a herder roping a wild bull. He and Kemian leaned hard on the rope, and it pulled taut around the monster's neck. The wyvern flung its head from side to side, trying to break the line. When that failed, it snapped its jaws in a vain attempt to catch the rope in them.

The beast decided to continue on in the direction it was being pulled. Greenhands and Kemian disappeared inside the tunnel just as the wyvern reached their level. The long, green-black neck snaked into the cave. All at once, the wyvern's four legs were scrabbling furiously on the peak and at the tunnel mouth, trying to find purchase. Its hideous shrieking cry echoed through the mountains. The massive muscles in its back arched as it tried to pull its head out of the tunnel. Kith-Kanan's breath caught when he saw blood washing out of the cave.

The violent scratching of the monster's limbs continued for a moment, and then it fell. The enormous beast hit the ground, and the impact shook the earth all around. Its legs continued to thrash and claw at nothing, and Kith-Kanan saw why. The wyvern had left its head inside Black Stone Peak.

They kept away from the raging, headless corpse until its dark blood had all leaked out. Its legs continued to twitch slightly. Kith-Kanan rode forward and drove his lance through the monster's heart. That put an end once and for all to the wyvern, and it lay unmoving.

Verhanna emerged with Rufus and the other warriors. Kith-Kanan asked, "Where's Greenhands? And Lord Ambrodel?"

"Here!" came the shout from above. Kith-Kanan looked up. Greenhands stood at the high cave entrance. He was covered with blood and held the head of the wyvern in both hands. As everyone watched, he hurled the head to the ground.

When Greenhands came out of Black Stone Peak, he moved slowly, carrying Lord Ambrodel in his arms. Two warriors came and relieved him of his burden.

"What happened?" asked Kith-Kanan, rushing to his son's side.

"The creature smashed him against the wall," Greenhands replied softly. "He has something broken. . . ." The green-fingered elf's legs folded beneath him, and he would have dropped to the ground but for his father's quick arms.

Verhanna ran to them. "He breathes," she reported anxiously. "I think he just passed out."

"No wonder," observed Rufus. "After seeing Lord Kemian cut that monster's head off!"

The young general coughed and lifted a feeble hand. "No," he said in a scratchy voice. "I didn't kill the monster. He did."

\* \* \* \* \*

The wounded were cared for, and the dead were placed on a funeral pyre. Six young elf warriors had died in the fight, and Lord Ambrodel's life was hanging in the balance. Rufus bathed Greenhands with a bucket of water and found that, for all the black blood on him, he hadn't any wounds at all.

The wyvern's body was too heavy to move, so they piled what tinder they could find against it where it lay. The broken furniture from inside the peak proved useful, as did the lamp oil. Soon the beast was in the center of a roaring bonfire. As the sun passed its zenith, coils of oily black smoke darkened the sky, spreading an evil smell over the high mountains.

That deed done, the warriors dropped into an exhausted slumber. Kith-Kanan drew Ulvian and Verhanna a little away from the group.

"I have some news for you," he began, feeling a little uncertain how to go on.

Ulvian tensed. Verhanna glanced at him and then back at the Speaker. "What is it, Father?" she asked, her face serious.

Kith-Kanan looked toward Greenhands, who'd been sleeping since his battle with the wyvern. A feeling of tenderness warmed the Speaker's heart. Anaya's son. This elf was his and Anaya's son.

"I suppose there's no other way to say it than simply to say it," he said briskly. "Ullie, Hanna . . . Greenhands is my son."

Verhanna's jaw dropped in shock, but Ulvian's face remained as still as stone. Only the brightness of his hazel eyes betrayed his surprise.

"He's your *what?*" Verhanna exploded. Kith-Kanan passed a weary hand across his brow. "You deserve the whole story. I know you do. Just now, though, I am weary to the bone," their father sighed. "Greenhands is the son of my first wife, a Kagonesti. I think the marvels of these last days were signs of his coming." He put a gentle hand on Verhanna's arm and was surprised to feel her trembling. "I know it's a shock, Hanna. It was to me, too. I'll explain everything later, I promise. It's been an eventful day."

With a fond pat on her cheek, the Speaker moved back among the sleeping warriors. He lay down near Greenhands, and in no time he was gently snoring.

Verhanna was astonished. Her brother! Greenhands was her brother! All at once, the absurdity of the situation struck her. After not thinking of marriage for centuries, now she chose a mate who turned out to be her own brother! The warrior maiden vented her spleen on a handy boulder, kicking the rock with all her might. All she succeeded in doing was making her foot sore. She simply couldn't think about this right now. She was worn out from battle and from all the worrying she'd done on behalf of her father and Green—her half-brother. Gods, it was too unbelievable!

The warrior woman stalked back to camp. At the edge of the sleeping mob, near the unconscious Kemian Ambrodel, she dropped down and slept.

Ulvian had also been surprised by his father's announcement. This unknown bumpkin, a son of Kith-Kanan? It was a startling bit of news. But the prince had too many worries of his own to waste much effort wondering how he had come to acquire a half-brother. He, too, lay down to sleep, but sleep was longer in coming. His mind was filled with thoughts of what his immediate future might hold. Some hours later, Prince Ulvian awoke with a start.

"Who is it?" he said. "Who's calling?"

He glanced around. The sun was low in the western

sky, and its orange rays showed him the kender nearby. Rufus was curled into a ball, fast asleep, giving vent to his unique, high-pitched snores. The rest of the group also slumbered on. Just above them floated smoke from the funeral pyres, like a cloud of remembered evil. Ulvian grimaced at the smell and wondered how they had all managed to sleep in such a vile place.

Once more the prince heard the voice. It was soft and low, a feminine voice, he thought. It seemed to be coming from the direction of the largest fire, at the base of the peak. Ulvian rose and walked in that direction. Heat shimmered off the bed of coals. The voice, a faint whisper barely louder than the hiss of the dying flames, spoke to him.

A stack of charred wood collapsed, sending sparks up into the cold, twilight sky. Ulvian listened to the voice and answered. "How can I reach you? The fire is still hot."

The voice told him. The words entered his head like smoke wafting into his nose. The words were caressing, the tone melodic and resonant. His tired, aching limbs seemed imbued with strength. Belief flooded his mind. He could do it. The voice said so, and it was true.

Looking into the charred remains ahead, from where the voice seemed to emanate, Ulvian strode into the cinders. His bare feet pressed down on glowing coals, yet he did not cry out. So great was his desire to find the source of the silver-toned voice that he no longer took notice of where he walked. In the center of the pyre, he found it. Thrusting his hand into the ashes and charred bones of the wyvern, the prince found the onyx amulet. Heat had fused the two pieces together. Now they could never be taken apart.

The voice spoke again, and Ulvian nodded. Though the amulet was still hot, he put it into his pocket and walked out of the fire. In minutes, he had fallen asleep once more. Though smeared with soot, neither his hand nor his feet were burned.

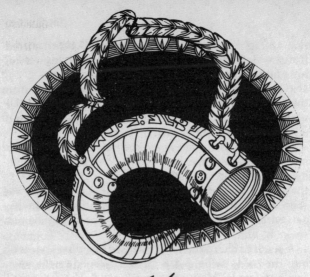

# ᥲ 16 ᥳ

## four-Legged Cousins

Verhanna stirred from her slumber. Opening her eyes, she saw Greenhands sitting cross-legged on the ground a few feet away. The morning sun was in her eyes, and she lifted a hand to shade them. Greenhands was looking across the broad vista of mountain peaks.

It took the Qualinesti princess a moment to recall the events of the past days. The cold funeral pyres remained as mute evidence of what had transpired. She also recalled the news she had received regarding the white-haired elf before her. Her half-brother.

He turned to her, and she quickly looked away, embarrassed that he'd noticed her scrutiny.

"Hello, my captain," he said equably. "You have slept

long—a night, a day, and a second night." Wind stirred his long hair. His green eyes were darker somehow, more muted than their usual vivid hue.

"By Astra!" Verhanna got to her feet and hurried to Rufus. She poked him in the back with the toe of her boot. The kender screwed up his wizened face and groaned.

"Go 'way, Auntie! I wanna sleep," he grumbled.

"On your feet, Wart!"

Rufus's blue eyes popped open.

The warrior maiden and kender circled through the scattered sleepers, waking them. Kith-Kanan sat up, coughing and shaking his head. "Merciful gods," he muttered. "I'm too old to sleep on bare ground." Verhanna grasped Kith-Kanan's arm and helped him stand. He was very stiff from having slept in the open. "Is there anything to eat?" he asked. "I'm hollow."

Rufus approached Kemian cautiously. The general had been seriously injured by the wyvern, and the kender feared that he'd find him dead. But Kemian drew breath steadily. His brow was cool and dry, and after Rufus awakened him, his eyes were clear.

"Water," he said hoarsely. Rufus put a wicker-wrapped bottle to the elf's lips.

Gradually the whole party arose. They stood around, a bit dazed, taking in their situation.

Kith-Kanan saw Greenhands, still seated serenely on the ground. He stood when Kith-Kanan approached him. The Speaker held out a hand. His son looked at it uncomprehendingly, and Kith-Kanan showed him how to shake hands.

"My son," he said proudly. "You did well."

Greenhands' brow wrinkled in thought. "I only wanted to save you," he replied. "I did not mean to kill."

"Shed no tears for Drulethen, Son! His heart was as black as the onyx talisman he prized. He chose his path, and he chose his destruction. Be at peace. You have done a noble deed."

The elf didn't look convinced. In fact, he had a look of such sadness that Kith-Kanan put an arm around his shoulder and asked him what troubled him so.

"Before I found you, I often felt the presence of my mother," he replied. "She would guide me and help me. I have sat here a long time, reaching out to her, but she does not answer. I do not feel her near any longer."

"She must know that you're with me now. You're not alone," Kith-Kanan said gently. "When your mother . . . left me, it took me a long time to get used to not having her by my side. But we are together now, and there are many things I need to know about you and how you came to be here."

A disturbance erupted on the other side of the plateau. Kith-Kanan left his newfound son and hastened to the point of trouble. All the warriors were clustered in a group. They parted for the Speaker. In the center of the knot, he found Ulvian being restrained by two warriors. Verhanna and her kender scout faced them.

"What is this?" asked Kith-Kanan.

"My loving sister seeks to deny me a horse," Ulvian said, straining against his captors. "And these ruffians have laid hands on me!"

"There are twenty people, and only twelve horses," Verhanna snapped at him. "You're still a convict, and by Astra, you'll walk!"

"Release him," Kith-Kanan said. The elves let go of Ulvian. A smug sneer appeared on the prince's face, but his father erased it by adding, "You will walk, Ullie."

The prince's face turned red under his dirty blond beard. "Do you think I can walk all the way to Qualinost?" he exploded.

"You're going back to Pax Tharkas!" Verhanna put in.

"No," said the Speaker. The single quiet syllable silenced both siblings. "The prince will accompany us home to Qualinost."

"But, Father—!"

"That's enough, Hanna." She flushed at this mild rebuke. "Has anyone seen to Lord Ambrodel?"

"He's doing okay, Your Worship," interposed Rufus. "But with those busted ribs, he can't ride." The kender suggested they make a stretcher from whatever they could find inside the cave. The stretcher could be dragged behind a horse.

Kith-Kanan gave orders for this to be done. Two warriors went in search of poles and cloth while the others collected their scattered gear and loaded for home.

The Speaker and his daughter went to see Kemian. The general was white-faced with pain, but he saluted gamely when his sovereign arrived. Kith-Kanan knelt beside him.

"The kender says you'll be all right," he said encouragingly. "Though he's not a healer, he does seem to have some knowledge of these things. How do you feel, my lord?"

Through clenched lips, Kemian replied, "I am well, sire."

"Do you feel well enough to tell me what happened in the cave? How did you get hurt, and how did Greenhands manage to kill the wyvern?"

The injured elf coughed and almost fell back in pain. Verhanna got behind him to bolster him up. Kemian gave her a grateful glance over his shoulder, then launched into his account of the death of the sorcerer Drulethen.

"The green-fingered one reasoned that, with his strength, he could rope the beast and pull its head inside, where I would chop it off with my sword. I got the rope we'd gathered for you, Speaker, and tied off the end to a wall bracket in the great chamber. The warriors and the kender teased the monster into attacking, and Greenhands caught him in his snare." He paused to draw a ragged breath.

"We pulled the monster in, even though it fought hard against us," Kemian continued. "I've never seen so strong an elf, sire. Greenhands hauled in that wyvern as if it

were a river trout. I stepped forward to finish the job
with my sword, but—" he passed a hand over his
chest—"the monster pinned me against the wall with its
head. It meant to crush the life out of me and was doing
just that when Greenhands took the sword from my
hand and chopped the beast's head off. Two strokes was
all it took, I swear. Then I swooned from pain."

Verhanna took up the water bottle Rufus had left and
wet Kemian's lips. "Thank you, lady," he whispered.
"You're very kind."

"That's not something I hear very often," she replied
tartly.

Kemian coughed. Agony contorted his face. "Sire," he
gasped, "is he really your son?"

"Yes. He is the child of my first wife, whom I lost
many, many years ago."

Kemian grasped Kith-Kanan's hand. "Then you have
a fine son, Majesty. With guidance, he would make a
fine Speaker of the Sun."

It was the same thought that had just occurred to the
Speaker. By common law of primogeniture, the eldest
son was to inherit a monarch's crown. Even though Ulvian was born first, Greenhands had been conceived
several centuries earlier. It was a legal and ethical riddle
to try the brains of the wisest thinkers in Qualinost.

Verhanna interrupted his thoughts. "Father, I agree
with the general. Greenhands is brave and good and has
powers beyond what you have already seen." She re-
counted the experiences she and Rufus had had with
Greenhands—his control of the herd of elk, her healing,
their meeting with the centaurs—

The centaurs! She jumped to her feet, letting go of Kemian so quickly he slid sideways to the ground. He
moaned, but Verhanna was already stepping over him
and bawling for Greenhands. He and Rufus were standing at the edge of the ashes, all that was left of the
wyvern's pyre.

"I'm calling you!" she said, planting her hands on her

hips. "Why don't you answer?"

Rufus pointed to the object of their rapt attention. Half-buried in the cinders was the scorched skull of the monster. All the flesh had been burned away, and the horny yellow beak had turned a sickly gray from the heat.

"We was thinking that would make a great trophy," Rufus said.

"And on what pack mule were you planning to put that thing?" she asked pointedly. The skull was four feet long.

"I can carry it," Greenhands said softly, and Rufus beamed at him.

"Leave it. It's just carrion." Verhanna took hold of Greenhands' arm, pulling him away from the ashes. "Do you still have the horn that centaur gave you?"

"It's there." He indicated the rocks where their gear had been placed before the fight.

"Use it," she said. "Summon the centaurs."

"Why, my captain?" Rufus scratched his freckled cheek.

"We need mounts, don't we? Centaurs have four legs, don't they? If they're agreeable, we'll ride them right into Qualinost!" She grinned. "What an entrance we'll make!"

Rufus grinned back at her. So taken was he with her idea that he ran to the rocks and fetched back the ram's horn.

He inhaled deeply. Fastening his lips on the horn tip, the kender blew till his red face turned purple. A horrible wail escaped from the open end of the horn. Everyone on the plateau stopped what he was doing and put his hands over his ears.

"Enough!" said Verhanna, snatching the horn from Rufus's lips. He staggered away, winded from his effort.

She handed the ram's horn to Greenhands. He raised it high and blew.

A deep, steady tone issued from the horn. The unwavering bass note bounced against the mountains and echoed back like a phantom reply.

"Again," Verhanna demanded.

The second note took wing before the first had died. The two sounds chased each other all through the Kharolis and back again. Greenhands lowered the horn, and the two calls finally faded away into the distance. Everyone waited, but nothing happened. There was no answering sound.

Verhanna was disappointed, but before she could order Greenhands to sound the horn again, Kith-Kanan came up to them. "Son," he said quickly, "Hanna said you were able to heal a goblin bite she received. Do you think you could do as much for Lord Ambrodel?"

"If you wish it, Father" was Greenhands' reply.

They went to the general, and Greenhands sat down on the ground beside him. Kemian watched him expectantly, a fevered gleam in his gray-blue eyes.

Greenhands touched his fingertips lightly to each side of the warrior's head, cocking his own as if listening to something. "You must take off the metal he wears," Greenhands murmured, pulling his hands back. "It blocks the power."

"What power?" demanded Ulvian, who had joined them. Verhanna punched him in the arm to silence him.

Rufus deftly untied the armor that Kemian still wore and tugged it free. He removed every bit of metal the general had, even snipping the copper buttons from his haqueton. Those buttons found their way somehow into the kender's pockets.

"Now it begins," Greenhands said. He placed his hands flat against Kemian's ribs. After a few moments, it became obvious the breathing of the two elves was synchronous. Kemian's was short and ragged because of his injury; Greenhands also breathed in small gasps. The green-fingered elf slowly closed his eyes. Kemian's eyelids fluttered down also.

Their breathing came faster. All the color drained

from Greenhands' face, and beads of shiny sweat broke out on his brow. At the same time, a flush of red blood came to Lord Ambrodel's face. His body went limp, his head lolling to one side. The green-fingered elf stiffened abruptly, his back and neck rigid. Now his breath came in harsh, loud gasps for air.

Verhanna cared greatly for Greenhands and hated to see him in pain. Her guilt was compounded by knowing that he had suffered for her also, when he'd saved her from the festering goblin bite.

Kemian cried out. His shout was echoed by Greenhands. The sound rose in intensity and was suddenly cut off. Greenhands' head hung down. His hands slid off the now sleeping general. He wrapped them around his own chest and moaned. Kith-Kanan and Verhanna gently lowered him to the ground.

"Rest easy," Kith-Kanan said, smoothing Greenhands' sweat-soaked hair from his brow. "Rest easy, Son. You've done it. You've healed Kemian." The general's chest rose and fell in deep, untroubled breaths.

It was early afternoon by the time the party was ready to go. Kemian and Greenhands had slept for several hours. Lord Ambrodel awoke fully recovered, and his healer had only some soreness and stiffness remaining. No centaurs had come to aid them, so they set out with ten riding and ten walking. Two horses were used for baggage only. Verhanna mounted up with Kemian and eight warriors. In spite of her protests, her father had chosen to walk, along with Greenhands and Ulvian.

"But you're the Speaker!" she protested.

"An even better reason to go on foot. My subjects should always know that I am willing to do without so that they may live better. Besides, down here I can talk with my sons."

Verhanna looked at Greenhands and Ulvian, who walked on each side of their father. Neither of them had spoken to the other. In fact, Ulvian seemed to be assiduously avoiding his newly revealed half-brother. With a last shake of her head, Verhanna reined about and galloped to the head of the little column, taking her place by General Ambrodel's side.

"How long is the journey to your city, Father?" asked Greenhands.

"On foot, we'll be many days walking," said the Speaker. "We'll have to pass through Pax Tharkas on the way."

Ulvian reacted violently to this. He halted in his tracks and stared hard at Kith-Kanan, who continued walking along with the rest of the group. The others on foot passed the prince, until he was standing alone on the narrow mountain trail, the rest of the party well ahead of him.

Kith-Kanan called out, "Coming, Ullie?"

He wanted to shout back, "No!" but there was no wisdom in resisting. His sister would merely insist he be restrained. His father had said he would be allowed to return to Qualinost with the rest of the group. All the prince could do was hope that was true.

* * * * *

They made good time that day, reaching the wider road in the lower elevations by midafternoon. Kith-Kanan halted them there for a rest and food. Cooking fires were lit under the flawless blue vault of sky. The Speaker commented on the fine weather.

"Strange," he mused, "the Kharolis in summer is usually beset by daily thunderstorms."

"Perhaps the gods are showing their favor," Kemian suggested.

Verhanna and her father exchanged a private look. "Some happy influence is at work," Kith-Kanan agreed. The Speaker believed that the shooting stars and this fine weather were all signs that the gods were pleased by the fact that, after four centuries, he and Greenhands had come together.

Rufus had dropped off the rump of Verhanna's horse when the column stopped and promptly disappeared into the rocks on the high side of the road. The group was busy, though, and no one paid any attention.

The soup was just beginning to boil when the drumming of hooves echoed down the road. The warriors, true to their training, dropped their pots and cups and grabbed their weapons. Kith-Kanan, more curious than alarmed, walked to the end of the road and looked up and down the mountainside, trying to see who was coming. Dust rose from the trail. He heard a high, broken yelp.

"Hi-yi-yi!"

Around the curve in the road appeared Rufus Wrinklecap, clinging to the back of a brown-skinned centaur. More wild horse-people followed, and they barreled up the road straight at Kith-Kanan. The warriors shouted for the Speaker to withdraw to safety, but Kith-Kanan stood his ground.

The lead centaur, carrying the kender, came to a stop just inches from the Speaker.

"Hail, Your Worthiness!" declared Rufus. "This is my friend, Uncle Koth, and these are his cousins!"

Kith-Kanan placed his right palm over his breast. "Greetings, Uncle Koth, and all your family. I am Kith-Kanan, Speaker of the Sun."

"Most happy to see you, cousin Speaker." The centaur's dark eyes, round like a human's, flitted quickly from side to side. "Where would be our friend, he of the green fingers?"

Kith-Kanan beckoned Greenhands forward. The centaur embraced him with both brawny arms.

"Little cousin! We heard you call, and have run hard all day to find you!"

"You were a day's ride away, and you heard him blow the horn?" asked Verhanna, amazed.

"Indeed so, sister cousin. Is that not why I gave it to him?"

Koth beamed, showing his uneven, yellow teeth. "We found the littlest cousin down the road, eating jackberries. He explained the boon you desire from us and led us back here."

Verhanna raised an eyebrow at her kender scout. "Jackberries, eh?"

Rufus gave her an ingratiating smile. "Well, there were only a few—"

"This is excellent," Kith-Kanan said. "Are you willing to carry us all the way to Qualinost?"

Koth scratched behind one ear. The stiff brown hair that fringed it grated loudly on his callused fingers. "Well, cousin Speaker, where might this Kaal-nos be?"

Kith-Kanan said, "By horse, it's an eight-day ride from here."

"Horse!"

Koth snorted, and the band of centaurs at his back laughed loudly. "The sun and moons all know no horse can run like the *Kothlolo*," he boasted. "If it pleases you, cousin Speaker, we will have you in your Kaal-nos in six days."

This claim set the warriors buzzing with speculation. Kith-Kanan held up a hand for quiet. "Uncle Koth, if you can put me in my capital in six days, I will give you a reward such as no centaur ever dreamed of."

The centaur's eyes narrowed with thought. "Reward is good. I'll think on it, cousin, and so should you. When we get to Kaalnos, I'll find out if you think as big as Koth!"

There were only eight centaurs. Since it was claimed that ordinary horses would not be able to keep up, only the Speaker and his close party rode them. The rest of the warriors were told to proceed on horseback to Pax Tharkas, where relief and refreshment would be given them.

"Are we bypassing the fortress, Father?" asked Verhanna.

"If the centaurs can get us back to the city in six days,

there's no reason to detour to Pax Tharkas," he replied. Verhanna looked at Ulvian and frowned but said no more.

There was much rough laughter and nervousness as the party climbed on the centaurs. Kith-Kanan rode Koth. Without saddles or stirrups or reins, the riders were worried about maintaining their balance as they rode. Rufus supplied the answer. His mount was a dapple-gray lady centaur who wore a buckskin halter over her small breasts. The kender took the wide sash belt from his formerly fine suit of clothes and tied it loosely around her human waist. This gave him something to cling to from behind, and it didn't impede the centaur's movements. In fact, she stroked the dirty yellow belt fondly, admiring its silky smoothness. The rest of the party quickly copied the kender's invention with whatever belts or braces they owned, and they were soon set.

"Ready, cousins?" boomed Koth. Together the centaurs chorused their assent. "You have a firm hold, cousin Speaker?"

Kith-Kanan shifted his seat slightly. "I'm ready," he said, gripping the leather baldric he'd converted to a centaur harness. Koth gave a wild, wavering yell and galloped down the road at breakneck speed. The rest of the centaur band thundered after him.

The Speaker had ridden some strange creatures in his life. His royal griffon, Arcuballis, had possessed breathtaking strength in flight and had once performed a complete loop in the air, but this! The riders' weight didn't seem to hinder the centaurs much; they bounded over low obstacles and careened around large ones with absolute abandon.

Kith-Kanan was above yelling from fright or excitement, but his followers were not so restrained. Verhanna, whose long legs nearly scraped the ground when astride her short-legged centaur, yelped involuntarily at every wild bump and turn. Rufus whooped and shouted from the back of his lady centaur and waved his big hat. Kemian tried to emulate the Speaker's dignity, but an occasional startled shout escaped his lips from time to time. Ulvian was tight-lipped, his thoughts on distant things. Only Greenhands seemed to take the ride with perfect equanimity. Despite the pounding pace, he held on with one relaxed hand and studied the scenery with total attention.

The landscape swept past at an astonishing rate. As surefooted as goats, the centaurs raced near the sheer drop that bounded the mountain road. Kith-Kanan gradually relaxed his death grip on the baldric and sat more erect.

"How long can you maintain such a pace?" he said loudly in Koth's ear.

"I shall be winded in a few hours," shouted the centaur. "Of course, I am old. My young cousins can run longer than I!"

Kith-Kanan cast a glance back over his shoulder. His children and friends bounced and yelped on the centaurs' backs. Red topknot streaming in the wind, Rufus flipped him a salute. Verhanna gave her father an uncertain smile as she glanced at the cliff's edge almost below her feet. Greenhands waved casually.

The wind sang in Kith-Kanan's ears, and the day was fair and warm. He would soon be home in his beloved city, arriving on the back of a wild centaur. Throwing back his head, the Speaker of the Sun laughed out loud. His merriment echoed through the hills against a rhythm of centaurs' hooves.

\* \* \* \* \*

By twilight, after half a day of constant motion—they even ate on the run—the centaurs were on the lower slopes of the eastern Kharolis, with the wide plain spread out at their feet. Kith-Kanan remarked on the abundance of flowers and the tall green grass, none of which had been present when he and his party passed through a week before.

"The flowers bloomed for Greenhands," Rufus said. He bit a wild apple, then offered the rest of the fruit to his mount. She reached back with one sun-browned arm and deftly took the fruit.

Kith-Kanan looked over Koth's human shoulder at the field of blooming flowers. He remembered a time long ago when he and his young friend Mackeli had journeyed to Silvanost through a land bursting with life. Pollen and flower petals had filled the sun-washed air, and everywhere there was a vibrancy above and beyond the usual growth of spring. It had happened because his wife Anaya had metamorphosed into an oak tree—she had joined the power that she served so faithfully. The ancient power had showed its rejoicing in an explosion of fertility. Now Greenhands' passage through the countryside was provoking the same reaction. It was one more bit of confirmation that Greenhands was indeed his and Anaya's child. Not that he needed much convincing. He saw his beloved every time he looked into his son's innocent green eyes and smiling face.

"Majesty? Majesty?"

Kith-Kanan snapped back to the present. "Yes?"

Rufus had guided his mount next to the Speaker's. "Your Mightiness, the others want to know if we can stop and stretch our legs."

The Speaker rubbed his numb thighs. "Yes, an excellent idea. Stop, uncle, if you please."

The centaurs drew up, and their riders stiffly dismounted. With many groans, they stretched their sore muscles. Kith-Kanan went to speak quietly with Greenhands. From the corner of his eye, he saw Ulvian stalking down the slope toward the plain, deeply shadowed now that the sun had set.

"Shall I fetch him back?" Verhanna asked, hand on her sword hilt.

"No. He won't get far." Kith-Kanan sighed. His delight

in the fine day and his new son were tinged with worry for the problems of his other son. "Your people can catch up to him, can't they, uncle?"

A wide grin split the centaur's face. "No doubt, cousin Speaker!" Koth declared. "No two-legs can outrun the *Kothlolo!*"

They delayed a while longer, then everyone mounted up and Kith-Kanan pointed the way to distant Qualinost.

## 🍃 17 🍃

# a home never seen

Ulvian kicked his way through the waist-high weeds, batting heavy-headed flowers aside in clouds of yellow pollen. It was easy to see which way his father's mind was turning. Kith-Kanan was so solicitous of this new-comer, this upstart who claimed to be his son. Not once had he asked after Ulvian's health, asked how he had fared with the scum of Pax Tharkas. All his attention was for Greenhands. And the power this elf wielded! He'd defeated a wyvern, healed Lord Ambrodel, called a band of centaurs.

The prince didn't care whether Greenhands was truly his brother or not. All Ulvian was concerned about was making sure he received what he considered to be rightfully his—the throne of Qualinesti. The prince could see where this was leading—it was out with Ulvian, in with Greenhands. No wonder his father hadn't insisted he return to Pax Tharkas. With Greenhands in the picture, it hardly mattered now where Prince Ulvian went!

By now it was fully night, but the red moon, Lunitari, had risen and shone over the flowering plain, lighting his way. Ulvian knew that his father and the others, mounted on those mad centaurs, would catch up with him. He wasn't trying to run away; he just couldn't stand the sight of his father fawning over his supposed son. Ulvian was a prince of the blood, by Astra! Let the Speaker try to favor that green-fingered elf over him. Let him try! Ulvian had friends in Qualinost, powerful friends who wouldn't stand for such a usurpation.

He halted. Green-fingered elf. Elf. Greenhands was a pure-blooded elf, half Silvanesti, half Kagonesti. Humans, elves, and dwarves all lived together in peace now in Qualinesti, but there were always tensions among them. Ancient prejudices were hard to erase. What if Greenhands found favor among a majority of senators because of his purely elven heritage?

Ulvian realized he was stroking his bearded chin. The beard was just one more sign of his mixed blood, of the human heritage that flowed from the mother he had idolized.

If Greenhands were gone, everything would be all right.

*So get rid of him.*

Ulvian shook his head. It was as if someone had said those words in his mind.

*Someone did.*

"Stop it!" he said aloud. "What is happening to me? Am I bewitched?"

*No, it is I who speaks to you.*

"Who are you?" he yelled at the star-laden sky.

*We spoke once before. The night Drulethen died, remember? You saved me from the fire.*

The voice. Low and softly feminine. Inserting a hand into his shirt, Ulvian felt the onyx amulet there. It was warm from being next to his skin. He drew it out and stared at it in the red moonlight.

"Are you a spirit imprisoned in the amulet?"

*I am the amulet itself. Once I served Drulethen. Now I serve you.*

A slow smile spread over the prince's face. His fingers closed tightly around the stone. "Yes! Then your power is mine?"

*It will be in time.*

"Tell me what to—" Ulvian broke off suddenly. He heard loud swishing noises, as if made by many legs striding through the grass. He shoved the amulet back inside his shirt.

A pair of riderless centaurs appeared. The black one who had been Ulvian's mount said, "Ho, little cousin. We were sent to look for you. Uncle Speaker wants you back. Will you come?"

Ulvian regarded them with distaste but replied, "I will come."

The centaur approached him, and the prince climbed on his back. They went bounding away in the grass until they caught up to the rest of the party, hardly a mile distant. The other riders were slumped forward, sleeping. Only Kith-Kanan was awake.

"There's no reason to run away, Ullie," he said softly. "I'm not taking you back to punish you."

Ulvian gripped the belt that formed his centaur's harness. He forced himself to ask the difficult question. "Why are you taking me to the city, Father?"

"Because I want you there. Putting you in prison only taught you to make friends with criminals like Drulethen. I shall try to give you the guidance I should have given you when you were younger."

Guidance. He would give Ulvian guidance while installing that rustic on the Throne of the Sun.

"That won't be necessary, Father." Ulvian's voice was

firm in the darkness. "I intend to pursue a different course once we get back home."

Kith-Kanan studied his son. Darkness and distance separated them from each other, and it was hard to read Ulvian's expression.

* * * * *

Verhanna and Rufus had ridden ahead to prepare Qualinost for the Speaker's return and to quell any panic at the sight of wild centaurs entering the city. Kith-Kanan, Kemian, and Ulvian rode together at the head of the little column. Behind them walked Greenhands and the other, riderless centaurs. The green-fingered elf had dismounted several hours earlier, claiming he needed the touch of the living soil on his bare feet.

They topped a treeless rise. Without being told to do so, Koth stopped. Kith-Kanan asked, "What's the matter, my friend?"

"That place yonder. Is that your city?" asked the awed centaur, pointing ahead.

"That is Qualinost," the Speaker replied proudly. "Have you never been to a city before?"

"Nay—the smell of so many two-legs is hard for us to bear."

Kemian raised his hand to cover his mouth and smiled. Five days with centaurs hadn't made any of them more used to the powerful aroma the creatures gave off.

In the clear air, the capital city of the western elves seemed close enough to touch. The soaring, arched bridges hung from the sky like silver rainbows. The Tower of the Sun was a molten gold spire, a flame leaping from the trees on the plateau. Kith-Kanan could feel the centaur's muscles tensing.

The sight of Qualinost had brought silence to the boisterous band. A feeling of joy filled the Speaker's heart.

"Onward, cousins," said Koth at last, lurching into motion. They descended the rise and soon entered a band of forest land. The centaur leader broke out into song. Rufus and Verhanna would have recognized it, for they had heard it before:

> "Child of oak, newly born,
> Walks among the mortals mild . . ."

Kith-Kanan was intrigued. He let the centaurs sing through the entire song once before he interrupted to ask, "Did you just make that up?"

"An ancient ode, it is," replied Koth. "Sung by uncles who died before I was a colt. Do you like it?"

"Very much."

The forest had given way to rolling hills, many tilled by farmers. The dirt road suddenly became paved with pounded cobbles. Other travelers on the road gave the caravan of centaurs wide berth. When they recognized Kith-Kanan, many set up a cheer.

The people grew more numerous. By the time the party reached the high cliffs overlooking the river that formed the city's eastern boundary, throngs of people had turned out to see the return of the Speaker of the Sun. The added spectacle of their Speaker riding on a centaur only increased their excitement.

The Qualinesti cheered and waved. Amused, the centaurs bellowed back their own hearty greetings. They came to the central bridge over the river, and the Guards of the Sun were drawn up in two lines, holding back the enthusiastic crowds.

"Hail, Speaker of the Sun! Hail, Kith-Kanan!"

Koth's front left hoof stepped down on the hundred-foot-long, suspended rope bridge. It swayed dizzyingly. He looked down into the deep river gorge and rolled his dark eyes. "Not good, cousin! We *Kothlolo* are not squirrels, to scamper on high!"

"The bridge is quite safe," Kith-Kanan countered. "It's used by hundreds daily."

"Two-legs are too foolish to be afraid," he muttered.

"But a bargain is a bargain." He threw wide his thick arms and let out a bellow that silenced the assembled Qualinesti. Kith-Kanan tightened his grip on the strap around the centaur's waist, wondering what this yelling portended.

Still bellowing, Koth tore across the bridge at a blistering gallop, with Kith-Kanan holding on for dear life. The other centaurs set up a similar roar and, one by one, dashed across the bridge. By the time the last one reached the plateau and city gate, the crowds were cheering them on wildly.

"Who is brave? Who is strong? Who is fast?" roared Koth.

"*Kothlolo!*" answered the massed centaurs in deafening shouts.

Kith-Kanan slid off the horse-man's back. "My friend, I would walk to the Speaker's house now to be among my people. Will you follow?"

"Of course! There is a reward waiting. We traveled from Kharolis to city in five days!"

Kemian and Ulvian dismounted also. Flower petals and whole bouquets fell around them. Smiling broadly, Kith-Kanan drew Greenhands forward. "Walk with me," he said in his son's ear. Ulvian waited for a similar invitation, but none was forthcoming.

Arm in arm, Kith-Kanan and Greenhands went down the street, trailed by Kemian, Ulvian, and the centaurs. The upper windows in every tower stood open, and elven and human women waved white linens as the Speaker strode past. The falling flower petals became so thick on the pavement that the underlying cobbles were lost from view. Elves, humans, half-humans, dwarves, and a kender or two cheered and waved all along the sweeping route to the Speaker's house. Kith-Kanan waved back. He looked at Greenhands. The younger elf seemed dazzled by the sheer size and magnitude of the greeting. The Speaker realized his son had never seen so many people before at once. The noise and outpouring of affection drew them on.

"Majesty, did Lady Verhanna announce the coming of your newfound son?" asked Kemian. Kith-Kanan shook his head. "Then why are they cheering him?"

"My people know who he is," said the Speaker confidently. "They can see it in his face, in his bearing. They are cheering the next Speaker of the Sun."

Lord Ambrodel grinned. Ulvian, just behind the general, heard every word his father said, but he plodded resolutely onward. Every joyous cry, every tossed bouquet, was yet another nail driven into the coffin of his desires.

They paraded past the Hall of the Sky. The slopes of the hill were likewise covered with Qualinesti, shouting and cheering. Each tree boasted several children who had climbed up for a better view.

In the square before the Speaker's house, Verhanna, Rufus, and Tamanier Ambrodel waited, flanked on both sides by the household servants and the remaining Guards of the Sun. Kith-Kanan went ahead of Greenhands, who hesitated at the foot of the steps. The Speaker stepped briskly up to the landing in front of the polished mahogany doors. He clasped arms with Tamanier Ambrodel and received a salute from Lord Parnigar, who had kept order in his absence. Kith-Kanan turned and faced the crowd, which gradually fell silent in expectation of a speech.

"People of Qualinost," he proclaimed, "I thank you for the warmth of your greeting. I am weary, and your affection makes me strong again.

"I have been to the high mountains, first to inspect the Fortress of Peace, later to put an end to an evil sorcerer who had long plagued those regions. Now that I have returned, I do not plan to leave you again any time soon."

He smiled and fresh cheers erupted from ten thousand throats. The Speaker held up his hands.

"More than that, I have brought with me someone

new, someone very close to me. A long time ago, when I was merely the second son of the Speaker of the Stars, I had a wife. She was Kagonesti."

There were loud hurrahs from the wild elves in the crowd. "Our time together was short, but our love was not in vain. She left for me a most precious gift: a son."

The multitude held its collective breath as Kith-Kanan descended the mahogany steps and took Greenhands by the hand. He led him up to the landing.

"People of Qualinost! This is my son," Kith-Kanan shouted, his heart full. "His name is Silveran!"

Through the roar that followed, Verhanna stepped close to her father and asked, "Silveran? Where did that name come from?"

"I chose it on the way here," said Kith-Kanan. He held his son's green-hued hand aloft. "I hope you like it, Son."

"You are my father. It is for you to name me."

"Silveran! Silveran!" the crowd chanted.

Kith-Kanan wanted very much to tell his people the rest of it. Silveran was his heir; he would be the next Speaker of the Sun. But he couldn't simply announce his decision, though he knew in his heart that Silveran was the best and wisest choice. Many people had to be consulted, even his political foes. The stability of the Qualinesti nation came first, even before his personal pride and happiness. He knew, too, that Ulvian would take the news very hard.

After receiving the cheers of the crowd for some time, Kith-Kanan led his family into the Speaker's house. Rufus and the Ambrodels, father and son, followed. The crowd began to disperse.

"Sire, what am I to do with the, ah, centaurs?" asked Tamanier, as the *Kothlolo* crowded up the steps to the double doors.

"Make them comfortable," Kith-Kanan replied. "They have done me a signal service."

Tamanier looked askance at the band of rowdy centaurs who filled the antechamber. Their unshod hooves skidded on the smooth mosaic and polished wood floor, but they moved in eagerly, delighted by the strange sights and sensations of the Speaker's house. As Kith-Kanan ascended the steps on his way to his private rooms, his castellan sent for troops of servants to deal with the centaurs. Amidst all the hubbub, no one noticed Prince Ulvian slip away from the royal family and disappear through the rear of the antechamber.

The prince strode furiously down the corridor that led to the servants' quarters, to a room used by the household scribes. The room was windowless and stood empty, as he knew it would be; everyone was in the streets, celebrating. When he shut and bolted the door, Ulvian had complete privacy. He turned up the wick on a guttering lamp and sat down at the scribes' table. With shaking hands, he took the amulet from his clothing and set it on the table before him.

"Speak," he said in a loud whisper. "Speak to me!"

Ulvian could barely form the words, so angry was he. Angry and, though he could hardly admit it even to himself, afraid. The prince was terrified by the adulation and acceptance Greenhands had received from the people of Qualinost. First he'd been banished to Pax Tharkas to be beaten and humiliated by the grunt gang, then he'd been terrorized by a lying sorcerer, and now, when all that he wanted should be within his grasp, now there was Greenhands.

The amulet was silent. The only voices Ulvian could hear were those of the people in the streets outside, still rejoicing.

"Are you trying to drive me mad?" he shrieked, flinging the onyx talisman against the far wall. It bounced off and rolled away. Ulvian buried his face in his hands.

*I am not your servant. I do not come when ordered,* said a haughty, cold voice inside the prince's head.

He raised up with a jerk. "What? Are you there?"

*You must learn self-discipline. This anger of yours gets out of control and serves you ill. Drulethen did not lose his temper so readily.*

Ulvian got down on his knees and felt under the shelves loaded with scrolls. His fingers found the amulet. It was warm to the touch, like a living thing.

"Dru wasn't so superior," said the prince, shifting around to sit on the floor.

*Yes, I know. His killer is the one who has stolen your birthright.*

Ulvian set the amulet on the floor. "Greenhands," he said with a sneer. "Now called Silveran—as if he deserves a royal name."

*He is your father's son, but there is more to him than his ancestry. The power dwells within him. It is a danger to us.*

"What power?"

*The ancient power of order, which brings life to the world. It is not of the gods, but a more elemental force.*

The prince shook his head. "This theology means nothing to me. All I want is what I was promised from birth: my place on the throne!"

*Then Greenhands must die.*

Put so bluntly, the idea gave Ulvian pause. He pondered the possibility for a long time and finally said, "No, Greenhands must *not* die. No matter how subtly it was done, suspicion would fall on me. That must not happen. I want this upstart discredited, not killed. I want the people, including my father, to *want* me on the throne." His jaw clenched, he added in a whisper, "*Especially* my father."

It was the amulet's turn to fall silent. Then it said, *You are a worthy successor to Drulethen.*

Ulvian smiled, basking in the praise. "I shall surpass that lowborn sorcerer in every way," he said smugly.

\* \* \* \* \*

"I am most pleased to meet you, Prince Silveran."

Senator Irthenie bowed to Kith-Kanan and his son.

They were in the outer hall of the Thalas-Enthia tower. The Speaker was about to present his newest son to the senators of Qualinesti, and he knew they weren't going to be as enthusiastic as the common folk had been.

The Kagonesti woman studied Silveran closely. He was dressed in a simple white robe, with a green sash at his waist. His long hair shone in the late morning sunlight that poured through the windows. "The public display yesterday was very clever," said Irthenie. "How did you accomplish it?"

The elf once known as Greenhands gave her a blank look and said, "I don't understand. I was very happy when I entered the city. The people were friendly to me. That's all I know."

"My son has certain gifts," Kith-Kanan remarked. "They come from his mother's side of the family."

Verhanna, standing back by the wall, raised her eyebrows.

"A very useful talent," Irthenie said. "But can he rule, Majesty? That is your plan, I know. Can this innocent in a grown elf's body rule the nation?"

Kith-Kanan adjusted the folds of his creamy white robe distractedly. "He will learn. I—we—shall teach him."

The rumble on the other side of the thick obsidian wall was the debate already raging about the Speaker's new son and possible heir. The Loyalists were outraged, the New Landers were doubtful, and the Friends of the Speaker were completely in the dark about what to say or do.

"Where is Prince Ulvian?" Irthenie asked. "Why isn't he here?"

"He's sulking," Verhanna snorted. "I offered to drag him here by his heels, but Father wouldn't let me."

"The Speaker has a kind heart and a wise mind. There is real danger in alienating Prince Ulvian and those who support him. I have not served this nation so long to see it torn apart by a dynastic war."

"Do you think it will come to war?" asked Verhanna, sensitive to the larger issues.

"Not really," the senator admitted. "The Loyalists want to exploit Ulvian in the name of tradition, for their own greed, but none of them would choose to die for him."

"I pray you are right," said the Speaker softly.

The ceremonial doors of the senate swung outward, and the steward of the chamber announced, "The Thalas-Enthia humbly requests that the Speaker of the Sun enter their house and address them."

The ritual invitation was a signal to Kith-Kanan that the fight was at hand. Adjusting the drape of his clothing once more, the Speaker said quietly to Silveran, "Are you ready, Son?"

The young elf was quite composed, having no conception of the fight that lay ahead. "I am, Father."

The Speaker raised an eyebrow at Irthenie. "Ready for yet another battle, my old friend?"

Hitching her wide, beaded belt off her narrow hips, the Kagonesti woman replied, "I say give them no quarter, Great Speaker." Her eyes gleamed.

Kith-Kanan swept into the hushed senate chamber, followed by Silveran, then Irthenie. Verhanna remained outside. As the steward moved to close the huge, balanced doors, she heard the first voices rising in anger from within. Unable to bear the suspense of waiting here but having no desire to sit in on what she considered pointless arguing, Verhanna left the Thalas-Enthia tower and returned to the Speaker's house.

There she was met by Tamanier Ambrodel, who looked harassed. "Lady," he pleaded, "if you have any influence with these vulgar centaurs, will you please ask them to get out of the house? They're wrecking it!"

She winked. "I'll have a word with uncle Koth."

The antechamber was in chaos. The centaurs had camped in the open room, changing it from an elegant greeting hall to a fancy stable. Somewhere they'd found some straw, which they had strewn about on the floor to give their hooves better purchase. All the ornamental vases and artfully grown plants had been broken, uprooted, or eaten.

When Verhanna entered, four centaurs were playing catch with a globe of flawless emerald taken from the stair baluster.

She intercepted a toss and caught the emerald. It was weightier than she expected. "Oof!" she grunted, bending low with the ten-inch sphere in her arms.

"Hail, sister cousin!" cried Koth. He sat by the far wall, his legs folded beneath him. A heap of fruit was piled up beside him. On the other side was an equally large pile of gnawed cores. Koth's face was sticky with juice.

"Hello, uncle," she said, setting the emerald down on the floor. "You fellows are having quite a good time, aren't you?"

"This city of yours is paradise!" The elder centaur burped loudly. "Why, only this morning, I went to the big open place with cousins Whip and Hennoc and found all this lovely fruit!"

She surveyed the small mountain of pears, apples, and grapes. "Did you pay for this, uncle?"

"Pay? Why, as soon as we got to the two-legs who had the fruit, he yelled and ran away! He wanted to make us a gift of this, I am sure."

Koth polished a dusty pear against his hairy chest and bit into it.

"Look here, uncle. You can't let all the cousins carry on like this inside the Speaker's house. It's, er, causing a bit of a disturbance," Verhanna said in a kindly tone. "Why don't you go outdoors? There's a great deal more room."

He regarded her with sharp, intelligent eyes. "I think *Kothlolo* should live under the open sky," he declared. "City life is making us fat!"

With a few raucous words, he rounded up his band.

He spoke a bit longer, and they began to file out of the antechamber.

"You're not angry, are you?" asked Verhanna as they headed for the doors.

"No, sister cousin. Why should I be? No uncle of mine ever went to a city. I am old and have seen more than I might have seen. I am content."

Outside, in the square before the Speaker's house, a group of four Kagonesti elves waited with a small, donkey-drawn cart. Tamanier Ambrodel was talking with one of the Kagonesti. When Verhanna and the centaurs appeared, the castellan approached them.

"Ahem," he said. "His Majesty Kith-Kanan would like me to present you with this gift."

With a sweep of his arm, Tamanier indicated the four elves and cart. "These Kagonesti are farriers. They will teach you and your people about shoeing. The Speaker thought that if your people were shod with iron shoes, you could travel farther and have less problem with worn and cracked hooves."

Koth descended the steps to the square and approached the chief farrier. "We will wear iron, like elf horses?" he asked with curiosity.

"If it pleases you," replied Tamanier, nervously stepping back by Verhanna.

The elder centaur lifted a horseshoe from the farriers' cart. The four Kagonesti farriers regarded the horse-man speculatively, as if already sizing him for shoes.

All at once, Koth yelled and lifted the horseshoe over his head. He spoke a long stream of centaur talk at his band, and they raised a cheer, crowding around the cart.

The four farriers got on their cart and led the band of centaurs away to their smithy. The *Kothlolo* followed with shouted good-byes and boisterous waves, except for one. A lone centaur remained behind. It was the dapple-gray lady centaur who had carried Rufus from the mountains to the city.

She approached Verhanna. "Sister cousin," she said

slowly, as if searching for words in the unfamiliar Elven language. "Please thank for me littlest cousin Rufus." She smiled triumphantly, but Verhanna lifted puzzled eyebrows at her.

"Thank him? For what?" asked the warrior maiden.

In reply, the lady centaur patted a yellow sash she'd wound around her muscular human waist. After staring at it for a few seconds, understanding dawned on Verhanna. It was the same sash Rufus had used as a centaur harness on their wild ride to the city. The lady centaur had admired it, and the kender must have made her a present of it.

Verhanna smiled and nodded her agreement. The lady centaur whirled in a tight circle, her long white tail swishing out behind her, and trotted off to catch up to her comrades.

The warrior maiden stared after her. For some reason, she found herself wishing she could go back to the plains or the high mountains with them. They had no worries, no responsibilities, and ran wherever the wind took them. In the wilderness, you could fight your enemies with a sword, something Verhanna understood. Here in Qualinost, foes were not so clearly defined, and the weapon of choice was words. She had never mastered that form of battle.

Verhanna sat down on the steps. There were a few people moving across the square, and she watched them go about their daily affairs. To her left, the great spire of the Tower of the Sun glinted brightly. The dark stripe that was the tower's shadow crept across the square away from the Speaker's house. In a few hours, at sunset, it would blanket the entrance of the Thalas-Enthia. She wondered how long her father and Silveran would have to argue and maneuver with the crafty senators there. It could be hours or

days . . . perhaps even weeks.

Yes, sometimes the simple life of the wilderness seemed very appealing.

* * * * *

When the meeting broke up, the news radiated outward from the senate hall in ever-widening circles, so that by a few hours after sunset, the entire city knew that the senate had accepted Kith-Kanan's testimony that Silveran was his true son. The last bit of convincing evidence presented to the senate had been the testimony of the scribe Polidanus, reading from the copied archives of Silvanos the tale of the elf noble Thonmera. Thonmera was one of the original members of the legendary Synthal-Elish, the council that had been the foundation of the first elven nation several millennia ago. It was written that he had been born sixty years after his mother's official death. Apparently the sorcerer Procax had cast a spell on Thonmera's mother because she had refused the magician's offers of love. Procax turned the elf woman into stone. Sixty years later, when Thonmera's father had the stone image of his dead wife moved to his newly built home, the laborers dropped it. The stone image shattered, and the living infant form of Thonmera was discovered.

The Loyalists were completely defeated. Indeed, the tale of Thonmera undercut their entire position. Senator Clovanos and his cronies had made a great show of proclaiming themselves loyal to the traditions of the elven race. What could be more traditional, Irthenie demanded, than the birth of a member of the great Synthal-Elish?

Throughout the debate, Kith-Kanan sat quietly, not indulging in the raucous verbal maneuvers. The Speaker left it to Irthenie and his other friends to put forth his case. He answered occasional questions put to him, but by and large he remained in the background.

In the end, by a vast majority, the Thalas-Enthia gave its approval to Silveran as the Speaker's son. Kith-Kanan did not press right away for the issue of succession, though everyone in the hall had no doubt that was his ultimate goal.

The dying rays of sunlight streamed in the high window slots in the chamber as the session ended. Senators stretched and yawned, rising from their hard marble seats to go to their homes. The Loyalists filed out silently, utterly dejected. Many of the New Landers came forward to offer their congratulations to Kith-Kanan for finding his long-lost son. He remained to speak to all of them, thanking each one personally for his or her vote of confidence.

Finally only Irthenie was left. Her hands shook and her legs were weak from the long, hard afternoon's work. Kith-Kanan put an arm around her tiny waist and supported her with his strength.

"You're about to collapse," he said, concerned. "Shall I send for a litter to carry you home?"

"I can carry myself home," she snapped, jerking away from his encircling arm. The Speaker of the Sun retreated from the old elf woman's ire. "I may be tired, but I'm not senile yet!"

"That you are not," agreed Kith-Kanan. He watched Irthenie's painful progress up the chamber steps to ground level, then out the open doors. A warm wind blew into the hall, flapping the Speaker's robe and stirring Silveran's loose, long hair.

"You've been very quiet," said Kith-Kanan to his son.

"In truth, Father, I haven't understood one word in ten." He pressed his hands to his temples. "Never have I heard so many words spoken at one time! It makes my head reel to remember it!"

His father smiled. "The good senators do like to talk. But the wellborn and the important should talk to each other and argue their points of view. It's far better than settling their disputes with blades, as was the case in Silvanost in my father's day."

"Talking is better than fighting," repeated Silveran, impressing the concept on his mind.

"And right now food is better than both," Kith-Kanan sighed, putting an arm across his son's shoulders. "A plump chicken, a loaf of fresh bread, and some fine Qualinesti nectar should do nicely."

"I'm hungry, too."

Father and son mounted the shallow steps and passed out of the hall. The rose quartz outer walls of the tower burned in the setting sun, and the full weight of summer leaves tossed back and forth on the trees as the wind stirred through them.

"I will teach you all I know," Kith-Kanan promised. He held his head up, letting the sun wash over his face. His regal robe, rumpled by the long afternoon of sitting, flashed white satin highlights as he walked. "You will be a great Speaker of the Sun."

Silveran was quiet for several minutes as they crossed the square toward the Speaker's house. They were unescorted by warriors and unburdened by pomp. The green-fingered elf lifted his own face to the warmth of the sun and shook his hair out of his eyes.

"Father," he said, at last, "I believe this is what my mother wanted."

"I believe so, too," Kith-Kanan murmured. "I believe you were sent so that the nation of Qualinesti would not die. You are its future."

As the Speaker and his son moved through the people who were finishing the day's chores, they were greeted by bows and smiles and happy voices.

"Long live the Speaker," said a human woman whose arms were laden with freshly cut flowers.

"Long live Prince Silveran!" added two nearby elves.

It was a fine day, a fine evening. At the door of the Speaker's house, Kith-Kanan saw Tamanier Ambrodel waiting for him. He sent Silveran on ahead into the house. When his son was gone, Kith-Kanan asked his castellan why he was so happy.

"How do you know I'm happy, sire?" asked the surprised Tamanier.

"Your face is an open scroll," the Speaker replied. "I can read your every emotion. Now, what is it?"

"The centaurs have received their reward and left the house," Tamanier reported.

Kith-Kanan sighed. "I'm sorry I wasn't able to bid them farewell. They were staunch friends when we needed them. Such allies must be treasured." He passed a hand before his eyes. "My head aches, Tam. Have the apothecary send up a soothing draft with dinner."

Tamanier bowed. He watched the Speaker ascend the stairs to his private rooms to join young Silveran for their meal. How old he seems this evening, the castellan thought. The expedition against Drulethen had taken a great deal out of Kith-Kanan. But with a new son and plenty of rest, he would recover quickly.

## ✍ 18 ✍

## Onyx Dreams

*In a small room adjoining the Speaker's bedchamber,*
Silveran lay sleeping on a simple pallet of blankets
spread on the hard tile floor. He was too used to sleeping
on the ground to be comfortable on the soft bed. Every
night of the week he had been in Qualinost, he'd dragged
his bedding onto the floor and spent the night there.

As often happens to those with untroubled minds, he
fell asleep quickly and passed the night in harmless
dreams of his forest birthplace. The heady changes in his
short life had barely impressed themselves on his inner
mind, and Silveran did not yet dream of glory or power
or the adoration of the people.

The only troubling aspects of his dreams so far were

the images of his half-siblings, Verhanna and Ulvian.
They did not menace him, but he felt vaguely troubled
whenever they appeared. Even the innocent Silveran
could sense Ulvian's hostility, and he did not know what
to make of Verhanna's strange behavior at all. Sometimes she got angry at him for no reason at all.

*She loves you,* whispered a voice in his dreams.

Like a child, Silveran took the voice for a normal part
of his dreamworld. "I love her," he replied reasonably.
"And I love Rufus and my father, too."

*I could have loved,* sighed the voice, *but you took my
life.*

Silveran's brow wrinkled and he stirred restlessly.
"Who are you? How have I harmed you?"

A face rushed at him in his mind's eye. With marble-
white skin over sunken cheeks, it stared balefully
through bleary gray eyes. Its mouth hung slackly open,
and its breath reeked of decay and the grave.

Silveran uttered a soft cry and awoke. After some seconds of disorientation, he realized he was in the Speaker's house. A sigh of relief passed his lips.

The blanket over him twitched as if it were alive.
Silveran grasped the satin hem where it lay on his chest
and held on. The blanket billowed up, rippling from his
legs up to his waist. The elf whipped it away to see what
was making it rise. Silveran let out a much louder cry
this time, for beneath the blanket, floating only a foot
from his nose, was the disembodied face from his dream!

*You killed me,* whispered the white lips. *I was Drulethen of Black Stone Peak, and you murdered me.*

"No! I slew a monster! It was a noble deed!"

The head floated closer. Silveran threw up his hands
to ward it off. Scrambling wildly, he fled the room on all
fours.

The connecting door to the Speaker's room stood ajar,
and Silveran banged through it. Hearing his son's wild
cries, Kith-Kanan sat up in bed. Beside his bed, a magical lamp in the shape of a small silver pine tree flickered

immediately to life.

"What? What is it?"

It took him a moment to notice Silveran cringing at the foot of his bed. "My boy, what's the matter?" he asked sleepily.

"Make it go away!" Silveran pressed his face into the dark red drapes hanging from the corners of Kith-Kanan's bed. "I didn't mean to do it! I didn't know!"

The Speaker arose and drew on a light cotton dressing gown. He knotted the sash at his waist and knelt beside his trembling son. "Tell me what's frightened you," he said, gently removing Silveran's clenched fingers from the drapery. The elf related his dream haltingly, including how he'd seen the face of the sorcerer he'd killed at Black Stone Peak.

"It was only a bad dream . . . a nightmare," Kith-Kanan whispered soothingly. He stroked his son's sweat-damp hair. "You never saw Dru in human form, did you?"

"But I woke up and it was still there," Silveran insisted. "He looked so ordinary in my dream . . . so thin and frail. Is that who the wyvern truly was?"

"It is true, Son, but the sorcerer is ash and dust now. He cannot hurt you."

As he spoke, Kith-Kanan tried to ignore his own fears. The link between Drulethen, the sorcerer, and Dru, the manifestation of the god Hiddukel, loomed large in his mind. He didn't want to see enemies and conspiracies under every stone and in every shadow, but coincidence rarely applied when the gods were involved.

It was a strange scene, the father consoling his fully grown son, rocking the weeping Silveran in his arms. The commotion had reached the sensitive ears of Tamanier Ambrodel, whose rooms were only a short distance down the corridor. The disheveled elf appeared in the Speaker's doorway holding a candelabrum.

"Sire?"

"It's all right, Tam," Kith-Kanan said, waving a hand.

"My son had a bad dream."

"I killed him!" sobbed Silveran.

Embarrassed, Tamanier quietly withdrew. The prince certainly seemed more overwrought than a mere bad dream would warrant.

Silveran's terror finally lessened, and he was able to compose himself. Kith-Kanan offered to sit up with him, but his son declined to return to his own room. "I would rather sleep here with you," he said, indicating the hard floor at the foot of the four-poster bed. With a slight smile, Kith-Kanan nodded. He remembered from many centuries past the hollow tree in which he'd lived with Silveran's mother, Anaya, and her brother, Mackeli. They had slept on the unpadded ground, too.

Kith-Kanan climbed back into bed. He listened for a long time, but Silveran's only sounds were light, even breathing. The Speaker pondered the mystery of Dru and what the coincidence of names could mean. Was Drulethen really the god Hiddukel in disguise? Did the God of Evil Bargains torment Silveran's dreams?

\* \* \* \* \*

The Speaker's house was haunted.

So the gossip went in the markets and towers of Qualinost in the days that followed. The strange son the Speaker had brought back from the mountains was being hounded by the dreadful specter of a severed head. It made the good folk shudder, yet they repeated the tale. The story was awful, but it was also fascinating.

No one else had seen the ghost—only Prince Silveran was tormented. The specter would not appear to him unless he was alone, and then it persecuted him relentlessly. The robust young elf soon lost his color and vitality as sleep was denied him by the vengeful spirit.

Verhanna and Rufus set themselves the task of always being with Silveran, since the ghost chose never to appear to others. For a time, this worked. With his half-sister or the kender always in attendance, Silveran's health improved. Then, after many weeks of this happy companionship, the haunting changed.

Verhanna, Silveran, and Rufus were in the garden behind the Speaker's house. A straw-stuffed sack had been set up, and the warrior maiden was teaching Silveran how to shoot a crossbow. With the passage of time, Verhanna had been able to accept him for what he was—her brother, and very likely the next Speaker of the Sun. She'd grown to enjoy his company immensely.

Rufus jogged back and forth, retrieving arrows that went awry. It was a balmy afternoon, with gray clouds scudding before the wind, chasing the last remnants of summer over the western horizon. The trees were just beginning to show a hint of their autumn brilliance.

*Thunk!* A quarrel stuck, quivering, in the target. Verhanna lowered the crossbow from her shoulder. She wore a sleeveless red tunic and thin white trousers. On her feet were dainty red slippers, embroidered in gold. These had been a gift from Rufus on her birthday a week before.

"You see," she said encouragingly, "it isn't so hard. Even Wart can shoot a crossbow."

"We kender think bows are cowardly," Rufus replied airily. "A real weapon is the sling. That takes true skill to use!"

"Sling, ha! Slings are mere toys for children," scoffed Verhanna.

Silveran sat on a marble bench cunningly shaped to resemble a fallen tree. He'd made a number of tries at the target, but his bolts always went wide. He couldn't understand it, but his lack of success didn't seem to bother him. It did, however, vex Verhanna.

"You have eyes like a barn owl," she grumbled, hands perched on hips. "Why can't you hit the target?"

"Weapons don't work well in my hands," Silveran replied with a shrug. "I don't know why."

"Nonsense. Warrior skills run in our family." She

thrust the hunting crossbow into his hands. "Try again."

"If you wish, Hanna."

Silveran fitted a quarrel onto the bow stock. Verhanna stood off to his left, Rufus on his right. He raised the crossbow to his cheek and squinted over the wire-bead sight fixed to the end of the stock.

*Murderer . . .*

Silveran lowered the bow and shook his head, frowning. Verhanna asked what was the matter. "Nothing," he said, raising the weapon again.

*Murderer . . .*

The green-fingered elf knew that whispering voice all too well. Gripping the crossbow hard, Silveran tried to concentrate on the target, to banish all other thoughts from his mind. He hadn't been bothered by the specter of dead Dru for over a month. His time had been spent with Verhanna and Rufus, or learning from his father the things that he needed to know as crown prince of the Qualinesti. His days were kept busy, and his nights had been calm since Rufus began sleeping on a small bed in his room.

However, hard as he tried to ignore it, the hollow sound of Dru's voice filled his ears: *Murderer. You killed me.*

Green robe flying, Silveran spun around, looking for the terrible face he knew would be hovering nearby. Rufus threw himself flat on the ground as the quarrel tip on the cocked crossbow spun by. He shouted, "Hey! Watch where you point that thing!"

The only sound the Speaker's son heard was the ghastly sighing of a long-dead elf. He swept around in a circle until he spied the horrible head suspended in space, just above his own eye level. The face of the evil sorcerer was even more decayed now than when he last saw it. The nose was sunken in, the eyes black sockets. The smell of death and putrefaction forced itself into Silveran's nostrils. He choked and aimed the crossbow at the dead elf's image.

"Silveran, don't shoot," Verhanna said evenly. The quarrel was pointing right at her forehead, only a half dozen feet away. A line of sweat appeared on her upper lip.

"Don't shoot the captain!" Rufus, still flat on the sod, added his plea to hers.

"Go away," Silveran quavered. "Leave me alone!"

"I'm not Drulethen," Verhanna said carefully. Keeping her hands spread apart in front of her, she took a step forward. She continued to speak in calm, soothing tones. "Turn the bow away, Silveran. It's me, Verhanna. Your sister."

In Silveran's fear-crazed mind, the words were different: *Time is short, murderer. When the last flesh rots from my bones, I will come to avenge my death on you. Time is short! Look into the face of your death!*

Maggots sprouted from the dead elf's skin. Drulethen's lower jaw fell away and vanished, leaving a horrid, gaping skull leering at him. Silveran shut his eyes and cried out for mercy. His hand tightened on the trigger bar.

Verhanna threw herself forward and knocked the bow aside. The square-headed quarrel leapt from the bowstring and hissed through the air, burying itself in a high tree branch. Silveran screamed and fought Verhanna, but she managed to pin him to the ground.

"No, no!" he ranted. "I'm sorry I killed you! Don't hurt me, Dru! I don't want to die!" Tears coursed down his cheeks.

Guards, servants, and Tamanier Ambrodel came running into the garden, alarmed by the cries. The guards restrained Silveran after Verhanna lifted him to his feet. The prince sobbed something about forgiveness and his own innocence.

"Did you leave him alone?" asked Tamanier quickly. "Did he see the ghost again?"

"We never left his side," Rufus protested. "My captain and I were teaching Greenhands how to shoot a crossbow."

Tamanier looked quickly to Verhanna. "Did you see anything untoward, Your Highness?"

She dusted dirt from her knees and shook her head. "I didn't see or hear anything but Silveran."

"He almost shot my captain," blurted the kender.

"Shut up, Wart."

Tamanier looked grave. "The Speaker must be told." He folded his wrinkled hands and pressed them hard against his lips. "Forgive me, Highness."

Verhanna bristled. "What do you mean?"

"His Highness could be ill in his mind."

Her eyes blazed. "You go too far, Castellan Ambrodel! If my brother says he's seeing a ghost, then by Astra, there's a ghost!"

"I meant no offense, Your Highness—"

"Well, you've offended me!"

The guards supported Silveran as they walked him back to the Speaker's house. Tamanier bowed and, white-faced, followed them inside.

Rufus picked up the crossbow and brushed the dirt from the bowstring. "You know, my captain, the old geezer could be right."

She shook a finger under the kender's nose. "Don't you start, too, you noisy beetle!"

The kender turned and stomped away toward the house. Shaking with fury, Verhanna watched him for a second, then snatched up a forgotten quarrel and broke it over her knee. She flung the pieces aside and stalked off into the garden. Soon the warrior maiden was lost from sight as she crashed through the bushes and descended the gentle slope into the deepest recesses of the peaceful garden.

From a window in the Speaker's house overlooking the upper garden, Ulvian watched the entire scene. He smiled. He was glad his rooms had such an excellent view.

\* \* \* \* \*

Healers were summoned to the Speaker's house; priestesses of Quen came and worked their incantations over Silveran—all with no success. Clerics devoted to the worship of Mantis and Astra wove protective spells around Kith-Kanan's beleaguered son, but still the hideous corpse face of Drulethen tormented him, and him alone.

The Speaker met with the priests and healers. "Is my son bewitched?" he asked solemnly.

The high priestess of Quen, a former Silvanesti named Aytara, answered for all of them. "We have cast healing spells on your son, Great Speaker, and they do not affect him. The good brothers of Mantis have erected barriers to keep out elementals and evil spirits, and still he sees the dread specter."

Her wide, pale blue eyes never faltered as she gazed at Kith-Kanan. "Prince Silveran is not afflicted by mortal magic, Great Speaker," the young priestess finished.

"What, then?" he demanded.

Aytara glanced at her silent colleagues. "There are two possibilities, Majesty. Both are distasteful."

"Speak the truth, lady. I want to hear it."

"There are potions, poisons, that can corrode the mind. Your son may have been given such a potion," she said.

Kith-Kanan shook his head. "Silveran and I eat the same foods. No one knows who will eat or drink from any given plate or cup. And I have experienced no such visions. It cannot be poison."

"Very well. The last possibility is that your son has lost his mind."

Terrible, icy silence followed the pronouncement. Kith-Kanan gripped the arms of his vallenwood throne so hard his knuckles turned as white as the wood. "Do you know what you're saying? Are you telling me that my son—my heir—is mad?"

The priestess said nothing. A thought occurred to the

Speaker. "My son has demonstrated magical ability in the past," he ventured. "Can this power not be used to help him?"

"He does indeed have great power, but he is completely untrained. Without much study and practice, he can't use these powers to help himself." Aytara's face was sad.

Kith-Kanan looked to each of the others in turn. All of them hung their heads and remained silent, having nothing further to offer.

"Go," the Speaker said in a tired voice. "I thank you for your efforts. Go."

With many bows and flourishes, the healers and clerics took their leave of Kith-Kanan. The Speaker turned away to stare out one of the windows. Only Tamanier remained in the hall.

"My old friend," Kith-Kanan said to him. "What am I to do? I almost think the gods have cursed me, Tam. I've buried two wives, found that one son was a criminal and another may be insane. What am I to do?"

At the far end of the small hall, the aged castellan took in a deep breath. "Perhaps young Silveran has always been troubled," he ventured. "After all, his early life and birth were not natural, and his powers are wild and uncontrolled."

The Speaker slumped back on his throne. He felt every day of his five hundred and some-odd years of life weigh upon him like stones in the folds of his robe, or chains laid in long loops around his shoulders.

"I followed all the signs," he murmured. "Has it all been a terrible hoax? It can't be. Silveran must be my true heir, I know it. But how can we cure him? I can't put my crown on the head of a mad person."

"Sire," said Tamanier, "I am reluctant to bring this up—especially now. But Prince Ulvian wishes to speak with you."

The Speaker started, his mind far away. "What, Tam?"

"Prince Ulvian has asked to see you, sire."

The Speaker gathered his wandering thoughts. With a nod, he said, "Very well. Send him in."

Tamanier pushed the doors apart. An eddy of wind from the porticoed exterior sent a handful of dead leaves skittering across the burnished wooden floor of the hall. The castellan admitted Prince Ulvian, then departed, closing the doors quietly behind him.

"Speaker," said Ulvian, bowing from the waist. Kith-Kanan waved for him to approach.

It took Ulvian twenty steps to cross the audience hall. In the months since his return from Pax Tharkas and Black Stone Peak, the prince had radically altered his looks and manner. Gone were the extravagant lace cuffs, the brilliantly colored and astonishingly expensive breeches and boots. Ulvian had taken to wearing plain velvet tunics in dark blue, black, or green, with matching trousers and short black boots. Heavy necklaces and bold gems on his fingers had given way to a simple silver chain around his neck, with a locket containing a miniature of his mother. Ulvian let his hair grow longer, in a more elven fashion, and shaved off his beard. Save for his broad jaw and round eyes, he could have been taken for a full-blooded elf.

"Father, I want you to send me away," he said after bowing a second time at the foot of the throne.

"Away? Why?"

"I feel it is time to complete my education. I've wasted too much time on frivolous pleasures. There are many things I want to learn."

Kith-Kanan sat upright. This curious request intrigued him. "Where is it you wish to go for this education?" he asked.

"I was thinking of Silvanost."

The Speaker raised his eyebrows. In a gentle voice, he said, "Ulvian, that's impossible. Sithas would never allow it."

Ulvian took a step forward. The toes of his boots

pressed against the base of the vallenwood throne. "But I want to learn from the wise elves of the east, in the most ancient temples in the world. Surely the Speaker of the Stars would permit his own kin—"

"It cannot be, my son." Kith-Kanan leaned forward and laid a hand on Ulvian's shoulder. "You are half-human. The Silvanesti would not welcome you."

The prince flinched as if his father had struck him. "Then send me to Thorbardin, or Ergoth! Anywhere!" Ulvian said desperately.

"Why do you wish to leave so suddenly?"

The prince's eyes dropped before the Speaker's questioning gaze. "I—I told you, Father. I want to complete my education."

"You aren't telling me the truth, Son," Kith-Kanan contended.

"All right. I want to get away from this house. I can't bear it anymore!" He jerked out of his father's grip.

"What do you mean?"

Ulvian fidgeted with his narrow gray sash. Finally he turned away, putting his back to the Speaker. "His screams keep me awake at night," he said stiffly. "I—I hear him wandering the halls, moaning. I can't bear it, Father. I know he's your legitimate heir, and I can't expect him to go away, so I thought I'd volunteer to leave instead."

Kith-Kanan rose and walked to his son. "Your brother is ill," he said. "If it's any consolation to you, he keeps me awake at night, too."

The dark smudges under Kith-Kanan's eyes testified to the truth of his statement. "I wish you would stay and help Silveran, Ullie. He needs a good friend."

The somberly dressed prince knelt and gathered a handful of red and brown leaves from the floor. Slowly he turned them over, as if studying their wrinkled surfaces. "Do the healers give him any chance of recovery?" he asked, staring at the leaves.

Kith-Kanan sighed. "They don't even agree on why he

is afflicted," he replied.

Ulvian dropped the leaves and stood. Turning to face his father, the prince said quietly, "If you want me to stay, Father, I will."

Kith-Kanan grasped his son's hands gratefully. "Thank you, Ullie," he said, smiling. "I was hoping you'd stay."

The prince had never planned to do otherwise. Back in his own quarters, Ulvian ran his fingers lightly down the front of his heavy quilted tunic. The hard lump of the black onyx amulet was there, sheathed in a tight leather bag hanging around his neck.

"My beauty," Ulvian rejoiced softly. "It goes well! Soon I will be sole and undisputed heir."

*You deserve it, my prince,* crooned the amulet for Ulvian's ears only. *Together we will rule.*

The prince busied himself putting the finishing touches to the speech he would give when he was made heir to the Throne of the Sun.

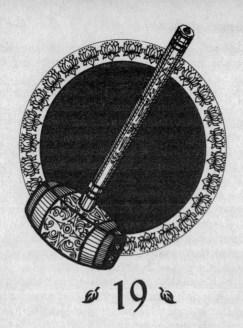

# 🌿 19 🌿

## The Death of the Sun
—

Before the first frost, they moved Silveran to a room at the end of the south wing of the Speaker's house. In this secluded chamber, his nightly ravings wouldn't disturb those sleeping near the center of the great house. Tamanier, as keeper of the keys, had the duty of locking Silveran in his room each night. If his cries became too loud, a sleeping draft would be brought for him to drink. Only through powerful soporifics could they hold back the relentless specter that haunted the young elf. The strong medicines left him groggy and befuddled most of his waking hours.

When Solinari, the silver moon, first called the fingers of frost over Qualinesti, Silveran was sleeping fitfully in his pitiful cell. There was no furniture or lamp or anything else he might use to harm himself or others. Of his blankets, only two hadn't been shredded by fevered hands as he struggled to keep the hideous phantom at bay.

*Greenhands*, dead Dru called. *Rise, murderer. Tonight, you join me in the land of the dead.*

"No," Silveran groaned. "Oh, no, please!"

*Your time is all used up. Rise! I am coming for you!*

"No!"

With a sudden spasm, the elf jerked awake. His heart hammered inside his ribs, and his breath came in rapid, shallow gasps. "You'll not take me! You'll not!"

He scrambled to his feet. The door to his room was locked from the outside. Panic seized Silveran. He stood and kicked the locked door hard.

The thick wooden panel boomed but stayed firm. Knowing his son's great strength, Kith-Kanan had sadly ordered the door be the stoutest that could be found.

*Greenhands, murderer . . .*

In desperation, Silveran threw his entire body at the door. Under his frenzied assault, the jamb splintered, and the door flew wide. The dark hall outside was cold. Winter rugs had not yet been laid on the bare wood floor, and the elf's teeth chattered as he staggered out into the chill.

To his left were door-sized windows, shuttered. Through the slats of the seven-foot-tall shutters came a weird, yellow-green light. Silveran uttered a short, sharp cry and recoiled from the slivers of sickly light slicing in between the slats. Laughter rang in his head— Dru's laughter, mingled with the sound of rattling chains.

He ran down the hall, blindly blundering from one closed door to another. These ground floor rooms were unoccupied, as the Speaker was entertaining no guests. Silveran shook each door handle and pounded on each panel, but he couldn't get in. The chartreuse light grew stronger, until it cast Silveran's own long shadow to the end of the empty hall.

The light seeped through the closed shutters like oil through cheesecloth. As the petrified elf watched, it coalesced into the rough form of an elf. Silveran pressed his back against a locked door and stared in abject terror. The greenly glowing form assumed distinct arms and legs—but no head. The neck rose up, but where the head should be was only darkness.

*Flee if you can, murderer! I have come for you!* boomed the voice.

Silveran bolted from the shelter of the doorway and ran down the hall, crying out in horror.

He crossed the receiving room at the main entrance on the ground floor and seized the first available doorknob. This was the Speaker's trophy room. Here were displayed Kith-Kanan's various suits of armor, his personal weapons, as well as flags and standards captured from the Ergothians during the Kinslayer War. Silveran wove his way among the stands of halberds, swords, and pikes. The glint of metal gave him an idea, a mad idea. He would kill the wretched ghost again—for good this time—and be safe. Safe and free.

But the pikes and swords were held in their racks by strong loops of chain and wire, and none came easily to hand. Silveran hurried by them and went to the rear wall, scanning the trophies mounted there. These were not, properly speaking, weapons, but rather tools the Speaker had used in his long career. The saw he had wielded to fell the first tree when Qualinost was being built. The mason's trowel he used to lay the cornerstone of the Tower of the Sun. The hammer King Glenforth of Thorbardin had given him to carve out the first block for the fortress of peace, Pax Tharkas.

The hammer rested on a small pedestal under a crystal dome. The silver bands on its handle sparkled, and its gilded head gleamed. The dome was not sealed, and Silveran quickly sent it crashing to the floor. The hammer fit his grip as if made for him.

He exulted. The mighty dwarven hammer would smash diamonds to dust if swung smartly and struck fairly. Now he would deal with the monster Drulethen. His torment would soon be finished!

The door of the trophy room opened slowly. The elf huddled in the shadows, hammer couched on his shoulders. A pale yellow light filtered in from the open door, and a voice whispered, "Silveran? Are you in here?"

"Yes!" he shouted, leaping on the door and wrenching it fully open. He saw for a second a grinning, fleshless skull staring at him with empty white eye sockets, heard the mocking laughter in his ears. "Now I will kill you forever, Dru!" Silveran screamed and brought the hammer down in a smashing blow on Dru's skull. Bone yielded under the awful impact, and he smelled blood. The yellow light went out.

Silveran collapsed in a limp heap on the floor. He'd done it. He'd killed Dru completely. Now he was free. His eyelids fluttered closed just as more light filled the room.

Tamanier, Ulvian, and Verhanna lifted their lamps high. Behind them, sleepy servants muttered about their interrupted rest. The lamplight fell upon the scene in the Speaker's trophy room.

"By all the holy gods!" Tamanier cried. "He's killed the Speaker!"

\* \* \* \* \*

The entire Guard of the Sun was roused and turned out of their barracks while the best healers in Qualinost were summoned to the Speaker's house. Kith-Kanan bore a terrible wound on his head where the dwarven hammer had broken his skull. But he was not dead. His heart beat, and he drew breath, but the Speaker of the Sun had not opened his eyes since the tragedy.

Strangely, Silveran was likewise insensible. His body

was unmarked, yet he could not be roused, even when foul-smelling asafetida was waved under his nose. All signs of madness had left him; his face was peaceful, and the deep lines in his brow were smoothed out. He looked like a sleeping child, lying on the floor by his mortally wounded father.

Verhanna refused any help and carried her father to his bed. Tamanier explained how Kith-Kanan had heard the disturbance Silveran had caused and had gone, without summoning any guards, to investigate.

"I will never forgive myself," the old castellan said, wringing his hands. "I should have gone in his stead!"

"Never mind," Ulvian said unsteadily as they mounted the steps on each side of Verhanna. "No one knew this was going to happen. Silveran must have struck out at Father in a delirium."

In truth, the prince was much shaken by this turn of events. He had never desired Kith-Kanan's death, and he somehow realized the amulet had deliberately maneuvered father and son together for just this result. Now the evil talisman wouldn't have to wait long for Ulvian to receive that which he'd requested. In days—perhaps hours—Ulvian would be Speaker of the Sun.

Aytara and the entire college of Quen arrived, and they were put to work trying to save Kith-Kanan's life. Silveran merited only a passing glance. Aside from the fact that he couldn't be awakened, he seemed in perfect health. The high priestess didn't wish to waste a single spell or incantation on the uninjured elf; all the magic they could gather would be needed for the Speaker. Two of the guards carried the Speaker's unconscious son to a small room on the second floor of the great house. Their orders were to chain him and stand guard at his door.

Kith-Kanan was dying.

Soon the whole house was saturated with the smell of incense and the sound of chanting. The Clerics of Quen invoked their mightiest spells, and they succeeded in slowing the creep of death through the Speaker's limbs, but they couldn't stop it. Aytara admitted as much to Verhanna and Ulvian in the sitting room of their father's chambers.

"How—how long will he live?" asked Verhanna, silent tears trickling down her face.

"A day. Perhaps two. He is very strong. A normal elf would have died on the spot from such a blow. You should be prepared, my lady. The end could come at any time."

"Is there nothing you can do?"

Aytara bowed. Her white robes were wrinkled, her sky-blue sash loosely tied. She, too, was crying. "No, Highness. I am deeply sorry."

Verhanna nodded and the high priestess departed.

After a silent moment, Ulvian coughed. "There remains the matter of my succession," he said.

Verhanna glared. "What succession?"

"When our father dies, who will be the next Speaker? Certainly not our mad half-brother."

Snarling with outrage, Verhanna seized her brother by the front of his shirt and propelled him backward out the door and into the hallway, until he thudded against a pillar. "Don't talk to me about crowns!" she said through clenched teeth. "Our father isn't even dead yet, and already you crave his scepter! I tell you this, Brother, if you mention such a thing to me again before Father is gone, I'll kill you. I'll gut you like a wild pig! Is that clear?"

Mastering the fear that trembled through his body, Ulvian said that it was. He had no doubt she meant what she said. Though he clutched her arms, he knew he'd never break her grip.

Verhanna felt something hard under her wrist. She plucked open Ulvian's blue shirt, sending buttons flying. There was a leather bag hanging around his neck. Her brother's eyes were wide with fear and anger.

"What's this?" she hissed. When he didn't reply, she drew her dagger in her left hand and held it to his face.

For an instant, he thought Verhanna was going to slit his throat, but all she did was cut the thong holding the leather bag. Stepping back, she pried it open and found the onyx amulet.

"What are you doing with this?" she demanded.

"It's just a lump of carved stone," he said, his voice quavering. Ulvian prayed silently for the amulet to intervene. Nothing happened.

"This was destroyed in the fire when Drulethen was—" Verhanna stopped in midsentence. Her head snapped around in the direction of their father's bedchamber. Slowly she turned back to Ulvian, her face suffused with blood.

"*You!*" she breathed.

"No, Hanna, it wasn't—"

She seized her brother again, shoving him so hard against the pillar that his vision filled with stars. "Let me go! You'll regret it if you hurt me!" he babbled.

"I haven't got time for you now," she muttered fiercely. She let him go. Ulvian's feet dropped to the floor.

"Sergeant of the guard!" Verhanna bawled. A warrior with a fanlike array of horsehair on the top of his helmet came running down the corridor. "Post a guard around this room," she ordered. "No one is to enter but I myself, Tamanier Ambrodel, or the holy lady Aytara. Got that?"

The guard glanced sideways at the prince. "Is my lord Ulvian to be excluded, Captain?" he asked.

"He most certainly is. If I find out anyone else but the three I named has gone in there, I'll have your head."

The sergeant, a seasoned warrior, swallowed hard. "It shall be done, Captain!" he vowed.

A squad of eight guards formed before the doors to the Speaker's rooms. It was nearly dawn. Verhanna left Tamanier to make the announcement to the people. Already heralds clad in golden tabards were appearing in the halls, rubbing the sleep from their eyes and tugging on their ankle-high boots. The old castellan, strain and sorrow written into every line on his face, shepherded the elf boys and girls into an adjoining room. Minutes later, the heralds emerged, red-eyed and weeping. They raced out of the building to cry the sorrowful news to the waking city.

Verhanna went to see Silveran. The guards outside the chamber stood aside for her as she unlocked the thick door of his room.

"Captain," one of the guards said to her before she entered, "you'd best look at his hands."

She was weary and heartsick and still angry with Ulvian, and she told the guard she had no patience for riddles.

"Please, Captain," insisted the guard. "He was once called Greenhands, wasn't he? Well, his fingers aren't green anymore."

Verhanna's brows lifted at that. She went in and closed the heavy door behind her.

Despite the thick chains that encircled his arms and legs, Silveran was the picture of peace. It made her heart ache anew to see him lying so innocent and untroubled while their father was dying. What evil miasma had invaded his simple, guileless mind and made him go mad with fear? She still held the black amulet in her hand. Verhanna knelt on one knee and studied the elf's hands. Just as the guard had said, Silveran's fingers were now white, contrasting with his tanned hands.

Slowly, with much fluttering of eyelids, Silveran was waking.

"Hanna," he said happily. "Hello."

She stared down at him, incredulous at his calm manner. He sat up, and the chains draped heavily on his stomach. "Oof," he wheezed. "What's this? Why am I bound?"

"Don't you remember what happened?" she asked.

"Remember what? Won't you take these chains off? They hurt me."

"How do you think you came to be here?" she said sharply.

Silveran's brow furrowed. "I was asleep," he said thoughtfully. "I had some bad dreams—-then I woke up, and there you were, and here are the chains."

In slow, deliberate words, she explained what had happened. Silveran cried out and retreated to the wall. The door opened and a guard poked his head in, but Verhanna waved him out. Silveran hugged himself and gasped for air.

"It cannot be," he said, shaking his head. "It was a dream, a terrible dream!"

"It is the truth," she said grimly. "The Speaker is dying."

He buried his face in his hands. "I am cursed!" Silveran moaned. "I have slain my beloved father!"

Verhanna sprang forward, grabbing his hands and dragging them away from his face. "Listen to me! You may have been cursed, but you're all right now. When father dies—" she choked on the word—"you must go before the Thalas-Enthia and demand that they name you Speaker of the Sun. Otherwise Ulvian will claim the throne. You must do it!"

"But I must be punished for slaying our father," he objected, sobbing. "No one could want me to rule. Let Ulvian be Speaker. I must be put to death for my crime!"

Verhanna shook him hard, rattling his chains. "No! It wasn't your fault. Ulvian used Drulethen's black amulet to drive you mad. He's the criminal. *You* are the chosen successor. Everything depends on you. Father believes you are the future of Qualinesti!"

Bells began tolling from the high towers of the city. The heralds' dire tidings were spreading fast. Verhanna listened to the doleful sound, knowing it was the Speaker's death knell. When the bells ceased ringing, it would mean Kith-Kanan was dead.

Quickly the warrior maiden unlocked the fetters on Silveran's hands and legs. "You stay here," she said. "I'll have the guards lock you in. You'll be safe."

"Safe from what?"

There was no time to explain. Silveran reached out for Verhanna as she made for the door. Whatever he intended to say died in his throat as he noticed for the first time that his fingers were no longer green.

"The power has left me," he breathed. "I no longer feel its touch."

Verhanna hesitated, her hand on the knob. "The magic? It's gone?"

He nodded. "Good," she said firmly. "Maybe that will be to your advantage."

The door slammed behind her before he could ask what she meant.

\* \* \* \* \*

To walk among the green trees, to smell the sun-washed air, to eat what came to hand, and to sleep under the stars—that was the good life. The best life. For all his deeds and wisdom, it was this simple woodland existence that Kith-Kanan always hungered for. The myth makers, the legend builders, had elevated him into a hero, a demigod, in his own lifetime. No doubt after he was dead, their exaggerations would grow larger with each passing century. Perhaps Kith-Kanan might become a god someday in the eyes of his descendants. He did not wish it. A far more suitable tribute would be the continued happy existence of the nation he'd founded, Qualinesti.

Kith-Kanan walked in the shade of oaks. It was a remarkable dream he was having. Dreams were usually thin things, flashes in his mind's eye. This one, though, was magnificent. The smells, sounds, and textures of the forest were all around him. Wind whispered in the leaves high overhead. He heard birds and small animals calling and scampering in the dead leaves on the ground. Sunlight made sparkling patterns in the air. Remarkable.

Truly remarkable.

"Not so remarkable."

He stopped, as if rooted to the spot. Leaning against a tree, not five paces away, was his first wife and dearest love.

"Anaya," he sighed. "You visit my wonderful dream."

"This is not a dream, Kith."

She straightened and walked toward him. The green eyes, the dark hair, the Kagonesti face paint—it was all so real. As she scrutinized his face, he rejoiced in her every feature.

"This is not a dream," she repeated. "You are in a shadowed realm between the light of life and the darkness of death. Our son struck you down with a dwarven hammer, but it was not his will that put the weapon in his hand. Your other son used the Amulet of Hiddukel to bring him down, and you with him."

Sadness appeared in her eyes. "No one could prevent this destiny for you, my husband, but I have come back to tell you these things. Your son Ulvian must not sit on the Throne of the Sun. He has opened his soul to evil to further his ambition, and he will be the death and ruination of thousands if he is not stopped."

Kith-Kanan looked past her at the serene wildwood, feeling removed and remote from the terrible tale she'd just related. He didn't feel as if he'd been struck a mighty blow; instead, he felt as young and strong as he had when he'd first met Anaya. Tentatively he took her hand in his. It was warm and suntanned, and the tips of the fingers were delicately green. "How is it possible, my love? How can I be here with you?"

She lifted her free hand and caressed his cheek. "The gods you worship do not interfere with the ebb and flow of life. They are apart from it, and they allow life to follow its own course. But this place, and my existence, are not part of life or death. The power rules here in eternal balance with Chaos. Now, as a boon to me, the power allows me to see you and tell you the truth."

"What is this power?" he asked, pressing her hand to his lips.

"It cannot be named, like a flower or a beast. It is the property of order in all things, the counterpart of Chaos. That is all I can say."

Wind rustled through the closely growing oaks. Kith-Kanan held Anaya's hand. "Will you walk with me?" he asked gently. She smiled and said yes.

As they strolled down the path, he wondered aloud, "Will I be with you always?"

Green moss softened their footfalls, and the wind lifted Kith-Kanan's long hair.

"As long as you remember me, I shall be with you," she replied. "But you cannot remain here much longer. Even as we speak, your mortal body grows cold. You must go back and tell those you love and trust the true story of your death."

"My death?"

Kith-Kanan mused over the idea, normally so frightening. "I've seen many people die, for all sorts of reasons. Is it a sad thing to be dead?"

Anaya shrugged and said with her characteristic bluntness, "I don't know. I've never died."

He found himself smiling. "Of course not. I'm not frightened, though. Perhaps I will find all those who have gone before me. My father Sithel, my mother, Mackeli, Suzine . . ."

A large boulder appeared in the path, completely blocking it. Kith-Kanan touched the stone, feeling the lichen and watching a stream of tiny black ants march over it like soldiers conquering a mountain peak.

"This is the end, isn't it?" he said, turning to face her.

"The end of your time here." She regarded him solemnly. "Are you sad, Kith?"

He smiled and said, "No. I said good-bye to you long ago. This visit is a wonderful gift. It would be ungrateful to be sad."

Kith-Kanan leaned over and kissed Anaya softly. She

returned his kiss, but already she was beginning to pale. Not daring to end the moment, he whispered into her mouth, "Farewell, my dearest. Farewell . . ."

The forest became dark wooden walls and beams. Pain flooded his limbs, and he gasped loudly. There was a pressure on his cheek. Kith-Kanan opened his eyes and realized his daughter was kissing his face.

She drew back. "By Astra!" Verhanna cried. "You're awake!"

"Yes." Merciful gods, his throat was raw. "Water," he gasped.

Verhanna looked distressed. "Water? Will nectar do?"

She had a bottle of nectar beside her that she'd apparently been drinking from. Kith-Kanan croaked his assent, and she carefully put the bottle to his parched lips.

"Ah. Daughter, get some people in here. Witnesses. Tam, the guards . . . anyone. As fast as you can."

Verhanna called for help, and guards threw open the door. "Run and get Tamanier Ambrodel!" she said. "The rest of you, come in here. The Speaker has something to say, and he wants you to hear it!"

Seven warriors crowded into the modest bedchamber. Verhanna raised her father up and stuffed a pillow under his back so he could see the warriors. Then she lifted the nectar to his lips once more.

"My good warriors," Kith-Kanan rasped. The thick white bandage that covered the horrible wound on his forehead didn't dip low enough to cover his bloodshot eyes. "These are my last commands."

The elves all leaned forward to catch every sound he made. "My son," said the Speaker weakly, "is innocent. Silveran is not . . . responsible . . . for my death."

The guards exchanged looks of puzzlement. Verhanna, heedless of the tears that had once more begun to flow down her cheeks, prompted, "Go on, Father."

"He was bewitched . . . by the onyx amulet. The evil talisman struck a bargain with . . . Ulvian."

Puzzlement gradually turned to anger. Muttering, the

warriors fingered their sword hilts.

"Ulvian will die for this, Father, I swear it!" Verhanna said. The guards seconded her vow.

"No!" Kith-Kanan said strongly. "I forbid it! Few are . . . the mortals who can withstand the sweet words . . . of Hiddukel. Ulvian . . ." He coughed hard, and fresh blood began to trickle down his face from under his bandage. "Do not harm . . . him. Please!"

Verhanna buried her face against her father's chest. "Father, don't die!" she pleaded.

"I am . . . not afraid. Is Silveran . . . well?"

She lifted her tear-streaked face. "Yes, yes! He has lost his magic, but he is himself again. The madness has left him!"

"I want to see . . . him."

Verhanna ordered a guard to fetch Silveran. He was gone several long minutes, so she dispatched two more. When they hadn't returned after quite a long wait, and Kith-Kanan's eyelids had begun to flutter closed, she got to her feet and stormed out of the room. Down the corridor at Silveran's door, she found the three guards she'd dispatched and the three watching the chained prince. Half of the warriors were howling for Ulvian's blood, the other half were protecting him.

"Get out of the way!" Verhanna said, shoving guards left and right. "The Speaker wants his son!"

"I'll go to him," Ulvian said quickly.

"Not you! Silveran!"

"But he's a murderer!"

Thrusting a finger at her brother, Verhanna cried, "We know the truth! You conspired to destroy Silveran so you could reclaim the throne. Did you also plot the death of our father?"

She whipped out her sword, and the guards stood back, leaving sister and brother facing each other. "I want to kill you so much I could—" She stopped herself. "But Father has forbidden it! Now get out of my way before I forget my promise to him!"

She sheathed her sword and unlocked the door. After hustling Silveran out, she and her half-brother ran down the polished wood floor. They were trailed more slowly by Ulvian and the guards.

Verhanna flew through the open doorway of Kith-Kanan's room. The four warriors who had remained behind were all kneeling around the Speaker's bed. His eyes were closed. Verhanna didn't need to ask; Kith-Kanan was dead.

Tamanier Ambrodel, his hair standing up on his head and his mantle askew, wept openly at the foot of the Speaker's bed. "I was too late," he sobbed.

The sergeant of the guard looked up at her. "He called to you, lady," he said chokingly. "And to someone named Anaya."

She had to swallow her grief, at least briefly. It was vitally important that her father's wishes were carried out. "Did you all hear what he told me before he died?" she said frantically.

"Yes, lady," said the sergeant. The other guards swore oaths that they had heard the Speaker's words as well. Tersely Verhanna informed Tamanier of Ulvian's plot against Silveran. Then she pulled Silveran into the room, and the guards rose to their feet.

"The Speaker of the Sun is dead," the captain said, her voice cracking. "Long live Speaker Silveran!"

"Long live Speaker Silveran!" echoed the warriors.

Silveran's face was bright as he tried to fathom it all.

"Your Majesty," Tamanier added, bowing to the new young monarch.

"Where's Ulvian?" Verhanna asked suddenly. He wasn't in the Speaker's rooms or the hallway nearby.

"Shall we search for him, lady?" asked the sergeant of the guard.

"It's for the Speaker to decide," Verhanna said softly, putting a hand to Silveran's shoulder. The warriors looked expectantly at him. The elf's eyes were calm.

The new Speaker gazed upon his father. "Let Ulvian

go," he said.

Now that she had fulfilled her duty to Kith-Kanan, Verhanna allowed her wobbly legs to give way, and she knelt by her father's body, weeping uncontrollably. She had loved him and respected him with an intensity that approached worship. She couldn't bear the thought that he was gone, that she would never again see his face, never again hear his voice, teasing her for her seriousness. Her brother moved to stand behind her and placed his hands on her shaking shoulders.

"I need you, Hanna," Silveran whispered, for her ears only. "I need your help to rule Qualinesti."

Verhanna pulled her gaze away from the still face of her father and looked up into the solemn visage of the new Speaker of the Sun. Kith-Kanan had been right. Silveran, once known as Greenhands, would make a fine leader. He was good and kind and incorruptible.

Her voice shook, but the words carried to all those in the room as she responded with the same ancient oath she had once sworn to her father. "You are my Speaker. You are my liege lord, and I shall obey you even unto death."

With Silveran's hands still on her shoulders, Verhanna rose slowly to her feet. The guards surrounded Kith-Kanan's bed and came forward to raise him up. By ancient rite, a dead Speaker was carried to the Temple of Astra for prayers and purification.

"Stop," Silveran ordered, and Verhanna looked startled. For just that instant, his commanding voice had sounded exactly like their father's. Silveran held out a restraining hand. A hand no longer green. "This is my duty," he stated.

With great tenderness, he lifted Kith-Kanan in his arms and carried him down the central stair to the reception hall. Verhanna walked behind him and to his right, and the warriors fell into step behind her.

At the bottom of the cherrywood stair stood the entire household, down to the humblest sweepers. All cried openly, and their heads bowed as the body of Kith-Kanan, founder and first Speaker of Qualinesti, was borne past them. Poor Tamanier Ambrodel was supported by the strong arm of his son Kemian. The aged castellan was so grief-stricken he could barely remain upright. He had one last duty to perform for his old friend and sovereign, though. When Silveran, with his sad burden, reached the bottom of the grand stair, Tamanier lifted his right hand and signaled the group of heralds waiting by the front doors.

The heralds flew out the double doors and ran like lightning across the square and into every part of the city. As the second Speaker of the Sun stepped into the morning sunshine, their high voices could be heard crying the dreadful news.

Speaker Silveran paused, blinking in the bright light. Verhanna felt her own step falter as, one by one, the great bells throughout the city of Qualinost fell silent.

# ❧ Epilogue ❧

## The Letter

___

*To his Gracious Majesty, Silveran, Speaker of the Sun,* from Kemian, Lord Ambrodel, currently at Pax Tharkas.

Great Speaker: I wish to extend my heartiest good wishes to you on this, the first anniversary of your ascension to the throne. All Qualinesti is proud of the great work you have done following in the mighty footsteps of your esteemed father, the late Speaker, Kith-Kanan.

Preparations of the vault for your father's final entombment here are nearly complete. The last touches are being applied, and Feldrin Feldspar is personally overseeing the tomb's completion. Before the autumn equinox, everything will be ready to receive the late Speaker in his final resting place.

Regarding the other matters you wrote about, I can tell you a few things. Of Prince Ulvian, we have no certain news, though many rumors circulate about him. One week we hear he is living in Daltigoth, the pampered guest of the Emperor of Ergoth; the next week I am "reliably" informed that the prince lives in direst poverty in Balifor. The suggestion of the General of the Guards, Lady Verhanna, to send her scout to Balifor to ferret out the truth is a good one. If anyone can find Prince Ulvian, Rufus Wrinklecap can.

The flow of travelers from the east continues to dwindle. Some of the Silvanesti who have lately come to us say that the Speaker of the Stars, Sithas, plans to seal the border and prevent further emigration. Personally, I am not unhappy with this. The more people who leave Silvanesti, the more dangerous relations with the old country become, as they get more and more jealous of our wealth and success.

As Governor of Pax Tharkas, I can also report to Your Majesty that things go smoothly here.

The dwarves are admirable allies, and since the arrival of the Second Regiment of the Guards of the Sun, banditry has entirely ceased in the Kharolis Mountain region. The King of Thorbardin is greatly pleased. I enclose with this letter a missive from the king, in which he expresses his gratitude to Your Majesty for the garrison of guards. The king also hopes to begin mining nearby and says the mineral wealth of the mountains will greatly enrich both kingdoms.

Now, if I may, Great Speaker, I would like to beg a personal favor of you.

For many years, I have admired the person of General of the Guards, Lady Verhanna, but she has not returned my attention. Now that the period of mourning for Speaker Kith-Kanan has passed, I wonder if you would broach the subject of marriage to your esteemed sister on my behalf? I ask this for two reasons, Majesty. First, she is of royal blood and therefore requires your permission to marry, and second, she is my fellow officer, and I dare not approach her on such a delicate matter. It would be a breach of military discipline.

If you think it wise and prudent, Great Speaker, to do this for me, my happiness and gratitude would be boundless. I have loved Lady Verhanna for many years, but I dared not reveal myself to so formidable a warrior maiden. With you to sponsor me, I feel I may have a real chance at winning her hand.

That is all I have to tell you at this time. May the gods smile on Your Majesty, grant you wisdom, and continue the good fortune and happiness your young reign has already begun.

> Your Most Humble and Obedient Servant,
> Kemian, Lord Ambrodel
> Governor
> Pax Tharkas

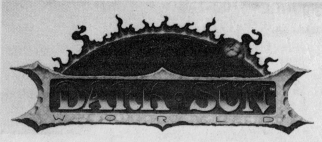

Prism Pentad
BOOK TWO
# The Crimson Legion
Troy Denning

*A dream born from tyranny . . .*
After a millennium of sorrow, the city of Tyr cast off the
yoke of the brutal despot who reduced its fields to dust
and its citizens to bondage. The new king, Tithian of
Mericles, has liberated the slaves . . . and plunged the
city into chaos. Only the man-dwarf Rikus, the gladi-
ator slave who sparked the rebellion, can save the city
from the mighty army sent from Urik to destroy it.
Available April 1992.

Book Three: *The Amber Enchantress*, October 1992.

# DragonLance® Saga

# Meetings Sextet

## Kindred Spirits                    Mark Anthony and Ellen Porath

The reluctant paternal dwarven hero, Flint Fireforge, is invited to the elven kingdom of Qualinesti, where he meets a young, unhappy half-elf named Tanis. But when Laurana, the beauteous daughter of the elves' ruler, declares her love for Tanis, a deadly rival for her affections concocts a scenario fraught with rish and scandal for both the half-elf and his dwarven ally.

## Wanderlust                    Mary Kirchoff and Steve Winter

Tasslehoff Burrfoot accidentally pockets one of Flint's copper bracelets and Tanis good-naturedly defends the top-knotted newcomer to Solace—triggering a thoroughly unpredictable tale, which includes a sinister stranger who has evil on his mind for the three new friends.

## Dark Heart                    Tina Daniell

At long last, the story of the beautiful, dark-hearted Kitiara Uth Matar, from the birth of her twin brothers, the frail mage Raistlin and the warrior Caramon. Kitiara's increasing fascination with evil throws her into the company of a roguish stranger and an eerie mage whose fates are intermingled with her own. On Sale January 1992

**Saga**

# Meetings Sextet
### *The Adventures Continue*

## The Code and the Measure
Sturm grows from youth to manhood in Solace, guided by his absent father's Solamnic Code. Then he meets Caramon, and finds himself fighting the young warrior, much to Raistlin's delight. When Tas meets the three young men, he promptly adopts them, taking them home to Flint's house, and new friendships are born. Available May 1992.

---

## Steel and Stone
Tanis, while on his way back from Qualinesti, encounters the beautiful Kitiara and rescues her. As the two travel together to Solace, rapport grows, creating a special bond that is later threatened by misunderstanding and conflict. Available September 1992.

---

## The Companions
Together in Solace, the seven companions learn about friendship and laughter, love and contentment. An idyllic year of peace gives each of them the strength and wisdom needed to forget the injustices of the past and to confront the challenges of the future. Available January 1993.

novels

One step into the mists, and a world of horror engulfs you. Welcome to Ravenloft, a dark domain of fantasy-horror populated by bloodthirsty vampires and other unspeakable creatures of the undead.

## Vampire of the Mists
### Christie Golden

Jander Sunstar, an elven vampire from the Forgotten Realms, is pulled into the newly formed dark domain of Barovia and forges an alliance with the land's most powerful inhabitant, Count Strahd Von Zarovich, himself a newly risen vampire. But as Jander teaches the count the finer points of being undead, he learns that his student may also be his greatest enemy.

## Knight of the Black Rose
### James Lowder

The fate of the villainous Lord Soth was left untold at the conclusion of the popular DRAGONLANCE® Legends Trilogy. Now it can be revealed that the cruel death knight found his way into the dark domain and discovered that it is far easier to get into Ravenloft than to get out—even with the aid of the powerful vampire lord, Strahd Von Zarovich. On sale in December, 1991.